The Farm From
ANYWHERE

The Anywhere Club: BOOK 1

M.R. ALGER

ISBN: 978-1-09832-058-4

Ebook ISBN: 978-1-09830-892-6

To my early readers:

My two sisters,

To Jack and Gabe, who gave me great feedback,

To my Dad, who believed in this project.

CONTENTS

CONTENTS

PROLOGUE

In Loving Memory

Fletcher called the thing a "pocket watch."

It *wasn't* a pocket watch.

It didn't even do pocket watch-like things. It did not tell time. It hardly ever clicked.

A more imaginative person would have called it something else. But even if Fletcher possessed the necessary imagination, he would not have possessed the interest to use it.

So, a "pocket watch" it remained.

And it was more erratic the farther he traveled West. Almost jumping out of his palm.

Another thing pocket watches rarely did.

This was to be expected, of course. Being so far out from proper civilization brought with it certain disadvantages. Calibrating nice, obedient, simple devices out here was difficult. And Fletcher's new pocket watch was anything but obedient. And not just because it was still mad at being misnamed.

It was downright moody, in a most *un-pocket-watch-y* way. Especially when it was cloudy, or when it was driven into a fit because the stars were out, or a moon-phase was not to its liking.

The night was moonless, windless, devoid of people on the abandoned old road. The stars had the room to shake their legs here. Maybe even strut if they were in the mood. All of them begging for some comprehension, or at the very least an audience.

But they were ignored. Fletcher was not a man who gave any time to something as gabbertoothed as Skywork.

It was hard to remember that sometimes. *Personalities could be like prisons, if you let them,* the man thought, *better not go too deep here.*

His prematurely lined face frowned.

It didn't tell time, but from what he was able to understand, he was going to be late.

1

Fletcher smiled.

This meant he was *exactly* where he wanted to be.

He felt so excited he could run the rest of the way. But he and his boots were not on good terms at the moment. He ran them hard the last few weeks. Fletcher could be horribly inconsiderate of such things. In any case, giddy running wasn't something a man like Fletcher did. It simply couldn't be allowed.

Without a word, and without any outward signs of positive emotion, Fletcher continued toward town.

He stopped himself in less than fifty paces.

No. no, no. He was late. This was good. But it could also be dangerous. If *he* was late somebody else could be later still. Perhaps even *just* later.

He looked up and around. There was a series of those things lining the road... what did they call them again...? *Electric poles?* An occasional yellow light buzzing away. That could be a problem too. Even out here in the frontier. *Especially* out here.

Fletcher was an unimaginative sort, but he was clever when he had to be. And most of all, *careful*. Fletcher's personality served him well on tasks like these. It's why he was chosen to do them.

He would take the Undertrail the rest of the way.

There were dangers in traveling the Undertrail with such Privilege—even stolen, borrowed, finagled Privilege like his—but ones Fletcher felt more capable of dealing with, should they arise.

He saw what he needed on the side of the road, the foundation and ruins of an old service building. Perhaps an old house. *Hopefully an old house*, but he wasn't expecting to get lucky. Not that he needed luck with crossing. It was one of the few areas in which the man considered himself exceptional, if he did say so himself.

Finding where he thought a door must have been, he focused, and did something like blurring and crossing his eyes while walking into the center of the foundation. Immediately turning around, he pushed against the center of the resistance—at just the right angle—and walked off.

He let himself relax. Looked around.

The foundation was now home to an old wooden shack. The electric yellow lights were replaced with gas burning lamps. The old cracked concrete road now gravel.

The whole area was likely this way. *A one-one convergence out here in the frontier?*

The pocket watch was as thrilled as ever.

Fletcher snorted—an indulgence for him—and continued to town.

He heard the town before he could make it out. The sounds of music and vehicles, of people fighting or laughing. The smell of cooking and powerful imp spices.

This was a much livelier town than he had expected.

The entire center of town was lit by flame. Colorful faeFlame all. He suspected the flames would line up perfectly with the electric lights up above. It was a party. Revelers shouting and laughing and dancing in the streets, next to pits of flame and grilling meat.

Fletcher wasn't noticed at all.

For all Bertrand's conceit of being a simple man, he never did travel light. A *one-one-convergence. An active town way out here, in Undertrail no less.* It was probably all *his* doing.

The two most active parts of town were a bar and a small inn. Parked in front of the bar were a collection of motorized bikes, a few horses—some of them flesh-and-blood—the odd caribou here and there. A few old automobiles parked on the side, next to a fine old puppet wagon. There were people and non-people and sub-people of all shapes and sizes. Talking, laughing, sometimes arguing. Poking their heads out windows, dancing in the street. A few Shadowkin lingered about in the corners, unnoticed.

He would have to be especially careful from here on out. Fletcher was talented at throwing off a scent. He had been dropping cracked hagstones for half a day now. A horrible expensive waste. But anybody could be at that bar. Or staying at that motel. Or behind him on the road.

He continued away quietly from the main part of town. Not knowing what he was looking for until he saw it. An ugly lit sign in front of an even uglier building:

Dignified Passing
Funeral Home and Undertakers

There it was. Staring him right in the face. Innocently, like he hadn't spent weeks of restless labor to find it. Like it hadn't been hiding from him.

He suspected the building wasn't any different in Undertrail as it would be elsewhere. Hideous decorations that attempted to look fancy and looked all the cheaper for it, surrounded by a somehow even more horrendous attempt at a cohesive garden. The man forced himself to look away. Fletcher didn't concern himself with things like aesthetics or symmetry or taste. A merciful disinterest, in this case.

He walked to the front door. The watch practically jumped out of his pocket.

The man threw away any semblance of Fletcher-y caution—and quite a bit of Fletcher's personality went with it.

He opened the door.

The room he entered was dark, the only light coming from the windows. Seats arranged in front of an open casket. A flower framed sign featuring a large picture of bald man with big clear text: '*IN LOVING MEMORY OF BERTRAND J. BERTRAND.*'

He took a flower off the sign and put it into his lapel before looking down at the casket and its occupant.

Bertrand lay there.

As motionless as stone. His hard but slightly pudgy face sat there calmly. Which was the most un-Bertrand-y thing the corpse of Bertrand could be doing.

Being a corpse didn't suit Bertrand.

It never did.

The man put his hand tenderly on the corpse's cold, stiff shoulder.

"Oh, Bertrand," he said.

Taking his other hand, he reached up, and slapped Bertrand's lifeless face.

The sound echoed in the empty room.

A few seconds later, he slapped him again.

And then again, harder. This slap followed by a series of smaller slaps, back and forth on Bertrand's cheeks.

"What?!" Bertrand yelled.

"Oh good, you're up," the man said, taking a few steps back. It was best not to be in grabbing distance when Bertrand got angry.

A stream of curses followed, a few of which even Fletcher hadn't heard of. "By bloody Hell and fire do you even know how much bad luck you just bought yourself?! Not even *you* could think this was decent!" Bertrand yelled and mumbled as he got himself up, still sitting in the casket.

"I just wanted to say goodbye to my oldest friend, forgive my sentimentality," he replied, noticing there were notes and cards and pictures stuffed into the casket with Bertrand. "Do you think it will stick this time?"

Bertrand looked at him. His eyes as angry as Bertrand's went. He looked like he was going to fling another curse or two, but then he said in a quiet voice, "You have no right to be here. You lost any right to be here years ago."

"I wouldn't have come if it wasn't important."

"What in that exhausted brain of yours could possibly justify interrupting a man's..."

"He's going to do it," the man said.

"... own funeral? You indecent excuse for a pocket picking horse thief..."

"... he's really going to do it. *Again.* He's going to open the Farm," he said with as much gravity as he could muster. Which was quite a bit of gravity, as he was trained in these things.

Bertrand paused. "You're lying..."

"You know I'm not."

"Madness," Bertrand said, stammering. "What's all this have to do...?"

"'Have to do with you?' I'm not going to beat around the bush here, friend. You know exactly what this has to do with you. You know *exactly* what I want out of you. What *we* need out of you."

He let that sit, and then continued in a softer tone, "I need your help, Bert."

Bertrand sat there. His anger depleted. Bertrand was all boil, no simmer. He always had difficulty holding on to anger. *Perhaps his life would have been a little easier if this weren't true*, the man thought. *The right anger could keep a man going.*

Bertrand took his first real look at the man. His eyes landed on the flower attached to his lapel.

"Flower is a bit much for you, isn't it...? *Fletcher...*?" Bertrand said, saying the name slowly.

The man smiled. "I could never deny myself for long, you know that."

"I can't do it again," Bertrand said. "Too much was lost. It's too hard."

The man walked over to the small hidden door of the office. Taking a piece of folded paper and tapping it twice with his middle finger, he slipped it under the door.

"It's going to be different this time," he said.

"How do you know?"

"The madman's *all-in* this time. There's no going back. Making a whole big stink about it. Allurements spread everywhere. Even the Mundafold."

Bertrand let off another stream of half-hushed curses. "How long do you think you need me for?"

"Hard to say. A few weeks. Months. A *lifetime* at the most."

"Alright. Well, if you're so on top of things," Bertrand said, scowling. "You're going to know what I want in return. What only *you* can give me."

The man had expected this.

"I'm... prepared to give that to you," he replied.

Bertrand looked at him, clearly surprised. "*And* I want it in writing. Clear, *bold* writing. In case you plan on dying to get out of it."

The man called Fletcher nodded.

Bertrand nodded back. "Alright then," he said, and put out his hand.

The handshake was hard, both men looking at each other in the eyes.

The man noticed Bertrand's hand was warm now. *Good.*

"Now help me out of this thing," Bertrand said. "I need to arrange a few things with the undertaker before we go. They don't like corpses walking away. Bad for business."

"Already handled," he replied, pointing to the door. "Slipped a note under the door telling them it was absolutely necessary that your casket remained closed."

"Presumptuous twat. They're going to know the casket is empty."

"Don't think so," he said, and put a hagstone into the casket, convincing it to add a little weight to itself, to look a little less like a stone and a little more like a bald corpse. He closed the casket when he was done.

"That's a criminal waste," Bertrand said.

"I've wasted far more for worse reasons looking for you," he replied.

"Speaking of, how *did* you find me?"

He took the pocket watch out and held it up to Bertrand.

Bertrand's ever-expressive face registered surprise, "That's one of *his*, isn't it?"

The man called Fletcher nodded.

"Stolen?"

"Freely given."

Bertrand leaned against his almost empty casket. "This is really happening, isn't it…?"

"Unfortunately, magnificently, *horribly*… Yes."

"I was hoping you were tricking me."

"I probably am without knowing it. Don't you worry, old Bert. I can always be counted on to disappoint you."

Bertrand managed a snort.

Walking out of the funeral home together. Bertrand far too well dressed in a burial tux.

The revelers were leaving the bars and taverns, taking even more of the party to the already crowded street.

"Quite the event you're throwing for yourself."

Bertrand laughed, "You know me."

"I'm glad to have you back, Bert."

Bertrand continued on, picking up his step a little. *As set on a course of action as Fletcher was, once it was decided.*

"Well, I'm happy you're happy," Bertrand said back.

"No you're not."

"No," Bertrand repeated, speeding up again. "I'm not."

CHAPTER
1
The Bag Under the Bridge

Phillip Montgomery had never been in a car crash before.

According to Aunt Kath, he had *still* never been in a car crash, since their car had not technically 'crashed' into anything.

Phillip considered this semantics.

The old gray sedan had—according to Aunt Kath—narrowly missed a deer, which resulted in harsh braking, which resulted in swerving, which resulted in spinning, which resulted in even more breaking, which ended in a harsh stop in the middle of the road facing the wrong way.

If that wasn't a car crash, it was car-crash-*esque*.

It was an *honorary* car crash, at least.

Plus, something *was* hit. Aunt Kath's forearm had—in a noble but misguided attempt to protect him—launched itself into Phillip's face. So, it *was* a crash, for his nose at least, and he had the bloody cotton-filled nostrils to prove it.

"It just came out of *nowhere*..." Aunt Kath had said for what had to be the ninth time, putting the same emphasis on *'nowhere'* that she had the eight other times. "I think I hit the poor thing."

"That sound was the car breaking down," Phillip assured her, who had not seen the deer or heard the sound. Which was odd, since both his eyes and ears worked properly and he wasn't sleeping.

"Yeah? What part of the car?"

"Transmission... coil. Regulator unit. Duh," Phillip answered.

"What car breaks down just because it spun? I swear I have the worst luck," Aunt Kath continued. "I think I killed a nun in a past life or something..."

"Sounds like the nun had worse luck," he said, going to the back of the car. "Do we still have those protein packs?" He opened the hatch at the back of the car and noticed Aunt Kath's Clinical Psychology textbooks were again stacked on top of the cooler. Her textbooks had a way of invading every flat surface like pests, no matter how fast Phillip tried to put them away. "You left your books out..." Phillip said, surprised they hadn't moved during the not-car-crash crash.

He then noticed that they did still have protein packs, but Aunt Kath had again forgotten to replace the ice, and they now floated at the top of an icy puddle.

"Get me the umbrella, it's bright out here!" Aunt Kath yelled from the hood.

The umbrella was now underneath a pile of textbooks and loose sweaters and clothes. Loose sweaters also followed Aunt Kath around. Too many of them for one person. A compliment to the loose textbooks.

He came back to the front of the car grumbling.

"Thank you," she said, opening the umbrella, holding it tightly to herself. "We only brought one? Darn."

"We could share..."

"It's so small though, fate is cruel. If only there was a way. Sad..."

It was surprising to people that Katherine Smith was Phillip Montgomery's sole legal guardian. There was a vibe about Aunt Kath that just didn't say 'I take care of myself *and* another person.'

Though the surprise—Phillip admitted—probably had more to do with how they looked than anything else. Thirty-year old Aunt Kath could look younger than she was, when she wanted to. She could sometimes be confused for an older teenager when wearing the right clothes. Similarly, thirteen-year old Phillip could pass for a short fifteen—or even a student at Aunt Kath's university from time to time. They looked similar. Both of them shared slightly longer faces, with the same wide-set, light hazel eyes. Though Aunt Kath's hair was auburn, while Phillip's hair could never decide whether to be brown, blond, or reddish.

They were confused for siblings, more often than not.

It was a confusion Phillip enjoyed, and Aunt Kath found irritating.

"What color eyes do deer have?" She asked suddenly.

"I don't know... *black* I think?" Phillip replied.

"Alright, no teasing."

"I'm not, I think they're black."

"I know you said you didn't see the boy deer..."

"Stag," Phillip corrected.

"... Whatever. I know you didn't see the boy stag. But I really did, and it was *huge*. I mean huge. And when it jumped in front of the car, I saw its face, like it was looking right in here. It had these big red horns..."

"Antlers."

"... *Antlers*, who cares? They looked red. I swear to God. And the eyes matched. Giant. Bright red eyes," she paused, to see his reaction. "I wasn't sleeping!"

"Aunt Kath..." Phillip responded with every bit of false seriousness he had in him. "Is the stag... *here* now...? Can you see it, Aunt Kathie?" This earned him a jab on the arm. "Does it talk to you? Is the stag telling you to do things...?"

"I don't like you anymore, you used to be cool. What happened?"

"I was cool before your nun-killing bad karma started crashing our car," Phillip said. "The deer is probably an omen. Punishment for sins like keeping your textbooks everywhere. Not to mention *abandonment*."

He hated that he said it the moment it came out.

Aunt Kath was smiling, but the smile got tighter. He had stepped on a landmine. Their relationship was riddled with landmines and pitfalls now. All caused by one big issue.

The town of *King's Hill* was their destination.

Home of Aunt Kath's sister Elaine Fairchild and Phillip's four cousins. Over a thousand miles away from their home in Portland, Maine.

Correction, Phillip thought, *King's Hill was my destination*. Aunt Kath was going out West for a special summer program at the University of California, Berkeley.

Phillip wanted to go with her. He had done the math. It made sense for him to go with her. Her accommodations at Berkeley were large enough, even with an extra plane ticket, she was spending more money dumping him in the Midwest with his other aunt than it would cost to go with her.

But she never changed her mind. "This was not a vacation, it's an intense program," she had said. He had never said it was a vacation. "Plus. It's good for you to connect with your cousins. Meet Matthew."

In the end—after much arguing that got progressively bitter—she had won for pure insistence. Something Phillip resented more than he let on, and he let it on plenty.

He had never been stonewalled out of decision making before.

He learned about his summer plans and the program at Berkeley at the same time. The plans were already made, and he was the last one to know.

It had never been like that with him and Aunt Kath before... she had never been secretive with him, not since she became his legal guardian five-years ago, or even before that.

What this meant was more concerning to Phillip than the prospect of spending an entire summer with his cousins. Even Steve and Harrison.

And now they were on their way, set to arrive in the afternoon before their maybe-imaginary-stag-induced-not-a-crash-car-crash detour.

"It's not..." Aunt Kath started. Phillip was ready to speak again before she did, make a joke to avoid the awkwardness. But Aunt Kath's phone interrupted them both. "The tow truck company," she said, answering the phone.

Thank God for the interruption.

He could hear parts of the conversation, but he only needed to hear Aunt Kath's side to know it was bad news.

Something about "an unusual number of incidents in the area" and the fact that they were in the middle of nowhere and there were only so many tow trucks. "So how long do we have to wait out here?" Aunt Kath asked. Phillip heard on the other end say "around 1:30 to 2:00pm" and he groaned. He looked at his cheap mechanical wristwatch. Three hours away. What were they going to do for three hours? There was nothing interesting for miles. A car hadn't even passed them since they crashed.

He tapped Aunt Kath on the shoulder, said "pee" and pointed to the side of the road, where a short barrier led to a small field and a woody drop-off. "Don't wander off, stay within shouting distance, don't go in the woods," she whispered back, "no not you," she said back into the phone.

He didn't need to pee, but he did want to move.

He was prone to wandering. Always had been.

Over the barrier was a small field, and then a thicket of bushes and trees. Beyond them there was a ravine or gulch he could just see from the road.

Phillip got through the bushes—less than fifty yards from the car—to find a gulch wider and deeper than he thought.

It went down a hundred yards or more.

There was even a bridge. Two of them. Both perpendicular to the road. Both abandoned, the roads or rails they connected to long gone. Just skeletal remnants of wood and steel beams. What deck remained was covered in soil, where plants and trees grew. They were lower than the gulch, almost looked like they were sunken into it.

"Neat," Phillip said, walking a little into the gulch.

He was about to turn and yell for Aunt Kath to take a look at this when an odd feeling hit his stomach. A sick rushing feeling.

It was almost in slow motion that Phillip realized he was *falling*.

He dropped to his knees, but the ground collapsed under his feet.

He was falling. Falling forward.

He tried to put his hands out but there was no time, he hit the ground hard. He closed his eyes as he started to roll and slide down the gulch. He planted his feet and stopped rolling.

He slid on his butt and back another twelve feet before coming to a stop. He was staring upwards. The blue sky above him obscured by the remnants of a bridge.

"Ow," he said. Not moving, seeing if anything was hurt or broken. Nothing hurt too bad. His hands were scraped, and he was dirty, but that was it.

He tried to get to his feet and found that he couldn't.

On one leg was wrapped a massive chunk of plastic debris. One big strip of clear plastic tarp. Wrapped around his leg, almost in a knot. "How the heck...?" He said, trying to pull his leg free and failing. He grabbed a stick and began puncturing and ripping the plastic wherever he could. "Stupid," he said, and he wasn't sure he said it to the plastic or to himself. He got up on one foot and tried to pull the plastic off as he hopped.

There was more than plastic wrapped around his leg. Some other material, like cloth, was underneath. He ripped at it as best he could. He grabbed the material and pulled.

The binding on his leg came off so suddenly he almost fell again.

His leg was free.

And hanging from his hand, the cloth material. Some kind of burlap sack.

But it wasn't a sack, it was a bag.

A light brown backpack or messenger bag. There were so many straps attached to it he couldn't tell.

On the bag were patches. Colorful stars and rainbows and a flying horse sewed on.

It was heavy. The bag was filled...

"Phillip!" Aunt Kath yelled. Her voice far away but still managing to make Phillip jump.

"I'm okay!" Phillip yelled back.

"Tow truck is here!"

Already? He thought, as he tried to dust himself off. There really was no damage, though he had lost the bloody cotton in his nostrils.

"Coming!" He yelled back, scrambling zig-zagged up the steep gulch one handed.

The other hand firmly holding the brown bag as he climbed.

CHAPTER 2

Wet Socks and the Red-Eyed Stag

The tow truck driver's name was Harold.

He had been married twice. He had four kids, three from his newest wife, and one from his first whom he rarely spoke to. He also had a brother he was in business with, a living alcoholic father, and a half-sister who was miserably married to a "certifiable dirtbag" who Harold implied had an addiction to prescription pain medications, among his many other faults.

Aunt Kath had gotten this all out of Harold within the first twenty minutes. She possessed an uncanny ability to get people talking, a skill Phillip regarded with equal parts admiration and fear, as she was unfortunately not also gifted with the ability to *end* conversations. Eating out with Aunt Kath could easily turn into a never-ending conversation with the server. Phillip thought that he might know more about the sometimes-torrid lives of the serving staff at the local diner than anyone else living.

"Good thing I was just driving by," Harold had said when he was still lifting their car on the platform. "It's a big season for us, you know. Come summer, entire industry works full time just to pick up the empties. Could have been out here for hours."

"What is that in your hand...? What happened to you?" Aunt Kath had said when she first saw Phillip.

"Nothing, just fell. I'm fine," he answered. She looked him up and down as he dusted himself off. He really was fine. "I found this bag..."

She had looked at the bag for a moment and looked like she was about to object but Harold asked her a question, which allowed it to slip from her mind. Phillip managed to put the bag under his feet in the back seat of the tow truck, and said no more about it. He waited until the conversation got more involved before pulling it out again.

The bag was weird. Weirder the more he looked at it.

It had seven different straps attached to it. Five of them looped but two of them loose.

There were zippers and small pockets riddled at odd angles, hidden under small folds. Most of the zippers had small suitcase locks on them. Which didn't budge no matter how much he tried.

There were flaps everywhere. He pulled on each one. None led to an opening. Spun it around at least a dozen times, trying each zipper and flap again and again. No luck.

He pulled at it randomly, and another flap appeared. Hidden by the patch of the winged horses. A fold sewed so perfectly to the bag almost didn't look like it was there.

The bag was open.

What a find, he thought, and chuckled.

"Well I'm glad you find my sister's botched nose job funny, she certainly doesn't," Harold said from the front seat.

"Huh?" Phillip looked up. "Oh, sorry. Was thinking of something else."

"It's fine," Harold said laughing, not offended at all. "Gotta laugh about these things, or life will seem tragic."

"Harold is going to take us farther than he needs to," Aunt Kath said in the front seat in her *'please-join-the-conversation'* voice. "A mechanic right near Gardenvale..."

"Gardenvale *Crown*," Harold corrected, giving the small town's full name.

"That's close to King's Hill, isn't it?" Phillip said. You always had to go through Gardenvale to get to King's Hill. "Thank you."

"Don't thank me, mechanic I know gives me throwbacks if I deliver cars to him. I don't have much power but I abuse what I got," Harold said, laughing again. "I'm a corrupt man on my own level."

A squawking voice on Harold's radio complained about something. Harold grabbed and answered in an equally argumentative voice. There was some argument about where he should be, and what he wasn't doing. Somebody named Carol was very upset...

Phillip didn't need any more invitation to look inside the bag.

Nothing was wet inside. Or dirty. The plastic the bag was wrapped in must have protected it.

There were books. Small books. Eight or nine at least. All children's books, all old and worn. Each one featuring the same girl in a pink witch's hat, surrounded by strange little animals.

The books were not in English. They were in Russian or Greek or something similar.

There were crayons and markers at the bottom of the bag. None of the brands Phillip recognized. None of them in English.

There were dolls. A stuffed bear with a baby's face. A perfectly round owl with squid tentacles instead of talons. A woman shaped doll made of wood, only wearing a skirt, which had limbs with joints. Phillip noticed there were little articles of clothing in the bag, a change of clothes for the wooden woman.

This bag must have belonged to a child.

A fact confirmed by his next discovery.

In a fold all its own, in an almost invisible pocket, was another book.

A notebook.

A faded, wrinkled, old-style pink composition notebook.

'COMPOSITION' was written in English on the front, accompanied by 'MANY FOLDED SHEETS,' 'ADAPTABILITY-RULED', and 'N.A. MADE/N.A. PROUD.' In the middle, in unmistakably child's writing, 'TOp sECrAT NOTEs!'

There were drawings inside, mostly in crayon. Child's drawings and unintelligible notes. 'WinDohs wont stay closed ANyMOOR,' 'Lowdr OUtSide,' was the only words he recognized.

"Wow," he said as he turned the next page, low enough that Harold or Aunt Kath didn't hear.

The next few pages were not filled with child's drawings.

Notes in fine calligraphy, in several different languages. Maybe Hebrew, mixed with Latin, a few that used the English alphabet. All mixed with quick notes, dotted with intricate geographical patterns. Some looked like chemistry notes, others geometry or math or science. Many he couldn't guess. One page was filled with star charts, others diagrams of objects or inventions, one was a drawing of a dissected animal.

Page upon page was filled with quick sketches and drawings. Some in color. Made by a very talented artist.

One gray drawing was so detailed Phillip first confused it with a photograph. It was a drawing of a lake, surrounded by mountains. The detail of the drawing such that he could see the clearness of the water, and the sun reflecting on the lakebed. There was a dock here, overlooking a small island at the center of the lake. On the dock, a small sailboat was tied, surrounded on all sides by birds that weren't quite seagulls and not crows or ravens, with larger beaks than either. He could even imagine what they would sound like, a shrill whooping, though he didn't know why he thought of that since he had never heard a bird call quite like it before. The sun was behind him, warming his neck as his feet were in the cold alpine water. He knew it was midmorning. In fact, if he just turned around, he knew he would see...

"Phillip?" Aunt Kath called. "Phillip?"

"What? Yeah?"

"Sorry, we're here."

It took a second for Phillip to realize what she meant. "Here? What?"

"You've been sleeping," Aunt Kath said. "We're about to pull in."

"Pull...?" Phillip looked around. They were on a smaller road. Harold was dealing with cross traffic. A strip of business that were so out of the way they didn't even earn themselves real names. 'Donuts' was next to 'NAILS' was next to 'MECHANIC & TIRE.'

"Sleeping...?" Phillip said, the pink notebook closed on his lap.

"That's right, we're here," Aunt Kath said again, a little less patient.

He was sweating. Car sleep did that, he supposed. *Why did his feet feel wet?* A pinched nerve from sleeping? Maybe when he fell at the gulch he stepped in water or mud and didn't notice...?

He opened the pink notebook. The fine graphs and drawings and notes were gone. The only thing that remained were the child's drawings and notes.

He had fallen asleep.

He put the pink notebook back in the bag as Harold drove behind the mechanic's shop. His feet really did feel wet.

My shoes must have been wet, he realized as he got out of the truck. Wet shoes that eventually soaked up into his socks, which now made wet squishy sounds as he walked.

——— o ———

Their car started immediately when the mechanic tested the engine. Something Aunt Kath found more distressing than the car crash or the breakdown itself.

"I swear we tried a hundred times, it wouldn't start no matter what!" She said to the mechanic, who promised to give it a courtesy checkup. Phillip spent the time draining the melted ice from the cooler and changing out his wet socks.

In less than an hour—after a call to aunt Elaine and another conversation with the mechanic—they were back on the road, in their inexplicably working gray sedan. "I would have been more comfortable if they found something..." Aunt Kath said. "Anyway, no more detours."

"Try to avoid deer," Phillip said, trying to interpret the directions he had received and match it to his map. Navigating to King's Hill was always a problem. Auto navigation and GPS never worked well, and everybody they asked give a different set of instructions.

"Noticed you cleaned out the cooler," Aunt Kath said. "That was my job. It was really rude of you to do it, knowing that I forgot, and then *not* complain about it. Made me feel extra bad."

"I'll make sure to complain more next time."

"Thanks, it's basic etiquette," she said back. "By the way, thanks for abandoning me in the truck. I don't think Harold stopped talking once in two hours."

A long bout of driving punctuated by confused direction and backtracking finally brought them to the outskirts of town. A colorful wooden sign greeted them:

WELCOME TO KING'S HILL!
"The Nine-Flagged City"

King's Hill was a modest city. A town really, but it had been steadily growing for years. Set aside and split by the Mississippi river, the town intersected the corners of three different states. Illinois, Iowa, and Missouri. Part of the reason it was called the 'Nine-Flagged City.' Three state flags, one national flag, and if you include the town flag... that would be *five*. He tried to remember. *What were the other four flags...?*

The Fairchild family ranch was out of town, so far out of the way it had its own road: *Fairchild Ranch Way.*

'Fairchild Ranch' had not been a real ranch for at least two generations. The small roads leading to the ranch were the only part of the drive they never got lost. The area around the property was more crowded than he remembered, almost a suburb now. The big black metal gate that said 'FAIRCHILD RANCH' welcomed them into his aunt and uncle's property, where his four cousins waited.

Phillip steeled himself for what promised to be a long night of socializing.

There were two homes on the property, two barns, and one stable. All unused except the main home, the newest addition to the property, built by uncle Jeff's grandfather and expanded greatly each generation after that. An oversized classic white farmhouse that was bigger every time Phillip saw it.

When his parents were still alive, they had stayed at the 'Dollhouse.' The name given to the smaller and older of the two homes—which was now used only for storage.

On the large porch of the main house was a light-haired woman with an infant on her hip. His aunt Elaine.

"Ellie!" Aunt Kath yelled out an open window of the car.

"Kathy!" Aunt Elaine yelled back.

Aunt Kath stopped the car on the wide gravel driveway. Opened the door and ran to her sister without stopping the engine or shutting her door. Phillip made sure the car was in park and off before joining them.

"Phillip!" Aunt Elaine yelled, giving him a one-armed hug. She had the same blond-brown-reddish hair as Phillip. She looked like an older, much more responsible version of Aunt Kath. "Matthew," she said to the baby on her hip, "this is your cousin, Phillip."

The infant stared at him blankly, Aunt Kath still trying to get his attention by cooing and poking him. He was carrying a small toy dump truck. "Hey Matthew," Phillip said, tapping the truck. "I like your truck."

Matthew considered this for a moment, looked at his truck, looked back at Phillip, before deciding to curl his face into a sob, letting out a wail as he hid his head in his mother's shoulder. *Bad first impression.* "Sorry," Phillip said.

"It's fine," Aunt Elaine said with a laugh. "Growing up with older brothers, makes him protective of his things. Phillip you've gotten so much taller."

"Is that Philly Cheeese?!" A voice yelled inside the home.

"Phiilllllly Cheeeese!" Another voice repeated.

"Hey Steve, Harrison," Phillip said back to his still-not-visible cousins. 'Philly Cheese' had been their nickname for him since he was little. He told them repeatedly he had never been to Philadelphia or eaten a Philly-cheesesteak sandwich, which just somehow solidified in their minds that he deserved the nickname.

His cousins were easy to mix up, despite the fact that they looked completely different. Their personalities were just so similar. He never saw one without the other. *'SteveandHarrison'* was almost one word. He still mixed up which one was in football, and which one in lacrosse, *or was it track and field…?*

The older brother, Steve, was almost exactly two years older than Phillip. Shorter and stocky, with his father's dark hair. He popped out of the front door smiling. He was immediately shoved out by the younger and already taller brother Harrison. Who was almost exactly a year older than Phillip. Tall and long faced and fair haired, almost every feature contrasted his brother's. "By god it is him, Steve, it's Philly Cheese himself!"

Both were wearing exercise clothes and covered in sweat. and both threatened to give Phillip a giant hug before ducking out of it and rubbing Phillip's head with their knuckles. "Leave him alone!" Aunt Elaine ordered before they could do more. "Make yourself useful and help bring in the luggage."

"But we missed him, mom," Harrison complained, already walking toward the car.

"I missed you too," Phillip said, following. "Haven't started a fire in months."

The brothers laughed.

Years ago, the brothers invited Phillip to try out some new fireworks they had gotten ahold of around some suspiciously dry leaves. Phillip was the lone dissenter, something that made him feel like a "fussy mom." In no small part because that's what Steve and Harrison called him. His worries were vindicated in a short time, but he still always felt like a "fussy mom" around them. Their energy was difficult to match. *'Energy'* is what Aunt Kath called it when she was being diplomatic.

Steve and Harrison began grabbing things out of the car with no thought of what should be pulled out first. It was getting dark and harder to see. Phillip tried to get there first, to avoid as much damage as possible, and his hand touched the course material of the brownish patched bag.

The bag! Phillip remembered. He had put it back in the car when they were at the mechanic.

He didn't want to explain the bag to Aunt Kath, let alone Steve and Harrison, they'd tear it apart if they saw it.

He took some of Aunt Kath's loose clothing and wrapped it around the bag, it just looked like a bundle now. He put on his backpack and carried a suitcase in the other arm. He walked fast toward the house. Harrison had grabbed a bundle of loose and small items, Steve had the cooler. "Same room, Phillip," aunt Elaine said. Holding the door open with a still-upset Matthew.

"Thanks aunt Elaine," Phillip said, stepping over one of the Fairchild family's two ancient dogs, a fat watermelon-shaped beagle named Rosencrantz, who made no attempt to move as Phillip stepped over her, not even registering that he was there. Phillip could see the other dog, the equally ancient mutt hound Guildenstern, sleeping in the other room.

The old upstairs nursery had always been his room when he stayed in the bigger home, connected to another room Aunt Kath used which shared a bathroom. Phillip was carrying too much, and his hands began to slip on the bag. He walked faster to compensate, making it to the room and dumping it on the bed before he dropped it.

He took the bag and shoved it under the bed. *There, safe.*

"What's in the unicorn purse?" He heard at the door.

It was Maddie, the Fairchild's only daughter.

"Just underwear and things," he answered.

"You keep your underwear in a purse?" She said with the most sarcasm an eleven-year-old could muster. Which was quite a bit, it turned out.

Maddie hadn't barely changed at all. She looked like an elongated version of the fair-haired kid he knew from his last visit, with a personality that was as far from Steve and Harrison's as was humanly possible. She was responsible, careful, deliberate to the point of boredom, and always a bit of a tattle-tale. Something Phillip was secretly thankful for when he was with Steve and Harrison. She would have come in handy in the famed fireworks-dry-leaves-incident.

"All the kids are doing it nowadays," he joked back. "Gotta get more out of the car, good to see you Maddie!"

He rushed back downstairs and Maddie followed.

"Dinner's almost ready. Madelyn Cathleen Fairchild, where are you?! I need help," aunt Elaine yelled from somewhere in the house. Maddie groaned behind him and said "Coming mom!"

Phillip went back to the car to see what else there was to bring in, only to find that that job was done. Steve and Harrison were thorough, he just hoped that too many of his things weren't lost or broken.

It was almost night, the sky a dark blue. The lights of the property had come on right when the wind picked up.

He turned to go in when he heard something.

A ticking.

A mild, rhythmic ticking, from somewhere down the driveway. So mild he didn't know whether he was hearing the sound or feeling it in his feet.

Curious, he walked towards it. Then walked a little more. Until he found he was almost at the end of the driveway itself. The sound felt no closer or farther away.

"Weird," he said.

Turning on the gravel driveway, he got the briefest glimpse of a red jacket and surprised face hurtling toward him before he was knocked to the ground.

Phillip, for the second time that day, landed on his back.

When his eyes cleared, he was staring up, at darkening clouds.

"I'm so sorry, oh my gosh I'm sorry!" Said the kid in the red jacket.

He was also on the ground, the bike on the ground next to him. "I got lost and wasn't looking where I was going and I was lost and trying to look at my phone and I'm sorry are you okay?"

"I'm fine," he answered, getting up. The kid, who Phillip now noticed was probably around his age, was a little shorter than him, a little wider, and a little darker.

"Gosh darn I'm sorry," he continued through Phillip's insistence that he was fine. "You're really fine?" The red jacket kid said as he picked up his bike and slung his backpack on. "Really, I'm okay," He said as he dusted himself off.

"I'm in a hurry. My phone's not working, and my mom is going to kill me! Sorry again," and then he threw something in his bike's basket, kicked off and yelled "sorry!" over his shoulder.

Phillip looked up just in time to see him go around a corner, into a patch of woods.

Phillip froze.

In the basket of the red-jacketed kid's bike, sat a notebook.

A tattered, *pink*, composition notebook.

And attached to the back of the bike with stretch ties, a miniature mounted head of a stag, far too small to be real.

With bright, luminous red eyes, and matching red antlers.

CHAPTER
3
Slipping Memories

"Hey, wait! Stop!" Phillip yelled at where the kid had been.

He ran after him, turning the corner he had gone, yelling all the way.

The kid was gone.

He must be going fast. The trail he went down was long.

He didn't even know what to think. What was the likelihood of all this? How many people own pink notebooks? Red-eyed stags...?

Wait, where was his notebook? The little girl's notebook?

He left it back at Fairchild Ranch. Under the bed.

He wanted to look at it after dinner. But he hadn't thought about it since then...

He jogged back to the Fairchild home, for some reason wanting to get back to the bag and the pink notebook. To make sure it was still there. That it was real.

He ran down the Fairchild driveway, but then slowed down.

Why was he jogging?

He tried to remember. *He wanted to do something,* he thought. He wanted to come back to the Fairchild house. But not to go to bed, not because it was late.

He thought back, what was he doing?

That's right! He ran into somebody on a bike, fell down, added slightly to his collection of scrapes and bruises. And then the kid got up, and...

The pink notebook! The red eyed stag model!

He had forgotten.

He remembered now, but he had *forgotten*...

He wasn't forgetful. He was never forgetful. And certainly not for something like this...

So why was he forgetting?

Come to think of it. He didn't think about the notebook or the bag or any of its contents at all. He forgot about them completely when he was greeting the

21

Fairchild family. He thought about it again when he was bringing in the luggage. When he touched the bag. That was normal, he had other things to think about...

But how did he forget when...?

When did he forget...? Forget what?

He stopped.

"Forget what?" He said. He turned around, confused. Felt the blisters on his hand from earlier, the dust on his clothes and pants. He had fallen earlier that day and...

No!

He had *just* fallen. Fallen because he was hit by a kid on a bike.

A kid on a bike... with a *pink* notebook in his basket, and a red-eyed stag model...

This was craziness, this was insane, he thought, heading again for the house, picking his speed back up. He must have hit his head when they swerved off the road.

He began mumbling under his breath, "bag, red jacket, red eyed stag. Bag, red jacket kid, red eyed stag." He had walked farther than he had thought, or maybe the trip just felt longer. It was getting genuinely dark now. The Fairchild family had installed low lamps all around the property. He kept up his little chant with his pace. "Bag red jacket stag..."

There were fireflies coming out now.

He reached the porch, still mumbling low, "red jacket, red jacket, red jacket."

Wait.

There was more. Red jacket and... what? He had walked and... yes, he had run into a kid in a red jacket and...

There it was.

He had forgotten, again. Forgotten in the space of five minutes.

Forgotten when he was thinking of almost nothing else...

"Bag red jacket stag. Bag jacket stag. Red bag stacket jag," he mumbled. Picking up a rock as he walked, holding it tight, trying to make it part of the memory.

He burst through the Fairchild door.

And almost ran into uncle Jeff.

"Hey there, Phillip!" Uncle Jeff said. "Look at you, you've gotten taller. Are you in a hurry?"

Phillip looked at the stairs. He wanted to go upstairs.

He was holding a rock. *Why...?* "I don't think so..." he said to his uncle.

Uncle Jeff was always exactly how he remembered him, if maybe a little more tired. He even wore the same clothes, which Phillip always described as 'dad clothes.' He had Harrison's height but Steve's dark hair. With a more prominent nose than both, framed by horned-rimmed glasses. He was a King's Hill local, unlike aunt Elaine, he even attended *King's Hill University*. "Good to see you, uncle Jeff," Phillip said, as his uncle put his hand out for an awkward handshake. He put the rock in his pocket.

Why do I have a rock...?

"You should take a shower," Aunt Kath said behind him. "Ellie lied about dinner timing, you have time."

"Ungrateful!" Aunt Elaine yelled from the kitchen.

"You should really, really, take a shower," Aunt Kath said, turning back to the kitchen.

Phillip bent down to pet a passing Rosencrantz as she went by. The dog barely registered. "I will," he said back to Aunt Kath.

"I'm saying you stink," she added.

"Got it," he said and looked back at uncle Jeff and gestured awkwardly upstairs. He was always a little awkward with uncle Jeff. His uncle gave him a tense smile and gestured back. He really did look tired, almost surprised to see Phillip, maybe it was the prospect of socializing...

He went to his room, sat on the bed, and made no attempt to get in the shower.

He took the rock out of his pocket, and stared at it for a long time. Putting it on the dresser and staring at it some more, for some reason feeling the cuts on his palm more when he did so.

He took a shower. Distracted by... *something* the whole time.

He got out, wrapped in a towel, and the first thing he looked at was the rock.

He saw underneath the bed, he saw just the hint of a brown strap.

And he remembered. Again.

Tears almost came to his eyes he was so relieved.

He lunged—practically dove—for the bag under the bed. Grabbing it and pulling it out to the floor. "red kid on stag, pink notebook bike!" He said, far too loud. Shushing himself, he refused to move. He remembered all of it.

He grabbed a pen from his suitcase, not letting go of the bag, he wrote: 'Car crash. Found bag under bridge. Aunt Kath saw Red eyed stag. Ran into Red JACKET, had Pink NOTEBOOK, RED EYE STAG MODEL. FORGOT!!' On his arm.

He waited. He still remembered.

He closed his eyes, his hands on the bag. He remembered.

He took objects out of the bag, placed the stuffed animals on the dresser. Put the books on the bed, and held the pink notebook. He never forgot once while he was doing this.

What was happening? He managed to think, as a knock at the door caused him to jump. "Dinner," Maddie said on the other side of the door. "Coming, just need to get dressed," he said back.

It was difficult to get dressed while holding onto the pink notebook, but no force would allow him to let go at this point. He wore long sleeves to hide the note he wrote on his arm. *Why was this happening? Did he have a stroke? What if he forgot again while he was downstairs?* He laid the objects from the bag around the room. *Was that enough?* He was remembering now. No struggle. Not like it was outside.

He took the pen again and turned to the first page of the pink notebook. Wrote:

PROPERTY of Phillip Mulford Montgomery
Portland, ME
If lost, please return. Reward.

He wrote his number and his full address.

It was a silly thing to do. But for some reason he felt better.

He considered trying to put the pink notebook under his shirt, but then put it on the bed. He would see it again when he came back to his room. He walked backwards out of the room, and only with great effort did he turn around.

He remembered, down the hallway.

He remembered on the stairs.

And remembered when he was downstairs. He remembered easily, with no struggle...

"Philly cheese!" Harrison yelled at the dinner table. "Do you remember that one year you came here and you had that big magnetic detector with you?"

"It was the 'Gold Hunter 9000' metal detector, favorite birthday present ever," Phillip answered. That had to be over six years ago. "Why?"

"I loved that thing! We looked for treasure all summer, remember? Never found anything," Harrison answered.

"I did find something," Phillip said, tapping his wristwatch. It was a cheap wristwatch, but he had found it with his metal detector by the river. It was broken when he found it, and his father had spent more money fixing it for him than it was probably worth. He had worn the watch almost every day since. The 'Gold Hunter 9000' had stopped working in less than a year. He still had it in his closet at home. Unable to throw it out.

"You still have it!" Harrison said again.

"Stop screaming, Harry," aunt Elaine chided, as Phillip sat down at the crowded table. It looked like aunt Elaine had cooked her entire pantry. "Phillip, we're going to take you into town tomorrow."

"Sounds fun," Phillip said, trying to rustle up the energy to sound sincere.

Dinners at the Fairchild house were loud affairs. He was always involved in at least three conversations at once.

And throughout the entire dinner, Phillip remembered. Remembered without struggle.

And he knew, in the morning—miraculously if he could still remember—that he needed to try to find the kid in the red jacket.

CHAPTER 4

Lost and Found

Something was pushing on his shoulder.

"Breakfast is almost ready."

Phillip opened and then immediately squinted his eyes, *why was Aunt Kath waking him? It was summer. And since when had she been so short? And why was her hair so light?*

"You sleep with stuffed animals?" Maddie asked.

He looked up, then down at his chest, the baby-faced bear was tucked under his arm. "Yes, I do," he said, hugging the bear tighter. "Didn't I lock my door?"

"Doors don't lock very well. And you wouldn't wake up when I knocked," she explained, as if it was obvious. "Why is the bear so ugly?"

"Well that's rude," he said, rubbing his eyes. "Let me get dressed."

"What are all these notes you put everywhere? Are you doing homework?"

"Dressed," he mumbled in a sleepy voice, gently guiding Maddie out the door.

He remembered everything, at least he thought he did, as well as last night.

He tested himself all night, wrote notes, refusing to let the object go. At some point he fell asleep. He pulled clothes out of his suitcase, deciding to wear the over-shirt he had to hide the pink notebook. He tucked one of the doll's dresses in his wallet, and put the pink notebook under his arm. He would have to find a better solution, but this would do for the morning. He checked his phone. Charged, with some bars but no internet. A problem that always plagued the Fairchild Ranch.

He had asked Aunt Kath the night before if she remembered if he was carrying anything from the gulch. She said no. He showed her one of the stuffed animals, she said it was cute, he brought it back to his room, and ten minutes later asked her, "do you know where that stuffed animal went?" "What stuffed animal?" She had said back.

She couldn't remember it either...

It was the most incredible thing he had ever experienced.

It was the only thing he could think about.

Breakfast was hectic, but getting the Fairchild family and the SUV ready to go into town more so. Nobody was ready at the same time, and there was always somebody missing when they tried to leave. Uncle Jeff helped, but would not be coming.

Phillip asked Maddie, Steve, and Harrison if they "knew a kid around here about my age?" None of them did, but Harrison implied Phillip's interest in the kid was romantic.

All seven of them somehow managed to drive into town together. Phillip in the back seat between Steve and Harrison, sometimes intercepting their frequent jabs at each other.

The town center of King's Hill, separated by the Mississippi with an oversized bridge, hadn't changed much. Classic brown and red brick buildings hosting a variety of tourist spot staples. Antique shops, restaurants, thrift shops, and about a dozen ice cream places. Aunt Elaine played tour guide, a significant portion of the tour devoted to how uncle Jeff was involved in the local politics. Something to do with the double-decker gazebo and the historical society was causing waves. Phillip wasn't really listening.

They stopped at an ice-cream shop Phillip had been to before, 'Over the Mooooon.' Which had fantastic cake square pops and an ice-cream shake called the 'Moopocolypse.' Steve and Harrison didn't join them, instead saying something about "crimson pride" and going off to shop.

"I think I'm going to look around for a bit," he said to the group.

"Don't go too far," Aunt Kath said, in a baby-voice as she was playing with Matthew.

"Take Maddie with you, she'll show you around," Aunt Elaine said.

"Groovy," he said, disappointed, and started walking. Maddie grabbed his arm, shook her head attached to her Moopocolypse, and dragged him in the opposite direction.

Maddie proved a far less enthusiastic tour guide than aunt Elaine. She mostly just had ideas on what not to see. The section of town she led him to seemed to be hipper and less family oriented. It was the college part of town. Advertisements for bands and petitions for roommates or cheap furniture dominated billboard stands they passed.

Maddie brought him to a cramped used bookstore filled with as many trinkets and antiques as books and immediately disappeared into the shelves, Phillip was too distracted to find anything interesting.

"This one's good," said a stocky woman with an arm full of books and a bird's nest of grey hair, she was pointing to a tattered yellow textbook, "cheap too. This whole section is. Shame."

A Complete Introduction to MindCraft and Associated Disciplines, it said on the cover. A library edition, still wrapped in protective plastic.

A psychology book?

Maybe he could figure out what was wrong with his memory, he thought with a chuckle, *what was wrong with all of them*. It was only $1.40. "Thank you," he said to the woman.

"Any time, kiddo," she replied with a wink from a glassy white eye. Her other eye a bright blue.

He decided to buy it. Holding it in a bag would give him an easier way to carry the notebook for the rest of the day.

Looking out the window of the shop, he saw a copy print store.

And he had an idea.

"Hey Maddie," he called to her, she was parked on a big armchair in a corner, looking through an illustrated Atlas that was almost as large as she was, "I'm going to go find a restroom, you okay here for a little bit?" She gave him a thumbs-up, the rest of her hidden behind the huge atlas.

The copy shop was exactly what he needed. He went to the computer. Opened up a document and began writing. He printed forty copies and bought tape.

He ran to the circular billboard, and taped three copies of his new flyers to it:

MISSING/LOST
Faded Pink Notebook
Red-Eyed Stag Model
Foreign Children's Books
(Red Jacket Kid who Ran into me on Bike)
If you know anything about these items, Please call.

His number was at the bottom. On the off chance that the red jacket kid would see this, he might just call.

It wasn't a great idea—it felt silly now that he was doing it—but it was the only one he had.

Running back to the bookstore. He found Maddie in the same spot.

"Where did you go? There's a bathroom in the back," she said.

"Is there? I didn't know never having been here before. Well let me check out and we'll get out of here," he said as her frown deepened, "Is there anything you want?"

Her frown turned into a look of surprise, "wait one second" she said, and went back into the maze of bookshelves.

"How much for the messenger bags?" He said to an old bald man behind the counter, pointing to the bags behind him.

"Twenty-four ninety-nine," he answered without looking up "You should know I don't think it's real leather."

"That's fine," Phillip replied. Perfect.

Maddie came back holding a large-ish picture book. Something to do with oceans and creatures of the deep. It was $15.00. *Ouch*. He was spending way too much.

"Thank you!" Maddie said to him, her tone suddenly very different.

Well at least he had won her over.

Putting the pink notebook in his new messenger bag, along with the yellow textbook, they went back to the ice cream shop.

"Mom, Phillip bought me a book!" Maddie said when they got back to the ice-cream shop.

"I wanted to win her over," he whispered to Aunt Kath, seeing her disapproving look. They were on a tight budget, and Phillip was usually the sensible one. But Aunt Kath accepted the explanation immediately. Trying to buy approval was a very Aunt Kath thing to do, after all.

He was able to get away from the group a couple of times. Once saying he had to go to the bathroom, something that didn't get past the ever-suspicious Maddie's attention, who only narrowed her eyes at him.

He put up ten flyers. Feeling sillier with each one.

Nobody noticed him, except at a different expansive used bookstore called 'McKay's', where one of the clerks asked where he had come from. Phillip just acted busy, said "yeah" and walked away.

It took forty minutes and two phone calls to find Steve and Harrison. Aunt Elaine was threatening to leave without them. They came back with a bag each.

On the ride home, Phillip asked what was in the bags.

Steve and Harrison grinned together.

And began to undress.

"What? Wait…" Phillip stammered.

"Steve! Harrison!" Aunt Elaine yelled from the front seat. Matthew laughed.

"Crimson pride, Mom" Steve and Harrison echoed together.

Just as Phillip was about to ask what 'Crimson Pride' was, and why it required undressing, his phone rang.

Unknown number, but he picked up.

"Hello," he said.

"Helloooo?" Came a small voice back.

"Yes, hello, this is Phillip."

"Hellooo?" A woman's voice.

"Yes, this is Phillip."

"Hello," she said again, "Is this the person who put up those flyers for missing items."

"Yes!" Phillip said.

"Yes, well, I was thinking…"

"Yes."

"… that since you're out in the world putting up flyers…"

"Yes."

"… if you wouldn't mind helping me find my lost kitty?"

He didn't answer right away.

"Well I really don't think…"

"He's a darling little orange tabby. Missing a bit of his left ear. Bit of his tail too..."

"I'm not really a local..."

"... but I'm sure you wouldn't mind just keeping an eye out? He answers to *Gingersnaps*."

He didn't know what to say. "Sure, I'll keep an eye out."

"Promise?"

"Sure, I promise," Steve and Harrison had grown quiet, and even more amazingly, had stopped moving.

"You mind telling me what he looks like, for I feel better that you know. I won't keep you much longer."

Phillip sighed. "He's a tabby with a missing ear and a short tail."

"... and what was his name...?" She continued.

"Gingersnaps," Phillip replied flatly. Harrison snorted. Aunt Elaine shushed him.

"Say again dear..." The soft voice said sweetly.

"*Ginger. Snaps*," Phillip replied.

"Yes! Yes! *Gingersnaps*. Gingersnaps. Little tabby Gingersnaps. Oh God Bless ya' dear. God bless ya'," she said, and immediately hung up the phone.

Phillip just looked at his phone. Steve and Harrison cracked up laughing.

"Who was that?" Aunt Kath asked.

"Just a wrong number," Phillip lied. "An old woman, wouldn't let me get off the phone until I promised to help find her lost cat." Everybody laughed at this.

Phillip had to admit, it was pretty funny,

"We're just happy to see you making it with women in town," Harrison said, and Phillip noticed what was on his head, what he was dressed in.

Steve and Harrison both were wearing identical red shirts, emblazoned with a gold heart, which had deer antlers poking out of it. On top of both their heads, a matching pair of felt antlers scraped against the roof of the car.

"Why are you wearing those?" Phillip asked.

Steve broke out in a wide smile, and grabbed Phillips shoulders "Crimson Pride! Philly Cheese, Crimson Pride!"

And suddenly Phillip remembered. It was the college. The local University. *King's Hill University*. The College spread across the town, with a massive campus just outside of town center. Its colors were red and gold.

"Crimson Pride," Phillip repeated, "That's the college, right. And the antlers are...?"

"The Crimson Hart!" Steve and Harrison said together, Harrison following up with a little rhythmic whistle. A game call, probably.

The *Crimson Hart* was a stag.

A stag with red eyes. And red antlers...

Phillip knew all this. He just never thought much about the college. Why would he think about his cousin's local university teams?

This meant the red jacketed kid could just be a fan.

With a mounted deer. A prop for a game bought at a gift shop. They probably sold pink composition notebooks by the dozens around here. Pink is close enough to red for marketing purposes.

Maybe the stag Aunt Kath had seen was a local prankster in a costume. Or... *no*, there was still too much that didn't make sense about all this, he thought as he grabbed the leather messenger bag.

But he was no longer so sure the red jacket kid had anything to do with any of this.

He arrived back at Fairchild Ranch, and he felt further away from the mystery than ever.

As the family made its way back into the home, his phone rang again. Another unknown number, he stopped walking and picked up.

"Hello?" He said, and an echoing voice said at the same time, "Hey!"

The voice wasn't just on his phone, it was also behind him.

Phillip turned around, and standing on the Fairchild driveway, was the red jacket kid. Still mounted on his bike.

Exactly how he looked when he ran into Phillip. A slightly shorter and slightly wider and slightly darker kid about Phillip's age, maybe Hispanic, with a wide, friendly face. Wrapped around his waist, a red jacket.

The red jacket.

The kid waved his phone at him, then hung up. "Just wanted to make sure it was you," the kid said. "Sorry about running into you last night. By the way, it's a *windbreaker*, not a jacket," he said, holding up one of the flyers.

Phillip laughed, looked back at the family going inside the house, only Maddie taking notice.

"My name's Dan, by the way... now, uh, if you don't mind me asking," he said, and then held up a pink notebook, "what do you mean you lost this...?"

"I found it. One of it, actually. A different one. I thought since I saw one in your basket you might..." he stopped, feeling silly again.

"You can remember it?" Dan asked in an excited hush.

The words hit Phillip like a cold bucket of water.

This was it.

Something was going on. *It was real,* not just his imagination.

This was all real. He said the first thing that came to his mind.

"We should talk."

"Yeah, we should," Dan replied, his smile wider than Phillip's.

CHAPTER
5

Comparing Notes

"**Aunt** Elaine, do you mind if I bring Dan upstairs for a minute?"

His aunt was already cooking, and somehow almost done with her first batch. Wrapped sausages were already coming out of the oven. "Of course, hon. Any time," she said, not looking up. "Who's Dan?" Aunt Kath and Maddie said at the same time. "Jinx," Aunt Kath said to Maddie, who was not to be distracted from her suspicion. "Just that kid I ran into," he answered.

Steve and Harrison screamed from the living room, uncle Jeff joining in. The King's Hill University *'Summer Quad-Games'* were on, played in Gardenvale Crown. At the same time, something began beeping urgently in the kitchen. "What game is on, is that the Olympics...?" Dan asked.

"You don't know? It's those University games. I thought they did it every year... C'mon," Phillip said, walking lightly on the stairs.

Dan followed, clearly suspicious.

"I'm Dan, by the way," he said.

"You told me," Phillip said, shutting the door to the bedroom. "Oh, sorry. I'm Phillip. Phillip Montgomery."

"Daniel Miguel Edwin Castellanos," he said with an exaggerated Spanish accent he didn't have. "When did you find the book?"

Phillip took out the pink notebook. Dan looked at it, smiled, and laughed. "I found it the same day you ran into me."

"Yours has writing on the cover... Same day?!" he said. "Took me months to figure out something was going on. I kept..."

"... Kept forgetting," Phillip finished, "I think I would have too! If you didn't run into me. Then everything..."

"...it all comes back to you at once!" Dan interrupted back, "That's how it works. It's all or nothing. You see the thing and you remember all the times you forgot about it, but then right..."

"... right when it's out of eyeshot, or you're not touching it, you forget again!" Phillip's heart was beating so hard it was as if he was sprinting.

"Have you seen any weird people talking to you or asking you to do things?" Dan asked.

"I don't... think so, no more than usual," Phillip answered. "But I've only been out once since I found it. Is that part of all this? 'Weird' people...?"

Dan looked at him with a serious look in his eye.

"Phillip, right? I can trust you, right?"

"Well, sure. I think."

Dan stared at Phillip. Then slowly nodded.

"Okay!" He said, his face losing all hint of intensity, replaced with a friendly smile. "Oh my god you just found it yesterday. We need to compare notes," Phillip looked at his pink notebook, "oh, yeah, I meant symbolically, but that too!" He laughed. "Tell me everything."

Phillip, not wanting to let the opportunity pass, really did tell Dan everything. He mentioned how he had found the bag, how he had forgotten about it. He even told Dan about the dream he had where the notebook was filled with writing and diagrams. Dan's eyes lit up at this. He looked like he wanted to say something every few moments. Phillip moved around the room, showing him the stuffed animals, the bag with the winged horse patches.

"This is great. Perfect!" He said.

"I don't know what language that is, I meant to try to look it up." Phillip said, "I think it might be Greek or Russian..."

"It's neither" Dan said definitively, "I mean, I don't know what it is. But it's the same language on the side of the mailbox."

"Mailbox?" Phillip asked.

"Yeah, yeah," he said quickly. "My turn."

Dan had discovered his book over a year ago. When he was riding around on his bike, on a trash heap, in an old square mailbox. "I wouldn't have noticed it except that I had gone by the garbage heap before and I just happened to notice that the little metal flag thing on the side of the mailbox, what do you call that? It was up the second time I came around. I sometimes notice stuff like that. Well on impulse I went over and looked inside and there it was, the pink notebook. I took the whole mailbox with me home, had all this writing on it, the same as these books. Almost just took the notebook! Thank god I didn't. Well anyway I forgot about the box and the notebook for months at a time. It took a few times forgetting before I even realized it was happening. Tried to show it to my mom. Same thing happened! Except it seemed worse for her or maybe she wasn't interested I don't know. And then..."

"...and then?"

"...and then, oh my gosh Phillip there's so much to tell you. I can't believe this is happening to somebody else too, I thought I was going crazy for half of this. Phil, This goes so much deeper I don't even know where to start."

"Just say it, say everything. Anything," Phillip said, smiling.

"Well then, the weirdest stuff started happening, I started..."

"Yeah."

"I started... getting mail."

"Getting mail? What do you mean?"

"I mean getting mail, Phil!" He said, "Mail. Mail in *the* mailbox, the mailbox I found. Even though it was in my closet! The little metal flag would go up when I wasn't around or sleeping. And there would be stuff in there!" He was staring at Phillip's face now, looking for signs of disbelief.

But Phillip believed him, he believed every word. "What kind of stuff?"

"Little things at first. Little notes that didn't make sense, or in a different language. Then a wooden pocket knife. These little carved masks. Doll size things. One time I opened it up and it was filled with bones! Rat bones, I think. I wanted to throw them out but then put them in a plastic bin under my bed. Gosh I hope my mom doesn't find those, don't know what she would think..." He trailed off. "Anyway, the last thing to come was the weirdest thing yet. The little stag head, but..."

"Phillip, you have to believe me that this really happened."

"I do, go on," he said.

"... It was in the mailbox, but, well if you saw it would make more sense. It's bigger than the mailbox, but it was also inside it. I didn't notice it was bigger until I took it out and..." seeing Phillip's confused look continued, "this doesn't make much sense. But it *is* bigger, and it did come from *inside* the mailbox. And now. Well now, I started noticing recently..."

"What?" Phillip asked, getting impatient with his pauses.

"The stag... goes away sometimes," he swallowed hard.

Phillip looked on, too surprised to respond immediately, "you lose the model, and then it comes back?"

"No, I mean. The mounted board is still in my room, or on my backpack. Only the deer's head goes away... and then comes back."

Phillip was quiet and let that sink in.

This was stunning, Phillip thought, all the more unbelievable because, despite everything, he found himself believing all of it. He knew Dan was telling the truth. He knew it at the very core of his being. They sat together in silence for a moment, and then began laughing.

"Thanks for hitting me with your bike," Phillip said.

"You're welcome, anytime," Dan responded with a laugh, then looked down at the pink notebooks on the bed. "Oh, wow would you look at that..." he picked up the notebooks and held them side-by-side.

They were identical.

Perfectly identical in almost every way. Every scratch, bump, and wrinkle the same. The only difference was the writing on the cover of one.

"Dan," Phillip said, mesmerized by the notebooks.

"Yeah?"

"This is the most amazing thing that's ever happened to me."

"Me too," he said. "And there's still a bunch I need to tell you... but. Well, it's best if I show you. I think. Do you have a bike?"

———— ○ ————

"Tell your friend he can stay for dinner," aunt Elaine said.

"He can't stay long, he was just going to show me around," Phillip explained.

"Take your phone," Aunt Kath said. Phillip patted his pocket in response.

The Fairchild family never threw anything away. A consequence of living on a huge property with multiple buildings. It was easy to find a bike in the barn that fit him. Harder to find an air pump, so he rode with almost flat tires.

"Which one was your mom?" Dan asked.

"Neither, those are my aunts. I live with the dark haired one up in Portland, Maine," Phillip answered.

"Oh, sorry, I thought the dark haired one might be your sister," Dan said. "I've lived around here my whole life. Those games on the TV, you say they were college games? They looked weird. My dad's always trying to get me into college game stuff. Big fan of the Vols. The younger girl there was giving me the stink eye. I don't think she likes me very much. Is that your... cousin?"

"Yep, Maddie," Phillip confirmed. "She gives the stink eye to lots of people. Don't take it personally. Let's get going."

"You have a pencil like I told you? I have an extra..."

"Got it. Now where do we go?" Phillip said.

"Well let's see," Dan said, tackling the question without hesitation. He took a small board and the pink notebook out of his backpack and attached it to his handlebars with an intricate system of ties and clamps. He opened it to a page of notes, small hand drawn maps. Some erased and redrawn, others scratched off. Dan took out a pen and wrote a note. Looking at his watch.

"You write in the book?" Phillip asked.

"Oh yeah, that's super important. I was going to tell you that on the way," he looked up, then got on his bike and went on to the main road.

"I meant to tell you upstairs. I don't think I'm forgetting like I used to. It wasn't for very long. But I remembered upstairs without any prompting right before you got here."

Dan nodded, he didn't seem surprised by this. "Same thing happened to me after a while. It kinda gives up trying to make you forget. Or maybe it was because of something else. I think it has to do mainly with the notebook. Writing in the notebook is important. Something happens. Did you write in the notebook at all?"

"No," he answered. "Wait, *yes*. Last night I wrote my name in there and my number."

"And have you forgotten anything since then? Are you losing track of time?" Dan seemed excited now.

"I...don't think... No, I don't think I have," Phillip said, thinking back. "I thought it was because I was holding the notebook. You think it's because I wrote in it?"

"Don't know. Maybe. Probably," he said, looking at his hand drawn map. "You'll see what I mean when we get there."

"When we get where?"

"It's sort of hard to describe. It's a place. Some property. It's like the notebook, all weird and... well, it's best if you see it," he said. They both sped up, Phillip's low tires making the trip difficult.

It was hard to tell how long they rode for. They took frequent stops at junctures as Dan looked at his map, sometimes mumbling to himself. They sometimes went down a road for thirty seconds, and Dan would stop suddenly, saying "this isn't right" to himself. "It's hard to find, you have to get there just right. Trust me. Trust me." They went through fields and through small alleyways between houses. The passed dozens of farms, houses, large abandoned silos and factories. At one point, they passed through a wooded trail, with woods far thicker and greener than he had seen around King's Hill before. Finally, they hit a trail next to a small river. "Here we go! Here we go!" Dan said.

"Is this place much farther upstream?" Phillip asked, "this river connects to the Mississippi probably, we could probably find a real map..." He suggested.

"Huh?" Dan said. "No, I think that's too far away. I told you. You have to get there just right. Normal maps won't do. Yes!" Dan said, as they approached the husk of what had to be once a massive oak tree. A ribbon was tied to it.

"This is it, this is it," Dan said, taking the book off his bike, throwing the bike on the ground.He went running up a wood covered hill, disappearing instantly. "C'mon!" He said to Phillip.

Phillip followed him up the hill, which turned out to be deceptively short. The thick green canopy of trees and bushes making it seem larger. Dan was waiting at the top, at a vantage point overlooking the river.

"Tell me what you see." he instructed Phillip, but before he could answer. "No, wait. Better yet. You see all those farm buildings on the opposite side of the river? Count how many you see."

Confused but not arguing the point, Phillip replied, "I see, what? Five? No, six different buildings."

Dan let out a quick "Hah!" And then walked away to the side, disappearing again into the bushes. "Follow!" he said, "avoid the poison oak," he cautioned.

Not knowing what poison oak looked like, Phillip tried to touch as little as possible. They walked for a short while, finally arriving at a different vantage point. Dan sat himself down on a felled tree.

"Now, do it again."

"What? Count the buildings?" Phillip asked impatiently.

"Yes. Yes," Dan said, smiling like a madman.

Phillip looked at the buildings across the way. A large farmhouse, a collection of barns, a few silos. "There's ten buildings, same as before."

"Ah hah! Amazing!" Dan said.

"What's this have to do with...?" Phillip started.

"Do me a favor," Dan said. "Take out your pink notebook. And draw the buildings."

"I can't really draw," Phillip said.

"Doesn't matter, just do a quick outline. Label them."

Phillip, assuming Dan would explain this to him and it would eventually make sense, followed his instructions. He took out the notebook, turned to the cleanest page he found, and drew the quickest outline he could of the buildings.

When Dan saw that he was done, he said, "How many buildings did you draw?"

"All of them" he said, holding up the notebook, "all twelve... of them..."

He had drawn *twelve* buildings. But he had said ten before, and before that...

"Do you remember how many buildings you saw the first time?" Dan asked.

"I saw... six, I said. Then I saw ten..." He had said it out loud to Dan. He said he saw six, and then he saw ten. And he didn't remember the difference.

Dan smiled and practically dragged him back to the first vantage point.

"Don't look at your notebook. How many buildings do you see?"

Counting, Phillip replied in a whisper, "Twelve."

"Twice as crowded as you remember." Dan stated, "When you're right here, there's five buildings. When you're over there, there's ten. When you draw it, the number turns into twelve, And suddenly there's twelve building's no matter where you look," he said, staring intently at Phillip's face. "Took me forever to figure this out. Now look at the page you drew the buildings on. I'll bet you five bucks the page has no lines on it, it was blank before you drew on it!"

Phillip looked down at the notebook. Dan was right... the page he had drawn on had no lines. It was like thick sketching paper... None of the other pages were like that. "Why...?" Phillip said.

"Happens when you don't think about it!" Dan said.

Too many questions came to Phillip's mind to handle at once. He looked back up at the buildings, all *twelve* of them, and just said, "What is this?"

"That, Phil," Dan said, pointing across the river, "is the *Farm*."

CHAPTER
6
The Campground
Outskirts

"Do you need a protein bar? I got extra," Dan said, taking one out of his sizable backpack and handing it to Phillip, who took it without thinking.

On Phillip's insistence, Dan had taken him across a bridge, and brought him as close to the Farm as possible. "This is almost as close as I've gotten," Dan said. They were on a wide dirt trail canopied by thick trees. There were dozens of travelers with backpacks ahead of them. "You can't get close to the Farm, but I think this is the entrance or something. Go a little further and you'll see all the tents. Huge campground! It doesn't make sense, either. The Farm's not in the right place. You think you should hit the river at some point but you never do..."

"What are they wearing?"

"It's the *weird* people, Phil," Dan whispered. "The ones who talk about the 'Farm' all the time. The ones all over town. Sometimes they dress funny. In cloaks and masks and junk. The tents too, none of them are nylon... Hey where are you going...?"

"Let's get closer," Phillip said.

"Last time I got closer it took me forever to get back home, it's easy to get lost," Dan warned, but followed. Phillip got off his bike and pushed it. Not wanting to go too fast or attract attention. There was music up ahead.

"Maybe it's a music festival or something...?" Phillip suggested.

"Don't think so, they've been pouring in for weeks, I think, hey...!"

Dan jumped like he had been shocked. Spinning and almost tripping on his bike.

Behind him was a scrappy dog with mangled and dirty fur. He cowered when Dan yelped, as surprised at Dan's reaction as Dan was with him. "Jesus..." Dan said.

"He probably smells your protein bars, he looks hungry," Phillip said, opening his own protein bar, taking a bite before bending down. "Don't you boy? Do you smell the protein bars?" He broke off a piece and offered it. The dog approached Phillip nervously, taking long sniffs before yanking the chunk out of his hand. "Good boy," Phillip said, patting his head. The dog lost any semblance of weakness. Spun on the spot and barked before running off.

"Energy bars are working," Phillip said, taking a bite himself.

"Probably shouldn't do stuff like that here..." Dan said, chuckling.

"Good day to make friends, good day!" Yelled a toad-voiced man behind them.

Both of them jumped this time. The man was slim, and no taller than Phillip. Almost emaciated. But had on a backpack that looked three times his size and four times his weight. "Making friends of any persuasion." Pans attached to the backpack clanked as he laughed. "Does my heart good, seeing young folks like yourself taking on the wide world. Getting into the right sort of trouble." He winked and cackled, the pans clanking again. "Speaking of the wide world. Things can get a little scary without some security. I assume boys as smart as yourself have already got themselves a fine skull-deal to make their way with. Hmm?" He glared at them. "Don't tell me you've come all this way without one! Well it's a fine day for you you've found me. I know all the right people..."

"... keep the bone-peddling to the Camp, Favian," another voice said. A girl's voice this time, behind them. They were doing so much spinning Phillip was getting dizzy.

"Ain't committing no crimes making recommendations to Earners!" Favian yelled.

"Doesn't have to be a crime to annoy the Pauls, bone-peddler," the girl said. She was maybe a little older than him, his height but much thinner. She was wearing shorts, a band concert shirt, and some kind of thin open black robe that went to her thighs. She was wearing high wooden shoes and thick black glasses she wore on the end of her nose. Her hair a bundle of black kept up in disorganized series of mismatched clips.

"Bone-Peddler?! Bone-Peddler?!" Favian repeated. "I'm a Skull *Merchant*. Proper Skull merchant. I'm licensed. Worked hard for what I am..." His complaints dissolved into incoherent mumbling as he turned and walked away, so insulted he couldn't cope.

"You did not have to insult the man, Andy," another girl said. This voice belonged to a girl with strawberry blond hair, long but cut carefully around her face, hair which seemed a few shades more luminous than it should have been. She wore a bright blue dress and was as unlike the first girl in attitude as was possible. She held a clipboard with a feather pen.

"He was picking on Choicers again," the first girl, Andy, said.

"Andy! What a thing to assume!" The girl in blue said, she looked at Phillip and Dan. "Not that there's anything wrong with that, of course..." She said—almost as an apology—and for some reason Phillip found himself blushing when she caught his eyes. She had the brightest blue eyes he had ever seen.

"Excuse my friend Emily, she's horribly inconsiderate, I try to restrain her but I can only do so much," Andy said, approaching their bikes. "Look at you two, all out of pamphlets. Well here you go." She then dumped about two dozen packets of paper into Dan's basket. "Andy!" Emily chided, taking the redundant pamphlets out. "Sorry. I'm Emily Morris, this is Andy Kanamori, we are the Welcoming Committee, for the time being. We can help you with anything you need, I assume you have your paperwork filled out?

A slight pause. "Yep," said Phillip, "sure" said Dan. Andy squinted.

"Delightful. If you find anything confusing. Just consult the 'Informal Laws, Suggestions, and Expectations' manual. The white one right at the bottom. Or ask for Emily, I'd be happy to help. The opening ceremony is tomorrow night, that's Farm time, at the Amphitheater, everybody is invited. Schedule should be in here somewhere..."

"Do you feel welcomed?" Andy asked.

"Um, sure. Yes. Very welcomed," Phillip said.

"See, Emily, we're doing fine," Andy said. "Now let's leave the Choicers alone, they got choicing to do. Don't you two sell your bones to a guy like Favian! I'll be mad at you," she said, grabbing Emily. "Oh, and one more bit of advice, don't trust people like Favian, but you have to start trusting somebody if you want to get anywhere. You know, use those Choicer instincts of yours."

"Good luck to you both, and welcome to the Farm," Emily said. "What were your names again?"

"Phillip, and uh, Daniel," he said, pointing to himself when he said Dan's name. He sounded like an idiot, *why did he sound like an idiot?* "Thank you!" Phillip yelled to them—far too loud—and waved as they walked away.

It took a few moments for them to recover.

"Like I said, weird people," Dan said, looking at the pamphlets. "Did that guy want to... *buy* our bones...?"

"The girls seemed nice. Andy and Emily..."

"You shouldn't have told them our names. These pamphlets are all in different languages..." Dan said, flipping through them. "Except this one," One small sheet of paper featured simple text:

OPENING CEREMONY

THE PAULS

MAIN GATES AMPHITHEATER

NOTHING FANCY

JUNE 20TH FIVE HOURS BEFORE DUSK, FARM-TIME

"Opening ceremony for what...?" Phillip said.

"And what's Farm time...? Ah crap!" Dan yelled, grabbing Phillip's left hand and looking at his watch. "How long have we been gone?"

"Crap," Phillip repeated, looking at the watch, "too long."

"I got to get back home."

"We're going to come back tomorrow," Phillip said, initially as a question but morphing into a statement halfway through.

"You bet your butt we are," Dan said.

———— o ————

It took less time to get back to Fairchild Ranch than it did to get to the Farm.

"Contact me when you get in, phones don't always work right so we need to know we can talk when I'm home," Dan said in one breath, already turning to leave. "Bring whatever we need tomorrow. I'll try to make an excuse..."

"My Aunt Kath goes to the airport tomorrow, in the morning, after that I think I'm free," Phillip waved goodbye and ran up the porch. There were no messages on his phone, the family was probably already eating dinner and wondering where he was.

"That didn't take long," Aunt Elaine said as he walked into the door, barely audible over the hoots and screams in the living room.

"Sorry about that, lost track of time..." he responded.

"What do you mean sorry?" She replied, "You were gone for less than fifteen minutes. Was everything okay with your new friend?"

Fifteen minutes? No, he had lost track of time but they were gone for... how long were they gone? An hour? *Hours?* He looked again at his watch. *When had they left?* Aunt Kath came out of the kitchen with another tray of food. She was still cooking. "You're back?" She said.

"Oh yeah, Dan had to get back home really quick, call from his mom," he lied quickly.

"Come and have something to eat." Aunt Elaine said.

"Eat the pizza muffins, they're way better than those gross sausages," Aunt Kath said with a pointed look at her sister, who stuck out her tongue.

Phillip sat down in front of the TV. The Crimson Hart's were competing in some game that involved throwing a heavy ball attached to a smaller ball with a rope. He hardly noticed.

"Fifteen minutes..." He said under his breath.

It was just as light out as when he left... he went to go look at the time in the kitchen, and then at his watch.

The time was off. Hours off.

He laughed. Following Dan's advice, he wrote what happened in his pink notebook. He was interrupted by his phone buzzing. Dan's number.

'DID u see the time???!?!!!' the message said.

'Just noticed.' Phillip wrote back.

'This is wild! What does it mean?'

'We are going to figure out tomorrow,' Phillip wrote, feeling at that moment that nothing on earth could keep him from the opening ceremony.

"Who was that boy?" Maddie said behind him, causing him to jump a little.

"Jeez, Maddie, don't sneak up on me," Phillip said. "It was Dan, he lives around here."

"I've never seen him," she said.

Phillip shrugged.

"Why were you putting up papers? The ones you printed when you were 'going to the bathroom,'" she said with air quotes.

She figured him out. Probably didn't question him because he bought her the book...

"That was just summer homework stuff," he said without a beat.

"You're looking for lost things," she said, and then held up one of the signs he had printed. It had tape on it. "Why?"

"Homework gets weird in Maine," he said.

"The Dan boy had one of the flyers. He came here because of them, didn't he? Why are you lying about it? What's in that bag...?" She said, drifting off at the end to look out the window. "Puppy!" She yelled so loud it made Phillip squint. She ran out of the kitchen and he heard the front door open.

"What was that?" One of the Fairchild boys yelled from the living room. "Oh God don't let it be a puppy..." He heard aunt Elaine say.

It wasn't a puppy. On the porch was a dog.

The same light-colored ragged dog he had fed near the Campgrounds.

"You?!" He said before he could stop himself. The dog spun around at least a half dozen times when he saw Phillip. Maddie was bent next to him, offering some food, the spinning throwing dust into her eye. The dog was very dirty.

"Do you know him...?" Maddie asked, and the dog wagged his tail all the more.

"Don't feed him, Madlyn, he's just a local," aunt Elaine said, holding Matthew on her hip, who pointed and babbled. "I think he's lost, mom," Maddie said. "Look how dirty he is..."

"Puppy!" Aunt Kath yelled, bending down next to Maddie and talking in a baby voice. "Do you have any dog food for him?"

"You don't know if he had diseases..." Aunt Elaine said helplessly, as the family—one by one—went to pet the dog or offer him food. "Don't feed him!"

The dog never looked away from Phillip. He was so fixated on Phillip that aunt Elaine asked, "have you seen this dog before...?"

"Nope," he answered. The dog smelled. Aunt Elaine wouldn't like that. Maddie was already arguing that they should clean him and bring him inside. "What are you doing here...?" Phillip whispered to the dog.

The dog looked confused—as if the question was so obvious the dog didn't know how to answer it. *Because you're here*, the dog seemed to say, and began wagging his tail again, so Phillip wouldn't be too embarrassed by his own foolishness.

CHAPTER 7

Drips

Aunt Elaine lost almost every battle that night.

The dog was fed, groomed, and given an enormous amount of attention. "What should we call him?" Maddie asked. "Don't name him, Madlyn, he probably has a home," aunt Elaine begged.

Maddie started calling him Fortinbras.

The name fit, Phillip admitted. Steve and Harrison called him "Forty" and Phillip joined along, which annoyed Maddie. Fortinbras seemed happy with either name, and answered to both.

"Maddie, we have a busy day tomorrow. Your aunt goes to the airport, your brothers have practice, and don't you have to get ready for the program?" Aunt Elaine said. Maddie rolled her eyes and was forced to leave the dog on the porch. "Program?" Phillip asked. "Young Scholars, at KHU," uncle Jeff answered. "They have a ton of free summer programs for locals, you should check them out, Phillip." "Maybe," Phillip answered, trying to sound interested. "I think your aunt is stressed she might have to take care of another dog, the baby keeps her busy," uncle Jeff whispered to him, and it took a second for him to realize he was talking about aunt Elaine and not Aunt Kath. "At least he looks young," Phillip joked, gesturing to the two sleeping bodies of the Fairchild's ancient dogs. Uncle Jeff gave a tense laugh back, his wife's stress concerning him more than he let on.

Fortinbras stayed on the porch—aunt Elaine's one victory. Uncle Jeff would take him to the vet tomorrow if he was still there in the morning.

The family tried, and failed, to go to bed early. It was after midnight when everybody went to bed.

Sleeping didn't last long.

Phillip spent the night looking through the pink notebook and planning for tomorrow. Dan sent him a message every few minutes. *'Should I bring a tent?'* *'Wut kind of tent??'* *'Never mind about the tent I can't find it.'* *'What about the stuff I got from the mailbox?'* The messages went back and forth for hours.

He heard aunt Elaine and uncle Jeff fighting in their room. Distant mumbling sounds in an unmistakable tone. He couldn't make it out, but thought he heard his name and Aunt Kath's.

Maddie woke him up by shaking him on the shoulder.

It was still dark. "What?" He mumbled, confused. "It's in here too!" Maddie yelled.

"What's in...?" Phillip said, he was uncomfortable, he felt wet. Maddie flipped on the light. When Phillip's eyes adjusted, he noticed little puddles of water on his bed. "It's really bad in here!" Maddie added.

Phillip looked up. The ceiling was leaking.

"Not Philly Cheese's room!" Harrison answered back. He came into the room carrying pots and bowls. "Get up Philly Cheese, sleeping in your clothes, Philly Cheese? Good thinking. Ah man it is bad in here. The whole bed is wet."

"Get the mattress out of the room before it's ruined," uncle Jeff said from the hallway as he opened the attic door.

"Dang Philly Cheese you're a deep sleeper..." Harrison said, manhandling the bed while he was still in it. Steve joined him.

Rubbing his eyes. Phillip moved his things as fast as he could. Hiding the pink notebook in his shirt. Throwing the unicorn bag and its contents into his suitcase. Steve and Harrison were too busy to notice. "Good thing you get nightmares, Madds, or Philly Cheese would have drowned," Steve said.

Pots and jars and bowls were placed in the hallway, being dripped into from the ceiling. Aunt Elaine was bringing towels and handing them to Maddie and Aunt Kath, who placed them on the floor. Uncle Jeff was yelling something from the attic. "What happened?" Phillip said, moving his things to the dry side of the hallway and trying to help. "Pipe burst," Maddie answered.

His phone was buzzing. Dan again. He looked at his watch. Almost 4:00am.

'_)() **&% Fiiii Fi FInd GUIDE, fiiiinnnd *&^%^%$ Bride**&Oopen stttead'

'Dan your phone is glitching, ur messages are not working,' Phillip wrote back.

"Harry? Where's Harry? Somebody get me the blue toolbox. The blue one!" uncle Jeff said in the attic.

His phone buzzed again. It wasn't a message, but a call. Dan.

"Hello?" Phillip answered as discreetly as he could.

A high-pitched screeching answered him. A scream—almost a cackle—followed, followed by a metallic clunking. He winced and held the phone away from his head.

At the same time, uncle Jeff gave a shallow yelp in the attic. A massive 'CLUNK' reverberated through the house. It took a moment to realize it wasn't coming from his phone, and Phillip saw in the open door of his room a part of the ceiling gave way and gallons of water poured into where his mattress used to be.

The screeching laughing on his phone continued.

He hung up.

He caught Maddie's eyes, who looked at him like he just committed murder.

"Jeffery, what just happened?!" Aunt Elaine yelled.

"Nothing! It's under control," uncle Jeff said, almost loud enough to be heard over the dripping.

"See, cursed," Aunt Kath whispered. "All that past-life nun killing…"

"Definitely cursed," Phillip said. Feeling the phone in his pocket and looking at the hole in the ceiling.

———— ○ ————

Thanks to Steve and Harrison's physical prowess, almost nothing was hurt.

Furniture was moved to the hallway or downstairs, and anything that was wet was put on the wide porch. Looked over by a curious Fortinbras, who did his best to help with encouraging barks.

Rosencrantz and Guildenstern were not nearly so enthusiastic, annoyed that their favorite sleeping spots were disturbed, they sat around Phillip's feet and grumbled.

Things didn't settle down for hours. Almost the entire upstairs was covered in towels and tarps and blankets and pots and pans and bowls. The dripping slowed. Aunt Elaine started making early breakfast. "I can get Donald here today, but it won't be a few hours…" Uncle Jeff said. Matthew had woken up in the commotion. "I'll drive Katherine to the airfield…"

"I'll take a cab to the airport," Aunt Kath interrupted. "It's only thirty minutes away, you need to be here." King's Hill had an unusually large airport for its size, shared with Gardenvale—*the King's Hill & Garden Airfield*—something uncle Jeff bragged about.

"Sorry about this, Katherine," uncle Jeff said. "This happened in this house when I was a kid, younger than Maddie, thought we solved the pipe problem…"

"Where are we going to set up the beds?" Harrison said. He was far too cheerful. Excitement did that to him.

'What's going on ON oN on on?' y all the _ -..??' Dan messaged him. Phillip ignored it. His things were spread around the living room and porch, he didn't know where anything was.

"Harry your bunking with your brother until we know your room is okay. We can set up a blow-up mattress in your room for Phillip. Maddie will sleep downstairs," uncle Jeff answered.

Sleep in a room with Steve and Harrison? Gallons of water pouring on his head was one thing, but *this* was something to panic about.

"What about… Uh," Phillip said. Thinking fast and petting Rosencrantz to look casual. He pointed outside. "What about the Dollhouse?"

Uncle Jeff seemed to think about this. He always looked intense and worried when he was thinking. His eyes darting between Phillip and the old beagle, "that's… not a bad idea."

45

"Yeah, I can just sleep there and keep my stuff there," Phillip said. "I can bring Forty with me, take care of him for aunt Elaine doesn't have to."

"But you'll be alone..." Aunt Elaine said.

"Only to sleep and use the bathroom," Phillip answered, worried that he was selling it too hard. "If it's a pain though..."

"No, it's a good idea. Isn't it Rose?" uncle Jeff said, talking to the fat beagle at Phillip's feet. "Best case scenario Phillip is sleeping in the boy's rooms or the living room, we need to get the ceiling fixed, and what happens when Katherine gets back? This solves the problem. Steve, Harry, we're moving your aunt and your cousin to the Dollhouse."

Harrison clapped his hands and began lifting the mattress. "We don't need that mattresses over there, just unwrap them and bring over bedding," aunt Elaine said.

"What are we doing?" Aunt Kath asked. "Moving," Phillip answered.

The whole family—save Matthew—helped move their things and bedding over to the smaller home. The sky still mostly dark. "C'mon Forty, we're moving," Phillip said to the dog, who obeyed, running from one porch to the other. "The dog really likes Phillip..." Aunt Elaine said. Uncle Jeff turned on the power and gas. Then tested all the water and toilets in the home by running them. Steve and Harrison unwrapped the mattresses from storage plastic, and the house was ready. "The fridge is temperamental, beyond that everything works, showers are fine," uncle Jeff said to Aunt Kath and Phillip. "Better shape than the new home right now. Does this work for you, Phillip?"

"Perfect," Phillip answered. "Thank you."

"Good," uncle Jeff said. "Should be no more problems then."

The Dollhouse was clean, if a bit dusty. Tarps were put over the furniture. A few of the rooms were being used for storage. In almost every way it was like a compressed version of the main house, though much older, the house slightly warped and cracked.

Exactly like Phillip remembered.

It even smelled the same. Like a library, old musty paper. He went upstairs to the cozy corner room with the blue wallpaper which had always been *his* room, and he realized he hadn't been in the home since his parents died.

That was a weird thought.

Phillip's things were spread across two houses and maybe the lawn, Steve and Harrison were efficient, but not careful. He had the pink notebook, and the brown bag stuffed in his suitcase, that was important. But he had lost track of some of the items. *Where were the stuffed animals? The doll? The books...?*

He was missing stuff.

He scrambled through all his things, putting his clothes away in the closet. It was light out when he stopped. He was definitely missing things.

This was not good.

Steve and Harrison probably thought the stuffed animals and doll belonged to Maddie.

"Phillip?" Aunt Kath said with a knock at the door as Phillip went through his suitcase again. "Phillip?"

"Hmm? What's up?"

"Phillip, I called the cab, it's on its way."

"Oh," Phillip said, looking at his watch and opening the door. It was later than he thought. Aunt Kath had showered and dressed. "Didn't think of that, I guess I can't come with you to the airport," he said with his back turned, still looking through his dirty laundry.

"You going to be okay here?"

"Think so, probably nap all day now..."

"I mean *here* here...?" She said.

"Oh, yeah, I guess so," he answered. Now the pink notebook was gone. Where had he put that? He thought he put it on the nightstand but...

"You sure...?"

"I'm sure," he answered, going through the drawers.

"I just don't want you to..."

"At this point the plans are made, right? Decisions already done. Doesn't matter how okay I am..." He said, surprised by how harsh he sounded. "Sorry," he said immediately. "Not what I meant. I'm just tired..."

"No, it's okay..." She said. "We'll talk later about this, I promise. It'll all make sense... Just, I promise we'll talk about it."

"It's fine, sorry," he said again, following her downstairs. Her open suitcase at the door. He had been holding the pink notebook all along. He really was tired. "Help me close my suitcase, sit on it," Aunt Kath said.

"Why are you bringing such a big coat? It's summer, you're going to California," Fortinbras barked on the porch, looking in through the screen door. "Forty aggress with me."

"Fortinbras," Maddie corrected, half-asleep on the couch.

"Madds, what are you doing over here?" Aunt Kath asked.

"Wanted to..." Maddie yawned, "...say goodbye, parents busy calling people..."

"I'm going to miss them, aren't I? What a weird day..." Aunt Kath said.

"It's because Aunt Kath killed a nun," Phillip explained to Maddie.

"Not me, Madds, past life me, Hey who's that boy outside...?"

Aunt Kath pointed out the window, and Phillip saw the person wearing a red windbreaker around his waist on a bike going towards the other house. "Dan...?" Phillip said to himself, opening the front door, which thrilled Fortinbras.

"That guy who came over yesterday? It's early..." Aunt Kath said.

"He ran into Phillip on his bike," Maddie added.

"Dan," Phillip called across the lawn, Dan turned around. "What are you doing here? It's early..."

"But you...?" Dan said, furrowing his brows, which widened again when he looked down at the blond dog that followed Phillip's feet. "You...?!"

Fortinbras barked.

"You know Fortinbras, don't you?" Maddie said pointedly behind Phillip. "Just like Phillip, you've seen him before. What are you up to? Why are you both acting weird?"

"Fortin..." Dan stuttered, a service truck was making its way up the driveway. "Have we met before?"

"This is Maddie, my cousin," Phillip said. "This is our new dog Forty. Hey Forty, why don't you go back to the house and protect the porch?" The dog gave a happy bark, turned around three times, and headed for the porch.

"Were you... talking to...?" Maddie started.

"Madlyn!" Aunt Elaine yelled from the main house. "Come help with your brother!"

Maddie groaned, Aunt Kath appeared behind her. "Hi Dan," she said with a wave.

"Hi," Dan said back awkwardly. "Miss Kath, right? I had an early thing, a summer school program, so I thought I'd come around and see if Phil was up and also you have a new dog and I'd thought I might see him. I love dogs and we used to have one but then it died and it was sad so we haven't gotten a new one yet..."

"Oh, okay," Aunt Kath said back. "Summer program, one of those ones at the University?"

Dan pause. "Yes..." he answered without blinking.

By god he was a bad liar, Phillip thought.

"Neat," Aunt Kath said.

"Why is all the furniture on the porch?" Dan asked.

"Aunt Kath killed a nun," Phillip answered.

"Only in a past life. Allegedly! Phillip I'm going over to say goodbye to everybody. Yell if the cab comes."

"Will do," Phillip answered, looking at her walk away. "What are you doing here this early?" He whispered to Dan when she was far enough away.

"What do you mean 'what am I doing here?'" Dan said. "You've been sending me things all night. You told me to get here as soon as possible. That it was urgent."

"I didn't..." Phillip stopped. Felt the phone in his pocket. "I didn't send you a thing... but you did. Last night, you sent me a bunch of nonsense stuff with random symbols."

"What? I..."

"Dan..." Phillip interrupted. "I got a call from *you* last night, before the pipe burst. It was just this sound. But then the pipe burst, and I could have sworn I heard it on the phone first..."

Dan was silent for a moment. "Holy dang moly, Phil..."

"Holy dang moly," Phillip agreed.

An unfamiliar car with no markings honked as it came down the driveway. That must be the cab. Phillip waved to the car.

"I brought the stuff over," Dan said.

"What stuff?"

"From the mailbox, like I told you about," he tapped his heavy bag on his back. "Brought the mailbox too. Like you... told me to."

"Jeez..." Phillip said. "Go inside the house, my room is upstairs on the left, the one in the corner with the blue wallpaper. Hide the stuff there before my family notices."

Aunt Kath was hugging uncle Jeff and aunt Elaine on the porch of the main house as Dan went into Dollhouse, Fortinbras barking to tell Phillip he was there. More service trucks came as the cab waited for Aunt Kath to pack her bags and then forget something and run inside the house, which she did three times. "I'm bringing too many books..." She said, her bag was almost unliftable. "Sucks that you can't go to the airport," she said to Phillip.

"Yeah, sure does," Phillip said. "So, I guess I'll see you in a month."

"Three weeks," Aunt Kath corrected.

"Right, you're back Thursday, July 12th," Phillip said. "Basically, a month."

She hugged him. "Try not to cause your family too much trouble, I think Ellie is losing her hair."

"Can't promise anything, you know me," he said back. "Don't be a bum. Do well at the University of Berkeley."

"University of California, Berkeley," she corrected. "And you're the bum."

"Try to avoid any animals on the road," Phillip said in the direction of the cab driver. "She killed a lucky nun and now the deer are after her."

<hr />

Dan had brought everything with him.

In the center of the room, a blue squarish metal box, with odd writing and symbols on the side. Next to it a plastic bin filled with what looked like rat skulls, jars with twigs in them, a bundle of origami swans, a foldable pocket knife with a wood and glass handle which Phillip picked up. Dan was in the center, writing in the pink notebook. "I'm lucky my mom worked late last night, she was all zonked this morning and didn't notice I left. Wrote a note saying I went to McKay's, hopefully she doesn't wake up too early," he said to Phillip.

Phillip wasn't listening. He was looking at the bed. Where a small model of a red-eyed and red-antlered stag lay. He picked it up slowly and put it on the dresser. "You say it... goes away sometimes?" Phillip said.

"Yep, thought I was crazy when it first happened. I looked it up on the internet and it said I might have schizophrenia."

"Was it gone the day you ran into me?"

"I don't know, I have to hide all this stuff for when my little cousins come over, they get into all my stuff."

"But you had it with you, when you were on the bike..."

"That's the thing, Phil. One of the things I wanted to talk to you about," Dan looked concerned. "I don't remember why I brought it. I don't remember making that decision. I still think I'm going crazy..."

Phillip didn't look away from the red eyes of the stag model.

"Holy dang moly," Phillip said.

"Holy dang moly," Dan agreed. "What do we do from here? With everything that's happening, are we still going to try to get to this opening ceremony whatever-it-is?"

"You bet your butt we are," Phillip answered.

"Good," Dan said. "First mission of the 'Farm Discovery Club.' 'Operation Infiltration.' That's the first thing I came up with, Phil, but I'm not too happy with it and am open to suggestions. I think we should form a club, by the way. It's the natural thing to do..."

"Sure, a club," Phillip said offhandedly. "And I say we leave to the Farm now, before we lose our nerve."

CHAPTER 8

The Amphitheater

A loose group black bears wove their way lazily through the campground. Occasionally stopping by a booth offering food or a camper who was holding something of interest, looking for scraps or gifts.

They were ignored by most, and shooed away by those who did pay attention.

One man offered to put masks on them. In the middle of summer! During midday! They declined as politely as they were able, being bears.

The unofficial leader—who was the oldest, fattest, and slowest by half—stopped suddenly. He had found two campers that didn't smell like the others. Nothing about them was like the others. They stunk of soap. Their hair smelled like sweet berries. What was odd was that they also smelled a little like bears. With his old eyes he could see, even in midday, the waving lines wafting off the two campers.

A proper stink, but not cultivated. It reminded him of home.

The two camper creatures, who were smaller than most others, became tense. Their fear adding to perfume of that odd smell of theirs.

What these campers had to be scared about, the leader didn't know. He pushed his head in close to the camper creature's face to take a longer sniff.

They both had bags on. Bags contained food. Camper creatures foolishly carried food with them. Maybe some of that rich sweet stuff some of these creatures liked so much. He wondered if food from these stinky campers tasted any different than food from the foul-smelling clean ones...

"Shoo! Shoo! Off with you then," a tall camper creature yelled at them. Flapping those useless paws at them. They were like birds, these creatures, always squawking about something.

He considered what to do. He looked at the tall camper creature and then back at the two stinky ones, one of them now holding one of those pathetic little claws these creatures sometimes had. He did want to see what was in that pack. But it probably wasn't worth the trouble. Closing his eyes and turning his hide to the tall camper creature for that it knew that leaving was his decision, he strolled off. The other bears following suit.

He lost all thoughts of these stinky little camper creatures before they were out-of-sight, when one of the brash and eager young bears noticed a basket of unattended food stuffs. Filled to the brim with all the foods these camper creatures, with their pathetic paws and weak jaws, never seemed to be able to eat.

The old leader spared no time to pity the camper-creatures as he tipped over the basket to enjoy their bounty.

— o —

"You can't let them do anything they want. They'll get all entitled and right miserable to deal with," the mustached man in the leather apron said to them.

Both Phillip and Dan were looking after the bears, who were now eating garbage

"Thanks," Phillip said as he slowly put away the wood handled pocket knife. "Are there a lot of bears here? In camp?"

"Running through the place like rodents, they are," he said. "They're supposed to stay in *their* camp most of the day. I suppose you can't do too much about it, with so many Canadians here," he grumbled as he walked away.

"You brought the pocket knife with you?" Dan asked.

"I guess I pocketed it without knowing..." Phillip said. "Sorry, I wasn't stealing it."

"No, I know," Dan said. "The stuff, Phil. It moves around, it's hard to keep it in one place... You move it without knowing it. I wanted to talk to you about that, I wish we had more time to talk. Excuse me sir?" Dan said to a tall man handing out papers. "Do you know where the amphitheater is...?"

The man answered back in angry sounding French and handed Dan a paper.

"What does it say?" Phillip asked.

"It's a schedule, but it doesn't make any sense..." Dan said. "It's a chart. It tells you the day, then it divides it up into four. *Prima... fold*? Mundafold, Camps, and Farm-time... '*Standard Relative Non-Contradictory Entrance Exit Dilation,*'" he read. "Today it says '*Two-moonrise and moonset. Plus-five, Exit midday... schedule is subject to change...*' What the heck does that mean? Phil, do you think this is why time here is weird and wonky...?"

"Who knows, let's keep walking," Phillip said, getting out of the way of two dozen men wearing tuxedos and top hats. There were similarly dressed kids with them, who starred at them judgmentally as they passed.

"Where?" Dan asked.

"We're not where we want to be, so anywhere, people seem to be heading that way."

The Camps were weirder the deeper they went in, and they had been walking for miles. Dan said they should have hit the river at some point, but never did. They were small streams and little bridges littered through the camps, with water so clear it was almost invisible. Tents and yurts and new wooden or brick structures and campfires and horse wagons littered the densely wooded campground in all directions. The tents were all cloth. And there were animals everywhere. Not just the bears. Dogs and cats, huge deer and elk, goats, pigs, horses. They heard a trumpeting blast in the distance that sounded suspiciously like an elephant. Dan said he saw a group of ostriches who "looked like they were wearing masks..."

But the people were the oddest thing.

Some were impeccably dressed, tuxedos or dresses. Fine suits. Some wore nothing at all, or were covered in blue body paint. Some wore masks and cloaks. Others furs and feathers. Many looked like backpackers or homeless people, interacting with people who wore gilded capes and shawls and looked like royalty. Phillip didn't recognize half of the languages around him.

"I think we're close," Dan whispered, everybody was walking in the same direction. He had given up trying to draw a map in his pink notebook, nothing made sense.

The tree line broke, and they were walking in a wide field. The trees were cleared here. Some trees were left standing, but their branches and bark were removed, with animals or faces carved into them at random angles. They looked like pillars in the ruins of an ancient city. Blocks of stone lay everywhere, as small as a car or as large as the Fairchild house. Some buried into the ground, some stacked, others jutting into the sky, looking like they were about to tip over.

"Hurry up! Hurry up! Everybody's invited but room is scarce and the Pauls won't wait!" A booming voice said.

Trumpets and drums were being played somewhere in the distance. Phillip couldn't see over the crowd, which was picking up its pace.

Black-clad people—wearing what looked like military uniforms—walked in the opposite direction, holding metal instruments that looked like large tuning forks. *Metal detectors?*

"Dan, we should go around..." Phillip whispered, interrupted by a tap on the shoulder.

One of the black-clad men, a youngish square-jawed blond, was holding up the tuning fork to Phillip, and frowning. The tuning fork made a higher-pitched ringing as he waved it near Phillip's pockets. Another woman in black did the same to Dan.

"Are you nopes compliant?" The blond man asked.

"Um, *nopes*...?" Dan said.

"What's the holdup, Brooks?" Said another man in black, older than the blond and not much taller than Phillip. He had darker, coppery skin.

"Nothing, Captain, just some nopes violations," the blond man answered.

The older man looked at Phillip and Dan. Looked down at his clothes, then sniffed the air and sneered, like he was looking at something disgusting and rotten and was about to gag. "Don't waste any more time, mark them and send them to processing," the Captain said.

"Yes, Captain Karo," the younger man answered, holding Phillip's shoulder a little too tightly.

"I... we don't need to..." Phillip started, not knowing what he was going to say but knowing he didn't want to go to 'processing.'

"That won't be necessary, Captain," a polite and familiar voice interrupted.

The blond girl in the blue dress—still wearing blue and still holding the clipboard with the feather-pen—stood behind them. Her name was Emily, Phillip remembered.

"They are with me, Captain. Guests," Emily said.

"I wasn't aware you were able to bring in guests, *Miss* Morris," Captain Karo answered, putting emphasis on 'Miss.'

"Excuse me for misspeaking," she said, just as politely as before. "I should say they are guests of the Welcoming Committee. Of which Lady Kanamori is a member, I'm sure you know."

"Hi, Emily," the younger blond man said in a low voice to Emily.

"Good to see you, Willum. Sorry, Private Brooks," Emily answered back, a bit sheepishly, and Phillip found himself not liking Private Willum Brooks very much, in no small part because he still held Phillip's shoulder. "As I understand it, Captain," Emily raised her voice. "Wallmen purification standards aren't to be applied at the Amphitheater, as everybody is invited, am I wrong in that assessment?"

Captain Karo looked like he was going to say something harsh, but a blast from fireworks in the sky followed by cheers interrupted him. "We don't have time for this," Captain Karo said. "Brooks, get their names and move on. Write that the good Miss Morris here will answer for them..."

And then the Captain was gone in the crowd. Willum Brooks let go of Phillip's shoulder, "This is Phillip," Emily said and pointed to Dan. "And the other is Daniel."

"Thank you, Lady Morris," Brooks mumbled, smiling awkwardly before turning and following the Captain.

"Thank you," Dan said.

"I'm Phillip," he blurted, cleaning his throat halfway through.

"Sorry?" Emily said.

"I'm... uh, I'm Phillip, this s Dan, Daniel."

"I'm so sorry for the mix-up," Emily said, sounding distressed.

"No, it's my fault, Dan's name is good. Daniel's name. So... you know, all good," Phillip said, and wished beyond everything that the bears would come back and maul him.

Emily smiled, a perfect dimpled smile that matched her shining hair. "Well, Phillip and Daniel, we better get going, the show's about to start and Andy might not save enough seats for all of us."

———— o ————

The amphitheater was dug into the ground. It was asymmetrical, like it was made from an uncareful scope of a giant spoon, one side much steeper than the other.

It could fit thousands of people—and did—all of the stone seats surrounding a triangular stage at the bottom.

Emily brought them through a special entrance. A staircase hidden between two rocks that led to a pathway barley wide enough to accommodate them. Dan had to take off his backpack and walk sideways. "Just a little bit longer," Emily had said, like she was trying to reassure him. "Oh, that's cool," Phillip answered. "I actually like small spaces and caves and... stuff."

"Why are you acting so weird?" Dan whispered.

"Shush!" Phillip whispered-yelled back.

The small entrance led to seats near the bottom of the amphitheater. The other girl with the wild black hair sat nearby, she waved obnoxiously and yelled for Emily, even after it was clear Emily saw her. She was sitting next to an Asian boy who was maybe a little older than her, dressed in what looked like a business suit mixed with a kimono.

"Hey, it's those guys!" Andy said to Emily. "What's their names, Dawson and Filipe?"

"This is Daniel and Phillip," Emily corrected, though Phillip was sure Andy was teasing. "Captain Karo was harassing them, so I said they were guests."

"Be careful, Emily, that has power here," the boy said in a serious voice. He was looking critically at Dan and Phillip. He wore a long knife at his waist, Phillip noticed.

"We appreciate it," Phillip managed to say. "Hi again."

"Tadaaki is just not in a fun mood, ignore him," Andy said, adjusting her glasses. Phillip noticed the lenses changed color when she did so. "If it annoys the Captain, we're happy to have you. Good job playing on Emily's sympathies to get better seats."

Phillip was going to defend himself, but drums cut him off.

He sat in front of Andy, next to Dan, who was having a difficult time deciding where to put his backpack.

Dan grabbed his shoulder and pointed to the stage. Dozens of men, covered from head to toe in blue overlapping cloth were walking to the stage. The audience began to quiet down. By the time they stopped, nobody in the amphitheater was speaking. The drummers sat statue-still around the parameter of the stage. It was bright in the theater, but the stage seemed somehow more illuminated than the rest.

Two men appeared on the stage from behind the drummers.

The audience began clapping.

The first man was large, wearing work clothes with a trimmed gray beard. He held his hands in his jacket pockets, as if bored.

The second man was smaller and older than the first, with longer hair and a shorter white beard. Tight and hard looking. Wearing similar clothes to the first. Despite being older he looked more energetic.

"I think those are the Pauls," Phillip whispered, who wasn't listening to him, instead writing notes in his pink notebook as fast as he could. "Oh yeah" Phillip said, taking out his own pink notebook and pencil.

The smaller man raised his hand up to the crowd, forming a fist. The audience went quiet again. The two men moved around the stage. Everything they did echoing across the deathly quiet amphitheater.

The larger man went to the center of stage, he somehow pulled a thin table from behind him and, reaching into his jacket, took out a crystal bowl that looked far too large to have fit in his jacket. Placing the bowl on top, he took a bottle out of his coat pocket and filled the bowl with clear liquid. He then took out a small flask and poured its contents into the bowl, taking a swig before emptying it completely. Some of the crowd laughed at this, but were hushed by others. The large man put his finger into the bowl, and then circled the rim, making it hum and ring. A sound which continued after he was done.

The smaller man was circling that stage all the while. He was drawing a circle with a stick on the ground, into a thin layer of dust that covered the stone stage. How he didn't make footprints, Phillip couldn't guess. He drew another circle, and then another. He placed simple angular symbols at points around the circle. Phillip drew the image into his notebook as best he could.

The large man joined the smaller man. Reaching into his pockets, he took out small metal objects and placed them where there were symbols. The smaller man clapped his hand, picked up the metal objects, and placed something else on the ground.

They both joined each other at the bowl. The smaller man threw the metal objects he had gathered into the bowl. The large man put his hand into the bowl, brought it up with a swish, and with two fingers held up, he stood there.

What were they doing? Phillip thought.

At least a minute passed.

The crowd murmured.

His hand came down.

CRACK! BOOM!

A noise so loud Phillip didn't even register it as a sound, it was like being hit by a wave, accompanied by a blinding flash.

CRACK! BOOM! Again.

Lighting.

Lightning was striking the center of the stage. Again, and again. Becoming weaker, less blinding, each time, but speeding up. Becoming a constant stream of light.

"Dan!" Phillip yelled.

"I know!" He replied.

He had dropped his book, he grabbed Dan's shoulder when the lighting struck, which was surprisingly bony.

"Ummmm…" He heard Andy say.

He looked to the right, and noticed he was wrong, he had not grabbed Dan's shoulder, he had grabbed Andy's knee, which sat near Dan's shoulder…

"Sorry!" He said, taking his hand away like her knee was a hot stove.

He heard Emily suppress a giggle.

"It's fine," Andy said with a chuckle.

The boy next to Andy—Tadaaki—clearly thought it was anything but 'fine.'

He found himself unembarrassed and not caring.

The lightning was still there. The focal point was the bowl. Blue and thin and seemed to be slowing down. Flowing in slow motion. The crowd erupted into more cheers.

"We said nothing fancy, and we meant it," the larger man said with a slight western accent. "We're going to keep this short."

"We suffer from no delusions," the smaller man continued. "We know why many of you are here. We expected this when we started this endeavor. We've planned for it. And I'm sure to the great surprise of the less naturally devious among you, have even welcomed it."

The crowd murmured.

"As a gift for accommodating you, we expect a certain level of behavior. Inside and out…"

"To be a tad blunter," the smaller man interrupted, he had practiced accent that sounded almost British. "We expect all of the Old Laws and rules to be obeyed. Even the unfashionable ones. The greater courtesies will be respected."

"As many of you have noticed, the Wallmen have been employed within the Farm," the large man said in a grave tone, "they have been given full privileges to expel those they feel are not respecting our wishes. Respect them. And do not make me get involved."

"'Me' not 'us'," Phillip heard Andy whisper, her head turned to Emily.

"We do this for a reason. The greater respect we show for each other. The further we can go together," the small man said. "The Farm will see the removal of all common restrictions. The camps in half-restriction."

The crowd erupted into cheers yet again.

"… the ones not covered by the old laws," the big man amended.

"Our laws are the only ones that matter here. Which brings me to the next order of business…"

A pressure. Like he was going up a fast elevator, pressed on Phillip's ears. It was growing darker in the amphitheater. Phillip looked down at his notebook and then up at the sky.

The moon.

It was larger than he had ever seen it.

And coming closer.

Falling into the amphitheater.

The sky was darkening still further. It was no longer day, like it was moments ago. The stars were out. But they too seemed to be descending. A few came into the amphitheater and floated above the crowd.

The moon continued to descend out of the sky and into the amphitheater. It took up about a third the space when it slowed and stopped, hovering above the stage, bobbing up and down as if it rested on a smooth lake. Light shone on one side, illuminated the many craters and dark patches on the surface. It rotated. Spilling the light on one side of the crowd, and then the other, as it did so.

Some audience members were holding objects up, bowls, which began to glow.

Gasps and shouts followed this, cheers and screams with them.

The pressure in Phillip's ears was overwhelming.

He could feel the weight of the thing. He felt as if it could flatten him if he let it, but also that he could fall into it at any time.

"The rules here are simple," the large man said, his voice still easy to hear despite the roaring audience. "But not easy. We have granted you the utmost respect. Please do us the courtesy of respecting us back,"

The moon floated out of the amphitheater, slowing going back to its correct position. Taking some of the stars with it.

"For those of you invited to the Farm, the rules are simpler still," the small man continued. "If you learn. you *teach*. If you accept generosity, you show courtesy. If you are a guest, you become a host."

"Good luck to all," the larger man said, turning around toward the doors.

"Celebrate! We have made a few donations to the local brewers. You are in our grace until sunrise. But please, don't abuse this generosity too much," the small man said in a cheerful tone.

"And for better or worse. Welcome to the Farm," the large man said.

The smaller man tapped a tall cane on the ground that had not been in his hand a moment ago, and the doors at the back of the stage grew taller. They grew to nearly the top of the amphitheater. The doors burst open. Revealing a meadow populated by a few barns, and a large silo.

It was daytime on the other side of the door.

The two men walked through the massive doors, which shut after them. The crowd got up at once and clapped and howled at the men. Some threw their hats in the air.

Almost the entire audience was moving or jumping or dancing.

All except two, who sat in stunned silence, staring into space.

CHAPTER
9
Open Door Policy

"That wasn't a bad show," Phillip heard Andy say.

"Excuse my ignorance," Emily responded, "I can't begin to fathom the trick they did with that moon illusion, or how it filled the moon gleam bowls, but how was the lighting the Pauls summoned any different from any Storm Parade I've seen?"

"There's a world of difference," Tadaaki responded. "It wasn't summoned or cooked here. What we saw was *made* right here before our eyes with nothing that would normally necessitate its making. Locally non-contingent. Pure Will."

Phillip was only half listening. He was still staring at the stage, occasioning letting his eyes move upward, to the large full moon that hung overhead in the dark sky.

It was *magic.*

He had seen magic tonight.

Because magic existed. Because magic was real.

Magic. Existed.

Magic. Was *real.*

"Couldn't it be a trick?" Emily asked.

"I'm certain a significant portion of the audience will say just that," Tadaaki responded. "Especially the city ink mongers."

"Stop asking my brother boring questions, look at this!" Andy said, holding in front of her a bowl with white sand inside, which glowed. "This is a week's worth of moon gleam. Do you know what that means?!"

"That the Pauls could radically change the industry if they went public with that ability," Emily responded.

"You sound more like your dad every day," Andy said.

"You say that like it's a bad thing," Emily responded.

Phillip and Dan began writing down everything they could think of. It was too dark to write accurately. The audience was moving out of the amphitheater.

Torches being lit. Small metal bows of glowing sand were hovering mid-air, casting gray, or pink and orange light on the crowd and the steps.

"S'cuse meh, boys. You's look like Mokumer types. Gots any honest flame in you's?"

Phillip looked up. The voice came from a man.

But he wasn't a man. He was short and thin. He had enormous features. Long arms that ended in hands with too many fingers. Huge flopped ears that moved like a cat. Skin that looked scaled at points. White blue hair that continued down his neck and forearms. His arms were almost as long as his body, ending in six fingered hands. One on which held a purple cigarette. He was wearing a tattered three-piece suit, the jacket patched.

He had a tail.

A tail with a little bit of fur on the end.

Phillip starred. Dan made a noble attempt to answer him, though no words or thoughts were conveyed.

The little tailed man's face went sour. He said something harsh in another language, all clicks and hisses. He said a few words in English under his breath, Phillip only heard, "Mundafolk country bumpkins," and "little-eyed nats," or maybe "bats..."

"I can help," Emily rushed in. Rescuing them again.

She blew into her hand, murmured something, and held out her cupped hand to the tailed-man. Something inside of her hand glowed. The little man bent down to Emily's outstretched hands. It lit. He took a few puffs and blew out bright purple smoke. It smelled like rotten fruit.

That was magic. Emily was magic too.

Of course she is, Phillip thought.

"Great kindness, Mams. Ands great kindness back," he said with a bowed head. He disappeared into the crowd. Phillip and Dan looking after him.

"Good thing you fellas don't speak Gremmish," Andy said. "Some of those insults about your mother's virtues would have cut deep..."

"So that was... he was a...?" Dan started.

"A gremlin, an Imp," Andy explained.

"Andy, language!" Emily said.

"And... the Imp, the gremlin, insulted our mothers, in Grennish?" Phillip said. "Which you speak."

"That's right Philharmonic. But it's called Gremmish, and I only understand a bit of it." Andy corrected. "Also, don't say '*Imp*', it's rude."

"Gremlins are the second most common creature here, besides humans," Emily explained. "Was that the... *first* time you've meant one...? How did you not notice them coming in?"

"They are very new Choicers," Tadaaki said.

"Brand new," Andy added, pushing her glasses up her nose, which always seemed ready to fall off.

"What does that mean?" Phillip asked. "The word you just used. Choice...ers?"

Phillip drifted off and looked up. There were more gremlins, a group of them. With greenish to bluish to greyish skin. But there were more than gremlins in the amphitheater.

Masks floated mid-air and drifted by. There were women with antlers like deer. Men with horns. Bald men who were as pale as sugar and nine-feet tall. Little dots of light flew in the sky and giggled as they went by. Men and women and animals wore masks. Lighting bowls and lanterns in their wake. Transparent shadows, which looked like people covered in sheets walked by. One creature as large as car which moved on its arms like a gorilla made its way out of the amphitheater.

"What are you looking at!" A man with goat like horns and yellow eyes yelled at Dan, who said "Sorry" and averted his eyes.

Was the crowd always like this? How had he not noticed?

"Choicers," Tadaaki repeated. "Means you were of the Mundafold, and now you're not."

Too many questions filled Phillip's head for any to come out.

"We have appointments to keep," Tadaaki said. Andy rolled her eyes.

"That's right!" Emily said. "Phillip, Daniel, will you be okay here? Do you know your way back?"

"Yes," Phillip said, though it wasn't true, for some reason desperately trying to sound relaxed and casual. "We're Choicers, we got choicing to do."

Andy snorted, surprised by the joke, and made her way out with Emily and Tadaaki.

Phillip and Dan didn't move from their seats. They took notes and gawked at the passing crowd while trying to look they weren't gawking, and failing badly. "Why didn't we notice...?" Dan said a few times under his breath.

"It's like notebooks, like all the stuff..." Phillip said, the thought coming out of his mouth before he realized he had it. "I bet it's like that, plays with your memory." But now they could see it... after the lighting hit. *Why?*

"It's nighttime..." Dan said. "That's possible. It's magic, Phil..."

"I know," Phillip said.

"I knew it was magic, or I was crazy. I went through a spaceman phase a few months back, but nope, magic. Magic is real, Phil. It's magically nighttime. That's possible..." Dan sounded dreamy and mild, like he was delirious.

"C'mon," Phillip said, jumping up. The amphitheater was almost empty. "Let's get going."

"Where?"

"Anywhere, there's stuff to see," Phillip said. "We're 'Choicers', apparently, we got to do "choicing." Let's go to the Farm."

"It's dark, we might want to get home."

"It's fake dark. Time is wonky, like you said, I bet when we get back home only thirty-seconds will have passed. Magic, Dan! C'mon. Let's do this. Let's go to the Farm. We might not get another chance, what if it all disappears?"

"Cool... cool, yeah. Let's do this," Dan said, his eyes getting clearer. "Where is it?"

Phillip shrugged. The shock was starting to wear off, leaving an almost intolerable buzzing of excitement. "The door. How about the door on the stage? It leads to the Farm, I think."

"Okay, the door," Dan repeated. "What the Hell, Phil, let's do this."

"Let's do it," Phillip said, and began walking down the wide uneven steps. Nobody was walking this way.

"What are we going to do if we get in?" Dan asked, and was much farther down to the stage than they expected. "What if that Captain guy finds us again...?"

"Who knows? Say we're with the Andy and Emily girl I guess," Phillip answered.

"Good idea," Dan said. "They seem nice. Did the one named Andy say that the Tadashi guy..."

"*Tadaaki*," Phillip corrected.

"Right, Tadaaki. Did she say that was her brother? I was surprised but now I can kind of see it. Hey, did you notice how pretty Emily is?"

Phillip took a second to answer. "Sure," he said nonchalantly.

"Wait," Dan said, grabbing Phillip's arm. "How long have we been walking down these stairs?"

"What are you..." Phillip stopped, looked at the stage, which was just as far away as it had been minutes ago "... talking about?"

"Whoa Phil, I think some magic is going on," Dan said.

"Let's keep walking. Don't look away from the stage this time," Phillip said, walking down the steps slowly, not taking his eyes off the stage and door.

It took another minute to see they weren't getting any closer.

"Whoa Phil," Dan repeated. "I have an idea, you take two steps at a time and I'll take one, then see what happens."

"That's a good idea, if only we had some string or rope..." Phillip said. Dan had taken off his backpack and was digging into it. He held a spool of twine when it came back out. "You brought twine...?"

"It came in handy, didn't it?"

"Alight give me one end, we should get farther apart if we do this, right? If we keep the line taunt, I should hit the stage eventually..." Phillip said. "Then I'll stay still and you follow the line, wrap it up and make it shorter."

"I think I should stay still," Dan said.

"Actually, that makes more sense..." Phillip said, already going down the stairs. "You ready?"

"Yep, I'll record how many steps you take," Dan said, taking out his notebook again.

He went down the stairs two at a time. Making sure to pull on the twine to keep it taunt as he let off more slack. Two steps. Two steps.

The stage still didn't get any closer.

"Dan..." Phillip turned around, looked up the stairs, and had to keep looking up to find Dan. "Dan?"

He was almost at the top of the amphitheater, much farther away then he should be. The twine was at its limit. Dan seemed to just notice, look around himself, then yell something back at him. All Phillip heard was "Phil!"

He pulled on the twine, taking one step backwards.

And ran into something. He turned around again, he was at the stage. "Dan, follow the rope and get down here!" He yelled, noticing Dan was already wrapping the twine and coming down the stairs. "You don't have to look at the stage!"

Phillip held the twine tight and watched him come down, not letting go of the stage for fear it would vanish.

"This is nuts, Phil," Dan said, a big smile on his face.

Phillip just nodded, then turned and leaped on the stage, Dan had a harder time with his backpack, there was nobody around. The door was small now, and there was nothing behind it.

They walked over the symbols—the symbols which had summoned the lighting.

Magic symbols.

Because *magic* existed.

Dan took notes before joining Phillip at the door. The amphitheater was dark and quiet and abandoned now. "What if the door doesn't open?" Dan asked. "Hey, there's nothing behind the door..."

"Magic," Phillip said with a shrug and grabbed the wooden handle, Dan grabbed the other one. The looked each other in the eye and without another word gave a small push.

The door opened without complaint, except for a small squeak.

Bright green fields, basked in sunlight, met them on the other side. The open door lighting the dark amphitheater. Behind the field, partially obscured by hills, was the silo, and a farmhouse on the hill. *The Farm.*

Shielding their eyes—and without another word—they stepped through the door.

CHAPTER 10
The Farm

Dan fished in his bag for a pair of sunglasses. Came out with two pairs and handed one to Phillip.

"You brought two pairs?" Phillip asked.

"Came in handy, didn't it?"

The door creaked and shut behind them. Like in the amphitheater the door stood with its frame and nothing behind it. There were no handles on this side. "Look..." Dan said.

The door began to dissolve, like tissue paper over a flame. It burnt away until it was gone, and they stood alone on the grass.

"Maybe we shouldn't have done this..." Dan said.

"What's the worst that can happen?" Phillip said. "We get kicked out or go to 'processing.'"

"Phil, that's not even close to the worst thing that can happen," Dan said. "Evil witches, people who want our bones for wind chimes, monsters, more bears..."

In front of them was a low white fence. The kind that surrounded ranches.

Just a little climb and they could be at the Farm...

No! This wasn't a good idea.

They probably had more to do in the Camp. It was dangerous to climb things. They had to eat and get their stuff. And hadn't aunt Elaine said she wanted him back? He really had no time to waste here. He had no idea what he was thinking. Putting everything else out of his mind, he turned around to walk back.

"Phil, where are you going?" Dan said. He would follow along, Phillip thought. He was a smart kid, that Dan. He would realize how foolish and pointless this was and follow him any moment.

"Phil? Phil!"

He could smell the campground food from here. He had never been so hungry, why hadn't he eaten anything today? That was dumb, he thought. Easily remedied, all he had to do was leave and...

Dan grabbed his arm. Pressed something into his hand.

"What are you doing?" Phillip asked Dan.

"You were walking away, I couldn't stop you," Dan said.

"No, I... didn't..." he stammered back.

Walking away? Why? What was he doing? Something about eating...

He looked down. Dan had pressed the pink notebook into his hands, still holding onto it himself. Realization hit him. His thoughts became clear and crisp.

"Dan, I didn't want to go closer to the fence. I wanted to do anything but get closer. It happened again. My thoughts... Dan, it was so much stronger than it was before."

"I think you better take out your pink notebook, keep holding it."

He did so, taking his pink notebook out and holding it tightly. "Fast thinking with the notebook," he complimented.

He touched the fence, and didn't feel any different. He looked to Dan, and they jumped the fence together. "Don't feel like leaving?" Dan asked. "Not anymore... You?" Phillip said back. "Nope."

For a moment Phillip thought he was dizzy, and then realized the ground underneath him was moving. Lifting and sinking.

The entire field was lifting and sinking. Swaying. Like a slow-motion sea made of grass. Boulders and trees bobbed on the field like ships.

"Phil!" Dan said urgently behind him. Phillip spun and saw something massive behind him. He jumped out of the way and ran into Dan.

It was a tree. Walking on its roots.

It moved around Dan and Phillip as if it was annoyed. Walked itself up to the top of the moving hill, and planted itself. The ground undisturbed where it walked.

"No. Way," Dan said, and Phillip gave a short nervous laugh before covering his mouth. It was all too overwhelming. There was another, much smaller tree making its way to the first. Birds followed the tree, jumping off and landing on branches whenever it moved.

"Dan, I changed my mind, I think we might just be crazy..."

"Definitely."

The tall grass only sometimes did what the wind said. The blue-green grass moved in odd patterns. Like the tree, going where it wanted. Even moving out of the way as Phillip and Dan walked.

"Storm cloud," Phillip said, pointing. A miniature storm cloud—not much bigger than the Fairchild's house—moved low along the grassy field. Dark and rumbling with lighting, the cloud was surrounded by maybe a half-dozen people in yellowish rain-jackets or cloaks, carrying long glowing spears.

They were herding it, poking it whenever it veered off course.

They walked past and toward the Farm without saying anything to people herding the cloud, who were too busy to notice them.

Another white fence.

Phillip held onto his pink notebook tighter, looked at Dan, who did the same.

Phillip jumped back from the fence when a massive bird, as tall as him, landed on it. It was a crane or something similar, wearing a thin porcelain mask. It looked right at them, though its eyes were covered by the mask.

"Early. Nightfall. Long. Night. Make your. Preparations," the bird said, in a deep and echoing voice, before turning and taking flight.

"Did the bird... just talk?" Phillip said stupidly.

"I think the mask might talk... or let the bird talk... I saw animals with masks in the amphitheater, floating masks too," Dan replied. "We're definitely crazy..."

"Look up," Phillip said as he jumped the fence. "Early nightfall..."

The sun was moving in the sky, fast enough to see, making its way to the horizon. Phillip looked at his watch, which told him nothing. "I hope time's not moving like that at home..." Dan said, looking at his phone. Neither of their phones worked.

The silo building looked less like a silo building the closer they got. It was made out of blocks of stone, and was carved with intricate designs. It looked like it was designed by a person who only had the most general idea of what a silo was or what it did. It almost looked like it was grown out of the ground, it was misshapen. Just a little bit off the more Phillip looked at it.

It went from afternoon to evening in the short time it took to walk there.

They were people all around them now. And not just people. Gremlins too. Phillip tried not to stare. Barns and low buildings and workshops and tents were all open. People worked with iron in one workshop, there were tents which looked like a flea market, people carved stone which seemed to be moving. Others were surrounding a small circle, cheering men in armor who were fighting. More moving trees lumbered along.

The Farm was an industrial district, an active tourist spot, a trade show, a fair, a concert or a sports event, a university campus. It was *everything*. Too many words described it and none completely. "Wild..." Dan said, looking in one barn that was filled with bright lanterns, where a man talked to a class.

A billboard contained notices. *'MINDWORKING Introduction moved to Old Stables'* one said. *'Rickshaun's Generator Course, held first night on Moon High,'* another said.

Phillip noticed the black-clad soldiers were putting up the notices, Phillip grabbed Dan's backpack and turned them both. "What are we...? Oh," Dan said. They walked towards the woods.

Lanterns were being lit. Sparks of light flew through the air. It was evening by the time they hit the trail to the woods. A sundown by the time they were in. It was crowded and well-lit on the trail. Camps and fires were scattered about. Music was being played. "Wild..." Dan said again.

Phillip grabbed Dan and turned off the trail when he saw another group of the black-suited soldiers. Towards a bundle of lights which looked like a building. A single person was talking, the voice echoing like it was amplified, a girl's voice.

"... firmly believes in the inductive approach," the voice said. "We're going to start at the beginning, with the earliest formulations of the ideas. You can't get a firm grasp of this without history." The woods and branches seemed to be grabbing for his clothes as he pushed through toward the voice. "Each discovery and counter-discovery are going to be covered. We're going to start in Greece, go to Rome. Backtrack a bit to the early Indo-states. From there we're going to quickly cover the formation of the concepts you've come here to learn. The first proto-Symbolarians. The evolution of the craft from its most arcane and mystical roots to what happened after the rise of strong formalization with the Shepherd revolution. We're going to hit on everything. Mental-Monistranarianism, Communimetrics, Germanic-Interactionalism, Void-theory, the eventual rejection of Willasticism after the Counsel of Old Berlin, why Bachmann dissented..."

Phillip pushed through, Dan accidently pushing him faster.

They almost tripped as they came into the clearing.

The speaker stopped talking. At least thirty people sitting in mismatched chairs and barrels and rocks turned around and looked at them.

It was a class of some kind.

At the head of the class, the speaker was the girl with the wild black hair.

A person he recognized.

Andy... he thought her name was.

"Dominique and Phebe! I'm glad you made it!" Andy said, she held in her hand some chalk, and she was surrounded by floating notes and symbols. "Everybody, turn around and stare at them intently."

An unnecessary thing to say, as everybody already was.

"Don't tease your students," an older boy said next to them who had black hair with blond roots.

"Peiter, you should know I only take advice from people who can decide on one hair color," Andy said to the boy, who grabbed his chest like he was injured. "Now Dishpan and Philargo, I am glad you're here. Do me a favor. The amphitheater was the first time you've seen the Pauls, right?"

"Um, yes," Phillip managed to answer, his throat dry.

"...and the first time you've *ever* heard of the Pauls, right?"

"Yes," Phillip answered, wondering if he could just say sorry and leave.

"Very good. Now do me a favor and give them nicknames."

Nicknames? Phillip didn't know what to do—everybody was looking at him—so he just answered with the first thing that came to his mind.

"Big Paul," he said, and Dan echoed him. They looked at each other, then both said "and Old Paul..." at the same time.

The class laughed.

"They're not laughing at you," the black-and-blond-haired older boy Pieter said. "Mostly."

"See what happened?" Andy said. Writing the word '*Memetacism*' midair with magical chalk. "You can ask a million people the same question and you'll get a million identical answers. And trust me, people have tried. A memetic thought virus? Something more direct? But with zero-convergence! zero drift from center! For as many years as people can remember. We'll study the different theories on how people think the Pauls are capable of this. Now, does anybody have any questions?"

Every hand went up but two.

"Good. That means you're curious," she said. "And smart enough to know how hopelessly ignorant you are. Unless you're one of those poor saps who only ask questions in class to talk and prove to the teacher how smart you are. Like Pieter."

"You misjudge me Madam Kanamori, I have a sincere desire to learn from you and bask in your wisdom," he said to her. His arm not going down.

"Twenty demerit points for sassing me and calling me 'madam,'" she said back.

"I wasn't aware the Farm had a demerit system in place..."

"Ten-thousand demerits then. To be passed onto your children when you die."

"Poor little guys..." he said.

"Why is everybody still raising their hands?" Andy asked the class. "I'm not going to answer any of your questions. I'm tired. Hungry. They're all probably dumb right now anyway. Go away. Shoo, shoo."

The class lowered their hands and walked out into the woods, following a path next to a barn or stable. All seemed to be in a good mood, with the exception of the group in white uniforms, who chatted amongst themselves. Dan and Phillip moved with the group.

"Don't leave," Andy said, drawing moving doodles midair with the chalk. "I want to know why you're obsessed and stalking me. Plus, Emily wants you to stay. Are you following us?"

"Not intentionally," Phillip said, Phillip noticed Emily, sitting next to the boy named Pieter, smiling at them.

"If you do not mind me saying," came a heavily accented voice. Maybe German. One of the men in the white uniforms, a man who would have looked young if he wasn't balding and sneering so much. "You have a bit of a stink about you that goes beyond normal for a sludgefoot. Am I wrong?" The other people in white-uniforms, who couldn't have been much older than Phillip or Dan, snickered as they walked passed.

Dan took a discreet sniff of his armpit.

"Don't listen to Sturmjägers about hygiene," Pieter said. "Those types will curl their noses at anything. I'm Pieter Vanderleer, nice to meet you, and I think you smell almost acceptable."

"Thanks," Phillip said. "I'm Phillip, this is Dan. We're Choicers, I guess."

"Oddly enough I picked up on that," he said, picking up his stuff and going. "Emily, always a pleasure. Andy, can your brother come over for a game later?"

"Going to have to ask him," she said, not looking up. Pieter gave a salute to Andy and left. "How did I do?" Andy asked Emily. Her floating fish doodles being eaten by a floating shark doodle.

"Fantastic!" Emily answered. "Though you could have been a little less abrupt with your students."

"Don't try to change me," Andy said. "Dan, Philargo, how *did* you find your way here?"

"That's an excellent question, Lady Kanamori," a familiar voice said. Captain Karo appeared, seemingly out of nowhere.

"Captain! Did you enjoy my class?"

"Unfortunately, I missed it, too many little things to take care of," Captain Karo answered. The other one, private Willum Brooks, was behind him, looking awkward again. "Like how these two sludgefoots you adopted made it here. What security entrance did you come through?"

"Um, we don't know the name of it..." Phillip answered.

"And where are you registered to stay?" Every muscle in the Captain's face tight.

"That... hasn't..." Dan stuttered.

"Is that the voice of the captain I hear?" A pleasant, deep voice said. It sounded British. A man walked out of the stable doors. He wore what looked like a business suit mixed with work clothes. An old-fashioned vest. He had tightly cropped gray hair and was smoking a long corn cob pipe. "I thought that was you!" He said.

But his mouth wasn't moving.

Because he wasn't the one talking. The British voice belonged to a gremlin, who appeared behind the man. Wearing similar clothes. The gremlin had thin glasses and a wrinkled face and a mustache. "Perhaps I can answer your question, Captain," the gremlin said, looking at Dan and Phillip with his massive eyes and giving them a wink. "You see, Captain, when you so kindly gave me this stable for my personal use and then so kindly registered all the animals as 'guests' to the stable so I had to take care of them, it seems you inadvertently registered me as the head of a boarding house. Can you imagine it? Me, a boarding house head? Really moving up in the world now. Henry is thrilled about it, aren't you Henry?" He patted the gray-haired man on the back, who ignored him and re-lit his pipe. "So, the boys are staying here. Right in the stable, booth twelve. Henry is making it real nice for them, aren't you, Henry?" The man named Henry puffed out colorful smoke, rolled his eyes, and went into the stable.

Captain Karo's mouth tightened. "I assume you're following purification standards as a 'boarding house head,' Mr. Haystacks?"

"Just Haystacks is fine, Captain. And as it so happens, I have a wrapping device here, makes my correspondents easier," the gremlin named Haystacks said. "I'm afraid I'm not an expert on the matter, if you could send over some Wallmen purifications, that would be greatly appreciated."

"I'm also thinking about making them members of the Welcoming Committee," Andy added. "Choicer outreach."

Captain Karo's eyes fell on Phillip. The contempt he conveyed was overwhelming.

Another person in black came up and whispered to Captain Karo. "He's arrived," Phillip heard him say. "When?" Captain Karo whispered back. "Just now." Captain Karo nodded and turned back towered Haystacks. "Good luck to you, Mr. Haystacks. Brooks, handle this, we'll follow up in the morning," he said quickly before leaving.

Private Willum Brooks came over to them, took out a hard notebook and a pen, and asked a variety of odd questions. *What is your preferred name? Your given name? Has any name been taken from you by force or coercion? Were you born in any unusual circumstances? Can you attest that you are fully human? Have you ever belonged to an organization opposing or in support of the Unificationists, the NALM, or the Greater Union of Primafold States?*

Phillip and Dan answered "uhhh" to most of these questions.

"Do you have any non-inclusionary belief systems that might be offensive to others, such as Primatarianism, Nonwillarianism, or Transapianosticism?" Willum asked.

"Um... I'm... *Catholic...*?" Dan said. Willum began writing it down, but then stopped. His frustration showed more on his face with each passing question.

"And what is your purpose here?" Willum asked.

Neither of them answered right away. "We're going to..." Phillip started, then looked at Andy, her magical notes floating around her. "We're going to learn magic."

"Magic...?" Willum said, with a bit of tone

"Yep, we're here to learn," Dan repeated. They both looked at each other and shrugged as Willum wrote.

Haystacks chuckled good-naturedly. "They were showing some interest in Rickshaun's generator course later tonight, he puts on a good show."

"That should be enough," Willum said. He gave a paper to Haystacks, who adjusted his glasses and looked at it. He turned to go. "Good to see you, Emily," he said before leaving.

"*Good to see you,*'" Andy repeated in a mocking tone to Emily once he left, a mischievous look on her face.

"Stop it," Emily said.

"He's a bit boring," Andy said.

"He's just earnest," Emily said back.

"Like I said, *boring.*"

"Why do you guys keep helping us?" Phillip said, the words coming out before he thought better of it.

"Don't let it go to your head," Andy said. "You're just pawns in a really petty fight we're having with the Wallmen."

"Oh, well thanks anyhow," Phillip said, looking at the gremlin. "Really, thank you."

"Don't listen to her. I'm doing this sincerely," Haystacks said. "Imps support Choicers. Annoying the good Captain Karo is just a bonus."

"Do we really stink?" Dan asked, to nobody in particular.

"A little," the gremlin said. "Now, boys. Daniel? Phillip, was it? We need to get moving to make this official. Henry's going to wrap your things. Then we're going to get you up to the big house on the hill, I assume you've seen it, it's called '*Crownshead*.' Inside you will find Adeline and her daughter Sarah, they practically run the place. Give them this and tell them you're staying here, after that. You need to go to Rickshaun's generator course, I was serious about that. I might be able to teach you some puppetcraft too, if you're interested, help establish yourself here."

"We are," Phillip said, and found he meant it. Dan nodded next to him.

Haystacks he clapped his six-fingered hands. "Good! Now what should I call my new boarding house? I'm partial to Haystacks' Hotel or Hostel, but I can be convinced otherwise."

CHAPTER
11
The Meeting

"This is a wild night, Phil," Dan said as they made their way to house on the hill, Dan was drawn instruction by Haystacks that had to be "followed to the letter" or "they'll end up somewhere else."

"Haystacks is really cool, like just normal guy, if you ignore the tail and six-fingers and everything," Dan continued. The path to the Crownshead house was dark but it was crowded out. "I can't believe he's going to let us stay at his place."

"Yeah, he is cool," Phillip agreed. *They knew a gremlin now*, he kept repeating in his head, his brain refusing to process the information.

Haystacks and Henry had 'wrapped their things.' Which was almost exactly like it sounded like. A large fish tank looking thing was filled with what looked like spider webs and small glowing mechanical worms. Henry dropped their things one-by-one in the tank and came out 'wrapped' in a clear softish coating covered in luminous symbols. They wrapped everything that wasn't 'inert.'

The pink notebooks were the only thing that fit that category.

"There's a little ball in each one, break it to undo the wrapping," Haystacks said. "Thanks. And, what does this do...?" Phillip asked, looking at his phone in the wrapping, which flashed at him, still not working correctly. "They're hard purification barriers for they don't mess with things, stops energy systems from interfering with each other," He answered. "You should wrap all your Mundafold stuff, it tends to be high-energy and prone to infection..."

"That word, Mr. Haystack...?" Dan started.

"Haystacks," the gremlin corrected. "And no 'Mister.'"

"Sorry, Haystacks," Dan continued. "That word you used, Mundafold, what does it mean?" Henry handed Dan his wrapped phone charger. Wrapped into a solid tube six-feet long.

"Good question, my boy," Haystacks said, twisting his mustache as if wondering how to answer. "When you live in Mundafold places—like where I imagine you two are from—and do Mundafold things, you are said to be in the Mundafold. It's the place but also the doing. It's geometry, but more than that."

"That's a terrible way to describe it," Andy said, wrapping her thin coat around her to the sudden cold. "Tell them the Primafold and Mundafold are like different sides of the same stretchy cloth, that shuts up Choicers for a little while."

"So, the Mundafold is like… where people act normal…?" Dan ventured.

"And *Choicers are*… what? People who come from the Mundafold to the Primafold? We're in the Primafold now? Is that why there's magic?" Phillip asked. Andy laughed.

"Close enough to work with right now," Haystacks said. "Now go up to Crownshead. See Adeline and Sarah, then get straight to the generator lab."

"I should hang around Choicers more, they're a blast," Andy said, she handed Phillip the silver metal instrument she had put in her pocket. "Try the Skychalk," Phillip waved it in the air with no affect. "You have to hit the button on the side," Phillip did so, and a line appeared in the air.

"Awesome," Phillip said, handing it to Dan, who did the same.

"See, Choicers are so fun and wide-eyed," Andy said. "Just between you and me," Andy whispered loud enough for everybody to hear. "How *did* you get in without Karo noticing?"

"We just sort of…" Dan started.

"… walked through the door, went over the fence…" Phillip finished.

To that Andy was silent and thoughtful—all of them were, Emily and Haystacks included. "We should probably inform somebody about that…" Emily finally said. Haystacks responded, "later. You boys go now to Crownshead, before Karo decides to get there first, we'll have your booth ready before you get back."

"Weird that Andy teaches a class here," Dan was saying on the way there. "She can't be much older than us, right? Is she the same age as Emily, you think? I can't really tell. Notice how she got called 'Lady Kanamori' and Emily was called 'miss?'"

"I did notice that, actually," Phillip said. "What was Andy's real name. Aleandra?"

Andy had written significant notes on the 'guest passes' she had given them, two slips of shining silver paper. Mostly it looked like Russian, though some was in English. She signed it at the bottom in Chinese or Japanese or Korean, Phillip couldn't tell.

Like the silo. Crownshead house seemed to be grown rather than built, and made less sense the closer they got to it. It was larger than expected. The wood and brick and stone that made it up all different sizes and shapes. It looked like four different builders built four different mansions and met in the middle. Red bricks gave away to wood paneling to round stones. Red tile roofing gave way to thatched roofing. A glass atrium could be seen behind the house.

They were met at the front door by an ape.

An ape wearing a thick wooden mask. An intricate carved mask which seemed to take a different expression depending on the angle.

"*What* is. Your Business. Here?" The masked-ape asked.

"I'm Phillip, and this is Dan. Daniel," he answered, not knowing what else to do. "We're here to see Adeline and Sarah."

He came up to Phillip's midriff as he got up and walked towards Phillip. He—and it was without doubt a 'him'—had colorful stripes on the bottom part of his body, and what looked like a little tail. The masked ape grabbed the paper Haystacks had written on, and seemed to be reading it, though the mask didn't have eyeholes. *As if it would be less remarkable if it did*, Phillip thought.

"Follow. Me," the ape said.

Dan and Phillip were so distracted following the ape the almost didn't notice their surroundings. The interior of Crownshead was filled with artifacts and antiques of all kinds, many displayed behind glass. It looked like a museum. They came to an open room full of taxidermied animals and displayed bones. Whale bones were suspended from the ceiling.

"*Wait.* Here. The Mistress Adeline. Will see you. Soon," the ape said, motioning to the full armchairs surrounding the room. "Always busy now. Miss Adeline."

With that the ape jumped on the desk. And took off his mask. The apes face was even more colorful than his bottom. The mask hovered in space when the ape let it go. It turned and looked at Phillip. The ape grew more excited after taking off the mask. He banged the desk and little bell on it, as if impatient. The mask floated off to a small tree planted in a pot on the side of the desk. When it approached, the tree sprouted fruit. Something that looked like a misshapen orange that sprouted little flowers on the top. The ape was thrilled, and picked as much fruit as he could carry, one on each foot, two in his mouth, and several more in one arm. The mask floated away to display itself on the wall with other masks. The ape walked out of the room, briefly becoming distracted by Phillip's messenger bag, which he opened with his free hand before decided it wasn't worth it and leaving.

Neither of them said anything for minutes after he left. They started chortling spontaneously.

"So, do you think we were talking to the ape, or the mask?" Phillip asked Dan.

"I think he was a *mandrill*," Dan replied. "They're monkeys, not apes. They're from Nigeria." Dan looked at Phillip. "What? I like nature shows..."

"Neat," Phillip smiled. "So, was it a magic *mandrill* or a magic mask that we were talking to?" Phillip asked again.

"If the mask can float by itself, I don't think it would bother being worn if it could talk by itself," Dan theorized. "Maybe it can't open doors? Animals act weird here but I don't think they can talk. At least we haven't seen that yet. I'm going to go with *both*. The mask needs the mandrill. The mandrill gets something out of wearing the mask," he motioned to the fruit making tree.

"Solid conclusion," Phillip said, affecting a bad British accent. "Well-reasoned."

"Thank you, good sir." Dan replied in a worse impression of the same British accent, tipping an imaginary hat.

"State your business," a woman said. She said it so abruptly they both jumped, in no small part because she seemed to appear behind them at the desk from nowhere. She looked impossibly old, but moved through the files in front of her at blazing speed, looking through glasses at least an inch thick and half the size of her head. Her skin was grey and wrinkled but also somehow hard, like she was carved out of granite. Phillip got the distinct impression that if he engaged her in a fistfight he would lose.

"Hi," Phillip said. "Are you Ms. Adeline?"

"State your business," the old woman said without looking up.

"We have to see Adeline and Sarah about where we're staying..." Phillip started.

"Go to the processing department," she said.

"Where's the processing depart..." Dan asked.

"Eighth door on you left, down that hallway," she said, pointing behind her. "Go in the red door, follow it straight, open the next door with the key."

"What... key?" Dan asked.

The woman moved a large bundle of papers, revealing an old brass key that sat on the table. Dan picked it up.

"You need a key to get in?" Phillip asked.

"Eighth door on the left. The red one. Go straight down the next hallway. Open the next door with a key," she repeated and they made their way toward the hallway.

Shrugging, they went down the hallway.

The red eighth door exactly where she said. Opening it. It led to a thin hallway lit with glass bulbs with glowing worms wiggling inside. The door shut behind them by its own accord as they walked farther down the hallway. The hallway became so thin they had to walk single file. Phillip was ahead of Dan and ran into the door first, which was not tall enough to walk through without bending down.

"Hand me the key," Phillip asked Dan.

"Odd place for a processing department..." Dan said as he handed him the large key.

"As odd as the rest of the place," Phillip said. He put the key in the lock, and twisted.

The door shook, the key disappeared from his hand. The entire hallway was swaying and shaking. Dan turned around and backed in Phillip, pressing him against the door. The hallway was getting smaller. Fast. The walls closing in thinner.

The red door on the other end of the hallway getting closer, rushing toward them. The hallway was contracting, the red door breaking the worm bulbs into nothing as it came closer.

"Open the door!" Dan yelled.

Phillip was already trying. The door knob wouldn't budge.

He slammed his body against the door as hard as he could. The red door was about to smash against them. Phillip closed his eyes just before it hit them.

The impact didn't come.

Phillip slowly opened his eyes. Dan was ahead of him, already shaking his shoulder and looking around.

They were outside. Surrounded by trees and flowering plants.

He was kneeling on the dirt, his hand still clutching a doorknob that wasn't there. Looking up, he saw that they weren't outside at all. There was a glass ceiling above them. They were in a greenhouse. One so thickly packed with trees and plants it was impossible to tell they were inside without looking up and seeing the glass roof.

"I don't think this is the processing department," Dan said in a half whisper, still out of breath.

"No, I'm starting to think that it's not," Phillip replied. "Maybe we should..." Phillip heard something. He shushed Dan. A person's voice. Several people. He stayed crouched to the ground. Dan seemed confused by this, he started to get up but Phillip pulled him back down, putting his finger up to his mouth to shush him again. He didn't know why, but he knew that revealing themselves was a mistake. *They probably weren't supposed to be here! They could be found out.*

He looked to his left and saw something that made his mouth go dry.

It was Captain Karo. Standing silently on what looked like a patio. He couldn't see them. Phillip pointed and Dan saw it. Without using words, Dan mouthed "let's go" and tried to pull Dan deeper into the trees and plants. Phillip shook his head, he tapped his ear. That would make too much noise. They were stuck here. Phillip knew that to his core.

"Gentleman you have gone to too much trouble for the likes of me. I am embarrassed by the riches you have set in front of me," the voice came from Captain Karo's direction. The voice was accented. Something like German but not quite. "It would be shameful for me to ask for anything else. But if you could, I would like my coffee to be a bit creamier. And my accompanying sweets a little... sweeter. Perhaps you have some Bundt cake on the premises? Lemon, by chance?"

There was a little shuffle and some clinking. It sounded like someone was washing dishes. Dan was paralyzed, Phillip got almost on his stomach. From here he could see a little through the thick bushes. There were a dozen people collected on a patio, a large table at the center filled with an assortment of food and drink on silver platters.

A man approached the table. It was Paul. *Big* Paul. He didn't seem particularly pleased when he lifted one of the silver platters covers, revealing some kind of food.

The blond man in the tight white suit on the other end of the table clapped. "You are truly a marvelous man!" He somehow managed to seem delighted and without any mirth. "I'm ashamed twice over. I'm afraid I've become something of a creature of comfort in my middle age. Never grew up with much, you know. And nothing makes a man addicted to comfort like poverty," the well-dressed blond man was busy filling his plate with everything on the table. A couple younger men in white uniforms helped him. There were men and women in

Wallmen uniforms around the patio, looking at the man eat in disgust. Phillip noticed Old Paul was here too. Sitting on the other end of the table. So still Phillip didn't notice him at first.

"General Waltz…" Old Paul started in a pleasant voice.

"Please, Paul," the blond man interrupted, his mouth full of food. "No honorifics or titles when we are here. It would humiliate me to hear my rank spoken by a man as great as yourself. Like putting a jeweled crown on a stray dog. Please, please. Just call me Waltzrigg while I'm here. Waltzrigg. I don't like my first name as much. Wilhelm. It doesn't sound right on English tongues."

"Waltzrigg, then," Old Paul continued. "We were hoping we could start this…"

"…and one more thing, if it wouldn't trouble you," Waltzrigg could barely be heard over the sound of his eating. "If you could find it in yourself to forgive me my little indulgences. For instance, I demand that all my subordinates laugh at my bad jokes," he pointed to the men in white uniforms with a fork full of food. "I know I'm making them do it but it makes me feel good. It's a petty little dignity I afford myself."

"I'm sure we can…" Old Paul began again.

"… now that we are done with idle chit chat, I was hoping we could move on to the meat of the conversation," Waltzrigg adopted a graver tone. "Do you know why I am here?"

"Why don't you tell us why you're here," came Big Paul's voice. *It would be impossible to interrupt him*, Phillip thought.

"In one word, *friendship*," Waltzrigg said without a pause. "I have been chosen, miserable lowly man that I am, to represent the interests of illustrious men and women. To represent the interests of friendship. *Your* friends. Equals. The friends you have chosen to humiliate, exclude. I represent *dignity*. The great but fragile dignity of the most dignified amongst us."

"It's not our intention…" Old Paul said.

"… please let's not talk of *intention*," Waltzrigg interrupted again. "There is nothing so meaningless in the hearts of great men such as you as *intention*. Let's talk about what you have *done*," Waltzrigg put another large bit of food in his mouth, followed immediately by a big gulp out of a mug, "and what you have done is, for lack of a better phrase, *thrown a bash*. A loud, exclusive little party."

He wiped his mouth and furrowed his brow, a look of mock concern on his face. "Those excluded from this party, who are not just uninvited but actively *excluded*! Are left wondering, what did I do wrong? What is he up to? I don't need to tell you there is nothing so dangerous as even a normal man left alone to his imagination. And as you know more than anybody, I represent the interests of far more than *normal* men. They fear the worst."

"A fine metaphor, Waltzrigg," Old Paul said. "But inaccurate. We are not throwing a party…"

"There are some unFae in the Camps I saw that would certainly disagree with you," Waltzrigg said, his men laughed a little.

"... This is just an informal get together. Nothing fancy. Nothing to get worked up about," Old Paul continued.

"... see that's where you have me confused." Waltzrigg said. "I am a man prone to confusion, of course. You will forgive me my density. But you say you are not throwing a party, and yet contracted with the brewers your opening night. You say this is informal, yet the Wallmen have been invited to monitor. There are invitations and bookkeeping and privileges being distributed. To me, and If I am not overstepping my bounds, to those I represent, your stated *intentions* seem wildly out of sync with your actions."

"The whole thing got a little bigger than we intended..." Old Paul said.

"...to say nothing of the fact that much of the source land your Farm sits on comes dangerously close to land that has been disputed," Waltzrigg continued eating. "Yes, yes. So much of what you have done has left me baffled. Which is nothing new, I admit. For instance, there is one thing I have been wondering about since I sat down for this wonderful meal you have blessed me with..."

"And that is?" Big Paul said, sounding annoyed.

"... why, with the Wallmen here, do you feel it necessary to hide a couple of your smaller men in the bushes?"

Phillip's stomach flipped. The only part of him capable of movement.

Waltzrigg turned in his chair and stared in Phillip and Dan's direction, Phillip got the distinct impression Waltzrigg was looking straight into his eyes.

The Pauls and the Wallmen seemed surprised. Phillip didn't think it was possible for his stomach to clench this much. Dan was pulling on his collar, urging him to get up and go.

But at the snap of Big Paul's fingers the trees and the bushes moved away from them. They were left alone, crouching on the ground, completely in view. Every eye on them.

"Sorry, we just came to get..." Phillip started.

"... to see Adeline..." Dan said.

"... we were looking for the processing..." Phillip continued.

"... there was this key and..."

"Captain," Big Paul said, turning to Karo. "I thought you cleared the nursery..."

"We did," Karo said, looking at Dan and Phillip, his face mutilated with contempt. "We were very thorough. I've seen these boys before. They've been skulking around. Choicers, both of them. Wallmen! Remove..."

"Choicers!" Waltzrigg said, his voice sounding happy and genuine for the first time. "Delightful, Paul. What a wonderful surprise. Boys, boys. You must join us for lunch. Come, come," he motioned to the table." Dan and Phillip didn't move. Neither did the Wallmen.

"They are not supposed to be..." Karo continued.

"I'm sure there is nothing to worry about," Waltzrigg said. "There is no place Paul would not go to make a guest feel comfortable and happy. And nothing would make me happier than having a couple of young Choicers join us for a bite," Captain Karo seemed unsure of himself, he looked to the Pauls for guidance, Old Paul just nodded to Karo.

Dan and Phillip went to the table and sat. Phillip knew Captain Karo was glaring at him without looking.

Waltzrigg only had eyes for them. "Try the cake, boys. And the coffee. And put some mint in it. That makes it better," Waltzrigg was making them plates and handing them cups of liquid. "Try. Try," Phillip took the cup, and took an awkward sip of the coffee. He wasn't a fan of coffee.

"Good?" Waltzrigg asked.

"Yes, very good." Phillip said back, nodding to the Pauls. "Thank you," Big Paul looked exasperated, Old Paul looked amused. Karo stood behind them glaring.

"Wait until you try the meats. Salted perfectly," Waltzrigg began eating, but continued looking up to check if Dan and Phillip were eating. "I have to say I love this word 'Choicers' you use in the States. So positive! The Danish word is not so polite. It's an old word. Roughly translates to 'Unwanted houseguest...'" He put some little sandwiches on their plates. "You know boys I am what they call a 'Choicer' as well."

"Really?" Dan said, clearly as awkward as Phillip.

"Yes, yes. I was a little younger than you are now. I became aware of some mysterious goings-ons of a neighbor of ours. A man lived near my family. He was an old-style Alchemist, you see. Not that I knew that. I would spy on him for months. Pester him when he left his house. He gave me no mind. Primafold men were far less accommodating in those days. This was just before academics invented the word 'Primafold', come to think," Waltzrigg looked up as if to remember something. "Eventually I became so desperate for knowledge that I snuck into his house when he was away. I grabbed the first book I could find. A cheap little alchemical mixtures book, not that I knew that at the time, and ran.

It was the wrong thing to do, I know that. Can youth be blamed for foolishness?" Waltzrigg said. "I was caught. The old alchemist had every reason to be mad, but he was a mean old coot. Demanded my hand be cut off. Luckily, I escaped that fate. Sentenced to hard labor. That was when hard labor was still being used. I was the son of a Mundafold cobbler, boys. A small boy. We lived poor but comfortable lives. And suddenly I was removed from my home and subjected to the utmost of cruelty and discomfort, my family having no idea where I was."

He shook his head. "But looking back boys I would not trade these experiences for anything. I learned more about myself in those years than I ever had an opportunity to at home. I never spent time on regret. I became more inspired to join this world than ever. And so much more was driving me than curiosity now, boys. I became what I needed to become. I learned that I was capable of *anything* to get what I wanted. That I would do *anything* for my goals."

He took another bite. A fast, aggressive bite. Not closing his mouth anymore when he chewed. "*Relentlessness* became my philosophy. When you are brought so low, boys, there is an impressive feeling that comes over you.

When nothing is left beneath you, amazingly, you find nothing is left above you either. There is nothing to lose and nothing more to be intimidated by," Waltzrigg gave them a pointed look. "It's not all gloom and agony, I don't wish to depress you. I was fortunate enough to find people who saw that I could be useful. And my life steadily improved."

His tone lightened up. "As for the old Alchemist. Times were not good to him. He was born a century too late for his profession. He mismanaged his inheritance. And a series of unfortunate accidents didn't help. I bought most of his property when it was seized to pay his debts, including that cheap little book I had stolen as a boy. His house too. The alchemist died without a penny or a bone to his name. I was told he could see the chimney of his old home from the poorhouse he was left in... My mistress lives there now, with our children." He wiped his mouth. "It is a sad and valuable lesson. No matter what you have, what you are born with, it can all be taken from you. Never get comfortable, boys," Waltzrigg wasn't looking at Dan and Phillip when he finished, he was looking at Old Paul.

"Let's move this along, Waltzrigg," Big Paul said. "Ask what you came here to ask."

"I am not here to satisfy my curiosity and play detective, Paul. I am only an instrument," Waltzrigg replied. "But since you insisted. There is one burning question I do have on my mind. What are you doing here?"

"Sharing," Old Paul answered, a hint of mocking in his voice.

"Are you *giving away* what you have?" Waltzrigg followed up.

"That's what sharing means," Big Paul said.

"So, you are choosing a successor?" Waltzrigg asked. "Many of the more learned men and women in the Camps think this is the case."

"That is not our intention," Old Paul said.

"Are you making a claim on the Frontier?" Waltzrigg seemed deathly serious now.

"The Farm's partial location here is a coincidence, nothing more," Old Paul answered.

"Fantastic, what a relief!" Waltzrigg said, using his cheerful voice without cheer. "Now that I have learned without a shadow of a doubt that your rude and provocative behavior, my client's words not mine, is nothing but an unfortunate mistake. I will send word immediately to your dear friends of their invitation to join you on the Farm. They are willing to pay for any trouble of accommodating them here, they have told me that themselves." He clapped his hands.

Neither of the Pauls spoke.

"... they won't want to be here for long, I assure you," Waltzrigg continued. "Just long enough to see that their legitimate and completely understandable concerns are without merit."

"They can come to the Camp all they want..." Big Paul said.

"... but their presence in the Farm would be disruptive," Old Paul finished.

Waltzrigg was calm now, a satisfied smirk crossed his face as he nodded slowly.

"That, is unfortunate," Waltzrigg said. "Not for me, of course. I confess I have turned my duties here into something of a holiday. I am enjoying touring the beautiful Washington Union countryside. Failing to resolve this issue allows me to see more of it. You know I met some Grannies? As you can see," he motioned behind him. Dan and Phillip noticed for the first time a woman in bundled furs and jackets. She looked like something between a Viking and a homeless person. They could not see her face in the bundle of clothes and gray hair. She was smoking a long pipe and didn't seem to notice she was being talked about. "Such an interesting cultural group, they are. So mystically oriented yet at the same time so stark and practical. They remind me of Eastern wagon-tramps back home." The women in furs snorted.

"I have met many people here. Extremist Weeping Men, disgruntled talking Shadowkin, greedy Imps and Fae of all stripes," Waltzrigg continued. "In the Camp alone, I have met so many new people. So many of them wondering and asking, like my clients, why they have been excluded. 'What are your criteria for inclusion and why don't they meet it...?'"

He rubbed his face hard with his napkin and threw it on the plate. "I do not need to tell a man as wise as yourself the fact that the only thing worse than not getting something you want is to see others getting it instead. There is not a king or serf or any creature that I have ever encountered who does not share this fatal character flaw. Shame, our shared natures."

He jumped up from his chair suddenly.

"Well, Paul," Waltzrigg said. "I apologize for wasting your time. Clearly, I was not the right man for the job. I could not persuade you to see the value of friendship and peace," he took one last gulp from his cup and then picked up another coffee cup and downed that also. "Even so, I will continue advocating for my clients, with every resource I have available to me. And If you will forgive advice from a man as lowly as me. My clients are *not* the types to stop advocating for themselves. And they have so much more to advocate with than words."

Nobody responded to him. Big Paul glared at Waltzrigg. Old Paul sipped coffee.

He turned suddenly to Dan and Phillip. "Boys, it was a pleasure to meet you. The greatest luck on your journeys. If you need any help, be sure to contact me, I am always looking for new talent." He moved in closer. "Bit of advice, avoid the earl gray pocket pies, they leave a bad taste in your mouth."

And with that he turned and left.

CHAPTER 12

Adeline and Sarah

Phillip didn't know what to do with himself. Did he keep eating? Look up and explain himself to the Pauls? Stand up?

Nobody had taken immediate notice of them since Waltzrigg left, with the exception Dan who was looking down as nonchalantly as he could, letting his eyes drift in any direction people weren't standing in.

"Mr. Paul. *Pauls.* Sorry about…" Phillip blurted out.

"Wallmen, take these two…" Captain Karo said at the same time.

"I told you we shouldn't have rushed this…" Big Paul said, ignoring Karo and Phillip.

"We should be happy we got this long," Old Paul responded.

Captain Karo's men circled Dan and Phillip.

"We didn't mean to be… We were told. We have a pass," Phillip said, three thoughts competing in one sentence.

"Hold on a moment, would you, Captain?" Old Paul said.

Everybody to stop moving.

"Security is my prerogative, you assured us…" Captain Karo began.

"I would never question your dominion here, Captain," Old Paul continued. "In fact, it's your competence that has me so curious. I judge you to be a competent enough man to clear a nursery of boys hiding in bushes. And yet here they are. My interest is piqued."

"I've seen them before," Karo said. "They've attached themselves to a few of the more privileged guests here. I think…"

"If you don't mind terribly, Captain," Old Paul interrupted. "I'd like to hear from them."

Phillip and Dan explained everything they could about how they ended up in the nursery. They talked fast at first and interrupted each other before Big Paul told them to slow down. The explained the guest passes. The mandrill in the mask. Meeting Adaline and being given the key. About the hallway and the door and the key.

"Adaline?" Old Paul seemed confused, and then turned. "Adaline, is that right?"

An unfamiliar older woman walked from behind Big Paul. Her greying hair was up in a messy bun. She looked ruffled, distracted, and overworked.

"I've been out all day, preparing for this," Adaline said.

"Can't keep their lies straight..." Karo started.

"There was a woman," Phillip interrupted. *The old women at the desk. She never did tell them her name was Adaline.* "She never told us her name was Adaline. I guess we assumed that. She was really old. Moved fast... Gave us a key."

Both the Pauls looked at the real Adaline. "Boo'jo brought them to the desk, that's what he's supposed to do," she said. "The woman sounds like the Lady, but she hasn't been seen for months..."

"And why didn't you announce yourself the moment you appeared here?" Karo said.

Phillip didn't answer right away. He had no good excuse.

"We got embarrassed," Dan said. "It took us a minute to figure out what happened and by that time you were speaking for too long and we got embarrassed."

"It was my fault. He wanted to stand up and I stopped him," Phillip said.

Karo looked as if he was going to continue. To sling another accusation. But both the Pauls began laughing. Old Paul was more restrained, Big Paul's laugh practically shook the ground.

"Been there," Big Paul said.

"There was a time I was trying to meet a friend backstage at this little theatre," Old Paul reminisced. "Accidently got caught behind a coat rack in the women's dressing area. I think my soul is still paying the price for what I saw that day."

"And what theatre was this, Paul?" Adaline said, her eyes narrowed.

"Far too long ago, I can't remember. Unimportant to the thrust of the story anyway," he said back. Adaline gave a judging but amused look to Big Paul, who seemed to be more embarrassed by the Old Paul's youthful antics than Old Paul was himself. "Adaline, will you help these boys with their 'guest passes.'" Old Paul said, turning suddenly back to the boys.

Dan and Phillip handed Adaline their silver sheets with perhaps a little too much enthusiasm and relief. Adeline said their names out loud, reading them off the passes. Captain Karo seemed as happy as Phillip would have expected at the turn of events.

"We need these boys for questioning," Karo said, his voice losing a little control.

"Captain no need to waste your valuable time here," Old Paul said in a dismissive tone. "I'm afraid you already have the culprit. It's me. With how busy I've been I've neglected to consider certain aspects of the Farm which are relevant to your job. Crownshead is a very old dwelling, Captain. And it's been mostly empty for so long and to suddenly be so full... I think she might be a little overwhelmed. A bit overstimulated. Likes to play little tricks and pranks when it gets that way. Especially at my expense. As passive-aggressive as a house cat, she is," he looked up, as if scolding the building. "I'll submit myself for question now if you want."

"No. Of course that won't be necessary," Karo said with a little nod of his head. "Sometime later I'd like to discuss what other *pranks* we can expect here. It would be useful to us."

"Thank you for your understanding, Captain," Old Paul said back. "Now, to ask these boys some really important questions," he leaned in and grew serious. "Phillip. Daniel. Tell me honestly, do the pocket pies really leave a bad taste in your mouth?"

They both laughed, from relief more than anything else. "No," Dan said. "Didn't taste anything bad," Phillip said at the same time. Which was almost a lie because he couldn't remember tasting anything during the meeting.

"You see. Tasted fine," Old Paul motioned to Big Paul and Adeline. "I'm starting to think Waltzrigg holds some animosity toward us..."

"I'm impressed, Paul, you're as sharp as ever," Adeline said.

"...and Mr. Montgomery, Mr. Castellanos. How about you? Do you think Waltzrigg is up to no good?" Old Paul continued. Phillip was surprised Paul knew both their last names.

"I think he was... hungry," Dan said.

"Yeah, I think he's up to no good," Phillip answered, surprised by his own honesty.

"Hmm, I think you might be right, there. Mr. Phillip," Old Paul said, getting to his feet. "Well as a thoroughly fussy but luckily very handsome woman once said to me, 'in the end you get the friends and the enemies that you deserve,'" he took one last long sip out of his coffee mug before throwing it into the bushes. "Come now, Paul, let's go earn ourselves some better enemies."

———— ○ ————

Adeline brought them through a series of bright wooden corridors to a room that couldn't seem to decide between being a small ballroom, a library, or a storage room. Dan asked if this was the real 'processing center.'

"The what?" Adeline replied. "This is administration, until we get the real offices cleaned. There's an infestation of memory weeds growing up the wall on the whole east wing. Don't tell anybody I told you that. The Wallmen will have us replacing our shoes six times a day if they knew."

"If the Pauls are in charge, why don't they just tell the Wallmen not to?" Phillip asked.

"Paul is not in charge of the Wallmen. The Wallmen are independent. The Pauls made a few deals with them before the Farm opened. They get access to the Farm and a few other things. In return, they bring the Farm and the Camp a little security and safety. They have been given some Privileges here. Excessive

Privileges, if you ask me," Adeline answered, somehow seeming both rushed and hurried but endlessly patient with their questions. "Taken over some jobs better left to administration. Not that I mind losing a bit of my workload. Paul likes to talk about order being spontaneous, which is a real poke in the eye to the one driving themselves mad maintaining it. *I'm* spontaneous order!" She chucked at her own joke. "Here boy's grab a cookie or whatever Sarah's throwing in these jars these days. God, I hope it's not fruit or nuts."

The jars did not contain fruit or nuts, they did contain something called 'northern grain-nut cookies' which Adeline said were almost as bad. This didn't stop here from grabbing some herself, and urging Dan and Phillip to take three each. "If I get rid of these, I can justify getting something proper in a cookie jar. Something with chocolate."

"So was that lady we talked to up front... real?" Dan asked, trying to cover his mouth, which was busy chewing the northern grain-nut cookies, which tasted a little like oatmeal if it was soaked in wine, "or was she, like, a mirage?"

"Beats the heck out of me. Never understood what Lady Crownshead could and couldn't do," Adeline said as she pressed a brass button on her desk. "Volumes could not be written on what I don't know about this house. And Paul only tells you stuff after it's too late. Poor fool is addicted to being mysterious."

"You called?" Came a voice of a woman who entered the room.

She had short blond hair, and was almost taller than Big Paul. She was younger than Adeline. Maybe just under middle aged, but it was hard to tell.

"Yes, good," Adeline said, gathering some papers. "Boys, this is Sarah. My coworker, subordinate when it suits her. In charge of filling the cookie jar. She's also my daughter, so be as nice as possible. Sarah, this is Daniel and Phillip. They've been given... *guest* passes."

"Guest passes?" Sarah said, and then a wave of comprehension took her face. "Ah, the Kanamori girl. Or was it Emily this time?"

"Probably both," Adeline said, handing Sarah the passes and more paperwork.

"And here I thought I humbled them when I stopped the Welcoming Committee from absorbing the pamphlet makers. Well, I guess gumption is a virtue," Sarah grabbed the papers, and began flipping through them. "You shouldn't have let them create their special bear and squirrel council..."

"The *'Diplomatic Resolution Council for Creature Welfare...'*" Adeline corrected.

"... That's what I said. Gave these girls too many wins, it's made them arrogant," Sarah said. "Well, Daniel. Phillip. For a couple of young Choicers with no invitations to the Farm you've certainly made some useful friends." Sarah turned to Adeline. "Are the Pauls okay with this?"

"They seem to be," Adeline responded. "He's in one of his... *dramatic* moods."

"... and what about the Wallmen?" Sarah continued.

"They don't seem to be," Adeline said. "Especially that Karo Captain or whatever-he is."

"Hah!" Sarah explained. "Well, that's good enough for me." She took that looked a little like a spoon out of her front pocket and taped both the sheets. A glowing orange symbol burned itself at the bottom of the silver sheets. Sarah took her thumb and brought it to her lips, blew on it, and then placed it on the burn mark.

"Guest passes will last for a week..." Sarah said.

"A week? Does it say it on there?" Adeline asked.

"... If the Kanamori girl and Emily can create fake guest passes I can create fake regulations for them," Sarah explained. "Anyway. They last from Sunday to Sunday. So, you boys are going to get a couple extra days on the first one. After that, you need to get them signed again by somebody with privilege in the Farm. So, keep doing whatever you're doing for those girls to make them like you," she handed them their silver sheets. The round symbols she put on there had a faint glow to them. There was a fingerprint and a signature to the side. "This way, the Wallmen might just stay out of my hair for five minutes and saying I'm making their jobs harder. Is that too optimistic, Mom?"

"It might be, kiddo," Adeline said. "You've been on their bad side ever since you moved the skyfish spawning grounds next to their training area."

"Heh heh, yeeeaah," Sarah said, as if remembering something fondly. "It's their fault for calling their field a 'gymnasium'. How was I supposed to know it was outdoors?"

"Skyfish? What are...?" Dan started.

"... A few more things, kids," Sarah interrupted. "You kids are Choicers. I hold no prejudice but, in my experience, sometimes that means you are a little green when it comes to the basics. I'm going to have you boys meet with Dr. Emmitt Bartly as soon as possible. He's our Physician-Healer. He'll check you out, give you some advice. Maybe answer some questions you boys have about this or that. Might want to cover hygiene while you're at it," she paused pointedly on these words. "I'm also going to have you do introductory Circles Class with Miss Julie. Paul is paying educators to keep the kids and parents happy. Being held any minute now. Don't scoff at it. If you graduate out fast, fantastic. Does that sound good to both of you?"

"Awesome," Phillip replied, meaning it.

"I see that your housing with Haystacks... is that right?" Sarah asked.

"Yeah, Haystacks is cool," Dan said.

"Yes, Haystacks is very cool. Good guy," Sarah said. "I guess the stables are better than those treehouses. Avoids motion sickness. Though it probably smells worse..." Sarah drifted off. "Personally, I think you lucked out. Imps are notoriously good hosts, when the guests are honest..."

"Sarah!" Adeline said. "Stereotypes, and don't use that word."

"Only *positive* stereotypes, Mom," Sarah said. "And kids, don't listen to her. I'm allowed to use that word. Got permission from an Imp King emissary when I was slumming it in Grass Alley. *You* don't use that word though, only I can."

"Imp...? I mean, the 'I-word'?" Dan asked.

"That's the one," Sarah said. "Now. I want you to be honest with me. Did my mom complain about the cookies I put in the jar?"

Adeline was mouthing "no" behind Sarah and turning her head back and forth.

"No. I liked them..." Dan said.

"No. She told us to try them," Phillip said.

"Hmm. Terrible liars, the both of you," Sarah said. "Just for you boys know a diet rich in grain-nuts will ensure a long, healthy life."

"When I was young, they were saying just the opposite," Adeline said. "Honestly, I'd rather die young and fat," she whispered to Dan and Phillip.

"What was that?" Sarah said.

"Just telling them how lucky I am to have a daughter who focuses so much on her mother's health that she decided to take away those few small comforts and joys that made life worth living," Adaline replied.

"That's what I thought," Sarah responded.

Dan took another large bite of cookie. "They really are good," he said. Phillip didn't agree, but gave a thumb up sign to Sarah all the same. Adeline said "perfect" and stuffed as many of the cookies in their pockets as would fit before they left.

CHAPTER 13

Circles Class

"**By** God we're lucky," Dan said. "I nearly pissed myself in that meeting. Can you believe how lucky we are?"

"Stupid lucky," Phillip agreed.

"Do we really smell that bad?" Dan said, sniffing his shirt again.

"Maybe by Primafold standards?"

"I think Haystacks wrapped my deodorant…" Dan said. "So, can people just, like, *learn* magic?"

"I guess so. We're going to class…" Phillip said.

"Do you think it's really the same time we left back home?" Dan said, looking up at the stars.

"That's what Haystacks said," Phillip answered.

Miss Julie's Circles Class was held in a few circular buildings that looked like raised beach huts. They were surrounded by people, and even more kids.

"Dropping off or picking up?" A young woman in a square hat asked.

"Uh, we're here for Circles Class," Phillip replied. "Are we in the right place?"

"And you're… here for yourselves?" She asked.

"Yes…?" Dan replied, both an answer and a question.

"Alright. That's fine. So what level are you at right now?"

"We… don't know much." Dan answered.

"Okay, okay. That's fine," she said, sounding embarrassed. "Tell you what, we'll put you in Level-A right now and if it's too easy for you just come to me and we'll advance you to where you need to go. Follow me."

Phillip was beginning to see the reason for her embarrassment. Dan and Phillip were the oldest people here by half. It felt like an elementary school. The oldest groups maybe eight years old. The youngest three or four, wearing hard yellow and blue hats.

"Miss Julie?" The woman in the square hat said, knocking on the sliding door of the hut. "I have a couple more students for you. Are you full?"

"Not at all, not at all," came an even higher and sweeter voice from a slightly plump woman with a mane of curly red hair. "Bring them in. We are just about to start."

Phillip and Dan walked in the room to Miss Julie saying, "Oh, they're so... *tall.*" There were fifteen other students in the class, all of them six or seven years old. Some as young as five. Every single one of them looking at Dan and Phillip. "Shut the door and grab a stick from the bucket," Miss Julia said. They thanked the woman who had brought them here and shut the door, then grabbed a two-foot-long bamboo stick out of a bucket, which all their other students already had. Dan and Phillip took turns saying their names. The class, including Miss Julie, repeated the name in unison with an enthusiastic "hello, Daniel!" and "hello, Phillip!"

Miss Julie sat on a raised circular platform at the end of the class. There were no desks, and the ground seemed to be made out of a firm sand.

Every student was sitting on a short stool on top of which was a pillow. After the greeting the class broke out into excited pleas. Every student wanted Dan and Phillip to sit next to them. They took the closest seats available. Which disappointed a few other classmates, particularly a girl on the other end of the classroom who crossed her arms and began to pout. Sitting down on the small stool, Phillip knees nearly reached his chin.

The boy next to Phillip—no more than six—was tapping his shoulder.

"Yes?" Phillip asked.

"Does your dad own a boat?" He asked.

"Uh, no. he doesn't," Phillip answered.

"My dad owns a boat," he continued.

"Oh, that's really cool." Phillip answered back.

"Shhhhhh. Shhhh. Shhh. Quiet down everybody," Miss Julie said as the lights in the room darkened. The students joined in with the shushing. "Marty, Maxus. Your sticks are not for poking. Don't make me take them away again."

She held up her bamboo stick to her nose, the class followed her. Dan and Phillip a second behind. She waited until everybody had done before she took the stick and began to draw a circle. The lights darkened further. The class followed along.

The tough sand on the floor didn't take to footprints, but could be moved around easily with the help of the bamboo stick. He drew the best circle he could, which was more lopsided than most.

Miss Julie hands raised again. Again, waiting for everybody to copy her, she clapped twice. The class followed along. She then placed the end of the stick in the center of the circle.

"Very good everybody!" She said, breaking the silence with a burst of enthusiasm. She got up with a sudden movement. The lights brightened as she stood.

The room lit up, with the exception of the circles on the floor.

They were still dark. From them emanated what looked like shadows in midair, pillars of shadow that almost reached the ceiling before fading.

It was as if the circles didn't allow any lighter than the light they were getting when they were made. *That's probably exactly what's happening*, Phillip thought.

From all except Dan and Phillip's.

Their circles were just drawings in the sand.

"Well, very good try, everybody!" Miss Julie said as she noticed Dan and Phillip's lack of success. "Follow along, follow along." She placed her stick back on the sand, and from the outside to the inside, drew a short line intersecting the circle. The pillar of shadow vanished. Fifteen other pillars followed.

"Who wants to listen to a song?" Miss Julie asked the classroom. The children in class cheered. "I dooo!" Some chanted.

She tapped a wall with her bamboo stick.

Music began to play.

The music was simple, cheerful. Bouncing back and forth in a predictable pattern. A male voice shouted out:

Well are you all ready for the circle song?!

"Yes!" came a resounding answer from the class.

Well there's no reason to wait then, is there?!

"No!" Came the class. The music picked up:

Wheeeeeeen yooouuu...
Have some stinky garbage
And you need the stink away
Just draw a wee circle
Clap your hands and save the day.

Clap, Clap, Stamp!
Clap, Clap, Stamp!
It's as simple as a
Clap, Clap, Stamp!

That class followed along, clamping when the singer said "clap" and putting both their hands on the floor when he said "stamp." Dan and Phillip followed along. Looking sillier for the effort:

IIIIfffff yoouuuuu'reeee...!
Trying to take a nap but the sun just hurts your eyes
Well draw a big ol' circle
Clap your hands and never rise

Clap, Clap, Stamp!

Clap, Clap, Stamp!
It's really just as simple as a
Clap, Clap, Stamp!

The song went on through a half dozen more examples, about subjects as diverse as a picnic that was being invaded by ants, an unfortunate dog that couldn't stop getting muddy, construction workers who were keeping a baby from sleeping, a little girl who though sunflowers would look better blue, and a fish tank that desperately needed cleaning to make the fishes happy.

The song seemed designed to get rid of some of the excess energy of children. Especially the last part, which had the students 'Clap, Clap, Stamp!' over and over to an increasingly fast beat. By the end of it, Both and Dan and Phillip—who wasn't the most athletic person in the world but could hold his own—were out of breath and covered in sweat.

Phillip looked to his right to the boat-owning dad boy. He didn't seem worn out at all.

Jerk.

Miss Julie was holding her stick up again to her nose again. Being quiet herself and staring at the glass proved more effective than shushing to settle the class down. She waited until there wasn't any movement in the classroom, before tapping a wicker basket twice she had on the podium. "Yes!" A girl explained. "Becca! Shhh!" Another one answered.

A figure climbed out of the basket, maybe six-inches tall. It had a bobbing wooden head with a long nose and cowboy hat. Its body was made up of a clear crystal. Its large comical feet complete with cowboy boots.

"Prism Pete!" Came a cheer from the classroom.

Prism Pete meandered around the classroom, sometimes waiving in random directions. His movements tight and mechanical.

"Wow," Dan said.

"I like Flyguy Freddie the most," the boat-dad kid said to Dan.

A second figure came out of the basket. Significantly rounder and fluffier than the first. It was a penguin. A little shorter than Prism Pete. On its head, a red bow. In the middle of its belly, a colorful camera like lens.

"Patricia!" The classroom said together. "Patricia the Projector Penguin!" One girl said, as if correcting the others.

Patricia the Projector Penguin made her way to the center of the classroom. When she noticed Prism Pete, she began flapping her little wings and jumping as much as her short legs would let her. Prism Pete didn't seem to notice. Patricia the Projector Penguin shook a little, opened her mouth, and shot a beam of light at Prism Pete.

The room became filled with thin strands of colorful light. Rainbow ribbons on the flow and climbing up the walls and sometimes bending in ways that weren't possible.

"All together now," Miss Julie said from the head of the room. "We are doing red first. Everybody repeat, red, red, red."

The classroom drew another circle, Miss Julie leading the way, and telling Devon not to jump ahead. But there was another step this time. They drew another, smaller circle about the main one. Miss Julie then instructed the class to draw a straight line from the middle of the smaller circle to the bigger one.

"What are we doing?" Phillip whispered to the boat-dad boy.

He seemed confused by Phillip's question. "Making only red light," he said. "See? You just draw a circle in the light. Then draw a tunnel to your bigger, your bigger circle. And then stamp closed your bigger circle closed," he clapped his hands.

"Thamus, no rushing ahead. Phillip, please pay attention," Miss Julie said.

"Sorry," Phillip and Thamus said in unison.

Phillip and Dan drew their circles. And then drew a line between the red light of the smaller circle to the large one.

"Phillip, can you tell me what we do now?" Came the unflinchingly sweet voice of Miss Julie from the front of the class. He guessed Miss Julie didn't trust Phillip not to talk without direct intervention.

"We, uh, snap, snap, clamp." Phillip answered, the class giggled. "I mean clap, clap, stamp..."

"That's right!" Miss Julie said. "Everybody together. Clap, clap, and stamp!"

The class followed along and 'stamp closed their circles.' The larger circles in front of the students instantly changed. All other light was emitted, the sand in the circles became a bright red. Some students stuck their hands in the circles, which also turned shades of red.

Again, all except Dan and Phillip's circles.

If anything, the ribbons of rainbows produced by Patricia the Projector Penguin and Prism Pete were brighter and more obnoxious than ever.

"Dangit," Phillip said.

"That's a bad word," Thamus said next to him.

"Sorry," Phillip said.

"I know other bad words," Thamus confided in a whisper.

Miss Julie led the class to drawing another line into the small circle to the big one. This time for blue. After which the circles in the class only allowed magenta. They drew a line crossing the red line, and the circles turned blue. They drew a line for yellow, and the big circle turned green. They crossed the blue line, and the circle turned yellow. They drew a large curling line from the corner of the small circle to the interior of the large one. The light in the big circle went back to normal. Which was a relief for Phillip, as neither Dan nor him had been able to follow along with the classes' success, though they did try to follow along anyway.

"You're not very good at this," Thamus said blandly.

To Thamus' credit, he tried to give helpful advice as much as he criticized.

The rest of the class proceeded in much the same way. With neither Dan or Phillip's success rate getting any better. *I think we're getting worse as this goes on,* Phillip thought. Thamus seemed to be growing more frustrated with their lack of success than Phillip was. "Just, stamp it. It's easy," he said.

Prism Pete and Patricia the Projector Penguin were soon joined by other wooden friends. This included Vicky the Viking, who would burst out into horrendous opera singing if the students didn't draw a circle around themselves to get rid of the sound. Stinkbug Stanley, who was a centipede in a three-piece-suit and a monocle who emitted a rotten egg smell and visible lines of green smoke. The kids got a kick out of this one. They drew a circle with jagged lines on the edges to protect themselves.

Finally, there was Flyguy Freddie, a turtle wearing goggles and big mechanical wings who was always looking for an updraft to float on. Which was provided by the most complex circle yet, involving circles within circles and about a dozen different lines. When done, the small circles produced a stream of air, which lifted Flyguy Freddie off the ground.

That was until Flyguy Freddie reached Dan's circles, and fell to the ground with a disappointing CLUNK, followed by an even more disappointed "ahhhhhhhh" from their classmates and a mumbled "sorry" from Dan.

Flyguy Freddie struggled on his back for a moment to get back up, he was upset—but apparently not being the kind of flying turtle to give up easily—went to the next working wind circle and began floating again.

The class wrapped up with a cleanup session. They cleaned all the circles off the sand with the long ends of their sticks—Phillip and Dan were even bad at this, they couldn't get the sand as smooth as everybody else—Miss Julie had to ask Thamus to help them. They put their chairs back in the right spot and returned their bamboo sticks to the bucket.

Miss Julie spent this time giving light orders that sounded like suggestions and distributing complements. "Fantastic job today on your color circle, Brian. Your reds were spectacular." "Sydney, I have never seen Flyguy Freddie fly higher." "Good Job setting an example for the rest of the classroom, Demer." "Perfect circles, Thamus." When she got to Dan and Phillip she said, "I have never seen any student work as hard as you two, and effort is the thing that matters most."

The class was to be followed by an outdoor break, then a snack, then a nap. "Come play with us," Thamus pleaded. "Demer has a big orbit ball to play with."

"Can't right now, Thamus," Phillip replied. "Dan and I have to go to the doctor."

Thamus was disappointed. But with a promise from Phillip that they would try to make the time to come play with him and Demer and the 'orbit ball' he eventually allowed them to go.

"So, Circles Class, how about that...?" Dan said after they left.

"Yeah... not going to lie, we really stink at circles class," Phillip replied. "My only solace is that I did better than you."

"What?!" Dan said, smiling. "My circles were perfect. Yours were all lopsided. I could tell, mine were close to working," Dan had taken out his pink notebook and was making notes. Drawings of the various circles. "Hey Phil, if it is possible to learn magic, do you think we should ask to be put in a lower class, maybe one with toddlers?"

"Nah, I think we should stick with this one," Phillip said. "Maybe we should hire Thamus as a tutor. His dad owns a boat, you know?"

───── o ─────

The medical tents looked nothing like tents.

They were made out of a series white triangular panels, forming almost random shapes. They had to walk around the tents two or three times before they found something that looked like an entrance.

"I think this is the right place," Phillip said. It was clean, bright, and barren inside. It felt sterile. There was something distinctly *medical* about the place. Things that looked like lab equipment were placed on long tables. Jars lines the walls filled with plants or specimens suspended in liquid.

The place was empty.

"Should we wait...?" Dan wondered.

"Wait for whom?" A man said, popping his head over the desk, as if he had been crouching on the floor. He had wireframe glasses he was cleaning, rubbing them on his lab coat. He was thin and small, and despite that had an oversized belly. He looked unhealthy.

"Were supposed to see Dr. Bartley," Phillip answered.

The man grunted, he seemed to be chewing something, and that something was not staying in his mouth very well. He put on his glasses and looked them up and down. "Thought as much, Choicers I imagine," he said, lifting a heavy leather box onto the desk. The leather peeling, revealing wood and colorful stickers underneath. "Dr. Bartley is out doing rounds in the Camp. I'm McMann, I keep telling them not to send more people, especially Choicers, it does no good, but do they listen? Come over here. I can help you."

He opened up the leather box. The leather peeling more when he did so. "Gotta get this old thing repaired, but the Imps want my bones to work it back to shape. Sentimental value, you know how it is," he said. "How much resonance treatments have you two been through?"

"Resonance treatments...?" Dan asked.

"Though so, could see it from a mile away," McMann took out several bottles of dark liquid. A label on the side said 'MIRACLE RESONANCE FORMULA #3.'

"I imagine it's been hard to do any magic, new Choicers like yourself," McMann continued. "What do they expect, eh? You've just got here. Have either of you used your Earners' Right? Do you have a Skull Deal under your belt?"

"Don't... think so," Phillip answered.

"Skull deal?" Dan repeated.

"Like I was saying an examination won't do until we get you fundamental resonances harmonically adjusted to this Fold's substratum," McMann continued. Pouring dark liquid which sparked blue into crystal glasses. "But we can jumpstart the process. Here drink this, my own formula."

He handed them the glasses of liquid, which they took, blue sparks almost touching their fingers. "What does it do?" Dan asked, taking a cautionary sniff.

"All safe. Use it myself. It's just a simple all-natural treatment, just like eating a vegetable. Simulates months of harmonic absorption," McMann answered. "Now drink it in one big gulp, it's better that way."

Dan took another sniff, a blue spark zapping his nose. Phillip, not wanting to scare himself in case it smelled bad, drank it with his nose plugged.

It was thick, like syrup. And as sour as anything he had ever tasted. His mouth, tongue, and eyes seemed to dry and shrivel with contact. It moved slowly down his throat, it was an unpleasant sensation, it felt like an electric current. Like he stuck his tongue in a wall plug.

He could feel the sparkvine going all the way down to his stomach, sending wave after wave of a jittering zaps through his body. "Oh God!" Phillip said through a cough. "Holy crud...!" Dan blurted out, his eyes watering.

"Nasty stuff, I'm the first to admit," McMann got close to Phillip, then Dan. Grabbed their hands and tapped their palms. Looked in their eyes. "Yes, yes. I think this is working well," He grabbed the bottle and poured two more cups. "I need you to take a second dose."

Any delusion that the 'second dose' would be easier than the first was shattered the moment the sparkvine touched his lips. If anything, the effect of the sparkvine was amplified, more acute. The buzzing didn't stop now.

"Do you feel sensation in your fingertips?" McMann asked.

"Uh... What? Oh, yeah," the room felt like it was moving. Phillip was having a hard time focusing his eyes on McMann. "It feels like I socketed them. I mean I put them in a socket. An electric socket, I mean. They're buzzing. Like, bzzzzz. Bzzz. Bzzz."

Dan laughed next to him. "*Socketed* them!" He said, and laughed again. Phillip laughed with him, it *was* pretty funny...

"Good. Good. I think we have the right mixture. What luck! One more dose ought to do you for today," McMann said, and poured again.

Turns out the third time was the charm.

The unpleasantness of the taste and the sourness seemed less now. The electric buzzing felt more like warmth moving through his entire body.

He lost tension in his body. He felt limber now. He could probably climb a tree or run without stopping for miles, no sweat. Probably draw those circles, too. Draw so many circles Miss Julie's head would spin. Give Thamus a run for his money. Show Prism Pete a thing or two with that stupid bobbing head of his...

"I feel... a little funny..." Dan said, hiccupping.

"It seems to be working well. Very well. Very well," McMann said, taking out new bottles and putting them in front of them. "I'm going to prescribe to you boys some of this concoction. Here, three... no, let's say four bottles ought to do you right for the entire treatment. Two each. Take it three times a day for a week. Now, not to pressure you boys or anything..." McMann said. "But how much do you want to donate?"

"Donate?" Dan asked, trying to drink from what was now an empty cup in front of him.

"Completely voluntary, of course. Of course," McMann said. "But healing and helping can get a little expensive and we do appreciate a little in the way of support. But if you boys are unable to give back ..."

"No, we'll give back," Phillip blurted out. He didn't want to be a burden, he was already getting help from so many people... "How much...? I only have dollars."

"That won't be a problem at all," McMann said, taking out a thin strip of glass and a matching glass pen. "You boy's tell me you don't currently do business with any skull or coin bank. That's no problem. No problem at all. That will certainly change in the future. Smart lads like yourselves. Just sign and print here and some donations will be transferred to us automatically when you open an account, almost anywhere in the Primafold. Now, I'll put you down for... You boys are young, so only ten great notes. Actually, since it's you boys first time being examined, I won't take anything more than five great notes from you. No, don't argue with me. I absolutely insist you don't go about five great notes. Each. I simply won't accept it anymore."

Phillip took the blue quill and signed the glass panel, on a line with an "X" underneath a long block of words, it said *'Gentlemen's Debt: Five-Great Notes in exchange for Two-Bottles of Miracle" Resonance-Formula #3.'* Dan was reading the identical glass document that McMann had put in front of him, squinting and rubbing his eyes to see clearer. *Classic Dan*, Phillip thought, but noticed Dan was already signing the document.

"Thank you, boys. It's much appreciated..." McMann said, he was standing now with his things, Phillip hadn't seen him get up. "Now just initial here... Yes, that's right. And here. And stamp your thumb here. That's it. Perfect," McMann grabbed the glass documents out of their hands. The quills too.

Throwing them somewhere within his coat. Phillip noticed that underneath his clean white lab coat there was a tweed suit that looked a little worse-for-the-wear, patched and a little dirty. *Being a doctor must not be as lucrative here,* Phillip thought, unable to take his eyes off a jelly stain on his undercoat. *It's a good thing we donated.*

"Well I have to be off, boys. Healing is a busy business. I'm sure you understand," McMann said, half walking away from them, half checking himself to see he wasn't missing anything. "You boys have anything exciting planned for your night?"

"Uh, yeah. The generator lab..." Dan started.

"The generator lecture, with Shauns... something. RickyShauns," Phillip added.

McMann stopped moving. "The... *generator lab* you say. That could be a little... dangerous. Have you two ever been there before."

"Nope. First time ever," Phillip responded.

"Good. Good. If it's your first time it will probably be all safety checks and rules. Stuff like that..." McMann said.

"Probably." Phillip said confidently.

"That's good..." McMann seemed hesitant, like he was going to say more, but then walked out the door without another word.

"Bye," Phillip said to the empty doorway. Dan laughed.

We should get going, Phillip thought, and got to his feet. He got up too fast and his head rushed a little, he grabbed the table for support.

"Where ya' go... going?" Dan asked.

"Gotta get."

Dan agreed, and they left, but then turned back within a minute when Dan realized they had left all their things in the medical tent. This happened one more time, when Phillip noticed they didn't bring the all-important bottles of sparkvine medical syrup stuff with them. They laughed when they realized they had left them. It was hard not to laugh at little mistakes like these. Circle Class was embarrassing but there were so many people trying to help them.

Yes. Yes, Phillip thought, nodding to himself, *they were very, very lucky.*

SPARKVINE EXTRACT

Fulgar-Sulfate, Cons. (Wash. U HPMS) U.S.P, (Patent Pending)

WARNINGS: Not to be used by anybody who is pregnant or expects to become pregnant with a halfFae child. Do not mix with resonance grounding concoctions. KEEP OUT OF REACH OF CHILDREN and nonFae. FLAMMABLE. DO NOT BOIL OR OTHERWISE Evaporate. NOT for use for IMPS, GOBLINS, TROLLS, or any non-human sentient creature.
Meant for correcting and healing resonance conditions associated with multi-Fold individuals. ++

USAGE: Take two dosages every 12-hours or solar setting until desired results are achieved.

INGREDIENTS: Extract of Sparkvine, Fulgar-Sulfate, Ethyl Alcohol, Migrating-MoonCorn-Syrup, Salt-Spark Extract, McMann's Flavorant #43, McMann's Flavorant #66, McMann's Flavorant #6, Troll Toe Gum (Ethically sourced.)
++ These claims have not been evaluated by the Washington Union Health Protection and Magickletic Services.

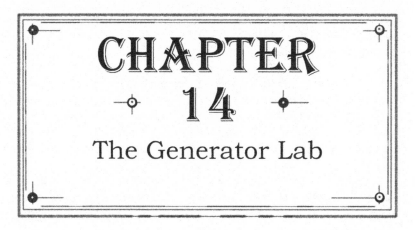

CHAPTER
14
The Generator Lab

It was remarkable Dan was able to lead them to the Generator Lab at all, given how much they got lost.

But found it he did.

Dan was a great guy, Phillip thought, rubbing his eyes.

He felt like he knew him forever. *He should tell Dan that*, but the thought was lost in a moment when his wrapped phone was buzzing in his pocket. It had been doing that. The screen was difficult to see through the wrapping.

He hoped that he wasn't getting messages. They had been assured by Haystacks that they would get back almost when they left, but how much could they trust Haystacks? What if Aunt Kath was already in California and he had gone missing and the Fairchild family was looking for him?

Aunt Kath.

He should tell Aunt Kath about this. Tell Maddie too, she knew something was going on, she was probably being driven nuts. Why was he being so secretive?

The phone buzzed again, the screen flashing.

Why should he tell Aunt Kath? She didn't tell him anything anymore. She made huge plans without consulting him. Going out to California. She had never done this, not since his parents died.

They were partners in everything. She had said so, they had both made a commitment. Not too long after his parents died, when he had gotten into the habit of sneaking out and walking to a local park—bringing with him his metal detector, which had by then broken but he always thought it would start working again if he just brought it with him.

He was nine years old at the time.

The world was painfully normal after his parents died. He remembered looking at a bus when he was told what happened, wondering why the bus was continuing to operate and make its normal stops. Why people got on and off the bus like nothing had changed. And nothing had changed, except everything. One day everything was normal, the next just a different normal. He remembered he wanted to shake it all loose, until the world finally acknowledged it that something was different.

So, he snuck out. The middle of the night felt nice and different.

Aunt Kath had followed him without him noticing. Sat down on the bench next to him without saying a word. They sat there in silence for a while, Phillip was going to apologize when she said, "is it too early for pancakes?"

It *was* too early for pancakes—Portland, Maine did not have many late-night diners—but they managed to find one they had somehow never been to before.

It was the birth of a tradition. *'Big Edna's'* became their go-to diner. The place where Phillip promised not to sneak out again. "I'm going to need your help here," she said. "We need to be partners in this. Cause spoiler-alert, I'm going to screw up a lot," he kept his promises.

Everything was shared with them. Finances, decisions to sell the old home, where to move, what furniture to buy for the new place. Aunt Kath had left school to take care of him, it was Phillip who insisted she go back. She had listened to him.

So why had she become so secretive now...?

God, what a way to ruin a good mood, Phillip thought, fighting off another wave of buzzing nausea and dizziness.

"Why are you walking so slow?" Dan said. "We're here."

"Sorry, thinking of something."

"What's that?"

Phillip thought, "I can't remember," he said, and laughed. Dan chuckled with him, before descending into an uncontrollable bout of hiccups.

The large stone building was slightly crooked, and looked like it was so heavy it sunk itself into the ground. Only half-dug out to gain access. Small windows on the roof were shining with gold coppery light, which shot out like rays.

The building was surrounded with hundreds of people, all in loose lines, all feeding into Wallmen who were checking their things. "It's crowded..." Dan said. "Maybe we should do something else. What's a generator anyway?"

There were floating signs on the grass with glowing gold lettering. *'Deposited all NoPES before entering.' 'Tunnel lashing safety required for entrance.' 'ASK an assistant before doing ANYTHING.'* Below the others, a sign said, in ugly handwriting: *'Alternative Entrance for Youngsters,'* with an arrow pointing around the building.

"Let's go this way," Phillip said.

"I think those cookies are making my stomach hurt," Dan said to himself. "What do you mean? Go where?"

"The sign said come this way. We're youngsters," Phillip said, impatient.

"Youngsters? What... sign?" Dan asked, but seemed to be more interested in keeping his cookies down than hearing the answer.

They pushed through shrubs and came to a small door in the back of the building, barley tall enough for Phillip to fit through.

The interior was impressive. Even Dan forgot about his ill-sitting snacks to look around. Phillip rubbed his eyes several times to make sure they were clear enough to take it all in.

It looked more like a brick and wooden church than a lab. High vaulted ceiling and large windows spilled light on the floor, which was divided into several levels, most of them containing long standing tables. The place was filled with large metal and sometimes stone or glass machines of all shapes and sizes. Some suspended from the ceiling on large chains made of crystal. There were tubes and wires running along the wall and suspended above them. Thousands of tubes. Some glowing and pulsating orange or electric yellow or green. Some moving back and forth, pumping like a human artery.

"Whoa. This place is great," Dan was looking up, and then noticed something at ground level. "Hey, everybody is wearing... What are those work clothes called? Over... Cover? Coveralls? That's it!"

Dan was right. Every person in the crowded room was wearing a single-piece work uniform. Phillip looked around. He had expected somebody to come up to them, to tell them where to go and what to do, but he guessed they were too busy for that sort of thing. It was crowded in here, after all. No need to be a burden if they could help themselves. In the spirit of helping himself Phillip looked around, and saw what he was looking for almost immediately.

"Over here," he told Dan, and walked over to a large bin, filled with coveralls. Picking through the bin, they tried to find the best size they could. They were all too big. They hastily put them on and tried not to attract too much attention as they dressed, a thick band of glowing wires provided them some privacy. Both Dan and Phillip looked ridiculous when they were dressed, they looked like children dressed in their father's clothes. The wrists and ankles of the coveralls grabbed them, so at least they didn't have to worry about the sleeves being too long or tripping.

"Get into position. Get what you need. We are starting soon and we aren't going to wait!" A booming voice announced at the other end of the workshop, where a projector and massive chalkboard displayed information. *'Generator Lab Introduction as taught by the illustrious Ailbeart Rickshaun,'* it said.

"We need the tube things," Dan said, and before Phillip could ask 'What Tube things?' continued, "... everybody has a metal glass tube-y thing in front of them at the tables we need one..."

Dan was right again. *Good ol' Dan*, he thought, giggling to himself, noticing things he missed. He was really indispensable.

"Here we go!" Phillip's mouth announced suddenly before his brain had a chance to catch up. He was pointing to another crate, this one marked with a purple triangle with purple claw marks on it, filled to the brim with shoebox sized 'metal glass tube-y things,' Phillip grabbed two of them and handed one to Dan. "Hurry, hurry." He whispered.

The sat at the first available seat, on the end of a long table. It looked like they were some of the youngest people here, the average age being somewhere around Aunt Kath's age or older. Phillip saw that there were a few people as young as them here, but not many.

The 'metal glass tube-y things' made more a 'CLUNK' when Phillip and Dan put them down then they had expected. Dan suppressed a laugh.

"Is something funny?" Said a black-haired man with glasses across from them.

"Oh... uh, no. Just a joke I was thinking..." Phillip began to explain.

Loud claps interrupted Phillip. A single person clapping, nobody else joining in, until the entire workroom was silent. Every eye in the building was directed toward the projector and the man clapping in front of it. The man at the front had dark black hair with a massive red and black beard which curled on the ends. He was wearing either a pointlessly fancy worker's outfit or an incredibly dirty business suit...

"My name..." he said in what sounded to Phillip something like a watered-down Scottish accent "...is Ailbeart Rickshaun, as you can see from the words behind me, I am both 'illustrious' and 'incredible.' If you do not know who I am, all I have to say is I'm sorry. I'm sorry your lives have been so colorless up 'till now. For those who do know me. Congratulations. I am pleased to bestow upon you the honor of meeting me," a few laughs and a round of applause greeted Rickshaun.

Phillip's phone was almost buzzing out of his pocket.

"Let me get a few things out of the way," he continued. "I am not nearly as happy teaching here as you will be learning. My time is better spent elsewhere. Every moment I'm lecturing dilettantes is time I'm not spending making the world a richer place with my incredible brain," a few more laughs. "Let's make a few other things clear while we're at it. I have a rotten personality. My *humility* is the best thing about me. I'm grumpy. Rude. Condescending. Demanding. Impatient. Prone to short periods of laziness and despondency. Utterly unfair to those who work for me, as they will likely tell you if you ever get a drink in one of them. I'm belligerent, stubborn, I'll forget your names and your birthday's and I'm a boring dinner guest. I am not proud of these traits, but I have learned to live with myself," he paused and looked at the crowd. "But one thing I *am*. Is *deliberate*. Deliberate. Burn that word into your head. I can teach you everything there is to know about my field. I can turn you into a walking reference manual, and it won't mean a thing if you lack *deliberacy*," Dan was writing furiously in his book now.

Buzz. Buzz. Buzzzz. Messages were coming in every few seconds.

"... I want to murder any wide-eyed delusions here before we start. We do incredible things here. We are cage fighting fundamental and half-understood powers of the universe. I can bottle an angry thought and have it light your living room for a year. We've done it. We have no idea how half of what we do works but we do it anyway. *Tedium* is the name of the game here. It's tedium and patience learning about generators, frustration and misery using generators, let alone managing to find that fickle lady we call *usefulness* in them. It's as boring at times as it is dangerous, and it's *always* dangerous…. By all accounts, I am ill-fitted for this field. Were it not for my magnificent intellect and my even more magnificent willpower, my naturally rotten disposition would have gotten me killed when I was still an apprentice, I expect from all of you, *deliberacy*." He paused, as if looking for disagreement.

"Which is why I don't expect any of you to complain when I start slow. I will explain things you already know and even if you're bored to tears, I expect you to pay attention as if you've never heard it. If you can't suppress a yawn you don't belong here. Go twiddle away your time collecting clouds or staring in each other's eyes with the Mindcrafters if that's your speed," there was some booing in the back of the room. "No disrespect for the simpler crafts, I wouldn't want to collect my own mist and have the utmost respect for those who failed out of any interesting career and are forced to do so…" The booing got a little louder, mixed with laughter.

"Now, I make any apprentice of mine go through five dry runs on any procedure before they are permitted to play with any power. For you, we are going to go through ten dry runs before I let any of you touch something with a current. If I catch any of you lot jumping ahead or ignoring my instruction, you will be politely humiliated in front of the group, laughed at, and tossed out. Hopefully never to fully recover from your humiliation. Trust me, a miserable sod like myself has no restraint when it comes to personal insults. I go for the throat…"

"Phil, Phil," Dan whispered. "I like Rickshaun."

"He's the best," Phillip agreed.

"Shhh!" A girl in tight ponytail shot them an angry glance.

"… What you have in front of you is a little training instrument provided by our gracious hosts. They have all been purified and tested before you got here so you don't have to worry about that. They are basic generator and converter combo. As simple as can be. Today, after you prove to me you are responsible, we are going to be working with non-purified moon powder. If we do everything right, we can convert it into some all-purpose sun-gleam. Ready for harvesting and storage. If the group of you are not complete idiots, we are going to convert it again into current, and power those baby chicken puppets a good friend of mine worked up for me for educational purposes," Dan and Phillip looked in the basket on the desk. There were baby chick dolls—or puppets—made of cloth and wood, all motionless. The projector behind Rickshaun had changed. Mathematical symbols, numbers, graphs and shapes now filled the wall. "Don't get intimidated, this is nothing you didn't learn in any good primary school. Basic laws of Convertance. I want everybody to be able to predict exactly how much sungleam you can obtain from how much moon-powder, and convert again into usable current. I hope you all brought some pencils…"

Buzzzzz. Buzz. Buzzzzz.

Phillip took the phone out of his pocket.

'*Where? Are YOU!!!!*' Phillip saw on the screen, was this from Aunt Kath?

'EMergeccccy cycycyc!!!'

Phillip pressed hard against the wrapping, desperate to get more information.

'Hurt? Huuurt???'

Rickshaun was still speaking in front of the class.... these generators will auto-convert anything you put in them to the outsource so long as..."

'Okay?'

"... which is why ten toadstone of powder will produce better convertance ratios than five..."

'Need you!! Where r u?'

Oh crap, Phillip thought. *Haystacks was wrong!* Time was moving normally out in the normal world.

He needed to find a way to get a message back...

"... what side is positive and what is negative is arbitrary, the important thing is to stay..."

Buzz. Buuuuuuuzzzzzzz.

'That it. Calling cops. COpss coppssss.'

His fingers found a hard point on the wrapping, like a little ball bearing right underneath the surface, there was a small red circle next to it. He pressed and pulled. Nothing. He grabbed it as hard as he could and twisted.

The wrapping snapped. It was an inaudible snap, but he felt it in his hands.

Just as he was hoping he didn't break his phone the wrapping began to unravel.

Slowly at first, a few threads got loose and burnt away into nothing. The wrapping gave away with a few crackles and pops, it smelled like hot glue. The wrapping was gone. His phone was free.

"Phil. Phil," Dan whispered next to him, "What are you doing? Follow along."

"Oh, yeah, yeah," Phillip answered, and looked to what the rest of the table was doing. They had flicked switched on top of the generators, and stuck black tube in the front which led to the bottom of the table. Phillip copied them. Turning his attention back to his concealed phone, the stupid thing was glitching again, the screen going blank and then flashing, coming back to life and going dead again.

"... you need to spend power to make power. Good life lesson there somewhere..."

The phone was just obedient enough for Phillip to look at his messages. There was nothing there. Maybe it would take a while to come back...

Dan and the other classmate were flicking switches on the top of the generators now. And then flicking another switch at the bottom of the table. Phillip followed along.

Stupid phone, he thought, making him miss some of the lecture.

"What are you doing?" The girl in the tight ponytail asked him.

Phillip looked up, confused. And then looked at the table.

His generator was different. It was the only one with a bright glowing wire.

It was making a sound too. A grinding growling sound...

Dan made a move for the switch underneath Phillip.

"Ah!" Phillip screamed as pain erupted in his left hand.

It felt like he was stabbed with a knife. It burned and seared, sending shock waves of pain through his body. Every muscle had gone tense.

It was his phone.

His phone was burning, stabbing him like a thousand needles into his hand.

He dropped the phone on the table.

The lab had gone quiet, all eyes were staring in his direction.

A faint humming sound filled the air, and a soft screech.

His arm hairs stood on end.

"Out!" yelled Rickshaun. "All hands out! Walk! Don't run!"

People got up but didn't follow his instructions right away, they were still looking over at Phillip's table. The buzzing and the screeching became more intense.

It hurt Phillip's ears. His phone had begun to vibrate, then jump inches off the table. Sparks of electric current were jumping from the generator to the phone. Until the phone seemed to explode. A bright yellow flash. The ponytail girl screaming.

The phone was moving of its own volition, it had grown arms out of the screen.

Bright sparking arms that only sometimes kept their shape. The phone was crawling toward the generator. Phillip didn't move, and neither did anybody at his table. He didn't know what to do. The humming was overwhelming, it sounded like laughing now...

"Dowse that thing before it touches any live circuit! Hit the master brake, man! For God's sake, hit the switch!" Rickshaun yelled.

The sparking arms of the phone touched the generator.

Boom! Boom! Boom!

Screams filled the lab as every generator on every table sparked and exploded. The generators in front of Dan and Phillip sparking brighter than all of them. Sending balls of light across the lab. Phillip's hair was standing on end and blowing as if he was in a wind tunnel. People had begun to run. Some ducked under their tables. The humming now had become a voice, an unmistakably malevolent and mocking voice. No, *voices!* Vibrating in his skull.

Something had begun to crawl out of the generator...

"Pull your cords, ya' fools!" Rickshaun screamed at them. His voice drowned out by the laughing.

A hunched creature made of lighting crawled out of the generator, laughing wildly. Followed by others. Smaller creatures the shape of lizards or centipedes crawled up the wires.

There were a dozen people including Dan and Phillip stuck on the far side of the lab by the creatures. Nobody moved an inch, nobody knew what to do. The man with the dark hair and glasses did something with his hands and slapped the table. The hunched energy creature turned to him and laughed all the louder.

It lunged for him as he made a feeble attempt at swatting him away. The creatures were not substantial enough to touch but it became clear they could touch others.

The hunched creature grabbed the dark-haired man. Smaller creatures made their way into his coveralls. "No! No! Ah!" He yelled, as they touched and burnt his skin, some trying to go in his mouth.

They succeeded and overwhelmed him as he fell to the floor.

He gave off one horrible scream, and then... evaporated.

He was there, and then he wasn't... his clothes lay on the floor without him. Moving now only because the hunched creatures were moving inside it.

The ponytail girl let out another scream, and then grabbed her chest as if she was trying to pull off her clothes or swat away a spider.

The light from the generators blinded Phillip. More creatures appeared. Each one more misshapen than the last. They moved slowly toward the other students, making sudden leaps at them. It was hard to see anything now but he could hear other students being attacked. Their screams suddenly cut off. Neither Phillip or Dan moved.

What do I do?! What can I do?!

This was all his fault. People were dying and it was all his fault and his stupid phone. Why had he come here? What did he think he was going to accomplish? He was stupid. And now he was here, standing like an idiot, staring at what he had done, wasting precious moments blaming himself. But what could he do? There was nowhere to run, nothing to fight with. How do you fight these things?

He noticed a girl on the floor, the one with the glasses, crawling away backwards from a taunting laughing figure.

No, he wouldn't let this woman die. He grabbed the closest thing to him, a stool, and threw it at the misshapen creature.

The stool slowed midair, cracked, and exploded.

The girl with the glasses looked all the more horrified. The creature had turned its attention to Phillip. Other creatures had made their way to the girl. She gave a short scream and continued to crawl and pull at the clothes on her chest. The creatures overwhelmed her like it did the others.

There was a pop and whoosh and sparks and lights. More laughing. Then it cut out completely.

And nothing was left of the girl with the glasses but her coveralls on the floor.

Dan grabbed some clothes on the floor and threw them at the creature now making its way toward them, he clutched his book in his arms and almost threw it.

The creature reacted. It dodged as if the book had been thrown...

Dan, noticing the reaction, swung the book at the creature again. It growled and laughed, but backed up...

The pink notebooks!

Phillip grabbed his notebook and mimicked Dan, they were swinging them in all directions as if they were trying to swat a fly. The creatures would scatter away, reconvene and then move toward them again. Dan and Phillip were back to back, swatting at any creature that got close to them.

Phillip heard another grunt, and a weak scream to his right.

"Dan! Dan! There's someone over there! We can help them, we have to help them." Phillip yelled.

Dan just nodded. Phillip moved as fast as he could, swatting at the creatures that approached, Dan walking backwards behind him.

They found another man passed out on the floor, the top of his head bleeding. Dan and Phillip positioned themselves over him, holding out their books like shields.

"Maybe we. Maybe we can pick him up? Try to carry him out," Dan said, out of breath. "Drag him maybe...?"

A centipede creature that had wings landed on Phillip's neck, shocking the skin. Phillip took his pink book and scraped the creature of his neck. Dan looked over and the creatures took the opportunity to get closer. They were getting closer. Their numbers were greater and they seemed less afraid of the books with each passing moment. Their cackle of laughter blending together into one long screech.

They were eight feet away. Then five. And then Phillip felt the heat and the energy of them on his skin...

A blast of wind and a crackle as another figure emerged. Man sized. Deathly white.

No, not white. Covered, from head to toe, in a white powder that smoked as the figure walked.

It was Rickshaun.

He was clapping his hands as hard as he could. Each time the creatures would scatter.

He made his way to them. He ignored Dan and Phillip and he crouched down to the unconscious teenager at their feet. Placing a hand on his neck and head, he reached on his chest. Grabbed what looked like a belt, and pulled.

The unconscious man evaporated.

Popping out of existence, leaving the coveralls behind.

"What?!" Phillip yelled, still swatting at the creatures. Not knowing what to think.

Rickshaun got up and grabbed both their collars, then felt around their chest as he had done the teenager on the floor, looking confused as he did it.

"What the bloody Hell?!" He yelled to them as he took something off his coat. "Of all the stupid people in the world!"

He threw a strap around Phillip, something like a belt that had chains and ropes attached. He attached Dan to it the same way. Just as he was about to ask what Rickshaun was doing, he pulled a rope on the belt...

Phillips skull seemed to separate from his body.

His skin was left behind from him bones and his nervous system wasn't far behind. His eyes no longer registered shapes just a blinding swirl of light. It felt like he was suspended in water but at the same time that he was traveling at incredible speeds. He had no sense of where his body was but felt somehow that some of his body was far in front of him and some of it behind. He was stretched and separated from his whole self...

That was until he crashed back into himself. His body smashing and blending back together as he came to a stop.

He could see again.

He was surrounded by small white balls. He ventured to move, and found his body felt a little alien and unfamiliar. He was still clutching his notebook and noticed he was upside-down in the pool of what felt like soft tennis balls. The spheres moved him as if he was on a wave, placing him gently on his back on soft cool grass.

There were other people here. Dan was next to him. Phillip sat up and noticed a little more than dozen people lying on the grass.

The black-haired guy with the glasses was here! And the girl with the ponytail, she was being hugged by another girl.

Nobody had died.

Everybody was in their underwear. Phillip looked down. Including themselves.

Such relief overtook him that he felt on the verge of tears.

Dan was a step behind him. "Ohhhhhh," he said. "Phil. I swear to God I thought people were being killed."

"Me too!" Phillip responded.

It was so calm on the grass it took Phillip a while to notice the flurry of activity around them. Men and women in work uniforms were running about. Giving orders. The lab behind them was surrounded by people. The interior looked like a firework show was going on inside. A window exploded outward as he was looking.

"Anybody else inside?!" A man yelled.

"Rickshaun is still in there!"

"I want every person to dowse the place if anybody sees even a single wisp escaping. Where are my sealers?!" He demanded back.

Rickshaun walked out of the front door.

He didn't run. He was met with applause.

He did a little hand signal, and the lab was then blasted from several angles by a jet of smoke and white powder. Rickshaun refused a blanket another person tried to hand him. He was walking straight for Dan and Phillip.

The powder he was covered in had worn away. You could make out the black and red of his beard again. His was smoking, and his clothes looked worse than they had before. But nothing matched Rickshaun's expression. A look of intense, focused anger.

He walked up to Phillip with such speed and force that he thought Rickshaun was going to strike him, and was surprised when he didn't. Instead he grabbed Phillip by his undershirt with surprising gentleness and looked straight into his eyes.

"There ya' are..." he said in a calm and humorous voice in stark contrast to the look on his face. "Don't worry, I just wanted to give you back this Mundafold gadget of yours, found it in my shop. Should repair nicely," He thrust Phillip's phone, now covered in white powdered, into his hand. "Let's have a chat, shall we?"

———— o ————

Phillip and Dan were together but separated from the rest of the people from the workshop in the medical tents. The Wallmen who came and took them here made it clear they were *not* to leave. They could hear Rickshaun outside, screaming to anyone who would listen.

They were in trouble. Huge trouble. And it was all because of him.

He needed to find a way to apologize to Dan but he didn't know what to say and kept quiet. He had a headache now, his blurred vision was back, he felt nauseous.

It was McMann's miracle drink! They had taken it before going to the lab. It made them feel funny.

Why did we think it was okay to go to the lab like that...?

A tall black man entered the room, he wore a wide brimmed white hat that sat high on his head. Phillip thought he might be a priest, his simple monochrome clothing looked almost religious... but he wore a practical lab coat with it.

"Hello," he said. "I'm Dr. Emmitt Bartly. Are you feeling alright?"

They told him they felt fine and he examined the small wounds they had, sometimes applying bandages. The burn on Phillip's neck was treated with a clear liquid he applied to the skin that alternated between burning and cold. Dr. Bartly looked them both in the eyes and smelled their breath.

"You're on something, aren't you? What is it...?" He asked.

Before they could answer, two Wallmen walked into the room.

"You going in to talk to them?! No, I want to talk to them!" Rickshaun burst into the room a second later. His expression still angry, tinged with a manic energy. "There you are. There you are. The good boys on the field took me away from you. All's well, it's just giving me more time to think about what I was going to say to you. I'll start by taking a little about your intelligence..."

Rickshaun was interrupted by another person who entered the room. Captain Karo.

He didn't look angry. Instead, his mouth set into a straight line, his face passive. "Somehow I knew it was you two the moment I heard."

"I am not done with my examination yet," Dr. Bartly told them.

"Nobody is asking you to leave, doctor. This won't take long," Karo said.

"... I get first swing at em'..." Rickshaun said. "My shop's a mess. And I need to take out my anger on somebody..."

"Can I at least dress these wounds before you 'take a swing at them?'" Dr. Bartly said, looking at Rickshaun, and then Karo. "Adeline or the Pauls should be here, and accident is not Wallmen business..."

"The Pauls and Adaline are indisposed at the moment. Left when you were out in the Camps, doctor. And I'm afraid you're wrong, this *is* Wallmen business," A Wallmen handed him a couple powder covered bags. Phillip and Dan's bags. With them some bundled clothing.

"Do these belong to you?" Karo asked them.

"Yes," Dan and Phillip said together.

Karo opened the bag, and took out one of the bottles they had gotten from McMann.

"... and these?" He asked.

"We got those from a doctor..." Phillip said fast. "They're for medical reasons... Making our bodies resonance... better."

"Oh, my bloody hell and the saints..." Rickshaun grabbed a bottle. "Are you telling me you boys came to my shop oiled up?!"

"You got them from Doctor?" Dr. Bartly asked, grabbing the other bottle and opening the cap. "What Doctor?"

"Doctor... McMann," Dan said.

"McMann? Red haired man, looks like a weasel?" When Dan and Phillip nodded Dr. Bartly continued. "McMann is no doctor. He's no anything. Had no idea he was skulking about. Did he tell you he was a doctor?"

Phillip and Dan didn't answer. They both tried to remember.

He hadn't.

"...No, McMann is no doctor. And this is not medicine..." Dr. Bartly continued, holding up the bottle. "Just make you act silly. Told you it had some fantastic medical quality, did he? Smells like mustard syrup and pure distilled sparkvine, if my nose can be trusted. It won't hurt you. But it's vile. Will make you stupid, maybe a little giddy. How much did he have you pay for it? He did have you pay for it, didn't he?"

"We... donated... five great notes... from our future bank that we use..." Dan said, sounding as stupid as Phillip felt.

Rickshaun and the two Wallmen at the door burst out laughing. Dr. Bartly looked angry.

"A month's wages for an apprentice, spent on this! I have to try some," Rickshaun opened the bottle, took a sniff and then a swig. He came back coughing. "Oh, my God. Doctor, you're right. That's vile," but took another swig.

"Captain, there's a man in the Farm taking advantage of people," Dr. Bartly said. "Are your men looking for him?"

"We'll talk about that later. Right now, I'm going to deal with them..." Karo responded.

"... Don't you go thinking I'm going to go soft on them just because some useless wonkytaddler bamboozled them," Rickshaun interrupted. "I have questions to ask! Biting insults to hurl...!"

"That doesn't matter..." Karo said.

"Doesn't matter? My shoes and socks it doesn't matter! Do you know how much has to go wrong for these snots to mess up to the extent that they did? It's impressive. I need them to tell me..."

"It doesn't matter, Mr. Rickshaun, because in less than an hour the Wallmen are using our Privileges safety to expel these two permanently from the Farm and the surrounding Campgrounds."

Phillip swallowed hard.

This had been expecting this. But he needed to speak up for Dan.

"... It was my accident, Dan had nothing to do with it..." He started.

"Expelled?" Rickshaun said." Do we do that here? Seems a little... I mean it seems like we're going easy on them. I want to punish them properly, not just send them away..."

"You said to one of the Wallmen outside that they weren't wearing a tunneling lash, which means they snuck in. You said this, yes?" Karo asked Rickshaun, who nodded.

"We didn't sneak in," Phillip said, desperate to say anything. "We used the... the youngster's entrance..."

"There's only one entrance to my shop," Rickshaun said.

No, he saw the signs himself, Phillip wondered. "I read the signs," he said, more to himself than anybody else. "There were... signs."

"... You also told me that they were dressed in tainted clothes," Karo continued....and that they had infected generators. Not only that, they brought in a dangerously infected Mundafold Nopes machine into your shop. These devices were wrapped earlier. They were able to confirm he not only brought this into your shop, but unwrapped it, right there at his table..."

"I didn't..." Phillip started.

"... are you saying they did this deliberately...?" Rickshaun said.

"... I don't know, and I stopped caring when it comes to these two," Karo said. "They either did this deliberately or are so incompetent they are dangerous to others. Either scenario deserves expulsion. It deserves more than that but since there's no proper jurisdiction to report to this will have to do," Karo was looking at paperwork now. "You'll be interested to know Mr. Rickshaun that this is not my first run in with them. I have it on good authority that they snuck into the Farm. They then snuck into a sensitive meeting with the Pauls. They've ingratiated themselves with a few of the more privileged guests here. It's the only reason they haven't been kicked out yet..."

"We didn't mean to..." Dan started.

Karo held up his hand "... I don't care. I am using my Privilege given to me for the safety and protection of this area to expel you. Since you're clearly just innocent little sludgefoots I'll explain what this means. It means you're not going to whine to your high-born or rich friends. Even the Pauls can't take away my decision without renegotiating our rights here. And they're far too old fashioned to do that. I can expel guests. And especially 'visitors.' And I will expel the two of you."

Karo snapped his fingers. "Wallmen, gather everything they have with them out the gates, including anything the left in the Camps. I want no trace of them. Give their description to every Wallmen and hired mask here. I want them out of here within the hour. And I don't want to see these faces again in my lifetime."

CHAPTER 15

Wild Night's End

Their things were already gathered by the Wallmen.

Everything the left at Haystacks, but even their bikes—which they left chained to a tree outside the Camp—were here, wrapped like everything else.

Wrapped, their things took four Wallmen and themselves to carry, the only Wallmen without something in his arms led the group, Private Willum Brooks. They were led through dark trails and woods, through old doors nested into corners of ancient looking buildings—Willum looked like he exchanged coins with a hand at one door.

Another door and they were on a trail.

The door floated in the middle of the trail, with nothing else behind it.

The Wallmen began dumping their things in a pile on the ground. "Be careful," Willum ordered. "Sorry about this..." he whispered to Phillip, and then said louder, "all paths lead out, take any one you wish. Follow the light, it is morning in the dominant Folds. If you find a path going back in, you are forbidden from taking it, by order of Wallmen and by the authority granted us here by the Inheritor Paul."

Willum Brooks gave them one more pitying look, before turning and walking back toward the door. The other Wallmen followed. Two lingered behind—one with a big broken nose the other in a soft hat—laughing amongst themselves, passing back and forth a bottle.

It was the sparkvine bottle.

"That belongs to us," Phillip said. The two Wallmen turned, as surprised at Phillip saying anything as Phillip was. "It's... ours. We paid for it. A month's wages for an apprentice."

"Really?" The hat Wallmen said sarcastically. He held out the bottle. "Prove it."

Phillip grabbed the bottle, looked the Wallmen right in the eye, and took a drink.

It took every ounce of energy Phillip to suppress the wince. He failed. The two Wallmen laughed and patted him on the back. "He said it was 'ours,' not just his," the Wallmen in the hat said, Phillip's eyes were too blurry to see which one. "Leave em' alone," said the one with the broken nose. Phillip was already handing the bottle to Dan. Who let out an annoyed breath, grabbed it, and took a swig himself, coughing when he was done.

The Wallmen laughed all the harder. "We're leaving!" Willum said from the floating door. "Yes, sir!" The Wallmen answered. "You two can loiter with us anytime," they said, with more congratulatory pats on the back, a few extra for Dan, who was still coughing.

The Wallmen followed the others out of the floating door, which began to shut.

Phillip got one last look at the lit silo building behind the trees before the door shut with an echoing clank.

The door began to dissolve into nothing. They watched it until it was gone. They were alone.

A wave of dizziness hit him as he turned around.

He suddenly regretted winning back those stupid bottles...

"I'm sorry, I don't know why I made us do that," Phillip said, burping. "For some reason I wanted to get them back..."

"It's okay, I get it," Dan said.

"... I don't know what I was thinking, Dan," he continued. "I did see those signs outside the generator lab shop, Dan I did...!"

"... I know."

"Really, you have to believe me, I didn't misread them or imagine them, they were right there..."

"I know."

"It was just, I don't know. I was feeling funny and not thinking. But Dan, those signs were there...!"

"Phil. I know. I believe you," Dan said calmly.

Phillip didn't know what to say to this. He wished he could take this whole day back and do everything differently.

"Why did you unwrap your phone in the lab, though?" Dan asked.

"I... I saw messages on the screen. They were saying it was an emergency..." Phillip answered.

"But it's impossible for messages to make it into the Farm. Haystacks said. Also, the Farm time..." Dan followed up.

"I know, I thought about that afterwards," Phillip said. "It just felt so urgent..."

"I bet it was the main house again. Yeah, that's what I bet it was." Dan said.

"What?" Phillip asked.

"The main house, *Crownshead* or whatever. The Pauls mentioned it liked to play pranks. Houses can do that here. It played a prank on us and we ended up in the meeting with the Pauls. I bet that's what happened here," Dan answered. "Yep. Yeeep. That's what I bet happened."

Phillip hadn't even thought of this. It all made so much sense. Just like with the Pauls and Waltzrigg, the old woman with the key.

Dan and Phillip were *pranked*...

"Opps, I still have Andy's skychalk..." Dan said, repacking his things. Phillip was trying to help as much as possible. Putting everything he could in his messenger bag. Dan hit the button on the skychalk and drew a line in the air. "Still works out here. Man, this is a weird night, Phil, I'm dizzy and think I'm going to hurl. Let's get home. It's over and I want to sleep."

———— o ————

They didn't notice until their eyes hurt that the sun was coming up as they made their way out.

Dan said it rose from the wrong horizon. Sunrise was a reversed sunset, which led to evening, then afternoon, then mid-morning as they got close to Fairchild Ranch—where time seemed to be moving at the right speed and generally the right direction.

It was spectacular. Dan even pushed past his malaise and dizziness to take notes.

The work trucks were still in front of the Fairchild Ranch when they got back. A good sign that time really hadn't passed normally. "Wild..." Dan said. "I'll message you when I get back. We'll decide what to do from here."

Phillip nodded. Dan was recovering fast.

At least seven different people were coming in and out of the main Fairchild house. Rosencrantz and Guildenstern watched from the lawn, so still they were unnoticed by the workers. Rosencrantz turned to look at Phillip when he approached, the old beagle had a tendency to stare at him.

"Have fun with your friend?" Uncle Jeff asked behind him, so suddenly Phillip jumped.

"Hi uncle Jeff," Phillip said. He noticed they left. "Dan wanted to show me this program he was in, at KHU." The lie was too elaborate and pointless, but he was still dizzy and didn't have the energy.

"Ah, that's good, your aunt Katherine tells us you're independent. That's good. You'll fit in around here, country kids tend to be independent, just be careful and tell us where you're going," uncle Jeff said, adjusting his horned rimmed glasses awkwardly. "Speaking of, I just wanted you to know. I heard you with Katherine today and I just want you to know if you want to ask me any questions, anything at all, that I'm here to answer them..."

Phillip didn't know what to make of this, and he was too tired to figure it out. "Thanks," he answered, then motioned toward the home. "How's the house doing?"

"Terrible," uncle Jeff answered. "but not as bad as we thought. There's some mold, big infection working its way up the wall, right next to your room. That's the worst of it."

A workman wearing a white hazmat suit motioned for him at the door. Uncle Jeff went to talk to him. Maddie appeared from behind the car like she was waiting to pounce. "Where'd you go?" She asked.

"To KHU with Dan, he's in a summer program," Phillip said, repeating the lie.

"Your clothes are dirty..."

"Dirty world out there," Phillip answered, looking at his phone to avoid looking at Maddie, which now seemed to be working almost normally.

"What's all that white stuff on your phone?" She asked.

"Just super illegal drugs."

"Why are you lying? What's going on?! Why is Fortinbras so well trained? What's with all the birds?! I know you heard the sound last night! Why won't you tell me...?!"

His phone rang, without glitches, it was Aunt Kath.

Phillip held the phone up to Maddie before answering. "Hello?" he said, deliberately turning around toward the Dollhouse.

"You have to try kolaches," Aunt Kath said, her voice echoing.

"Kolaches?"

"There like this sausage thing in dough, it doesn't have to be sausage. Big Texas thing, or Turkish, something like that, I met a lady who's opening a chain of them, nice lady but wouldn't stop talking forever."

"A chain in California? How's the weather?"

"California? I'm still at the airport. I've only been at the gate for an hour," Aunt Kath said. "You okay, you sound tired."

Fortinbras met Phillip at the porch with typical enthusiasm.

"Just tired," Phillip answered. "Long night... went to KHU with Dan, he has a program there."

"I heard, speaking of, how do you like the campus, it's a really good school you know..." Aunt Kath stopped talking, an electric voice was echoing in the distance on the line. "That's my flight, it's boarding. I'll talk to you when I land. You suck, by the way," she said, giving their traditional goodbye.

"You're a bum and will never amount to anything," Phillip said back. "Eat kale or whatever in California..."

A few more rushed goodbyes and they hung up. Phillip made his way upstairs to his room, Fortinbras following along. He didn't even take off his shoes before falling into bed, thinking of all the life-changing things he learned today, and everything he lost, before sleep took him.

———— o ————

He couldn't have been asleep for more than fifteen minutes when Maddie woke him up.

Why was Maddie always waking him up? And why was her voice so loud and grating?

"... I said we're going out," Maddie said, petting Fortinbras. "Mom says the chemicals in the house are going to kill us if we don't eat out so we're going into town for dinner."

"Too early..." Phillip said. He had the worst headache he could remember, the light outside the windows was painful. *Was the sun brighter here?*

"It's almost five-o-clock," Maddie said judgmentally. She was the worst waker-upper of people he had ever known. He might have preferred Steve and Harrison.

He was so dazed getting up and ready that he was surprised to find himself in the car, wedged again between Steve and Harrison on the way to town. The talking in the car didn't make his headache any better. Something about how King's Hill "fudged up" the summer games with Gardenvale because of a "cruddy" new strategy... At some point a KHU hat appeared on Phillip's head. Put there by Steve or Harrison he imagined, but couldn't remember when.

They went to 'The White Sea Lookout.' The "white sea" in the lookout was the Mississippi river. They sat outside on the massive raised deck. Phillip, who had a Mainer obligation to be suspicious of any Midwestern seafood, ordered the 'curry and rice omelet' which was half covered in a deep red sauce. It was pretty good, and he thought his headache might be getting better.

"Phillip, don't move," aunt Elaine whispered.

"What?" he said, freezing. He caught his reflection in the window next to the table. On top of his KHU hat was a bird. A tiny yellow bird. Aunt Elaine was trying to get out her phone to a picture. She shushed Maddie who was moving too much. Phillip gave a little thumbs up and the picture was taken. The bird was just hungry. Impulsively—moving smoothly and slowly—Phillip grabbed a small clump of rice off his plate and placed it on the brim of his KHU hat. The bird made a happy sound, grabbed the clump of rice, perched on the end of the hat and looked down as if to thank Phillip, and flew away. "Darn, he's gone," aunt Elaine said. "Look I got a picture."

"What kind of bird was that? I don't think that was a local bird..." Maddie started.

"You shouldn't feed em' Philly Cheese. It's a waste of good food I could be eating," Harrison said while helping himself to some of Phillip's rice. "Stay on your own plate Harry," uncle Jeff said. "Just pretend I'm a bird," Harrison whispered to Phillip.

Aunt Elaine wanted to avoid the "mess at home" as much as possible. So, after dinner they separated for walks around the river park and shops. "Meet back here in an hour," aunt Elaine said. "Steve, Harry, and *hour.*" Phillip managed to pretend he was going with Steve and Harrison but turned and separated at the last moment, for that he was walking alone alongside the river park, which contained so many raised gardens it was easy for him to hide.

He looked across the river, and wondered if he would be able to see the Farm if he went to the same vantage point Dan showed him.

Phillip was so deep in thought he didn't notice the man walking the other direction, until they almost ran into each other and their eyes met.

"Why if it isn't the young lad, I had the pleasure to meet earlier!" The man said

It was Waltzrigg. Holding what looked like a cup of ice-cream in his hand, wearing a light, casual suit which somehow looked militaristic when he wore it. He smelled like smoke and rotten fruit, but Phillip realized that wasn't him. Somebody was smoking nearby.

"Mr. Waltzrigg..." Phillip said, feeling for some reason that he should run. "Sorry..."

"Please, call me Wilhelm, I hate the name but I'll make an exception," he interrupted. Phillip had a hard time imagining calling him by his first name. "I was just out for a stroll, enjoying the local flavor, as it were. How about you? Is the Farm everything you expected?"

"Um, yes. I mean no. We got kicked out. But I'm just walking right..."

"Kicked out?" Waltzrigg said, his pleasantness overwhelming, almost aggressive. "Whatever happened?"

Dangit. Why did he say that?

"It was nothing."

"I'm afraid my curiosity has peaked," Waltzrigg said. "You must free me from the pain of it before it ruins the experience of my iced cream, which is already terribly bland."

"It was nothing, really," Phillip said. Waltzrigg didn't stop looking at him. "I just made a mistake, and the generator lab got... blown up."

Dangit! Why did he tell him that?!

He needed to walk away.

Waltzrigg gave a hoot of laughter. "Well done, big failures proceed great successes, you're halfway there. So, what are plans now, you and that other boy?"

"Plans? We don't... have any plans right now. We don't have access to the Farm or Camps so we don't know what to do next."

Waltzrigg stirred his ice-cream with his spoon. "I confess that I am somewhat disappointed."

"I'm sorry...?"

"Not in you, specifically," he said, as if apologizing. "I just heard so much about the American *can-do* attitude I began to believe the myth was true. The young of Washington Union had fires in their bellies, that's what I always heard. But perhaps this is not true of Choicers and Mundafold citizens. Perhaps it's this was just a bit of, what do you call it? *False advertisement*? As you have clearly given up, and from such an early failure too... shame."

"We haven't... *given* up. It's just..." Phillip answered.

"Happy to hear it!" Waltzrigg interrupted again. "It's indecent for the young to be dejected so easily. Would you mind a piece of advice?"

Phillip felt stuck in place, like his feet wouldn't move. "Um, sure..."

"You are in a wonderful position now, do you know why...?"

"No."

"... it's because you have no idea what to do next, because you don't have much to lose. It's wonderful," Waltzrigg said. "Almost any action you take is as good as any other. You can do anything. And anything can happen. So long as you *do anything*. It reminds me of my first disastrous steps into the greater Knowing. You'll remember this time with exhilaration, Mr. Phillip, I promised you. Now, what are your plans?"

"I..." Phillip said, pausing, "don't have any..."

"Perfect!" Waltzrigg began to walk away, looking at the darkening sky. "From one Choicer to another, I wish you the best of lucks. Remember, Mr. Phillip, not knowing anything is no excuse for not doing."

"Thank you..." Phillip said, not knowing what else to say, a little too late as Waltzrigg disappeared behind a raised garden, the smell of smoke and rotten fruit going with him.

———— o ————

Phillip was silent on the way home. So much so that his aunt asked him if he was okay several times. He blamed his silence on a lack of good sleep and a headache.

His headache was gone.

He was silent because he was thinking about what Waltzrigg said.

He was silent because *Waltzrigg was right*.

Too many thoughts, too many half-plans and half-conclusions got in the way for him to engage with the family. Maddie said several things about the bird but he barely heard.

He needed to move. To *do anything*. As soon as possible.

And he needed Dan with him.

"Uncle Jeff, aunt Elaine, mind if I ask you something...?" He said when they got back to the house, two of the work trucks were still there. "Dan, the kid you met, he's in a program at KHU and he's doing this recruitment thing he wants me involved in that sounds fun. Would you mind if he came over late if it's okay with his mom? Maybe even stayed the night? If it's too hectic here that's fine..."

Again, the lie was too elaborate, but he couldn't come up with a better one.

"What program is he in...?" Maddie started.

"No, that sounds fine, Phillip, bring him over anytime, the home is your home while you're here," aunt Elaine said, interrupting her daughter. "KHU has great summer programs."

"Thanks..." Phillip said, surprised that it worked so well.

He went back to his room in the empty Dollhouse, Fortinbras following again. Messaging Dan while he walked. His phone was glitching again, and still covered in the white substance. *'Call me,'* Phillip wrote several times.

He took out his things. The things Dan left over, some of the things he found by the river, and put them on his bed. The pocket knife, the pink notebook, the bag, the bottles of Sparkvine, the blue mailbox.

They lost the Farm, but they still had this.

Dan called him as he was making his way downstairs—he needed to arrange more with aunt Elaine—he picked up the phone as he got to the porch. "Dan!" He yelled into the speaker.

"Phil, what's up?" He said.

"Dan, my aunt's okay with it, ask your mom if it's cool if you come over, stay over for the night. We can make her call aunt Elaine and arrange things. Bring over the skychalk."

"Okay… that actually might work out, she needs to work on this project tonight… Phil, what are you thinking?"

A flash of movement on the porch. Something bright landed on the railing.

A small yellow bird. Tweeting expectedly and looking at Phillip.

Phillip laughed, bending down to stop Fortinbras from barking.

"Phil…?" Dan asked.

"I think we need to do something, Dan. *Do anything*," Phillip said, going inside to get food for the bird. "Dan, I think we need to do *magic*."

CHAPTER
16
Something from Nothing

Aunt Elaine was so accommodating of Dan coming over that Phillip worried he was abusing her good nature, but was also too excited to care.

He offered to take care of all the animals as payment. "All of them...?" Aunt Elaine said, too distracted by something Matthew was trying to swallow to listen. The arrangements for Dan to come over didn't take long. Aunt Elaine spoke with Dan's mom on the phone—they exchanged addresses, which was surprisingly difficult to do—King's Hill had a bunch of unofficial and personal roads.

In less than an hour, right before the sun was going down. Dan appeared on his bike at Fairchild Ranch, with more luggage than usual. "I'm surprised your family is cool about this, with all that's going on..." He said, after thanking aunt Elaine and uncle Jeff profusely.

"Me too."

"And they're just letting us stay in the empty home?" Dan said. "That's really cool."

"Yeah it is."

"Okay, Phil what's the plan?" Dan said as he put his bike next to the porch, noticing the yellow bird eating rice. "What kind of bird is that?"

"New bird, followed me home..." Phillip answered, wanting to get inside.

"Followed you home?"

"Yeah. Anyway, here's the plan," Phillip said. "I say we... *try stuff*."

"Try... stuff?" Dan repeated.

"Yes. Try stuff. Try anything. Keep doing stuff. You know... until something happens again, until something shakes loose," Phillip said, feeling a little embarrassed.

"Do stuff... Okay, I can get on board with that," Dan said. "Got to do *something*."

"Right?! Just like Waltzrigg said," Phillip said. "We are Choicers, which means we are Mundafold and not Primafold, or something. Got to do stuff to become Primafold, like Haystacks said."

"I think the Primafold is more like a place, and we're in the Mundafold right now. But yeah, I get it. What did you say about Waltzrigg?"

"I'm thinking we play around with that Skychalk you stole from Andy, try some Circles Class stuff, see what happens. Is all your magic stuff in the backpack?" Phillip asked. Dan nodded. "Good, I say we go into the woods over there. There's a clearing over the little hill."

"What woods? Why don't we just do stuff here?"

"My little cousin has been snooping around."

"Why not just tell her?"

"Because she'll tell everybody, and that will get messy," Phillip said, burping. The taste of the Sparkvine coming up again, an electric buzz traveling down his spine.

"Still burping that junk up, aren't you?" Dan said. "Me too. I have the worst headache earlier Phil you wouldn't believe it."

"I believe it, I'm going to bring it with us," Phillip said, holding up the backpack.

"Why?"

"You ever heard of a placebo?"

"Sure, it's like a sugar pill or whatever that makes you think it's real," Dan answered.

"Close enough. There's all this research that says placebos can still work even if you know they're placebos."

"Cool, but what does that have to do with the Sparkvine junk? Won't your family notice we're in the woods. And how do you know about placebo research?"

"Aunt Kath is getting a degree in clinical psychology, I sit in with her classes when they go late and I can't get home, Dr. Lewis is great," Phillip answered. Impatient to get going and feeling dizzy again from the burp. "My family is mostly asleep. Steve and Harrison get up at three in the morning, the baby is on an early schedule and that keeps aunt Elaine busy, trust me they have a lot going on and won't even notice, I said we're doing a summer program project. Let's get going. What do we need the Farm for? Let's do this."

Dan nodded, and seemed to be thinking. "Okay, let's do this," Dan repeated, picking up some of Phillip's energy. They were back outside, packs in hand, heading for the woods in less than a minute. Fortinbras yet again disappointed that he was to be left on the porch.

The clearing was exactly where he remembered it. Stumps and felled trees and thin grass. It felt safe and private. It was dark by the time they got there, Phillip forgot to bring a flashlight. Luckily, Dan had two, and a headlamp besides. Which made Phillip laugh for some reason.

Dan took out the Skychalk, pushed the button on the side, and drew a slightly glowing white line in the air. "Awesome," Phillip said, almost grabbing the chalk out of Dan's hand. "It works here," Dan said. "I tried it at home and it didn't work. Whoa, the stars are really bright tonight..." Phillip was too busy drawing fish in the air to look up. They floated in the air but didn't move like Andy's had.

Phillip went close to the ground, drew a circle, shined his light on it. "Clap, clap, stamp," he said, trying to close the circle. He turned off the light. Nothing was different.

Dan grabbed the Skychalk and tried the same thing, with the same results. Phillip found a stick and continued drawing circles in the dirt. Referencing Dan's notes. They tried everything they saw, with no effect. "The Skychalk works, does that mean we're doing magic? Or is magic like something you do yourself, and this is like a tool? Everybody implied Choicers, or whatever we are, can do magic, what do you think we're doing wrong?"

"It's psychology," Phillip said, fishing in his backpack. "I bet it's psychology. Dan, describe what it's like to know you have to go to the bathroom..."

"Weird question, I guess it's... I don't know, like pressure or something..."

"See, it's really hard to describe!" Phillip said. "Like describing how a color looks, there's this whole area of psychology about it. I forget what it's called. There has to be shared experience... I think those kids, Thamus the boat dad kid and the others, are doing something in their heads they don't know how to describe. Which means, I think..." Phillip took out the bottles of Sparkvine and put it on felled log "... we need a placebo. It's dumb, but what else are we going to do?"

"That stuff's gross Phil."

"Dr. Bartly said it wouldn't hurt us, who cares if it's fake? We need to change our brains up," Phillip said. "What's the worst that can happen, another headache?"

"Look, I think you're onto something, Phil. I was thinking about it, and the circles are on the ground, but they block light. Light doesn't travel on the ground, so I think the circles are like metaphors or something..."

"Right! That's why we need a placebo..."

"... but I was going to add that I think it's more than that," Dan said. "It's like what they taught me in Sunday school about rituals. It's like this mixture of things, what's going on in your head, what you're doing, that's supposed to make it real. It's the repetition too. I think magic is probably like that."

"I think it's all in your head, but that's a cool idea," Phillip said. "Here's another one, let's try to make it a ritual like you said, but every time we fail, we take some of this nasty syrup, just a cap full. *This syrup will definitely make us be able to do magic.*"

"Why do you want to drink that stuff so bad, Phil?" Dan said. "Fine, deal."

They drew more circles. Drew with the skychalk. With a stick on the ground. They carved them into the wood and wrote them in their pink notebooks. Nothing happened. Each time drinking a small bit of sparkvine out of the cap, which made them wince but got easier each time. "One, two, three, go!" They said each time they did it.

"Dan... get your notebook, the one with the notes from the amphitheater..."

"... there's only one notebook..." Dan said with a laugh.

"Yeah, that one. And get that twine you have..."

"You're talking really loud..." Dan said.

"Am I? Sorry," Phillip said. "Get that twine and maybe some coins and the skychalk. We also need some kind of bowl or..."

"Bowl? I have a glass jar..."

"You brought a glass jar?" Phillip asked, rubbing his eyes to look at his notes.

"Came in handy, didn't it?" Dan said, and they both laughed.

He got the jar out of his bag and followed Phillip to the largest stump in the field. "What are we..." he burped, "doing...?"

Phillip didn't answer, he led Dan to stand on the stump. Grabbed the string and put the end in Dan's hand. Moving away from Dan a few yards, he put the sky chalk close to the ground and pushed the button, then walked around Dan in a large circle, the twine allowing him to create an almost perfect circle out of chalk which hovered a few inches above the ground.

"Do you have your notes, Dan?" Phillip asked. "The notes you took the night of the amphitheater?" Dan nodded yes. "Good, let's do magic. *Big* magic," Phillip guided Dan off the stump, and put the jar in the center, then filled it up with water.

"I think we should start smaller..." Dan said, but was smiling and opened his notebook, complaining no further.

"This is what I'm thinking. Listen up. This is what I'm thinking," Phillip said after they had copied the rest of the circle from the notes. "We learned from Miss Julie and Prism Pete that circles do a few things. They filter stuff, they keep stuff out, they amplify or, I don't know, *concentrate* things," Phillip rubbed his eyes. "We also know that what the Pauls did in the amphitheater was special, Andy's brother Tenshu..."

"*Tadashi* ..." Dan corrected.

"Right, Tadaaki ..." Phillip continued. "He said the lightning was created right on stage. Not summoned. Not the result of some process or something. This is different than what most people were used to. Some people thought it was a trick! But if it wasn't a trick, I think that means the circle was there to isolate the Pauls and amplify them..."

"I think there's too much we don't know..." Dan said.

"... Not knowing anything is no excuse for not doing," Phillip quoted, and then looked down at the circle he made. "I think I should have put it lower on the ground. Here let me redraw it."

"What if this doesn't work?" Dan asked.

"Then who cares?!" Phillip yelled. "We'll do something else..."

Dan was nodding his head again. "Okay," he said in a small voice. "Oh-Kay!"

A manic kind of energy took them as they read their notes and drew in the rest of the circle, discussing their own theories and taking turns disagreeing or reassuring or dismissing the others doubts.

It felt like the amphitheater all over again.

Like something was cut loose in his chest and he was at risk of exploding.

He tried to settle himself down, tried to concentrate on what he was doing and trying to achieve, but every time he thought he succeeded he would find himself pacing fast on his feet, smiling like an idiot.

"Do you have coins?" He asked Dan. He did. Of course Dan did!

"How should we do this?" Phillip asked, and Dan went to his notes and read what the Pauls had done on stage. Draw the circle. Draw a few more circles. Draw the angular symbols at points around the stage, Dan and Phillip's notes contradicted on how these symbols looked, Phillip decided to follow Dan's notes, as he was better at it. Then, after that. Put down the coins, have the other person pick up the coins and replace them. Throw the coins in the bowl. Do something with your hands, and make lightning...

"Do you think it will work," Dan said.

"No," Phillip answered. "I think we have to think you know... *lightning-y* thoughts."

"Done," Dan said, but laughed.

"Take this seriously," Phillip ordered, but was also laughing.

So, they went through the process they had seen the Pauls do. Phillip placed the coins, Dan picked them up and replaced them with the cookies they got from Adeline, since that was all they had, joined each other at the center of the circle.

There was no surprise when nothing happened.

"You know..." Dan said, after they had erased and redrawn the circle, careful to go counter-clockwise this time since that's what the Pauls did. "I think it works like... You know, a ritual. Like, it doesn't mean anything by itself, but then you do it, and... and I don't know..."

"Explain. Explain," Phillip had no time for Dan's shyness.

"... It's... just like Sunday school. You do things repetitively and it doesn't mean something but you do them enough and it's real. At least that's how it's supposed to work. I'm not explaining myself right..."

"Going through the ritual..."

"Right! Right... going through the ritual. Then the circle does mean something. The whole thing becomes real... And *magic*. I think that's what magic is," he grabbed the jar and poured it out, then went to his bag to fetch what he was thinking about. "Here, I have an idea."

Phillip brought out the bottles. "Sparkvine. Makes sense," he said, and filled the jar. But this time he did something different, he took a drink of the Sparkvine syrup, before putting more in the jar. "There, know what's inside the jar is inside me. And what we put on the end of the circle will be in the jar... It's a ritual. Here, you do it too..."

"I don't think I can take any more of that stuff..." Dan said, but grabbed the bottle.

"Only one more sip," Phillip said. "And then pour the rest into the jar."

"Let's make this one count," Dan said as he winced from the sparkvine. "Only... lighting-y thoughts from here on out... Don't laugh! I'm serious..."

Phillip gave the thumb up sign and tried the best he could to reign in his energy.

They went slower this time, at each point Phillip tried to think about what he was doing, he had to stop himself every few moments from his thoughts drifting. He thought about lightning. He thought about nothing else as best he could. *Lighting. Lightning. Lightning.*

Dan was mumbling something as well, doing the same thing Phillip was.

He took off his shoes, because it felt right to touch the ground. Touched the end of the chalk before drawing with it.

Dan joined him at the center of the circle and dumped the coins in the jar. They dipped their hand in the liquid, and with flourish that lacked all self-conscious irony, threw their hand up, then down.

A moment passed. Another. A minute.

Dan and Phillip began to look around.

Nothing.

"You know I was thinking…" Phillip started.

"…I think maybe we should draw the symbols like you…"

CRACK! BOOM!

Phillip was thrown from his feet, or maybe he jumped back, he didn't know. He landed hard on his back.

He opened his eyes on the ground and realized that he couldn't see.

No, he could see. His eyes were just shocked and just now coming back into focus. They were shocked by the explosion of light and energy.

Energy coming from the sky and landing in the jar still on the stump.

Lighting, flowing into the jar. White and blinding before turning blue.

Lighting.

Lighting *they* had made.

"Dan! Dan where are you!" He looked around him and found Dan on the ground next to him, staring wide-eyed at the jar on the stump. "Dan are you seeing this?"

"Ye… yes," he answered.

"Are you seeing this Dan?" Phillip asked again and got to his feet.

"Yes," he said, still dazed.

"Are you really, Dan?" Phillip said, helping him to his feet. "We did it, Dan."

"We… did it?" He repeated.

"We did it!" Phillip said again.

"We did it," he said, as if trying out the words for the first time. "We did it! Phil, Phil, we did it! We made lighting, Phil!"

And then they were hugging each other and whooping and dancing, Phillip screamed something to Captain Karo but he couldn't remember what. All the while not taking one eye off the jar in the middle of the stump, for fear that it would stop existing the moment they looked away. They could feel the charge around them, but Phillip couldn't tell if it came from the lightning or their own excitement.

The lighting had died down to a thin blue string, and then nothing.

The jar was now filled with a bundle of vibrating violent energy.

"Phil…" Dan said as he slowly closes the lid of the jar, tapping the side with his finger.

"Yeah Dan?"

"Let's do it again."

"I'll find another stump. Do you have another jar?"

Dan did, amazingly, have another jar.

They found another stump not fifty yards away from the first, and began repeating the process as they did the last time, reminding each other to "stay serious." Phillip emptied the second bottle of miracle sparkvine whatever-it-was and was surprised to find he now had enormous affection for it.

They went through the process again, almost as slow as the first time. Phillip making an effort, and near impossible effort, to rein himself in and get his mind in order. Dan was mumbling again.

They stood at the new jar, threw their hands up, and then down.

A long time passed,

So long Phillip thought they failed, he was about to admit it when a *CRACK! BOOM!* broke from nowhere…

Phillip didn't fall back this time, neither did Dan.

"We did it…" one of them repeated, Phillip didn't know if he said or Dan did.

They didn't jump up and down and congratulate each other either, the smiles on their faces the only hint that they were happy. They sat on a log and watched the lighting burn itself out. It lasted longer this time, much longer. They didn't speak a word to each other as they watched. Phillip noticed the little sparks escaping the jar and traveling to the end of the circle before flashing out.

It was one of the most beautiful things he had ever seen.

"We should maybe… probably…" Dan started, but then bent over and threw up. Phillip patted him on the back. "We should probably do this a few more times, do different things each time… see… what changes," he threw up again on the ground.

"I think maybe we should get home," Phillip said, Dan wasn't done emptying his stomach.

They burst out in laughter and started talking nonsense as they gathered their things. They gathered up the lighting in the jars last. The top of the jars was tight but they didn't know if they should trust them in the bags. They glowed brightly, especially when held. Dan wrapped them both in cloths and stuck them in his backpack.

The walk home felt like a dream.

But it was too real for a dream. Too unreal. More real than real life.

Phillip couldn't describe it. Every moment felt infinite but at the same time they moved on the road as fast as light. He might as well have been floating. Even the stars—and it seemed there were more stars than usual—seemed more vibrant, like they were trying to talk to him themselves…

The road stretched ahead of them and Phillip knew that it led to another town and another discovery and more people and more magic and a whole world behind that! They had everything they needed.

Everything in the world was possible. Everything was theirs.

They didn't talk. They didn't need to.

But Phillip broke the silence anyway, "you know Dan, it's been a really great day..."

The normalcy of the Fairchild Ranch was almost more surprising than the lighting. Everything was the same. Nobody was looking for them. It was as if no time had passed at all.

Which, Phillip thought, *might be possible.* Then laughed at his own thought, it couldn't stop himself laughing. Even Dan joined in.

They were on the porch when they heard the ringing bell.

Diiiiing. Diiing. Ding. Ding. Ding.

"What's that...?" Phillip said, Fortinbras barked.

"That's..." Dan started, then opened the door and ran inside. He was halfway up the stairs before Phillip entered.

"Dan, what is it?" He said, following with Fortinbras.

"The box!" Dan yelled.

It wasn't until Phillip was in his room that he knew what Dan meant. "The box..." Phillip said. The blue square mailbox—on his bed—was ringing. A little flag was up.

"I think there's mail," Dan said. "It did this once before..."

"Get it," Phillip said. Dan approached the box like it was about to lunge at him.

The dinging stopped when he touched.

The little flag went down when he opened the hatch. The hatch shot open like it had been pushed.

Inside were two small, thin wooden boxes.

Dan and Phillip went to grab them. It felt as if the space of the box got greater as they reached for it, like it was farther away than they had expected and their eyes had fooled them. When they grabbed the boxes and took them out, they found them much wider than the box they had come out of.

"Cool," Phillip said.

"Yeah, I told you about that. Weird, isn't it?" Dan said.

The boxes were oiled and shined, they had a locked front. The reddish wood looked ornate. On the top, in gold lettering, were their names:

DANIEL MIGUEL EDWIN CASTELLANOS

And on the other:

PHILLIP MULFORD MONTGOMERY

"I think this one is yours," Phillip said, trading boxes.

"Should we open them at the same time...?" Dan asked, but Phillip was already trying.

Phillip found it, an almost unnoticeable tab next to the lock. The top clicked open. Inside was a single piece of paper. Carefully laid on a bed of black velvet in the thin box. It was a letter:

> Dear Phillip Montgomery,
>
> It is with the greatest joy that I have written this letter to inform you of your invitation to join us on the Farm. It is with even greater joy that we are prepared to over you FULL PRIVILEGES within the Farm.
>
> But we must ask you to put aside the great jubilation you must be feeling right now to issue a small word of warning. Full privileges come with responsibilities. We expect all given privileges within the Farm to adhere to the Old Laws and the moral principles that gave them rise; those given FULL privileges more so. We expect this of you whether you are *inside the Farm or at home.*
>
> You have proven yourself worthy of this great honor and we would hope that you join us soon. As a part of your guesthood here, we ask–but don't order– that you attend one class, once a week, in the silo building, for the foreseeable future. Miss Adeline will provide details.
>
> If your answer is YES (and we see no reason why it should not be), sign and stamp your thumb at the bottom of this letter, then put it in your mailbox.
>
> With Great Wishes and Hopes,
>
> Paul

"Phil. Phil let me read yours, does it say the same as mine...?" Dan asked. They switched letters, except for the names, the letters were identical.

"Should we sign them? What does ' The Old Laws' mean?" Dan asked, but then looked over at Phillip, who was trying to find a pen in his bag.

"I think we should talk about this," Dan said.

"What's to talk about?" Phillip responded.

"Well we don't know what the Old Laws mean... or what 'Full Privileges' means," Dan said back. "It might mean we have to... I don't know, eat a baby every full moon or something..."

"I'd eat a dozen babies to sign this letter," Phillip responded.

Dan laughed, and looked like he was going to talk again, but Phillip got their first...

"... What could it mean? We'd kill ourselves for the rest of our lives if we didn't sign," Phillip said. "If they ask us to eat babies... we just *won't* eat those babies. Worst case scenario, we get kicked out again or lose all these privileges..."

"I don't think that's close to the worst-case scenario," Dan responded.

"... probably not. But are we going to let that stop us...?" Phillip asked.

Dan considered for a moment, resolution setting in on his features the same way it had in the field. "No, I guess that won't stop us. Okay, Phil. We're in this together. Give me a pen."

They found a pen and with a final look to each other, signed their letters. There was a momentousness to it. Every stroke and scratch of the signature seemed to echo across the room. Across the entire Fairchild Ranch.

They put their folded letters back in the mailbox and closed the door. After a moment, Dan thought about raising the flag again. The mailbox shook, and the flag went down. They opened the mailbox again, and the letters were gone.

With another almost intolerable burst of excitement and tribulation, Phillip knew there was no going back from this. His life was changed the moment he found the bag, the instant Dan ran into him, when they had snuck into the Farm, when they had summoned... no, *made* lighting. But this, this was the real moment of significance.

There was no going back...

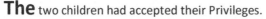

The two children had accepted their Privileges.

The Things reported this, the nearly lifeless dark eyes set on an even more lifeless face could see through the window in which they had done it, but it was also capable of feeling the change on the ground it stood. It would be felt by any being or thing of the greater Knowing.

The living creatures the Things were made from felt it too. They struggled against their impossible restraints inside the Things, feeling again their own pains and miseries. The proper flow of misery helped power the Things. The creatures were greater now, being a part of the Things. Serving a master instead of their own frail instincts, their natural suffering being granted purpose, instead of wasted on themselves.

The Things reported again, and again. It was redundant to report the first time, but the Things did not possess thoughts as thoughts were understood.

It did possess a kind of desire, a kind of desperation and begging, for purpose. Shall it continue to *watch*, master? To *intervene*? To *hide, master*? To *Kill*? To *Kill*, master?

The Things received new orders, burned into its nature by its remote master. *Continue to monitor, fall back, stay hidden. Stay close.*

The Things obeyed immediately. It was followed by other Things. Taller Things. Different Things. The screamer Things and the cutting Things and the watching Things.

They all fell back at once. To monitor from a safe distance. To monitor from the very edge of Anywhere. To keep their teeth and their claws sharp and their misery flowing.

To wait until their master ordered them again.

CHAPTER
17
The Next Day

A solitary crow sat on his usual perch.

He was mourning. Not anything serious. Not the loss of his mate or their nest. He was mourning the loss of what was once a prime gathering ground. Not serious. But he was a dramatic crow, being male.

It had all gone very bad very fast...

He used to have an ally here. One of those animals, the ones that knew enough to stand on two legs but couldn't muster the wisdom to fly. Worried, burrowing little animals those. Pitiful, really. But despite all that he had made a friend. One of the smaller ones, with the longer fur on top. It brought him food of all kinds.

In turn, he brought it what treasures he could find. Shiny things. Little things. Not the best things, those were for his mate, but good things still... These animals liked their treasures, they were often covered in them. The little animal seemed pleased by this, and collected the treasures.

It was good to have allies.

The little big animal made sounds sometimes in what the crow could only guess were these pitiful creature's attempt at communication. Not wanting to be rude, the crow always listened patiently, waiting for something to make sense. He sometimes tried to teach the little big animal things.

But it was a terrible student. These animals were as bad at learning as they were at flying.

Now it was all different. The little big animal was now too worried, too distracted, too scared to bring him food. He saw the little big animal from time to time, its schedule had been disrupted, it was tired and worried.

The little big creature's nest was being invaded. Stolen. While it was still there!

He knew which one was the invader immediately. It had come not as day ago and worked fast. It was the same kind of animal, taller than his ally, but with shorter fur. He wondered why the other animals didn't simply fight him off... but these creatures so rarely did what made sense.

He imagined that the invader animal was a tricky one, he had tricked the other animals to offer it food before the invader started his takeover.

The invader, despite moving in and un-nesting the ally, seemed utterly incapable and managing the nest.

A cloud came with the invader, he could see it. Grabbing the grass and crawling up the wooden sides of those ridiculous burrows. This cloud had attracted others. Enemies and parasites. Curious flying ones from far away, some with shapes and colors and accents that even he didn't recognize.

The nest was being mismanaged by the invader. This was clear.

What a shame.

He looked at where the invader was now resting. These animals always rested, often at the most productive times of the day and night. Silly animals these...

Something had happened before the sun came back up, he could feel it. The allegiance of the dirt had... shifted. The ground was usually not a fickle thing... Not like trees, not like clouds. These animals were always changing the dirt.

He was an older crow with plenty of experience to draw from, he had seen this before, when he was young, before he mated. When one of these animals had convinced him to wear a mask for a short time. Something he didn't enjoy and never sought again...

The invader was trying to stretch the dirt into a different shape. These animals did this sometimes. He guessed it was to fool other animals dumb enough to fall for it. These animals were always so confused. Not crows though.

His poor ally. The ground being changed under its feet while it was still there!

This invader animal was cruel. Dangerous. These animals were sometimes cruel to each other. This was nothing new.

He flew from his perch and landed outside the clear hard stuff these animals sometimes built their nests out of. It was risky, getting so close to an enemy animal, but he needed to get another look. He needed to wake this lethargic animal so he could get a proper look at him, and so made some sounds. Just sounds, nothing that meant anything. It was hard to wake these animals sometimes. What pitiful things. The invader more so. For his ally to lose its nest to this animal...

The crow found it all very sad.

———— o ————

There was tapping somewhere. Squawking.

Phillip opened his eyes and reached for his nightstand to turn off his alarm clock, only to find he was facing the wrong way and looking at the wall, and there was no alarm clock anywhere...

But the tapping continued.

A crow. Or maybe a raven. *Were ravens bigger?* Tapped on the window, looking in, almost aggressively. *It probably thinks its reflection is another crow,* Phillip thought.

Phillip got up to go to his bag, only to sit back down on the bed as he had one of the worst headaches he had ever experienced. It was an icepick going into his skull, right through his eyes. *God,* he thought, *no more McMann stuff,* he promised, but then remembered the lightning and amended, *unless it helps with magic...*

He pushed through the pain—almost stepping on a sleeping Dan on his air mattress—and grabbed the remnants of a cookie. *When did they go to bed?* They talked about magic and the Farm, signed the papers, ate, saw the family, Phillip talked to Aunt Kath on the phone... he couldn't remember when he went to bed. "No more McMann stuff..." he said out loud, opening the window just a crack.

He slipped the cookie under the window, moving slowly and trying to convey friendliness.

The crow looked from the cookie then back in the room—or his reflection—conveying an almost unbearable confusion. "Just food," Phillip said. The crow bent down and grabbed the food, looked Phillip right in the face as if to say, *"I'll take this but I don't trust you and I know you're up to something,"* and then turned and flew away into the morning sky.

"What was that?" Dan asked on his air mattress.

"Crow," Phillip responded. "Came right to the window. Gave it some food."

"Oh, cool. Cool," Dan responded. "Maybe shouldn't have done that though, now he'll wake you every day... Oh, jeez, my head is killing me..."

"Mine too. Let's cut down on our lighting juice, cool?"

"The mailbox flag is up..." Dan said, as he rubbed his head.

He was right, the flag was up again, but it wasn't ringing. Phillip jumped up and opened it, there was a single small folded piece of paper inside.

"Dan, look at this," he said, opening the note:

Glad you two accepted our offer. We
will be in contact soon.
- Paul

"Soon?" Dan asked, and just as he did Phillip's phone rang.

"Hello?" Phillip answered.

"Phillip?" Aunt Elaine said. "Did I wake you? Sorry. There's someone here for you."

"Someone for me...?" Phillip asked.

"From KHU..." Aunt Elaine continued, he could hear her fussing with Matthew.

"KHU...?" Phillip said.

"KHU...?" Dan repeated.

"... she says she's with the young scholar program, a woman named Adeline..."

"Oh! Adeline! That's right. Um, we'll be right over," Phillip said, hanging up the phone. "Adeline is here!" Phillip said to Dan who at the same time asked "Adeline is *here*?"

They rushed to dress and get out the door. Luckily, they were both still in their clothes. Phillip put Fortinbras on the porch and gave him some water "look for intruders," Phillip said to the dog.

There were already work vans in front of the Fairchild home—they had been talking about this last night, Phillip remembered—there was a mold inspector, and two plumbers. There was another car, an older style of car, a brand Phillip had never seen.

Phillip just went through the door and into the kitchen, where he heard voices.

Adeline sat at the kitchen table—her greying hair in a tight bun—playing with Matthew, as aunt Elaine and Maddie prepared breakfast.

"There you are!" Adeline said cheerfully, which caused Matthew to crack up.

"Ms. Adeline, how are you...?" Phillip said, stepping over Rosencrantz and Guildenstern, and narrowly missing a large work woman in a white suit walking from the door to the stairs.

"You're probably wondering why we're here," Adeline said, not looking away from Matthew.

"Hey kiddo," another voice said in the kitchen.

It was Sarah, she had put on an apron and was cooking. "I see what you're doing over there Sarah," Adeline said. "Mrs. Fairchild, don't let Sarah put anything too green in those eggs."

"It's a frittata, mom, you put things in frittatas," Sarah responded.

"You heard me, Mrs. Fairchild. Ms. Maddie, you keep an eye on her too," Adeline said with more urgency.

Aunt Elaine laughed. Maddie was staring too intently at Phillip to notice.

"Phillip, Adeline was telling me you're really fitting in at the program..." Aunt Elaine said, a hint of question on her voice.

"Which program?" Maddie asked.

"Same one you're in dear, but for an older age group," Adeline answered.

"I've never seen you on campus," Maddie said.

"I'm afraid I don't get out of the office much," Adeline answered. "Now Phillip, like your friend Daniel here, I'd like you to come to the program on a more official basis. Enroll you. I've already talked to your guardian Katherine Smith on the phone this morning, I didn't know she was in California and I woke her, I'm afraid, she's fine with it if you are. It's your choice, of course."

"Aunt Kath?" Phillip said, then looked at his phone. He already had a dozen messages and a missed call from her. "Yes... I mean yes, I'd like to join the program. At KHU..."

"Delightful! I knew you would," Adaline said in a baby voice to Matthew.

"What do you do at the University?" Maddie asked Sarah.

"Hand-to-hand and sword combat, military history, modern dance, long-travel etiquette, deep woods survival," Sarah said without missing a beat. "The basics."

"Madalyn, can you get your brother set up in the living room?" Aunt Elaine asked.

Maddie signed, but obeyed. Adeline waved to Matthew as he left the room, who laughed all the way.

"Phillip, Dan," Adeline said to them. she turned to look straight at them, and her voice took on a mild echoing quality. Phillip was sure aunt Elaine couldn't hear her. "Do you know what Privilege at the Farm entails...?"

Phillip shook his head, Dan did the same.

"It means a lot of things," Adeline said. "It means what you say, and what you lie about, matters. The powers of the Farm will stretch itself to accommodate you... for instance, if you need a bit of privacy..."

A woman in the white work outfit popped her head in the kitchen. "Ellie? I'm sorry to interrupt but there's something you might want to see..."

Phillip looked at Adeline, who was smiling as she lifted a coffee cup to her mouth.

"I can finish up here," Sarah said to aunt Elaine, taking over her spot at the stove.

"Oh, thank you, I shouldn't have tried to cook," aunt Elaine said, following the woman in the white suit out of the kitchen and then upstairs.

"You... did that?" Dan whispered.

"No, dear," Adeline said. "I asked for an outcome. The Farm, the *Privilege*, did that. Maybe. You have to be extremely careful with what you say. Especially your lies. Neither of your families are in the Know. Revealing the truth or concealing it both have consequences..."

"Mom, stop being mysterious," Sarah said over the oven, putting eggs on plates. "Kiddos, basic rule of thumb, don't ask for too much, don't make your lies too ridiculous, don't wish for anything you wouldn't want happen, respect the Old Laws."

"That's... incredible," Dan said. "Why would the Pauls do this for us?"

"Captain Karo said that the Pauls wouldn't be able to let us back in, was he lying?" Phillip asked.

Adeline smiled. "You know what my night was like? I got a report that somebody, two boys matching your description, blew up poor Rickshaun's lab. Then the Wallmen are telling me they're using their rights to banish two kids from the Farm and Camps. Then Rickshaun is in my office, complaining that the Wallmen kicked these two kids out before he was able to punish them properly. Then Karo comes to my office, to restate the whole matter. Then I'm visited by

Ms. Morris and Lady Kanamori, complaining that the Wallmen overstepped their bounds. Haystacks and Henry came too, with a big momma bear in tow, no less, to ask where their new tenants went... I was explaining what happened to him when a wild eyed Purificationist tells me someone made some lighting in a field, two boys, of all things. I just finishing your expulsion paperwork when Paul calls me, and tells me that two teenagers were to be offered Full Privileges, just in time for Ms. Morris and that Kanamori girl and Haystacks to come back with a new list of complaints..."

"*Full*. Privileges," Sarah said. "Not even those new friends of yours have Full Privileges, not even the Wallmen. So, tell me, how'd you do it?"

"Do it...?" Dan asked, sounding embarrassed.

"The lighting in the field, how?" Sarah said, sounding somehow both casually disinterested and pointed. "I looked at your performance in Circles Class, how do you go from that to what you did?"

"We just sort of... did it," Dan said.

"We repeated what the Pauls did on stage," Phillip said. "It just... worked."

"And the first day you were at the Farm, tell me, how did you get past the Wallmen?"

"We just went through the door, on the stage, then jumped the fence..." Dan said.

Adeline paused. Even Sarah stopped what she was doing. "So, the combined might of the other Inheritors couldn't get a toe in the Farm without permission but you two... '*jumped the fence*?'" Sarah said.

"I guess so...?" Dan said.

"Sarah, stop bothering them, we don't have time," Adeline said, taking a long wooden box with a handle from behind her skirt. "This is a compressed library. You'll find a big book on the Old Laws here, and a smaller book. Some stuff on hygiene and nopes compliance..."

"What is nopes again?" Phillip interrupted.

"Non-Purified Energetic Systems, N.O.P.E.S. *NoPES*," Adeline said. "Like that Mundafold do-dongle you blew up Rickshaun's lab with..."

"Oh..." Phillip said.

"There Are other books here covering the basics for fresh Choicers. Do me a favor, don't tell Paul I'm including the Mr. Magnificent series in here, he hates the guy. 'Psudomagical nonsense,' he says."

Phillip picked up the box, two wooden panels were open in the front to reveal a miniature library filled with thumb sized books. When he reached for one, he found his hand grabbing a normal sized book, which grew as he took it out. "It works like the mailbox..." Dan said with an intake of breath.

There were dozens of books in there. *The Old Laws: A Summary... A Complete History of the Imaginary... Understanding Many-Geometry: Introduction to the Knowing of Folds... The Undividable Self... The Sky as My Reflection... Kinship, Honor, and Why You Should Always Serve Drinks to Enemies: A Lesson from the Northmen... Good King Shepherd's Revolution, Illustrated... Law beyond Law, the Vincent Someday story... A Working Man's Guide to New*

Faroese... Minding your Temple... Mr. Magnificent, the Magnificent Magic Man, Educational Series: Circles to Apprentice courses and PSA's... My Fold, Your Fold, His Fold, Her Fold, a children's guide.

"If you have any questions, ask me or Sarah or those girls you've been stalking," Adeline continued. "And wrap that fool Mundafold device of yours and don't use it the Farm or in Camp, you can do most things in the Omniaspace anyway..."

"Okay now what's that...?" Phillip asked.

"... We haven't set one up in the Farm yet. Too much going on. Modern thing, called the Wire in most places. It's just the way most people in the Primafold communicate nowadays. I hate it. Give me a whisperstone or reasonclay or a dollaphone any day. More personal. More art to it... now on to important stuff. Daniel, I'm going to contact your mother, we're going to have change the story a bit, but keep the basics the same. It can't be KHU, of course..."

"What's... KHU...?" Dan asked.

Both Sarah and Adeline stopped moving again and looked at Dan.

"Holy turd balls Mom they don't know...!"

"Don't say 'turd balls,'" Adeline ordered.

"Know what?" Phillip asked, as Dan stuttered.

"Mom, let me tell them," Sarah said.

"Quiet Sarah, I get to," Adeline said. "Phillip, Daniel, do something for me. On the count of three, say what town this house is in, okay? One, two, three..."

"King's Hill," Phillip said.

"Knoxville..." Dan said at the same time. "Tennessee...?"

Sarah laughed. Dan and Phillip looked at each other. "Why did you say...?" Phillip started. "Where's King's Hill...?" Dan said. "I live twenty minutes from here...in Knoxville." "No, Dan, what are you...? My family lives in King's Hill, always has..." "I found your flyer in McKay's bookstore, I've been going there since I was a baby... In Knoxville. This is some magic stuff that's manipulated your brain again..."

Sarah laughed all the harder, almost falling over.

"Slow down, boys," Adeline said.

"... I've been coming here all my life, it's in King's Hill..." Phillip continued.

"I've never even heard of King's Hill...!"

"Neither of you are wrong, slow down," Adeline said. "But right now, Phillip is more correct, this house is in King's Hill, one of the main source points for the Farm. There are of course many other source points across the main Folds, including *Knoxville*, Tennessee."

"I'm... not in Tennessee right now? But I rode my bike here... where am I? My mom talked to Phillip's aunt, they gave each other directions..."

"Things have a way of working out that way around the Farm, it's from *Anywhere*, after all," Adeline said. "Close your mouths, you two, it's undignified for people with Privilege. Now, Dan, you're in King's Hill, which is set on the Mississippi river, intersecting three different states in the Mundafold. Iowa, Illinois, and Missouri. Home of King's Hill University."

"I'm like, a thousand miles away from home right now...?" Dan asked.

"Depends on how you measure space," Sarah answered. "But it's more like six-hundred miles."

Dan sat down, eyes darting around, not landing on anything. "That's why the weather's been so weird..." He said, almost to himself. "It was raining then sunny, then raining, then colder, then humid. Oh dang, Phil, this is nuts."

Phillip agreed. Somehow, they both managed to laugh.

"We have to get going, there's a dozen little breaches that need patching and the Wallmen are useless," Adeline said, getting up. "You do know of the conditions of accepting your Privileges, the class you will... attend?"

"Yes," they said at the same time.

"And do you plan on going back to the Farm today?" Adeline asked.

Dan and Phillip looked at each. "Yes," they repeated.

"Glad to hear it," Adeline said. "And do me a favor, could you? Try not to blow up any more buildings for a little while. The paperwork is horrendous."

CHAPTER
18
Back by Invitation

Dan couldn't get over the revelation that he wasn't in Knoxville.

Neither could Phillip, but at least Phillip could walk back to the Dollhouse without stopping every few seconds to say something else about it. "But that means... no that's dumb..." Dan said to himself, writing in his notebook. Phillip was carrying the little library. Adeline had also given them a thick folder of papers and pamphlets. "Do you have a map?" Dan asked, pausing again. "A paper one?"

"I have road atlases in the car, actually I think there inside the house now..." Phillip started.

"Who was she, really?" Maddie said on the porch of the Dollhouse. "And why do you need road atlases?"

"Hey Maddie," Phillip said. Maddie was petting Fortinbras. "Forty, I thought I said to look for intruders...?"

The dog barked back happily, unashamed.

A crow cawed on the closest tree to the home. Phillip looked at him. He was sure it was the same crow that woke him up.

"I don't think that crow likes me..." Phillip said, as it cawed again.

"Are you feeding him?" Maddie asked.

"No," Phillip said. "Well, this morning I did..."

"Then why do you have birdseed on the porch?"

"Not birdseed, that's leftover rice," Phillip answered. "And that's for a different bird."

"A different... bird...?" Maddie repeated, looking confused. She recovered and stared right at Dan. "How long have you been going to the special programs at KHU? How long have you lived here? I've never seen you around..."

"Oh, I guess... Um, we moved here from Houston when I was like six, so I don't miss it or anything. Houston, I mean," Dan replied. "My dad's in the Army Corp of Engineers and my mom's a freelancer illustrator, so I don't know why I'm telling you that..."

God, Dan was a terrible liar, Phillip thought for what had to be the tenth time.

"Maddie," Phillip interrupted. "I think there might be something happening at the main house, your mom..."

Aunt Elaine's voice interrupted him. She was yelling from the main house's porch. "Maddie?! Are you out here?! I need your help for a minute!"

Maddie groaned and got up. "Coming mom!" She yelled back. "This is not over," she said to Phillip as she ran past him.

"Okay Maddie, I'll see you later," Phillip said back, walking into the home with Dan and Fortinbras, the crow giving out one last angry caw.

"Man, Phil I can't keep lying like this, I got lucky with Maddie but I don't know if I can hold up. By the way, was that 'Privilege' you used? Saying something was happening at the house and then it did? That's wild, Phil. But why don't we just tell Maddie...?"

"She's a tattle-tale. You heard what Adeline said about telling people. Just trust me," Phillip said, putting the compressed library on the floor. "I'm surprised she didn't see I was carrying this..."

It was like a shrunken wardrobe with a handle on top. They opened the door to look at the little books on the other side. Dozens of them. Dan and Phillip reached for a book at the same time. The arms traveled for longer than was possible, by the time they got to the book, it felt as if the world was distorted, not the library... Phillip looked around, and the distortions hurt his eyes. Only the library looked right. Their hands grabbed a heavy, full sized book, and they pulled it out, the world returning to normal by the time it was in their hands. "Hah!" Dan yelled.

The book was heavy, he probably couldn't even hold it if he wanted to read it. *'THE OLD LAWS'* it said on the cover. "Adeline and Paul implied whatever the 'Old Laws' are is important..." Dan said. "Hey where's that map?"

"On the table near the door," Phillip answered.

"Awesome," Dan said, fishing in his backpack and coming out with a square folded map.

"If you had a map why do you need mine?" Phillip asked. His phone rang in his pocket. It was Aunt Kath. "I need to take this."

"To compare them, Phil!" Dan said, answering the first question. "I'll be upstairs."

"What do you want?" Phillip said into the phone.

"I want to know why you're joining summer programs right and left?" Aunt Kath said back.

"It just sort of happened, I ran into Dan and then he showed me the classes and I mentioned it was cool, and then people started signing me up," Phillip said. He put his hand in his pocket and his fingers touched something cold. He took it out. It was the wooden pocket knife, he had pocketed it again without thinking. "King's Hill is weird..."

"Sure is. So, you like King's Hill?" Aunt Kath said. Phillip opened the pocket knife. He found he could open it with one hand. It felt heavier than it should have, and he found he could twirl it around his fingers easily.

"You know I kind of dig it here, we should move here…" The tip of the knife made contact with the then drawer near the doorway.

CRACK. POP.

Phillip jumped at the sound. "What was that…?" Aunt Kath asked.

"I don't…" Phillip started. The sound had come from the drawers. He placed the knife carefully on the top. He tapped the drawer. Nothing looked different… he pulled the top drawer.

Only half the drawer came out.

The other half remained, cut at an odd angle. He saw it now, a thin line traveling across the entire thing. The drawers were cut. Sliced in half, with such a thin cut it remained together.

"Phillip…?" Aunt Kath said.

"Sorry…" Phillip said. "Just being a dork and a dropped a bunch of stuff." He picked up the knife slowly, held the phone to his shoulder as he closed the pocket knife, as carefully as he could, and placed it back on the sliced drawers like it was a sleeping baby.

"Stop being a dork, I'm tired. You know I was already up when that Adeline women called me? Lab starts early, I thought Californians were supposed to be laid back…? Anyway, that dumb book I stole from you kept me up all night…"

"Dumb book…?" Phillip repeated absentmindedly, not taking his eyes off the knife as he played with the now-half-drawers.

"Yeah, the yellow one. Says 'Mindworking' on it. I thought it was one of my textbooks so I packed it last minute," Aunt Kath said.

And Phillip remembered.

The Mindworking book. He bought it at the used book shop as cover. He hadn't even thought about it since then. *Mindworking.*

'Mindworking' was a magical thing. The Andy girl had mentioned it…

"… I get why you bought this weird thing, it's like in nine different languages. There's English in here but not much. It's about meditation or psychology, maybe neurology… I can't even tell! I keep discovering new parts of it. Why didn't you tell me about this?"

"I guess it just… slipped my mind," Phillip said. Aunt Kath had a magical book, what would that do?

There were sounds on the other line. Mumbled voices in the background. "Phillip, sorry I have to go. I'll talk to you later, okay?"

A couple rushed goodbyes and Aunt Kath hung up. "Phil!" Dan yelled at the top of the stairs. "You won't believe what I found Phil!" He came down the stairs, blinded by the three open maps he was carrying. "I was comparing… hey what happened to your drawers?"

"The pocket knife… I'll explain later," Phillip said. "What did you find?"

Dan smiled and fumbled with his various maps. Finally handing him one. "Find King's Hill on this map…"

Phillip went to the table, placed the map down, and did what Dan asked. King's Hill was a prominent dot. "Here," Phillip said. "Now what...?"

"Now find King's Hill on my map..." Dan said, placing down the unfolded map on top of the other. It was a trail map of Tennessee. "Sorry," Dan said, and flipped it to reveal a map of the US.

"Okay..." Phillip said, and went to go point at the town.

Only to find it wasn't there.

King's Hill wasn't on the map... Instead it was a smaller town on the Iowa side. 'Keokuk.' And a town or area called 'Hamilton' in Illinois.

No King's Hill anywhere.

The familiar roads he navigated on were gone too. Gardenvale was also gone...

"It's not there..." Phillip said.

"It's not there!" Dan repeated, smiling from ear to ear.

"I've been coming here my whole life..." Phillip flipped between the maps. Trying to find any differences. "Dan, where the heck is King's Hill...? Where are we...?"

"What does it mean?" Dan said.

Phillip didn't answer, he kept glancing at one to the other, expecting them to change at any minute. The ground underneath him feeling a little less solid. "I don't know. But we're probably not going to get answers here. Let's get ready as soon as we can, I want to get back to the Farm."

The Camps had changed.

Or maybe, Dan had said, *they had changed.* Like the first night with the lighting, they saw things they just didn't notice before. Which raised the question, how much weren't they seeing now?

There were almost more non-humans then humans. People with horns or antlers, or animal-like faces. "One of the pamphlets Adeline gave us said people with horns are most likely halfFae," Dan whispered. Gremlins were some of the most prominent. More animals wandering around, many with masks on. "More. Spare. Nuts?" A squirrel in a mask stopped and asked them, Phillip shook his head and the masked squirrel moved on.

Dan had stopped trying to make sense of where the Camps were in relation to the river. Nothing made sense about the place. The geography of Camps varied from place to place. Even the time of day seemed optional.

There was activity everywhere. People putting up buildings or more tents. An uneven wooden tower was built, covered in tents. Giggling balls of light swept around them herds of colorful flowers moved on their own little feet across the trail. Everybody was eating or partying or working or selling something.

They were walking through a market area. Every tent was selling something. Mostly food and something called 'gremlin offering stations' next to food tents and wagons. A part of the market that looked like a mixture of junkyard, a library, and a thrift-store.

"Hey Phil, look, they have skychalk things here, that came in handy," Dan said, picking out boxes with metal instruments inside. "We should get our own. It says 'Used: 12-Shepherd Notes' on them. That's money, I think. You think they take dollars?"

"Orbit ball..." Phillip said, picking up an uneven black rubber ball about the size of a grapefruit. He gave it a toss to the side. It swirled around Dan before coming back into Phillip's hands.

"You break anything you buy it!" A heavy man sitting behind a table said.

"Sorry..." Phillip said, still smiling. Reading the tags on the objects in front of him. *Many-Travel-Cans. Reaching-Gloves. Lashing-Gloves.* "What do you think a lashing glove is?"

"You probably find somebody to take Mundafold money, but the exchange is a pain so most people don't prefer to deal with it."

Phillip turned to find the voice of the older boy they had seen in class with the blond and black hair—Pieter—standing behind them. "As for the lashing glove, it does what it sounds like," Peiter continued, picking up the lashing glove off the table and putting it on.

He picked up the metal cups, putting them together, then did a motion with his gloved hand, two fingers out, tapping the cups. Silver strands shot out from the back of the glove, winding around the two cups before vanishing. When he handed the cups to Phillip, they were bound together, so tight it was like they were made that way.

"Neat!" Dan said. "Very cool," Phillip said. "You try," Peiter took off the glove and handed it to Phillip. It had a ring on the top and wires that connected to a small stick made of stone with. "It's a cheap one, made around a Nekss rod, try to de-lash it, spin the top to make sure it's on, then use a chopping motion."

Phillip chopped at the cups. The silver lines appeared again just to snap out of existence. The cups were free. "Very, very, cool," Phillip said. "It draws power from you, so be careful, eat sugar."

"This is not a playpen! Go somewhere else!" The big man yelled.

"I'll give you twenty for the lashing glove, and two of those old skychalk dispensers," Peiter yelled to the man.

"Forty!" The man yelled back.

"I'll give you thirty, and for that you'll throw in this old orbit ball," Peiter countered.

"Deal!" The big man said. Peiter threw coins at him, the man caught them in the air without looking up.

"Don't say I never did anything for you," Peiter said, handing them the orbit ball, the lashing glove, and two skychalk dispensers.

"Wow, thanks! But why did you do that?" Dan asked. "We don't really know each other..."

"Nonsense, Andy teased you in class and she teased me, we're practically siblings. You're Phillip and you're Daniel, I'm Pieter Vanderleer," Pieter said as

Phillip lashed together the orbit ball to the skychalk box, and then de-lashed them. "I've just bought two new friends, as friends go you two came cheap. Worst case scenario you'll end up being useless. But as I hear it if I ever need some spare lighting, you're the two to talk to..."

Phillip stopped lashing. Using the glove made his mouth dry. "You heard about that...?"

"Practically everybody with an invitation heard about that. Question is, why'd you decide to blow up Rickshaun's lab?"

"We didn't do it on purpose..." Dan said.

"Damn, that part's true?!" Peiter said. "You guy's going to the Farm now?"

"We were going there, we got sidetracked," Phillip answered. "Hey thank you for all this stuff..."

"Don't mention it, like I said I'm purchasing your friendship," Peiter said. "Where are you going on the Farm? Haystacks' place?"

"Yes," Dan said.

"Mind if I come with you?" Peiter asked.

"How can we say no to our new friend?" Phillip answered.

"See, it's worth the money already," Peiter said, leading the way.

———— o ————

There was a different entrance for people with Privilege. One of Adeline's papers showed them where to find it.

A vine covered stone wall, with a broken door barely large enough to let them through. An old woman in a cloak sat outside, smoking a pipe, when they approached, she tapped the stone, and the door opened behind her. Dan thanked her, but she didn't react.

"The powers that be keep moving poor Haystacks around," Peiter said, walking and combing his hair. "Retaliation is getting intense. This breach is making the Wallmen worse..."

They walked along straight lines of trees. Thin trees—almost vines—kept up by wooden frames which rose as much as a hundred feet. They grew orange-red fruit the size of coconuts, which fell from the trees and landed with soft thuds. Phillip picked one up. They were soft and their color changed when touched.

There were figures moving under the dark canopy with them.

Huge, lumbering creatures, almost eight feet tall. Their bodies jerked around but their long arms moved for too smoothly, picking fruit from the trees or off the ground.

"What are they...?" Dan asked, as Phillip realized they weren't creatures at all. Their bodies and arms made of logs, and bound together by noisy copper joints. Their heads looked like Tiki masks. The wooden things picked up the fruit and put into their frozen mouths.

"They..." A familiar accented voice said, slightly out-of-breath, "are antiques. Old harvesters I found just sitting around the Farm. And at this point fixing them is a hobby I wish I didn't start..."

Phillip and Dan looked around to find Haystacks, he was on top of one of the wooden harvester things. Perched on its back with tools and goggles, doing something to the back of its wide-eyed head which involved a bundle of golden orange light like a tumbleweed. His tail moved back and forth to keep his balance as the harvester moved, trying to grab a remarkably calm raccoon which sat in front of it. "No, no," Haystacks said reproachfully.

"So, they're like robots?!" Dan said, losing all control of his volume.

"What is a robot?" Haystacks asked.

"Mundafold word," Peiter answered. "Like a machine that can move on its own."

"Ah, like an autotons," Haystacks said, wiping away the golden bundle of light. "No, these are not autotons, more like puppets, made before puppetcraft was developed. Their logike all *intent* and *phantom* driven. Hell of a thing trying to work it back to shape, I've resorted to Nexxing, Peiter don't tell anybody." He knocked on the head of the harvester, who turned. "This little guy here is the least obedient of them all, I call him Dryrot."

Phillip held the fruit in front of Dryrot—whose eyes were just holes but none-the-less starred at it like a lot of thinking was going on—Dryrot grabbed the fruit, held it in front of himself, then threw the fruit at his own head, where it bounced off and fell to the ground. "Almost Dryrot, you're getting better," Haystacks said with another encouraging pat. Dryrot somehow managed to look disappointed in himself. "I can teach you boys some puppetcraft if you want. I'm supposed to teach a class if they can stop moving me around."

"Yes!" Dan accidentally yelled, all of them laughing as Dryrot picked up the fruit and dropped it back to the ground over and over.

"Good!" Haystacks said with a clap of his hands, jumping off Dryrot and landing light on his feet. "Peiter it's good to see you, how's your father?"

"You know, same as always..." Peiter said. "Don't think he knows what I'm supposed to be doing here, but also knows I'm doing it wrong. That little scramble I had with that Muki tribe didn't help..."

"I heard about that, your father should have taught you to never gamble with Muki," Haystacks said. "And tell him *none* of us know what we're doing here."

"Comforting. But that's why I latched myself to these two," Peiter said, pointing to Dan and Phillip, who were busy looking at Dryrot, who was lumbering behind them, picking up whatever they saw. "Bought them some second-hand junk and now they're super loyal to me."

"It's true, super loyal," Phillip said, lashing together two of the fruits together with the magical silver strands. His mouth went dry when he did so. He held up his work and it was grabbed by Dryrot and thrown in the air before he could admire it.

They all laughed, which probably just made Dryrot feel worse.

"What do you mean 'that's why I latched myself to these two?'" Dan asked Peiter.

"Because you're the talk of the town!" The echoing voice of Andy said from somewhere. It took a moment to find her and Emily standing one tree line over. *Why is everybody able to sneak up on us here?* Phillip thought. "Everybody and their farts have heard about what you did to Rickshaun, then what you did after!"

"Andy, don't be crude!" Emily said.

"... why'd you do it to poor Ricky?" Andy said, ignoring Emily as Dan tried to explain they didn't do it on purpose.

"Leave them alone, Andy! They're my friends!" Peiter said with a dramatic voice, putting a protective arm around Phillip and giving him a wink.

"Get off it, Peiter, we're all here to spy on them, same as you," Andy said, also winking at Phillip.

"So how does it know what to do? Why is Dryrot confused...?" Dan asked. "Spy...?"

"Uh huh, supposed to get close to you, see what you're all about and what makes you special," Andy said. "It's supposed to seem natural, for you don't suspect me, do you suspect me?"

"Not at all," Phillip said.

"I know Emily's a dead giveaway, she can't hide when she's being devious," Andy said.

"I can too. And I'm not being devious," Emily defended. "My father's far too busy in summer to send me on foolish errands. Speaking of, Daniel, Phillip, we'd like to offer you..."

"... you're joining the Welcoming Committee, you have no choice in the matter," Andy finished.

"Cool," Phillip said.

"Hey wait now I'm offended, you're offering them a spot in the Committee and not me?" Peiter said, feigning outrage.

"Don't take it personally, Pete," Andy said. "It's just that we don't think you're reliable and a potential stain on our organization's reputation."

"Oh good, I thought the explanation might really hurt my feelings," Peiter said.

"I think you should join," Emily said to Pieter. "Non-humans trust you more than they trust us, you can outreach to people we can't..."

"Oh God now you're offering me responsibility...? That's worse than Andy's insults."

"Speaking of non-humans... Haystacks! You should come by our tents in the High Camp. Some of your cousins work for us, you might want to meet them," Andy said.

"Yes, I heard about that..." Haystacks said. "Heard other things too, some intense conflict amongst the tribes with their masters. Causing some debate within the Imp community."

"They're just squabbling with the Yōkai, they always do that," Andy said, sounding a little awkward.

A bird landed on Dryrot's head. One of the large birds they saw before, wearing a mask. "Early. Sunset. Long Night. Purification protocol. Prepare," it said, then flew off. Dryrot didn't seem to notice.

"Another short day?" Emily said. "Breach must have been worse than they said..."

"I heard the breach was caused by that swamp Fae lady," Peiter said. "Have you heard...?"

"Oh my!" Emily interrupted, just as the wind gusted and the sun slipped out the sky, afternoon turning into night so fast it skipped evening altogether.

The dark so sudden it was impossible for Phillip's eyes to adjust.

Andy and Emily seemed as surprised by this as Dan and Phillip.

"So, this is not normal, even for here?" Dan asked.

"Nope, nothing's normal about the Farm," Andy said. "There's a little work-time engine in Mont Marseilles Academy but they get maybe a few days out of it a year if they're lucky, and it costs them a ton. Nothing like this."

"The Under city still has pockets of it, and some of the rich snobby families like the Kanamori or the Rurik's," Peiter said. Andy scowled. "It's one of the lost wizard sciences."

"Work-time...?" Dan and Phillip asked at the same time. "Is that what this is?" Dan finished, pointing at the sky.

"It's work-time. *Looping compressed time with a variable and dynamic starting state*," Andy said in an airy intellectual tone. "Means you can get some work done, but can't do other things, like grow a beard or age or grow crops. You won't be able to sleep or eat as much."

"Whoa..." Dan said. "That's wild, I was worried about aging! I did the math, the schedule says there's usually like, five to thirteen days, or sunsets or whatever, each day. That means if we're here a month we would age like six months to a year. My mom would probably wonder why I grew so much. But you say we won't age?"

"Only age as much as time from your starting point," Andy answered.

"Whoa... that's a relief," Dan said.

"When did you do the math?" Phillip asked.

"Last night, you fell asleep looking at the library."

"We'll arrange a tour of the engine!" Emily said in a delighted tone.

"Do you two live together?" Andy asked.

"No," Phillip answered. "He slept over. In fact, we just learned that we are six-hundred miles apart, but for some reason he's able to ride a bike to me."

"How do you not know that about each other? Don't you guys talk?" Andy asked.

"We just met," Phillip said. "And we just kind of assumed we *weren't* magically a thousand miles apart..."

"You know I'm happy about the early night, I'm old and can use a nap," Haystacks said, changing the subject. "Speaking of, boys, Henry has your booth all set up, he won't say it but he's very proud."

———— o ————

If Henry was proud of the work he did in their booth, he hid it well.

Henry barely turned to look at them when they came into the stable. Phillip thought he was going to say something, but instead he just re-lit his corncob pipe, and continued shoveling hay.

What Henry had done in the booth was incredible.

It didn't even look like a booth anymore. There were carpets on the floor, a burning stove in one corner, pleasant lamps, and curtains covering the small window. A hammock was strung along the booth, with a cot underneath. "I call the hammock!" Dan yelled.

"The lamps look like Mundafold lamps but have faeFlame inside them. Untrained but they will adapt with some discipline. There's a bathhouse about twenty yards out back. Fresh cleansing stones, everything you need," Haystacks explained. "Is this... suitable for you boys?"

"It's perfect!" Dan said, making the mistake of jumping in the hammock with his backpack on.

"It's fantastic," Phillip agreed, there was a painting of a steamboat on the wall. "Haystacks... Is us staying with you a big burden? We just didn't want to ruffle any more feathers with Captain Karo, we didn't want to put anybody out..."

"Are you kidding?! You boys have been a blessing, with you staying here I have some influence," Haystacks said with a chuckle. "Now if you don't mind, I'm going to take advantage of the early night and catch up on some sleep. I suggest you do the same, Farm keeps you busy."

The lamps and lights in the stable dimmed as Haystacks spoke, as if realizing that a nap was a good idea. Phillip realized how tired he felt.

He hadn't slept a whole night since he ran into Dan...

"Dang, I forgot to give Andy back her skychalk..." Dan said, as he tried again to get in the hammock, finally stabilizing himself.

Unfortunately, neither of them got much sleep.

Phillip and been awake when the storm moved through. He had briefly drifted off, only to be awoken when he heard the of the stall slide open. He looked up to see nothing before he noticed small black figures in the stall. He thought it was raccoons at first.

They weren't.

They were bear cubs, three of them.

Phillip almost told them to go away before a larger bear, who he guessed was the mother, waddled slowly to the stall and grunted at the three cubs, who ignored her, too interested in smelling and tugging on Phillip's blanket to listen. "What do we do?" Dan whispered to Phillip, who had no answer. The mama bear seemed annoyed at the cubs, eventually gave up and went into the stall herself. Finding a comfortable place right next to Phillip and laying down. Pinning one side of Phillip's blanket down.

"I don't think I can get off without stepping on her" Dan said, "Should I try to get Haystacks?"

"I... I don't know." Phillip responded.

The next few hours were spent staring wide eyed at the rafters, both of them as still as corpses.

Sunrise came as suddenly as nightfall, skipping dawn altogether.

Mama bear didn't wake up, but the cubs did, and began to fight on top of her and Phillip.

"Buttercup, we talked about this," Phillip heard Haystacks say at the stall door. "This is their space now. Come now. Out, out." The Mama bear got up with a groan, giving Haystacks a look before exiting the stall. Two of the cubs continued fighting on Phillip's chest. Mama bear grunted at them and they jumped off to follow.

"Sorry boys, but you should have woken me," Haystacks said. "It occurred to me how much you boys don't know. You'll forgive me the off assumption or two. You probably don't know much about bonding and beast kinship. Speaking of things you don't know..." he said, handing Phillip a book. 'The Young Gentleman's Guide to Cleaning Up and Getting the Girl' it said on the illustrated cover, a dapper man tipping a hat to a blushing woman in a Victorian dress. "It's all I can find on short notice, help you get... cleaned up, unless you want to join one of the naturalist schools, which I don't suggest."

"We still stink, don't we...?" Dan said, as if he was just remembering.

"A little, not that I mind, this is a stable, but as I understand it you're going to be attending classes. *Indoors*. And you might want to conform yourself a little more to the standard."

"How bad do we stink?" Dan asked.

"Better than Buttercup, but worse than some of the birds," Haystacks said.

The bathhouse was a stone building dug into the ground. Completely abandoned on the inside with the exception of large birds that cleaned themselves in some of the many pools. There were steam rooms and hot baths the size of swimming pools and cool springs where water flowed upward out to grates on the ceiling. It wasn't until Phillip saw the private showers that he realized the building was much larger than it should have been.

They followed the illustrated book as best they could to clean themselves, which mostly involved little rituals involving dark stones and branches. Afterwards they didn't feel any different, if just a bit wetter.

The toilets were another problem.

There was no toilet paper. Instead there were five colored ropes to the side. "Maybe it's like a bidet...?" Dan suggested as he went into one of the stalls.

Dan yelped and there was a sound like boiling water. Smoke appeared under the stall. "Are you okay?!" Phillip yelled. "Don't pull the red one!" Dan yelled back.

With enough experimentation they learned the ropes *did* replace toilet paper. It didn't work like a bidet, or anything else they knew about...

"I don't know if I like this," Dan said.

Phillip agreed, and they both decided not to talk about it.

Haystacks helped them understand how to read the schedule when they got back to the stable. Each real day was divided into sunrises and sunsets and sun-highs and moon-highs.

It was through this that they realized they were going to be late for the class the Pauls wanted them to attend.

They ran all the way to the silo building—Dan not even taking his backpack—they had no idea what would happen if they were late. *Would they lose their Privilege? Their invitation?*

It was difficult to follow the directions the Pauls gave them. *Go upstairs, immediately go downstairs. Take a left down the small hallway, then turn around.* The navigation was made harder by the dark interior, the building only lit by glass jars of glowing worms.

A thin hallway led to an opening and a heavy door with a lion crest on it. *They had made it.*

The classroom itself was lit by large windows behind the teaching podium. It was as crowded in the building as it was quiet. Every eye in the room turned toward them when they walked in. The class was impatient. *At least we didn't miss anything,* Phillip thought.

A second later they noticed Emily and Andy sitting next to Peiter and Tadaaki. They waved for them and sat down. "Did we miss anything?" Phillip asked Andy.

"Nothing," she answered.

"Any idea what this class is...?" Dan whispered.

"Nope. Nobody does," Andy said.

And just as she said it the lights began to dim.

Curtains were folding slowly on the large windows. A blackboard floated down from the ceiling. Bright gold letters appeared on the board:

WILL & POWER
HOSTED BY THE PAULS

Some cheering and clapping and excited gasps filled the room. Pieter and Tadaaki bumped fists. Emily said, "How thrilling."

The writing hadn't stopped. The board continued to be filled slowly letter by letter. It said:

GUEST LECTURERS:
DANIEL CASTELLANOS & PHILLIP MONTGOMERY

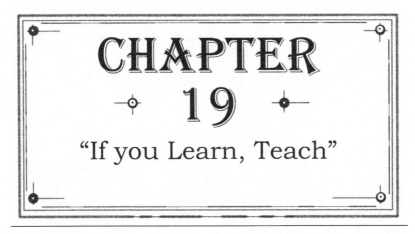

CHAPTER 19

"If you Learn, Teach"

Phillip didn't react.

There was nothing to react to. What his eyes were telling him didn't make the slightest bit of sense. It was stupid. It was silly, in fact.

"Who are they?" He heard a girl whisper behind him. He didn't answer or turn around. There was some similar mumbling spreading around the classroom.

He could tell from the corner of his eyes that Andy and Emily were alternating between looking at each other and looking at Dan and Phillip.

"That's a twist," Peiter whispered to Tadaaki.

Dan hadn't looked up since their names appeared on the board. Instead, he was shuffling around the paper he had gotten from Adeline. Being as quiet as he could. He stopped when he found the little map that showed the way to the classroom, it had gold writing on the back they hadn't noticed before.

Dan handed it to Phillip.

Daniel and Phillip,

>*I would love to teach this class today, but I'm afraid I have been called away on urgent (some would say life altering and world-shattering) business.*

>*If you could do me one great big favor, please teach this class until I get back and my situation resolves itself. Shouldn't be more than a couple days, a week or a year at the most.*

>*Study materials and the curriculum is on the podium. If you need any supplies that are not in the classroom just ask Adeline.*

>*If things start getting hairy, just trust yourself and wing it. I have every faith in you. And DO NOT let students see the fear in your eyes, they won't respect you.*

155

Thank you so much for your help in this matter. You're earning your keep already.

Good luck,

PAUL

"This can't be real..." Phillip whispered.

"Phil. Phil. I'm starting to think it is real..." Dan said back. Andy and Emily were looking at them, waiting to see what Dan and Phillip would do.

There was no way around this, his brain allowed him to think. The longer he sat here the worse it was going to get. Was this what 'Privilege' meant? Would they lose it if they didn't do what the Pauls asked? They agreed to be at this class when they signed their acceptance letters. *Stupid assumptions!* He thought they would be learning... *Stupid, stupid assumptions!*

Dan and Phillip looked at each other. They had to get up. They had to walk to the front of the class.

They both stood up.

The attention they received was painful. It's like every pair of eyes were a powerful heat lamp he could feel on his skin...

They walked to the podium which—judging on how long it took to get there—was at least five miles away from where they were sitting. He noticed the floor squeaked when he walked on it, or maybe that was his shoes... Why were his shoes so squeaky? Confused whispers broke out as Phillip and Dan went to the podium. A few chortling laughs.

He tried to remember what the Pauls had said in their letter...

Don't show fear.

Wing it...

"Sorry about the delay," Phillip said, surprising himself that he had spoken and his voice was audible. "We didn't expect to be teaching today because we... don't teach," he looked in the podium, there were stacks of papers and books on top and in cubbies. Dan was looking through them.

There was more mumbling. More snickering.

"I'm, Phillip Montgomery. And this is, Dan. Daniel, I mean. Daniel Castellanos."

"Why are you teaching this class?" A girl said somewhere in the third row.

"We're trying to find the Pauls notes now..." Phillip said instead of an answer.

"... I think they are the ones we heard about this morning," came an accented voice. "There are two guests who were able to create some lightning last night, out of nothing. The ones granted full Privileges..."

Phillip was able to see the source of the voice. It was the older balding man in the white uniform, the one who was in Andy's class, and was rude to them about how they smelled. Did he ever get his name...?

The mumbling continued, though it had a distinctly different tone now.

"… but I am confused as well. What can they possibly teach? They are clearly unprepared," the balding man continued. "I am increasingly convinced of those rumors floating around the Pauls' mental capacities. Such incompetence would never be allowed in my schools…"

"Well nobody's making you stay," Pieter said, turning around to stare. "If the Farm is not to your liking. Why don't you leave, Müller? Go back to teaching Village Burning 101 or whatever the Sturmjäger schools decide is important…"

There was a clatter around the man in the white outfit, as some giggles traveled around the classroom. Müller sat unmoving, looking at Pieter. His only movement to put a hand on the shoulder of a younger person in a white outfit to stop him from standing. "You are of course right, Mr. Vanderleer. I have much to learn. And I have not had the benefit of being raised by a family as *illustrious* and noble as yours," now it was the white outfits turn to snicker. "How about, for educational purposes, we go outside. Test our respected educations against one another…?"

Pieter stood now. Emily was trying to keep him sitting. Müller was standing as well.

"Stop!" Phillip said, and then froze on the spot as the entire room looked at him. "Stop" he repeated in a smaller voice.

Why had he done that?

Someday in the future he hoped some distant scientists would dissect his brain and discover the reason why he had done that for that nobody would repeat it ever again… "We are just trying to find the Pauls notes," he continued. "Please be patient. And don't… *test* each other…"

Pieter sat down, followed by Müller who was glaring at him. Dan was looking at Phillip in shock, holding some papers. It seemed just as confused by what Phillip had said as Phillip was. "Here, look at this," Dan whispered, handing him a disorganized stack of paper of different shapes and colors.

They looked like notes. But only in the most general sense. Most were not in English. They alternated between runes and what looked like Russian. It was messy, written fast in black pen, with red pen crossing out lines and providing notes on the side, as well as doodles of cartoon ducks… There were diagrams and geometric shapes. What looked like a drawing of a dissected human heart. Then one of a brain with fast handwriting next to it in red ink *'Ref – physiological and emotional stress, associated AND direct.'* There were several pages of more doodles, one of the Pauls really liked birds… and another listing out references to texts and people Dan and Phillip had obviously never heard of. He turned to another page. *'Teacher Instructions,'* it said at the top.

"Dan, I think this is it." Phillip whispered.

> *Teach Will magic. Go through the process, etc.*
> *SAY something about <u>resonance!</u>*
> *Hit on major points of curriculum. Involve the class.*

Focus on the lighting. People love lighting.
Students must learn the learning of a thing before
they learn a thing!
Set the STAGE! Daniel, Phillip.

Ignorance is forgivable. Intellectual cowardice
is not. The universe is a sadistic punisher of sloth
and cowardice, but also a great patron of patience
and prudence, as well as boldness. Find the sweet
spot between these and the universe is yours!

Trust yourself. Be honest.

Just Wing it. You'll do fine. I have every
confidence in you.

P.S. – Do try to avoid blowing up the classroom
this time. Adeline complains about it terribly.

Phillip stared at the notes in disbelief. This couldn't be it...
"That's it?" he said to Dan.
"I think, yeah. I think that's it," Dan said back, flipping through the papers.
"May I perhaps ask a question?" The balding man named Müller said.
"Um, yeah. Sure. Go for it," Dan said back.
"If you are the ones that created the lightning, if that is a thing that is truly possible in reality and it is not some sort of trick or workaround as a great many learned minds have suspected. Can you teach us the process? Why keep everything such a mystery?"
Phillip didn't know what to say, did he tell the truth? Whatever he did, he had to do it with confidence...
"Well, you have to learn the learning of a thing before you... learn a thing..." Phillip said, realizing he neither sounded confident nor made the slightest bit of sense. For the looks around the classroom, the people in the room agreed with him.
"A mystics puzzle...? Is that the only thing...?" Müller started.
"How do you solve the energy transference problem...?" A girl asked.
"... And how do you get around the laws of displacement...?" Another teenager added.
"Where does the lightning come from? I know it's made on the spot, but does it start as a thought and then become material...? Does performing Willastic magic support the Platonic Revisionist theory of fundamental material delusionism?"
"... Why did the Pauls need a containment circle...?"
Phillip didn't know how to answer anything. He didn't know what to say. The class was buzzing with questions now.

"Phillip, follow my lead. I have an idea," Dan said.

A heated debate had started in the class. Four boys and one girl were screaming at each other about something. The word "idiot" was thrown around a lot... most students were talking amongst each other, if they weren't watching the debate.

"Excuse me," Dan said to the class, he was ignored. "Excuse me!" He said louder, the class quieted down just enough to hear him.

"We... need a few more minutes... how about we go around and get everybody's name," Dan continued. "We'll start over here. Just give the class your name and something about yourself..."

Dan might actually be a genius, Phillip thought.

This was the best time-waster he could imagine, and it was legitimate! The class was large, this could take a while...

People took turns giving out their names, and a short biography. When the biography was too short, Dan prompted them for more. "I'm Katie Caster... um, my parents wanted me to come here... We live in the greater heights and my dad runs a compression shop in Old Jersey." "Name's Branton, I honestly have no idea why I'm here. I'm an apprentice foldguide..." "Pieter Vanderleer... Just call me Pieter. I'm a layabout who came to the Farm to get out of hard work. So far so good..." "Call me Andy, I'm some kind of Nihonkin Lady or secret halfFea or something... Who knows? But I just came here to give Pieter a hard time about being so lazy..." The next person was Emily, who didn't stand but seemed to rise a little in her seat, "I'm Emily Morris. My family are specialists in enchantment-based agriculture. They decided I should be the one to accept the invitation on my family's behalf. I'm deeply honored to meet you all..."

A dozen more people spoke. Many with accents Phillip didn't recognize. Not one of them from a location Phillip recognized. Dan was writing down names and location in his notebook.

"I am Mr. Antony Müller, and I am sad and very bored..." Some laughter from the class. Müller was one of the last people... "But if you must know. I am a salaried instructor in the most illustrious Sturmjäger academy on the Eastern coast of Washington Union, the 'Brick and Hammer Academy.' I teach mystical combat history and theory and am currently wondering if this class will provide any value..."

There was a murmur of humorous agreement that spread through the classroom.

"... Do you mind if I ask again...?" The girl named Katie asked. "How does... this sort of thing, the lightning I mean, get around the energy transference problem...?" There was another round of shuffles, like people were priming up their own questions.

"One at a time..." Dan said. Phillip had no idea how Dan would answer any question. In his opinion, it was better if they interrupted each other... "That is an excellent question. Your name is Katie...? Can you first define the 'energy transference problem?"

"Okay…" Katie seemed nervous to be put on the spot. "It's… the tendency for systems to become less energetic over time, especially when transference occurs… People say this means both Willastic *magic* and especially zero-plus magic is impossible because it's impossible to avoid energy decay and also any energy added to the system would cause rebounding… At least I think that's right…"

"Thank you, Katie," Dan turned to the class. "Does anybody have any ideas or theories about how lighting… *Willastic magic* gets around this problem…?

For the third time in less than an hour, Phillip found himself thinking that Dan was a genius. He might just be the foremost genius of his time. He deserved awards and praise. Phillip could not think of an award great enough to give to him. It was surprising, he had never seen Dan handle something so well…

The class rushed to answer the question. Dan pointed to people as they answered, not saying they were right or wrong, and moving immediately to the next person. "It doesn't solve the problem…" One man said, "It's a trick." "They draw energy from a greater source, there's no zero-plus…" "No, I agree it's a trick, it's some local power…" "The energy transference problem is incomplete…" "It is real! Why do you think we're all here?!"

Dan acted as moderator to the debate, never answering a single question but turning it around to the classroom as soon as they came up. Phillip joined in, simultaneously taking notes because it looked better than standing on the front and it gave him something to do with his hands.

This was working, but how long could they keep it going?

In the middle of a passionate speech from a large man named Grenn about how the counsel of Old Berlin were a bunch of "old fools trying to control the world with lies!" A long soft bell rang out…

Confused, but only for a moment, Phillip jumped on the chance. "Alright, that's it for today. Think about what we talked about today. We meet again… Soon."

The energy of the classroom would not be spilled so easily. But lucky for them, the bell rang out again, and this sparked a general movement toward getting up and leaving. People left looking more confused and unsure then when they came in. Except for Antony Müller, who smirked and gave them a sarcastic little bow before leaving.

Dan and Phillip stood by the podium.

Neither of them capable of processing that it was over.

"Dan, that was incredible. How did you come up with that?" Phillip asked him.

"My mom was a substitute teacher for a while. I sat in some of her classes. She told me if you don't know the answer to a question, you can just turn around and ask the class and it works ninety-nine percent of the time. We got lucky," Dan said.

Andy, Emily, Pieter, and Tadaaki were the only ones that didn't leave. They waited till everybody else was gone and the door was shut before talking.

"Well done, sirs!" Pieter said.

"That was incredible!" Andy said. "Almost nobody noticed you were complete fraud!"

"That was the idea..." Phillip replied.

"Well I think you did a generally good job, considering the circumstances," Emily said.

"And what was that thing you said, Phillargo...?" Andy asked. "That you have to 'learn the learning of a thing...' You sound like a wise old mystic. Will you teach me your ways? Do I have to carry rocks up a hill for twenty years just to learn the power was inside me all along...?"

"Well, for starters..." Phillip said back, laughing.

"Really though, do you think we could get away with having the students carry rocks on Thursday?" Dan asked, and everybody laughed.

"If you get Tony Müller to carry rocks up a hill, I swear I'll put you in my will," Pieter said.

There was the most incredible feeling of relief now, even though he knew they weren't done with this. A relief that Phillip suspected wasn't just felt by Dan and Phillip, but somehow by Emily and Andy as well.

"Why would the Pauls set us up like this?" Phillip asked.

"Maybe they have faith in you...?" Emily suggested.

"Two possibilities I see as most likely," Andy said, looking through her glasses as she shook them, the lenses changing color. "One, it's true what they say and the Pauls have gone bananas. Or two, it's a prank to get back at Dan and Phillip for destroying Rickshaun's lab..."

"I hardly think the Pauls would waste students' time in such a manner..." Emily said.

"A lot of people are saying the whole Farm is one big prank. That's the rumors in the Camps, anyway," Pieter said. "Speaking off, I'm leaving early today for the Camps, got some of my dad's business to attend to, who's going to join me...?"

"Oh, man. You know, speaking of Rickshaun, we should probably make it up to him or apologize or something..." Dan said.

"I would love to watch you apologize to Rickshaun," Andy said. "That would be the show of the year."

"I suggest flowers, He looks like a guy who would appreciate a bouquet..." Pieter added.

"I think it's a wonderful idea. Just..." Emily chimed in, "you might want to wait a week or so. Maybe start with a letter. Then find some ways to make it up to him. Symbolically, of course..." Emily was lost in thought, as if navigating apologies and niceties was a difficult game of chess.

The bell rang out again.

"By the way, what's that bell?" Phillip asked.

"Another night coming," Andy answered. "Another emergency cleansing session."

"Another breach, I saw it this morning," Tadaaki said, sounding serious and looking out the window. Andy rolled her eyes at her brother.

"Daniel, Phillip," Emily said, getting their attention. "The second Farm day, what are your plans, we'd like to get you introduced to the Welcoming Committee as soon as possible."

"We don't really have plans, we were going to talk about where we should go," Phillip replied to Emily.

"I'd like to go to a puppet class, or a puppet workshop. Haystacks teaches them," Dan added.

This was a good idea. Dan showed interest in 'puppets', and Haystacks was already a friend. There was also an unspoken rule that Dan and Phillip would stay together.

They agreed to go back to back to the stable with Dan and Phillip.

Night was coming again in the Farm. Though not as fast as last time. The sun be seen moving in the sky toward the horizon. This caused some activity amongst the animals, especially the birds. The trees moved around each other, seeking the best view of the sun. It was hard to tell with a tree, but they didn't seem pleased at their shortened day.

Lights began to turn on. Lanterns like they had seen the night of the amphitheater show, little sparks traveled from lantern to lantern. People rushed around, yelling orders to each other.

"We were talking and we'd also like to take your class," Phillip said to Andy, who was left out of a conversation between Pieter, Emily, and Tadaaki.

"Good. I need somebody to pick on I can trust not to make me look dumb," she said back.

"Perfect. Just one question..." Phillip continued.

"Go for it..." Andy prompted.

"... what is your class?"

Instead of answering right away, Andy snorted. She was terrible at keeping down laughter... "Introductory course on Mindworking. The Western European stuff I'm good at, Bachmann disciples, stuff like that. Nothing Eastern. So, stop assuming."

"Ah, yes. That's what I thought..." Phillip replied.

"...do you want me to define it for you...?" Andy said.

"Well I mean if you're going to do it anyway..."

"It's the study of the nature and the manipulation of the mind. It ties to a whole bunch of things. I started studying it to be rebellious but darn it I started liking it for real."

"Is that how you act out in the... Kanamori family?"

Andy shrugged. "My parents have never shown any anger at me. In fact, they're painfully supportive. Makes it really hard to be a brat and feel good about it... but yeah, I had certain expectations placed on me, so I started delving into the furthest thing from old Nihon mysticism, Germanic Mindworking. The ugly experimental stuff..."

Phillip gave out a small chortle.

"You find my passion funny...?" Andy asked.

"... Oh, no. I was just thinking that where I come from, when a person wants to rebel against their parents, they turn their hair a different color or sneak out, not... study hard," Phillip said back.

"Heeeey, I'll have you know that for the standards of the Kanamori family I'm a huge embarrassment," Andy tilted her head up. "Plus, changing my hair color is still on the table."

They reached Haystacks stable right when the sun set. Fireflies, or something like fireflies, sparked in multiple colors around them as they entered the lit barn.

"... Nothing risky about it. Don't argue with me anymore Henry, you're exhausting me," They heard Haystacks say as they walked in. Henry was dressed in a leather apron and was holding a large hammer and what looked like a glass pair of tongs. Haystacks was smoking in the rafters. He took notice of them as soon as they came in. "Welcome back boys. And you brought company with you!"

"You won't believe what happened to us in class," Phillip led.

"You'll find I'm more open minded than I look." Haystacks said.

"We went to the class we were supposed to go to and..." Phillip started.

"... they signed us up as teachers!" Dan finished. "They want us to teach a class on 'Will and Power...'"

Haystacks paused for just a moment before bursting out in laughter. Andy and Emily joined in. "A surprise a minute here. Have to stay on your toes," Haystacks said.... But come to think of it that is consistent with some of the Old Laws. You learn, you teach..."

"And what do you do if you don't know anything...?" Phillip asked.

"My old craftmaster back in Britannia always said that true competence was a myth. A mirage. Competence is a destination that never gets closer, a conversation you have with yourself," Haystacks responded. "But he was an idiot. I wouldn't take his advice. I don't know what to tell you, boys. Make something up? Wing it?"

"That's what the Pauls said to do!" Dan exclaimed.

"... I'm in good company then," Haystacks said.

The outside was filled with the sound of children playing. Nobody was ready to go to bed again just because it was night, the kids least of all.

Henry served tea and small sandwiches as Dan and Phillip spent their time comparing notes. Phillip's watch was acting funny again, clicking too loud and the arms going the wrong way.

"Broken watch?" Haystacks asked him.

"It's been going haywire sense I brought it into the Farm," Phillip answered.

"Do you mind if I take a look at it?" Haystacks asked. Phillip nodded and handed him the mechanical wristwatch. Haystacks held it up to his ear, then took a sniff of it. "Yes, it definitely has something nesting in there. Nothing dangerous, by the smell," his slender six-fingered hand manipulated the watch, there were small tools in his hands, and his fingers were moving so fast Phillip couldn't follow them. The watch seemed to come apart and be put back together in his hand before Phillip could react. "Phillip, do you mind if I fix this up for you... alter it a bit?"

"It's never worked very well. I found it with a metal detector on the beach. My dad got a new battery in it and I've worn it every sense. Keeps terrible time. Sentimental value."

"Well I won't alter it too much. Might need to dump that Mundafold battery though..."

"Well if it's not too much trouble. Yeah, having a working watch here would be great," Phillip replied, a little hesitant.

"No problem at all." Haystacks said, and pocketed the watch. "Now there's something I want to talk to you about..."

"What is it?" Dan asked.

"I'm not much of a salesman, so I'll just get right to it," Haystacks said. "How would you boys like to make use of your Earners rights, a make a little money?"

CHAPTER 20

Odd Job

Haystacks was overjoyed that Dan and Phillip accepted the job, and even more overjoyed that they wanted to attend his workshops.

So much so that he forgot to tell them what the job was. "Henry will get that all ready," he said with a wave of his hand.

Haystacks didn't stop moving or talking and puppetcrafting for the next hour. He didn't even notice when Andy, Emily, and Peiter excused themselves.

First, he went up to the rafters to retrieve an ornate wooden box of tools. "I don't know where... It's a good idea to..." Then he went to his workshop and brought with him crates... kids are always wanting to jump right to the modern autonomous stuff, but you have to understand the fundamentals..." He brought in wheeled tool chests and tables, chiding the raccoons when they tried to open the drawers "... Cloth, leather, wood, and brass were the materials I learned in but there's so much going on now! Woven glass. Incredible! My great niece, you should meet her I think you three would hit it off, is a savant when it comes to new materials. I give her all the help I can but she's beyond me on so many things..."

Dan was already taking notes. Phillip had too.

"... Come and look at what we made up for the workshop," Haystacks said to them.

Haystacks had set a pile of cloth and odd mechanical pieces on the worktable. He was nagging a faeFlame lamp to provide him with brighter light when he grabbed Dan by the shoulder and pointed to the table.

"See all this? Put it all together and you got yourself a simple puppet. Made them to teach with. When you're done with stage one, you get this..." He took a bundle of cloth out of his pocket. It was a stitched mouse with button eyes. "Pure puppet," Haystacks said, the cloth mouse moved over Haystacks hand and onto the table. "Put some of yourself in it and it will move for you, just like you're moving your hand. Simple as I can make them." Haystacks moved his hands. The cloth mouse moved with them. "Stage two is this..." He took out another mouse.

But this one was more intricate. It had wood and metal legs and front paws. It moved differently than the first one, but Phillip couldn't put his finger on why. "We are going to start moving into autonomous puppets. This little guy might not be able to find his way through a maze without help, but he could probably make it through a hallway," he put the mouse puppet on the table. Unlike the first, it continued to move when Haystacks stopped paying attention to it....and stage... I guess this would be stage five or six...is this," another mouse puppet came out of a pocket. The one moved around Haystacks cupped hands like he was having trouble controlling it. It had more metal and wood attached to it, and its movements were natural. Like a real mouse, it even sniffed the air with a nose that wasn't there. "Almost completely autonomous. He doesn't have his own power, and you can't look through his eyes or anything fancy. But it's a good project to get people introduced to the craft..."

"Haystacks, this is amazing," Phillip said. Putting his finger up to the third mouse, who sniffed it before scurrying away behind the box.

Dan had taken on a look of a person in an intense state of concentration. His face moved closer to his notebook as he wrote. "This. Is," Dan said as he tried to draw a picture of the third mouse, "the. Best..."

"I'm glad you boys like it," Haystacks said with a laugh. "I know it's become a cliché to have an Imp work in puppetcraft. But I'd swear to you I'd choose it no matter who or what I was. I knew this was going to be my life since I saw a crane puppet unload crates on in the Isle of Dogs when I was barely a hatchling... you know I'm going to get myself into quite a lot of personal trouble by showing you boys this..."

"Really? Why?" Dan asked.

"Puppetcraft is one of the few industries dominated by gremlins," he replied as he put away the mice. "We're starting to get some stiff competition. Some trade secrets have been stolen. Especially on the weaving side. There's an attitude amongst the gremmish community that we should look out for our own. Keep our secrets, our advantages close to our chest. I've even received a letter of concern from the Imp King himself!"

"And you don't agree with most gremlins?" Phillip asked.

Haystacks took a minute to answer. "I understand the concern. I really do. There was a time where I could see myself falling headlong into the fear and resentment that's baked deep into the gremmish community. One of my brothers did, turned himself into a fanatic..." He looked distant. "Greed, I suppose, saved me from his fate, if that's not too indecent a thing to say... I *wanted* things. I loved my craft and was willing to bite through all hate and bile to get to it. Moved myself away from my family, here to Washington Union, to pursue it. Worked and studied harder than anybody I knew. Achieved some success. Brought my whole family over, except for my fool brother, he joined a little group called the 'Bad Apples', a rot loving group. He's probably still there, devoting his life to petty sabotage. Making life worse for everybody..." Haystacks said with contempt. "Please don't think I'm complimenting myself, boys. I'm no sparkly-eyed integrationist either. I'm just trying to help you understand why I'm willing to swallow all the hate and suspicion of my kind to do what I do. There's a very rude gremmish word they use on me, to describe Imps who integrate too much into human life. Those accusations have followed me my whole life. But no matter how hard I tried I couldn't get myself to hire some disinterested idiot Imp just because they were an Imp... Or worse! Turn away a talented soul just because they were five-fingered."

Haystacks looked like he was repeating an argument that was played out dozens of times in his life "... they can criticize me all they want," he continued. "But at the end of the day, it's paid off for me. The Imps who want to hoard their knowledge think it makes them safer. It's exactly the opposite! If you're not growing your shriveling. You want to know why, boys? Because every talented soul interested in the craft in all of Washington makes their way to my shops. I give them the knowledge, the tools, the support they need. They sometimes do great things. And I help them. And they get rich, and I get richer. And then I get to live in a world where they added to it. Pure selfishness on my part, boys. And it works for everybody. More Imps working in my shops than were than were working in the *entire industry* when I arrived in Sentinel Bay. Don't get me wrong. There's more competition than ever. The Baker Brothers are doing amazing things, incredible things. I'd be a fool not to admit it. But to think that the best way to deal with competition is to hide from it! Saying that I'm not a *real imp* because I won't throw away possibilities for growth by only hiring gremlins! Well I find nothing more blood-boiling than that..."

Haystacks speech had left him agitated, breathing hard. He had climbed onto the table.

"Haystacks?" Dan asked.

"Yes, Danny?" Haystacks answered.

"Can I ask one question?"

"Anything, my boy..."

"Alright..." Dan took a breath. "With the puppet mice... It's the wood and metal components that make them *autonomous*, right? Why can't you do that with the first one? Is it hard to control a puppet? Can I try now? Also, why does the autonomous one sniff the air and act like a mouse? Is that just for fun or do puppets, a puppet of a mouse, I mean, have to act like a mouse...?"

Haystacks looked down at Dan, and instead of answering right away a smile broke on his long face. The fire he had during his speech had died out. "You two should meet my great niece," he said, jumping from the table. "She's around your age, I think you would like each other..."

Henry had come back into the stable, hauling packages with him.

"... Here I am talking a mile a minute and I forgot I wanted you to do something for me," Haystacks said. "Bring the packages over here... Alright boys. Here's the deal. I'd like you to do a quick delivery for me..."

"Delivery?" Dan asked.

"Yep, just a quick one. A little north of here. Well, one of the 'here's' that the Farm sources from. Shouldn't be more than two-hundred, maybe two-hundred and fifty miles away... With all our time spent at the Farm, Henry and I are getting a little behind on our correspondences."

"Two-hundred miles...?" Dan asked with a frown.

"That seems far..." Phillip added.

"... which is why you will be taking these..." he handed Phillip and Dan a palm sized silver object, with a chrome lever on the side. "Go ahead, try them out."

Not knowing what to expect, since almost anything could happen, Phillip moved slowly, trying to trust that Haystacks wouldn't do anything that would hurt them but finding it hard. He pulled the chrome level.

Ding! A clear bell rang. Dan did the same.

From the bottom of the bell a silver tube appeared. And then, just a fast, disappeared.

"Keep pulling that lever boys, you'll see why in a minute," Haystacks ordered.

Phillip pulled the lever again and again. Each time the silver tubes appeared and contracted, getting larger and brighter the more he did it. He pulled the lever faster. *Ding! Ding! Ding!* The tubes made an image, they were growing more solid. They had made their way to the ground. The sound of the bell pushing them like a wave.

"... you don't need to do it that fast..." Haystacks told them.

Phillip continued to pull the lever. It was heavy now, it stopped making the ding.

It was done. The light and the tubes had formed an object.

It was a bike.

An old style bicycle. The silver bell it came out of was attached to the handle bar. The one in front of Phillip a lime green, Dan's a fire-truck red. They stood in front of them without falling down, without the need of a kickstand.

"These..." Haystacks said with a flourish of his arms, "are '*Mr. Hanson's Many League Bikes.*' They're not mine, they belong to the Farm, probably why they still work, so be careful with them. But they should get you where you need to go in no time. Henry's already tested them."

"How fast do they go?" Phillip asked, allowing himself to touch the bike. There were more tubes and gears than a bike usually had...

"Speed is not really the word to use, you'll see what I mean when you ride them," Haystacks answered. "Incredible experience, if I do say so myself. Makes me hate those War Charters all the more. Mr. Hanson should have been swimming in money for this invention. Shame he was born at the wrong time..."

"What do you want us to deliver?" Dan asked.

"These parcels, to a friend of mine, a banker, up North a little way. It is a little town called Chadwick Cove. Henry has a map and directions for you both," Haystacks answered.

"If you don't mind me asking..." Dan said. He was, like Phillip, giving the bikes a look over. The wheels were slightly thicker than normal bikes. "There are mailboxes here, in the Primafold, I mean. I found one. Why don't you just use those?"

"You mean the Mailers and Postal Guild boxes? You have one of your own? The floating ones can be expensive, you're lucky. You should give me your address!" Haystacks said. "But no, the Mailers Guild won't do here. Now listen up, this is a very fundamental concept here. So fundamental most people won't mention it, they'll just think you'll know. *How* a thing got somewhere is important that it got there at all. This is not always true, but it's a good rule to know exactly what you are dealing with before you move it. Enchanted crops, for instance, can't be sent through the mail. The shortcuts they take rot them out. It's the same reason you have to go by boat if you want to get from Britannia to Washington Union," the concept was hard for Phillip to follow. "Which reminds me. The special gears on these bikes will only work in the Primafold. And then, only work well on well-traveled paths, be sure to keep to those... now let's talk about your pay..."

"Oh, okay." Phillip said, he had forgotten Haystacks intended to pay them.

"I was thinking forty minor notes for each of you," Haystacks took a square leather wallet out of his breast pocket, he shook the wallet until it turned into a sizable leather box with a drawer. He grabbed some coins out of it and handed five each to Dan and Phillip. "Here's twenty now."

"That sounds great!" Phillip said. "I don't want to sound greedy, but is twenty... minor notes... A lot?" The coins seemed to be made out of wood, with a circle of glass in the middle with the number '4' printed on it.

"Nothing greedy about wanting to get paid well, boys," Haystacks said. "You're not going to impress any Clock Village ladies with forty minor notes, but I'd say it's above market wages for a short delivery. I like to think I pay good wages."

"Thanks. This is great," Phillip said with Dan agreeing.

"Don't act too appreciative, boys. People will start to think you're not worth it and try to exploit you. People less ethical than me, that is," Haystacks said with a wink. "Now, let me tell you how to use these things..."

———— o ————

Haystacks said that their normal entrance road to the Camps was the perfect place to start. There was some confusion on where "here" meant.

They learned their usual entrance was the King's Hill entrance.

Sunrise had occurred less than three hours after it had set, which was more jarring than Phillip wanted to admit... There was a scheduled short break in Farm time, where they could leave and come back without missing Farm days.

They were traveling light. Which meant only a messenger bag and his pink notebook for Phillip, but meant a small backpack—he had brought a *spare* backpack inside his big one—for Dan.

Dan had also brought goggles. And gloves... And a first aid kit. Two maps. A compass. More string. And a dozen other items. Phillip had benefited too many times at this point from Dan's overpreparation to criticize him, but he did want to say something about how weighed down he looked... The brown packages lashed to the bikes didn't help. At least Phillip's bike had a basket in the front, which made carrying his own things easier.

They each received their own map. "Follow it to the letter," Haystacks said. The instructions were simple enough. Only a few turns. But also included advice like *'Do not trust any hitchhikers!'* and *'Possible forest crossing. Watch the road'* and *'Unmarked graves. Tread lightly'* and *'If you run into snow or desert, you've gone too far.'* They were going to a small town and meeting a banker named Mr. McKroft, who was expecting them.

"Alright, you ready to do this?" Phillip asked Dan when they had reached the main road. A clear and empty gravel road.

"Yes. Just give me one... No. Give me a sec," Dan said. He was going through the checklist Haystacks had given them.

Phillip had mounted the bike. Henry had adjusted them to their size already.

"They work just like normal bikes when you don't mess with the gears. We'll only do that when we're both ready, like we agreed." Phillip said, trying not to pressure Dan but wanting to get going.

"Alright. Alright. Okay. I'm ready. Wait... No, I'm ready. Let's get..." Dan said mounting his bike and giving it a push forward.

It did feel like a normal bike... *Mostly*. It felt more stable than a bike did. Phillip found he had no trouble taking his hands off the handlebars when he traveled in a straight line.

"Dan, try this!" he said, and took out his map and read it as if he was a passenger in a car.

"Be careful!" Dan said with a laugh, and gave it a try himself. "I've never been able to do this!"

"Let's try one of the special gears," Phillip said.

"Wait until we get on one of the long stretches of road." Dan said. "It's just a couple of turns."

"C'mon, Dan. There's no better time to try it..." Phillip said, the gravel road they were on stretched into the distance.

"Alright, sorry..." Dan said, putting his hand on the gear. "I'm just thinking too much. I'm ready. First gear?"

"First gear on three," Phillip said. "One..."

"Two..." Dan said with him.

"Three..."

They both flicked the gear. A green display went from a dash to 'I'.

A buzzing under Phillip's seat. The pedals became harder to push.

Nothing felt different, until it did.

Dan and Phillip realized what was different at the same time, as they both said "wow!" At the exact same moment.

Haystacks was right, it didn't feel like going fast. The wind blowing past Phillip's face felt slower. If anything, the world around was calmer.

It felt like the world had become smaller. Like he was riding on a miniature version of the path they were just on.

He could see ahead of him, thousands of yards as if he was looking across Haystacks stable. He felt larger and taller than he had, but still taking up the same space on the ground.

He moved past trees and cow farms with a single rotation of his pedals.

How did they look from somebody who was just standing on the path?

"Dan, this is great!" Phillip said, Dan nodded back. They had no trouble hearing each other. The voices echoed. "Dan, let's go into second gear."

Dan nodded. They said "One, two, three," and flicked the switch again. The display went from 'I' to 'II.'

More buzzing under his seat. A pop and spring as something shifted on the pedals.

The effect became more intense. The world became smaller and clearer still. It was like they were pushing a toy bicycle along a gravel road. Haystacks was right, it was easy to ride these bikes. Exhilarating.

"There's a turn up ahead." Dan said. They had no problem seeing the yellow sign which marked the different road.

They both stopped pedaling when they went to make the turn. The world became normal, if only for a moment. They pedaled out of the turn and the world was pushed back into a living model of itself.

It felt like flying. Like floating over the ground.

The road they had turned on was made of brick. Bright Red brick. It was a thin road, and nobody was on it but them. What did it mean for a road to be part of the Primafold? Phillip was having a hard time imagining it. "It's a matter of geometry" Haystacks said when Dan asked... which explained nothing to Phillip.

"Look," Dan said, and pointed to a green rolling field ahead of them. It looked like there were giant hermit crabs grazing on the grass. Hundreds of them.

"Are those animals?" Phillip yelled to Dan.

"I think they're puppets!" Dan yelled back.

The red brick road was going to lead right into the center of 'Chadwick Cove' which was "mostly Primafold community which loosely lines up with a Mundafold town." The maps had detailed instructions on where to go once in town.

The passed a field which was grass but flowing up and down like waves, just like the field outside the Farm. There saw hundreds of animals, mostly buffalo and elk. A gated Farm or ranch on the right contained hundreds of low thunderclouds, which were grabbing the ground like fog and gave out sparks of lightning.

Dan and Phillip had to stop for over twenty minutes to let trees go by the path. An entire forest of trees moved on their roots. Signs on the side of the road said 'Migrating Forest Crossing Area, Please Stop' and 'Migratory Forest Viewing

Area' and another *'Please do not Water the trees.'* Birds and animals moved with the trees.

They moved dozens or hundreds of miles in less than an hour. Phillip had a hard time calculating, especially without his watch. It could probably go from his hometown of Portland Maine to King's Hill in a few hours, instead of the two days it took in the car. *How high did the gears on this bike go? Why didn't everybody travel this way?*

"Here's the town," Dan said.

Already? They had to be moving faster than Phillip thought...

'WELCOME TO CHADWICK COVE' a sign on the side of the road announced.

They did what Haystacks said and got off the bikes, took off the packages, and then pulled the secret red lever on the bell.

The bikes disappeared into their own bells like a roll of tape. "Awesome," Dan said. "Really awesome," Phillip agreed.

'Frontier Bank, Financing and Speculation,' was near the center of town. The town itself seemed mostly normal—and abandoned—except for a few gremlins walking about.

McKroft the banker was a small man with twinkling eyes wearing a fine suit in an old style. He was beyond thankful to receive the packages and offered them a good deal on "new accounts for Earners. We don't do any Skull banking ourselves..."

They thanked him and said "maybe later," implying they had more deliveries, before leaving and getting back on the road.

The ride back was more fun than the ride there. Not having to navigate as much they were able to enjoy the experience more. "Imagine if we had these," Phillip said. "We could explore the whole country and come back before dinner!"

"You know, this is the first job I've ever had."

"Me too," Phillip said.

They had twenty minor note coins in their pockets. He had no idea how much that was but felt happy that it was there. Felt like he was really starting to be a part of all this. Getting back into the Farm with privileges, whatever that meant. Being able to experience something like these bikes... Even with this class the Pauls were making them teach, things were working out in their favor.

——— o ———

They were much more comfortable with the bikes by the time they got back to the main road leading to the Campground. Turning and changing gears were no problem. Even avoiding obstacles was easy now.

He could see Dan ahead of him, moving farther away. He looked odd on the bike when they weren't traveling the same speed. Like he was also on a treadmill.

Speeding up again to catch up with Dan. They were back in first gear now. One disadvantage Phillip found was that once you got used to the gears going back to traveling normally felt painfully slow and grueling. His Aunt Kath would love this. Come to think of it, if he had access to this, he could probably visit her in California, and then be back again same day...

An orange object jetted in front of Phillip's path.

He had just enough time to turn and skid and not hit it. The effect of the special gear going away when he turned the handle bars. He had overcorrected. The bike wanted to stand and move forward, it felt different than a normal bike, he wasn't used to it. He came to a stop in a skid, having to place one foot on the ground to stop himself from falling over.

He looked around for the object he had avoided.

It was a cat. An orange cat. It's back arched as if it was scared.

"Sorry about that..." He began to say to the cat, but then noticed a rustle in the bushes, the cat was backing up, letting out a low whining sound.

Something dark jumped from the bushes. It was the size of a dog. So dark he couldn't make out any distinguishing features, just that it had a hunched back and thin raccoon-like forepaws.

Without thinking Phillip took off his messenger bag and threw it as hard as he could at the dark creature.

The creature stopped in its tracks, turned towards Phillip for just a moment, before jumping back into the woods and fast as it had come out of them. The cat was still in the middle of the pathway. Back arched, its head now turned towards Phillip.

"It's alright, come..." Phillip said to the cat, bending down, but the instant Phillip started talking the cat ran to the opposite side of the path, and hid underneath the nearest bush.

"What's going on? Why'd you stop?" He heard Dan's voice say behind him. Dan had come back to look for him.

"I swerved. There was a cat in front of me, I think something was after him," Phillip said. "If I can get him to come out of these bushes..."

"If it's a stray it probably won't come to you."

"No. I guess it won't," Phillip said. Dan was right, but he didn't want to give up just yet. That dark Animal or whatever was still out there. The cat wasn't safe here and he didn't want to leave it...

"Dan, we took our time getting back. Haystacks needs those delivery receipts and to see if we're okay. I'm going to try to help this cat out, I'll be right behind you..." *There was no reason for Dan to stay here,* Phillip told himself.

"You sure?" Dan asked.

"Yeah, I'll be right behind you. Meet you at the stable." Phillip said. *Dan was a distraction here.*

"I'll stay," Dan said.

"No, he's less likely to come out if there's two of us here anyway. Thanks Dan, but I'm fine here. I'll be five minutes. Ten tops..."

"Um, alright." Dan said. Hesitant but turning around. "I'll meet you at the stable."

"Yeah. Stable." Phillip said, looking at the bushes.

Phillip sat on the ground. The cat was more likely to come to him this way. He made soft clicking sounds. He didn't know why this worked, he remembered he saw his mom doing this one time to a stray cat in the park.

An orange head popped out of the bush.

"There you go. Come here," He said, putting his hand out, palm up, like he was holding something. The orange cat took one tentative step out of the bushes and then, deciding to go for broke, ran to Phillip's hand. He smelled and licked Phillip's hand. He had a collar on. Part of his ear was missing, his tail too...

Wait. Phillip thought.

He slowly looked at the tag on the collar. In bold lettering on the front it read: *'GINGERSNAPS.'*

"No. Way," Phillip said to himself.

The women. The old women.

Well... maybe not old, but she *sounded* old. The woman who called him in the car and asked him to help find her missing cat since he was "looking for things anyway..."

Her cat was named Gingersnaps.

He didn't remember the conversation until now. This was her cat!

"I think I know your owner," he said to Gingersnaps, who was rubbing himself on Phillip's side.

This couldn't be a coincidence... It was too improbable.

He picked the cat up, Gingersnaps didn't struggle. He picked up the bag he had thrown. He made sure he hadn't injured anything and put Gingersnaps in the front basket of the bike.

Maybe this was how magic worked. Big coincidences happening. He gets a call about an orange cat and he happens to find it... Maybe this was what it means to have 'Privilege?' Adeline said something about how the world would make sense of the things he said and thought... on some of the notes she had given them she made the same vague point. *The world around the Farm will accommodate you*, whatever that means...

Another theory popped into his mind. The woman who had called him, *she* was from the Primafold. That explained her odd behavior, which he chalked up to senility at the time. Maybe this was how people looked for their pets here...?

He was off the bike now. Walking with it back to Haystacks stable. He couldn't go back now, Dan would wonder where he was. Haystacks stable could accommodate one more animal for the night. Gingersnaps had made himself comfortable in the basket.

The old women at the special entrance to the Farm took no notice of Gingersnaps. People bringing animals into the Farm wasn't special enough to warrant attention. "Good thing you're back. The break is about to end..." She said in a way that implied she was judging him for his brush with tardiness.

The weather was particularly nice. Especially inside the Farm. It was an almost cloudless day. The clouds Phillip did see—he realized as he walked to the stable—were not large and in the sky, but small. The size of buses and cars. Floating just twenty or fifty or so feet in the air. Sometimes moving with spurts in different directions, as if they were moving themselves. Like bacteria under a microscope.

Gingersnaps grew agitated when he went into the Farm. He stood in the basket, his head jutting around. Looking for threats.

"It's alright Gingersnaps," Phillip said while petting him. "You get used to it."

Gingersnaps was not comforted. If anything, Phillip trying to calm him down had the opposite effect. The cat wanted out.

"It's okay Gingersnaps. It's okay," Phillip said. He went in to pet the cat again, but he didn't want to be touched. He held the collar, but the cat struggled and got itself loose of both the collar and the basket in one movement.

"Gingersnaps, no," he said, but it was too late. The cat leapt out of the basket and ran as fast as he could to the nearest cover, which was a hundred shipping crates and barrels stacked between two barns.

He looked for the cat for over an hour.

Going back and forth to likely hiding places. Sitting on the ground and making the same soft clicking sound he made outside. What a stupid thing for him to do. Of course, the cat was scared when he came into the Farm. He should have tied him better, or taken a quick trip home. Drop him off at the Dollhouse. Dan would understand...

"There you are!" He heard Dan say. "I came looking for you."

"Dan, I'm glad you're here." Phillip said. "Help me find the cat..."

"You found another cat?"

"Same cat, got away," Phillip said and, realizing his explanation was inadequate, explained what had happened. He also told Dan about the phone call.

"What are the chances?" Dan said. "Do you think magic has something to do with it?"

"I was thinking that. I think he went somewhere in the barrels."

Dan and Phillip together were as successful as Phillip was alone. At the point where he was looking in the same crate for the third time, Phillip had to admit to himself the cat wasn't coming back.

"Sorry about that, Phil," Dan said as they walked back to Haystacks stable. "But don't worry. If the cat is owned, he's pretty safe in the Farm..."

"How do you know?" Phillip asked.

"I was reading some pamphlets about animal kinship and the laws, The Old Laws, I mean oh my gosh Phil it's so involved you wouldn't believe it. But there's a load of stuff about how to treat animals and interact with them. There's this whole section on what meat you can eat, there's a whole word for it... Forget what it is though. Anyway, the cat, if it's owned, is kinned to its owner, and will be safe from other kinned animals or owners... Or something. It somehow ties into the homestead... something. Ethics! 'Homestead ethics.' Which is connected to something called the 'Law of Hearths.' Phil, you have to read up on this stuff, it's crazy."

"Huh," Phillip said, feeling better. "That's good. Maybe I'll put up signs too. He's a pretty distinct cat. I feel bad I brought him in here just to get lost... Now he doesn't have his collar on," Phillip said, holding the collar in his hand then putting it in his messenger bag.

Haystacks was in a great mood when they came back to the stable.

"Thanks for doing that, boys. Huge help!" Haystacks said. "Henry was a little worried about you going so far on your first outing, but I knew you could do it. Now, tell me. How was it? Great, wasn't it!"

They talked about how thrilling it was and what they saw. Haystacks had never experienced it either until a day or so ago. When Phillip and Dan asked why these bikes weren't more common, Haystacks explained that there were travel restrictions in place put on almost the entire world after the war. "Going on a hundred years of the harsher air-amendment travel restrictions, too. Shame. They say it makes the world safer. No more armies and warships showing up out of nowhere."

"So why can we use them?" Phillip asked.

"The Pauls have advantages, their Inheritors, after all..." Haystacks said. "They can break all the rules they want, if they want to." He looked off, as if thinking about something, before speaking again. "Almost forgot! Here is the rest of what I owe you." He handed them both five more coins. Phillip didn't admit he had forgotten about payment. "And if you don't mind, hold on to those bikes for me. I might have you do a few more deliveries for me. Just don't break them, I don't want to have to explain myself to the Pauls."

This day just keeps getting better, Phillip thought. He didn't even know what to say Haystacks except "Thank you," multiple times.

"Now what did I tell you about showing too much appreciation?" He said back with a smile. "But since you want to thank me so much. I might as well give this back to you now."

He handed Phillip his watch. It was almost the same, except now it had a few more dials and twice as many hands.

"I added some functionality. Didn't throw anything away, given that it has sentimental value to you," Haystacks explained. "Except for that Mundafold battery, that thing was too infected to salvage. There was an incorporeal parasite nesting in there. Decided to work with the little guy instead of against him. He's still in there. He'll keep the springs tight so long as you wear him. It's a good deal for him and he's harmless to you. Longer lasting than one of those fool batteries too. You see the longest hands? Those will keep the time of wherever you set them... No matter what. Now tap the top. Yes, that's it. The blue and black lines tell you the time of day of where you are currently standing. I stole a moon and sun dial from another watch and put it in there. There's also a stopwatch which will count your personal time. Underneath that, if you spin plug on the side, is a work-time stopwatch. So, you can know how much you're being compressed," he pointed to the front of the watch. "You'll see that I've had it running almost since you gave it to me. Right now, about twenty-four hours is equivalent to about four in non-work biological time. Which is an amazing degree of compression... You'll forgive the shoddy craftsmanship, Phillip. Any gremmish jeweler would probably try to have me killed for the insult I've done to their craft..."

"Shoddy craftsmanship?!" Phillip said. "Haystacks, this is incredible. It's the best thing I've ever seen. You did this in only a few hours...?" Phillip put it on his wrist, trying it out. It felt the same.

"... and I won't have you thanking me anymore either. I consider my responsibility to help you two. That's not just the spirit of the Old Laws but the oldest gremmish laws... I might be a heartless self-compromised goldbride, but I do have some small sense of my responsibilities. So please don't thank me, it makes me feel bad thinking about all the responsibilities I've neglected over the years..."

Neither Dan or Phillip followed his advice.

"... bleh. But that does remind me," Haystacks said, "Henry is done putting some more lighting in your stall, and I have to say, the chandelier looks wonderful."

CHAPTER
21
Useless Friends

'Privilege' worked well. Sometimes *too* well.

Every lie and excuse Phillip made landed with the Fairchild family. Even the bad ones. Even *Dan's* bad ones. One day they would say they needed to leave just before sunrise, they didn't even say why, the next they said they wanted to go to a group night biking event for students with no specifics... *and it worked!*

Mostly worked. Nothing seemed to land with Maddie.

"Phil, my mom's usually way more curious than this," Dan said on the way to the Farm. "Is this Privilege magic doing something to her brain...?"

"Maybe..." Phillip said with a shrug. "I think it works like the pink notebooks. Like you can't pay attention to it right. I'm sure it's not dangerous, Adeline would have said."

"Who said anything about 'dangerous?'" Dan said, a look of concentration on his face now. "Oh god Phil is Privilege dangerous for people's brains?"

They didn't think about this for long. They had other problems.

Nothing they tried worked.

Nothing.

Magically, they were as inept as the first day they snuck into the Farm.

At first, they blamed the location.

Magic seemed to be location dependent. Almost nothing worked for Dan in Knoxville, except the mailbox and the pink notebooks. Almost everything worked at Dollhouse. *Sometimes.* It was more proof to Dan that King's Hill was in the Primafold. *But if it was in the Primafold*, Phillip would counter, *why doesn't anybody here know about magic or the Farm or gremlins...?* Then Dan would show him the collection of maps he was buying—from stores or gas stations in King's Hill or Tennessee—only half of which had King's Hill on them. It was usually a long unproductive conversation before they admitted they really didn't understand what the 'Primafold' or 'Mundafold' were—or what 'Folds' were, for that matter.

Haystacks explained it by taking a strip of elastic cloth, stretching it out, and folding it. "See? If you look from the top it looks the same size as before, but now there's more, and you can do more with it," he said. "Some with places, but we're stuck looking at the cloth from only one end at a time, so it can get confusing."

'Folds' were like space. Extra space. But could also refer to actions... or were created by actions... they weren't sure.

In any case, if King's Hill was in the Primafold, it didn't help them.

They tried everything they knew about from Circles class or the books Adeline gave them. Simple circles. Simple 'Magicks.' Simple crafts. Simple 'Nexxings'—whatever those were. Nothing worked.

Even Haystacks failed to teach them basic puppetcraft—much to Dan's disappointment.

Another wave of disruptions—caused by another breach—cancelled Haystacks' class again, as well as made it impossible to maintain solid faeFlame, which was prone to disobedience at the best of times.

The stable was lit with Haystacks' own brand of flying puppet lamps. Shaped like birds, their chests were lamps. They opened their wings and shined light wherever it was needed, so long as they weren't distracted by seeds. Henry spent a lot of time chasing them or stopping Buttercup from swiping at them or Dryrot from trying to grab them.

Haystacks had them assemble the simplest puppets. Think about the cloth. Think about the string. Put some of yourself in the stuffing.

The puppets looked like mice, but they never moved. Even Haystacks had a difficult time moving them. He allowed them to jump ahead, to start assembling more advanced mice puppets with external logike components. "It's good to learn the process, don't worry boys, you'll get there," Haystacks assured them.

Dan was disappointed but worked diligently. He had taken apart his mouse and pout it back together three times already. "I think it moved that time!" He would say. "No, never mind..."

Going to Andy's class was much more productive when Phillip knew what class it was.

He even understood something from time to time.

She talked about 'mind-modeling' and how it related to the modern practice of 'mind-mapping.' She had a habit of calling on Phillip and Dan. "Phillargo, what is the self in relation to day-to-day experience? I'm just kidding, don't answer that nobody knows." "Dan, tell me the most emotionally disturbing experiences of your life." "Philargo, try to describe to me what the sun would sound like..."

Andy was one of the few teachers who said "magic." Two people who believed different things about the structure of thought, she said, would have two different outcomes if they tried identical mind manipulation techniques. It was one of the big proofs that magic worked—at least in part—on a *'primacy of belief.'*

Phillip didn't understand five-percent of it, but wrote it down anyway.

After a long discussion and some convincing from Emily, Dan and Phillip decided to go back to circles class. "A good foundation is your most important asset," Emily said. "Just try not to murder the children by summoning lighting." Andy added.

Murdering children wasn't in the cards, it turned out.

They arrived back to Miss Julie's class, who said "Phillip, Daniel, I'm glad you're back. I admire your resolve. Gotta get right back on that horse..." They asked if they could sit in the back of the class and observe but Miss Julie insisted on participation.

They were as successful in their second class as they were the first.

Lucky for Phillip, his friend Thamus was always there to offer some helpful advice like "just do it like this," and "why are you so bad at this?"

Miss Julie used the figures again, with a different song. They were introduced to a new doll. *Toby the Thieving Termite*, who grabbed qualities from one circle and snuck them into others. The class learned how to stop Toby from sneaking into their circles, but also how to let him in and make him go to sleep. All except Dan and Phillip, who Toby had an easy time stealing from.

———— o ————

The Welcoming Committee met in Crownshead.

The club consisted of Andy, Emily, Phillip, Daniel, sometimes Tadaaki, and Boo'jo the masked Mandrill if he had nothing better to do.

Andy gave Phillip and Dan the title of 'Secretary and Governor of special projects and other boring junk,' before Emily corrected "we just need somebody to meet with other Choicers like you, who might be more willing to talk to somebody like them," to which Andy responded, "that's what I said. 'Boring junk.'"

"Maybe we should be a little more focused. There are other things to attend to today," Tadaaki said, wearing the same business suit kimono he wore at the amphitheater, not looking up from the book he was reading.

"Excuse my brother. He's moody because he's been overeating for days and hates himself." Andy said to Phillip and Dan.

"Dan, Phillargo," Tadaaki said back. "You will excuse my sister. Procrastination loves company."

"Phillargo, Danny," Andy continued. "Please find it in your heart to forgive my brother. He was born with a debilitating medical condition in which prevents him from taking any unpermitted joy from anything..."

"Daniel, Phillargo..." Tadaaki began.

"... maybe we should talk about what we have to do today," Emily interrupted, raising the volume of her voice as far as politeness would allow. "We have a whole new group of people coming to the Farm, they're expected next week. I've said before that there's an usual amount of Choicers here. Young

Choicers, traveling alone. That's where Daniel and Phillip come in. I've brought some maps…"

Their first mission was new Choicer outreach. Emily had a detailed map and list of names to visit in the Farm. "We are doing better accommodating new guests," she said. "Even without Sarah or Adeline here…" She handed Dan and Phillip a box of reading material and pamphlets to deliver to the guests. "Tell them you're Choicers, and make sure they know that they can ask us for any help they might need. I've written out a list of things you should say."

They spent the rest of the Farm day meeting with Choicers. Most were older, in their twenties or thirties, but a lot of them were just a little older than Dan and Phillip, the youngest was an eleven-year-old boy who said he was a runaway until he found out magic existed. A black kid named Davis. "You can call me Davy though," he said. He was completely alone at the Farm, except for some friends he made. "Come by where we are staying," Dan told him. "Yeah, you're welcome at our home anytime." "Might just take you up on that," Davy said, sounding nothing like an eleven-year-old.

Davy was the exception and not the rule. It turned out that most Choicers knew more than they did. Knew about the Mundafold and Primafold their entire lives and recently made the decision to integrate into the Primafold. "I couldn't get into any of the reputable schools. Came to the Farm when I heard about it, it's been great!" One man told them. They were asked a lot of questions they didn't know, but told people they would try to get the answers, as Emily instructed.

It was tedious and awkward, but Phillip liked doing it. It gave them a chance to see more of the Farm, and there was far more here than they thought, the place seemed to be growing by the day, and it gave Phillip a sense of purpose and success that was enjoyable.

"You guys want to see something neat?" Andy said when they came back.

"See what?" Dan asked Andy. But she was too coy for that and she told them to follow her. Leading them deeper into Crownshead.

"They let me in when they were doing their last purification, that's why night was so long. And I figure since you both have full Privileges and you enjoy gawking at things…"

"I *do* like gawking," Phillip replied.

They met Emily in a dark hallway that led downward at odd angles to a door that might have once been square before years of warping. Andy knocked and the door opened. Emily blew into her hands and then put out her palms, which lit the wooden hallway beyond. Andy led them to another door. "This way is faster," she said.

The door had a round sign on the front which looked newer and cleaner than the hallway or the door itself. It said *'Brother and Sisterhood of Gathers'* around it and in the center, was an image of a thin man grabbing a cloud and floating above farmlands.

It was bright behind the door. Bright like daytime. But they were still indoors. The light came from a few of the dozens of bright blue wooden doors that lined the long room. The blue doors that were open let in pure sunlight. There were dozens of people in the room. All manning these doors.

The doors opened to the sky.

They could see miles and miles of clouds, and a distant landscape underneath. The men surrounding the door were holding ropes and pulling them. When they reached the end of the rope, they dragged clouds with them. "Got too much moisture with this one, get the heavy bucket," a man yelled to a boy about Phillip's age. The cloud was placed in a tall wicker basket. Other boys with long spears with glowing tips shoving the cloud in from above.

"Incredible," Phillip said in a whisper.

"They're cloud gathering, Phil!" Dan said. "I read about it."

Andy shushed them and Emily smiled. "Cool, isn't it? They're not allowed to operate these doors most of the time, but since they're in the Farm they're taking advantage of the loose restrictions," Andy said. "But that's not what we wanted to show you..."

They walked as slowly as they could while still following Andy and Emily. Some of the blue doors led to sky above farmlands, they could see mountains in one, the ocean in another. The one at the end they could see what they thought was the large silo of the Farm underneath.

Andy led them down through more stairs going down. The walls went from wood to stone, and the doors they went through metal and raised of the ground, like the ones Phillip saw when he toured an old battleship on a school trip.

"Alright, get ready," Andy said, and banged on the metal door.

"Get ready for what? You haven't told us anything..." Phillip said.

The door opened and a small man with glasses looked at them. Then rolled his eyes when he looked at Andy beckoned them in.

The room was enormous. A massive circular tube that extended hundreds of feet above Phillip's head and below the metal walkway. A thin waterfall— flowing far too slowly— could be seen on the other side of the massive chamber. But the room was dominated by what was in the center.

It looked like a series of giant glass light bulbs stacked end-to-end, but there were also tubes containing large metal balls which slid around the machine. Hundreds of things were spinning and moving. Some hand sized, others looked like glass windmills the size of the Fairchild house. Phillip noticed the glass... Pulsated, moved like a beating heart or sometimes rippled on a smooth pond. It stretched from the top of the chamber to the bottom where it was submerged under water. It was surrounded by a curtain of a flowing light, like an aurora. He went into his bag to get his pink notebook. Something metallic clanked below him. He looked around, had he dropped a coin? But he couldn't find anything when he looked.

"What is it?" Phillip finally asked, Dan staring with his mouth open.

"Farm time," Andy said simply.

"This is what makes Farm time possible. It's a work-time engine," Emily said.

"The biggest one I've ever seen could fit in a puppet wagon," Andy said.

"I can't even imagine the power it takes. Don't look too much into the bright light at the center, it will hurt your eyes. My ears are already starting to hurt from all the pressure," Emily said.

Phillip looked around. "What bright light?" he asked. "All I see are light on the top."

"And what pressure?" Dan followed, not taking his eyes off the machine.

"Light at the top...?" Andy said, adjusting her glasses, the shades of which turned blue. "You don't feel the pressure of it? You don't see the bright light?" When both Phillip and Dan shook their heads, she said. "Hmmm, maybe you have to be in the Primafold longer to see it..."

"That's enough. Get your fill. This place is not for people," the small man in glasses said to them.

Emily thanked him previously for letting them see and they left. Dan talking about what they had seen, but Phillip unable to stop thinking about the question of why they couldn't see the light or feel the pressure of the machine, and what that lack of perception could mean...

<hr />

Will-class day rolled around in direct opposition to Phillip's wishes. Farm days were almost infinite—nine or twelve days to a day now—but they still weren't long enough.

He was starting to think he would have to stand in front of that class again.

He thought they would be able to talk to the Pauls or Adeline and Sarah, but they were always gone now. On some important business away from the Farm.

"Andy, I need you to do something for me," Phillip asked.

"Do I have to...?" Andy responded.

"I need to come up with some questions you can ask in the class, something I can answer," Phillip said. "If it looks like things are going South you can interrupt..."

"You want me to help you commit fraud?"

"Yes, exactly," Phillip said. Andy snorted, and suggested some questions.

The class was not half as full as it was last time. There were almost no people in the white uniforms anymore. Only three. Antony Müller and two students. Phillip thought he might choose to triple the size of the classroom if it meant getting Müller out.

Dan and Phillip had come to the classroom as early as possible and drew with their skychalk as meticulous a drawing of the circle they used to summon lighting as they could. This was Andy and Emily's idea. Give the class something to focus on.

He was able to find a book about Resonance, and another one about the history of Willasticism. They cost seven minor notes together and neither one was the slightest bit useful. Both texts were as dry as he had ever read, both assumed a level of knowledge on his part that he simply didn't have.

The smaller class size turned out to be a curse. People were less likely to get in their own verbal battles and interrupt each other, and there was much more focus on them. Phillip tried to go through the basic concepts of Resonance he had learned from Emily, but sensed he wasn't doing well and turned the questions back into the class. Dan's trick he learned from his Mom was proving less effective as the class went on. This was when Andy, Emily, or Pieter would throw them the softball questions they had planned earlier.

"Mr. Phillipe Monterrey," Andy said in a sweet voice, raising her hand the same moment she talked. "Does will based magic have anything to do with the ancient Greek concept of the seven layers of reality...?"

"Good question..." Phillip said, and then recited the seven layers—*Form, Material, Concept, Thought, Sense, Self/Identity, Existence*—before turning the question back to the classroom, as planned. "Does anybody think this is a good concept of Will magic...?"

The class took the bait.

"You're so smart, Professor," Andy said to him when the class got loud enough that she couldn't be heard. Emily was poking Andy to stop. "How do you do it?"

"Years of study," Phillip answered.

"I'm learning so much just being around you..." Andy said dreamily.

The class ended early. Another bell was announcing a sudden unscheduled break from Farm time. Phillip looked at his watch, twisted one of the knobs and saw the sun rushing to meet back up with outside time. "I wonder what's going on?" A student said to bell. Müller left the classroom without a word. He had been silent the whole class.

"That class was more successful than the first," Emily said.

"We can't keep doing this..." Phillip said back.

"Maybe we should just come clean, admit to the class we don't know much?" Dan suggested.

"It's too late for that," Phillip said, feeling more like the fraud than ever.

———— O ————

"**We** need to try it again," Dan said as soon as the girls left them outside of Crownshead.

Phillip, knowing exactly what he was talking about, "I don't think that's a good idea right now, who knows what could happen..."

"And what are you 'trying again', exactly," a familiar voice said behind them.

Captain Karo walked toward them, his hands behind his back and his head tilted slightly back. "I would hope that you inform us of anything dangerous you are doing, for that the Wallmen can plan ahead. *Master* Phillip. *Master* Daniel," he said with enough venom that the word 'master' became an insult.

"Nothing," Dan answered. "Just some magic we were talking about doing..."

"*Magic*," Captain Karo repeated. "That's good. That's good. We've been keeping an eye out for you since you got back. Seeing as how important you've become. We've been cataloging your... *successes*. Very kind of you to not show off your talents to a jealous public. But if you don't mind me saying I think you're taking it tad far. People might start thinking you don't belong here. That you're nothing but a waste and a danger to yourself, and that the old men who granted you full privileges have made a horrible mistake..."

"We will, thanks," Dan said.

"Yes, thank you," Phillip said with far less kindness.

"And please tell if there is anything the Wallmen can do for you," Karo said, walking away.

A funny kind of energy stuck Phillip as he watched Karo walk away.

"We need to try again," he said to Dan.

"Really?!" Dan said surprised, trailing behind Phillip who was walking ahead.

"We'll wait until Farm time ends. Get outside the Farm. Find a place without people. Try it again," Phillip said. "What's the worst that could happen?"

Farm time ended early again. The announcement was made just moments before. They heard rumors about animals running amok due to some infection, or a parade of Shadowkin or something else they didn't understand.

Dan and Phillip tried to trace back their route to the field. But they couldn't find it. They settled for an overgrown abandoned football field and stomped down the grass the best they could. They drew the circles with skychalk, carefully following their notes, getting out all their supplies, put out a fresh jar.

"Let's do it exactly how we did it last time," Phillip said, looking at his notes, wishing that he recorded better his thoughts and feelings when it happened. He remembered he wasn't quite himself last time.

"If this works, we should demonstrate it for the class," Dan said.

"It will work," Phillip said, imagining the blue lightning.

They were meticulous and followed their instructions the best they could. They even took drinks of the sparkvine miracle potion. When they were done, they stood at the center of the circle, waiting for the sun to reach the point it was the last time.

"Ready?" Dan asked.

"Ready," Phillip confirmed.

They did the hand motion.

Moments passed, then a minute, then two.

Nothing.

"One more time," Phillip said.

And again, nothing happened.

They redrew the circle, redid the ritual. Phillip telling Dan to start thinking like they had last time, which was hard because neither of them really remembered. They switched places. They drew the circle in a different spot. They waited longer.

Nothing.

Nothing every time.

"What are we doing differently...?" Dan said, looking at his notebook.

Phillip had his notebook open but was not staring at it or even the circles, but the setting sun. What *were* they doing differently? Looking down at his notebook, the notebook filled with strange notes and which could do things nothing else could do, he thought a painful thought, *maybe nothing*. Maybe they were doing the same thing, but they had nothing to do with why the lightning happened. He did read that lowerFae liked to play pranks on people...

"What does it mean...?" Dan said, to himself more than Phillip.

"It doesn't mean anything," Phillip answered. "We know this stuff is sensitive. Anything could be different. We'll try again later. Keep going. But I need to get home right now."

Dan nodded, and they left.

They were quiet on the ride back, Phillip suspecting they were both thinking about the same things. They said goodbye at the road split.

Then thoughts didn't get any better on the way home, the voice of Captain Karo echoing in his head, *'don't belong,' 'don't belong,' 'don't belong.'*

———— ◦ ————

Maddie had gotten sick and was bedridden most of the week, which allowed Dan and Phillip to go to the Farm almost uninterrupted. "I think it's the lack of sleep," aunt Elaine told him. "She's always been prone to insomnia..."

Phillip got most of his sleeping done at the Farm in Haystacks' stable. Sleeping on Farm days was different, like taking naps in the middle of the day. He spent his nights at the Fairchild ranch studying the books Adeline had given him. Most of which were incomprehensible. He and Dan would send each other messages all night, prompting each other to read this or that or to ask for help.

Fortinbras spent his time in Phillip's room, sometimes he used him as a sounding board and asked him various questions... linguistic standardization lent itself to the eventual formulation of standardized rhetorical power systems...'" One text said. "What the heck does that mean?" Phillip asked Fortinbras, who would wag his tail when he heard his name but never answered.

Fortinbras was a terrible study partner, but not bad company.

His Aunt Kath would always call him later than she wanted to. She kept forgetting that there was a time change between California and King's Hill.

Conversations were difficult since Phillip discovered the Farm, as he had to work around telling her any details about the Farm. He would try to turn the conversation around, as how California was. While Aunt Kath had plenty of stories, she was too astute a conversationalist not to turn the conversation back around. "Tell me what you're learning..." she would ask, and he would answer her by talking about Emily and Andy. He could talk about them as much as he wanted, almost without lying.

"You've really taken to King's Hill," Aunt Kath said.

"It's a nice place," Phillip agreed.

"I want to meet these friends you've made when I get back."

"Maybe..."

"Unless I'm not cool enough..." She said, picking up on his lack of commitment. "It's not because I'm not still cool, right? I'm super cool."

"Oh, no, yeah. Still super cool," Phillip said. "I have unrelated reasons why I'm embarrassed by you."

"That's good. So long as I'm still cool."

He had been falling asleep without realizing it. He always felt rested but his schedule was messed up. He was also having a harder time distinguishing dreams from reality. There were times when he thought he found new pages of his pink notebook but then discovered that it was morning and he was still in his clothes. Bizarre recurring dreams about the Farm and the missing cat Gingersnaps. Sometimes Haystacks looked like a standing racoon version of himself.

Some nightmares too, feeling like he was stuck at the bottom of well... bright lights flickering at the corner of his eyes. The deep feeling that something important and horrible had to be remembered but then it was lost...

For the third morning in a row he woke on Sunday in his clothes, surrounded by books. Clutching the pink notebook to his chest. At least he had taken off his pants this time... Fortinbras had jumped on the bed at some point during the night. It was early morning. The sun had just risen. He squinted his eyes out the window and saw something that didn't make sense to his waking mind.

Tents.

Three of four tents about fifty yards from the house.

Rubbing his eyes and trying to get his thoughts in order he rushed down the stairs. Stopped just long enough to put on his shoes, not bothering with pants. Fortinbras was with him.

He opened the front door and nearly tripped on a bundle of brown cloth on the porch.

It was a person. A man. Sleeping on his porch.

He started getting up.

"Pardon me. Pardon me," he said. He was bald and his clothes looked old. "I came in last night and didn't want to wake you, So I slept on the porch. By any chance do you have a bit of drink...?"

"I'm... sorry... what...?" Phillip stammered, backing up from the man.

"I'm being right rude," he interrupted, grabbing Phillip's hand with two of his and shaking it. "Asking for a drink before introductions. I'm getting old. So old. The names Bertrand. Bertrand J. Bertrand. But I'd be much more comfortable if you called me Bert."

CHAPTER
22
The Ancient Laws of Xenia

Bertrand let go of Phillip's hand as soon as Fortinbras came out.

"Hello there! Who's this?" He said as he bent down.

Fortinbras couldn't have seemed more overjoyed to see him.

"I'm sorry." Phillip said, trying to add an edge to his voice. "I don't think you can be here... this is my family's..."

"Usually..." Bertrand said to Phillip. "A host gives their name after a visitor gives theirs. At least that's how they did it my day."

"I... my name's Phillip," he replied. "But I'm sorry you can't..."

"Might I say, master Phillip." Bertrand said, still not looking at him, "that I've never been much of a boxers-man myself, but I might change my mind if I had a pair of those. Are those cartoon elephants...?"

Phillip looked down and noticed that he had not yet put on his pants.

"Wait one second," Phillip said, covering himself and going inside.

"I'd be much appreciative of some water, if you have it..."

Phillip ran inside, went upstairs and grabbed the first pair of pants he could find. He tripped when he tried to put them on and they got caught on his shoes. Limping from the fall, he went back for his phone.

He ran back to the front door, but with a moment's hesitation went into the small kitchen and got a bottle of water.

"Here," he said to Bertrand, handing him the water.

"Ah! Much appreciated. Much appreciated. Your dog speaks very highly of you. You can tell a lot from a person by how they treat their dogs."

"Uh, Thank you. Mr. Bertrand..."

"Bert," he corrected, downing the water.

"Mr. Bert," Phillip continued. "This is not my house. My uncle..."

"Bleh. Mundafold water," he said as he put the bottle down. "Has a funny taste to it."

Phillip stopped talking. *Of course, this person was from the Primafold*. He knew this before. It's why he didn't go to his uncle or call somebody the first moment he saw the tent... The tents! Plural...

"Wait. How many people are here?" Phillip asked.

"I'm just here with myself. Came in late, like I told ya'. Those fellows are Ramblers, I suspect. Northmen. Hard to say how many there are, they pack a lot to a tent... Me? I follow the Greek rules. Speaking of here are my stamps..." His hand went into his breast pocket and it came out with a small leather book.

The leather booklet felt ancient in his hand. As soon as he touched it, glowing symbols appeared on the cover and sides of the pages, simple things that looked hand drawn. He opened it to find more symbols, and notes, hundreds of thousands of words of notes. Most of them not in English. There were hand drawn maps and postcards and stamped leaves between the pages.

"You'll find on my travel log I've never gotten a bad mark. I take my duties seriously. I've been doing this for a long time," Bertrand said. "Just started up again, in fact. Can you believe that just a few weeks ago I was planning my funeral?! Real blow-out of a thing too, shame I couldn't be there... But when adventure calls it calls, I suppose. Mr. Phillip, you ever hear the expression 'purpose makes the body grow younger...?' Well I'd like to find whoever was fool enough to say that and beat them senseless," he drifted off. "Master Phillip, by any chance can I get a look at your guest book...?"

"Guest book?" Phillip said. "There's no guestbook, this is not a hotel. It's not even my..."

"No guest book...? Place like this?" Bertrand said in an incredulous voice, staring at Phillip as if for the first time. Looking him up and down, and then a rush of comprehension hit his eyes. "You've never played host before, have you? That explains so much! How long have you laid a claim on this home...?"

"That's what I'm trying to tell you. This is not my home, I don't even live here!" Phillip said.

"Hate to break the surprise to you, but I think the home feels differently," Bertrand said.

Phillip opened his mouth to argue, but Bertrand got there first, "Before you say anything else. Let me stop you. You're a... what do they call it now...? A Choicer, I suspect. Am I right? Nothing wrong with that. But you need to educate yourself on some of the basic principles we hold dear here... One of the oldest, and in my opinion one of the most important, is 'Xenia.' Spelled with an 'X' for some fool reason."

"Xenia...?" Phillip replied, getting annoyed at the situation.

"How do I explain Xenia...?" Bertrand asked himself. "I might as well try to explain friendship or laughter. Or love and family! I don't have the wherewithal to take on such a big task. Especially when I've been walking with no stops for five days straight, built up quite a sleep debt, I have," he said with a yawn, as if just remembering he should be tired. "Do you, Master Phillip, have a book on the Old Laws?"

"Um. Yes," Phillip said.

"Good. I mean it's bad. Books can't tell you what Xenia is. But it's a start, I suppose. Go and read that book... Come back to me and I'll try to fill in the gaps. Maybe bring a little something to eat. My love of dried travel meats has its limits."

Phillip, without another word, went inside the house, but instead of immediately going for the book Adeline had given him, he took his phone and sent a message to Dan.

'Are u Up??'

When Dan didn't answer he called him while looking around his room for the book.

Dan answered. "Hello...?" he said, half asleep.

"Dan, sorry about..."

"Phil...?" Dan said.

"Yes. Dan, this is Phillip. Look, I know you've been reading the book about the Old Laws..."

"Phil, it's early," Dan said, confused.

"I know, Dan. I'm sorry. But I need your help really quick. What do you know about Xenia?" Phillip continued to look around his room. *Where did I put it? How did I get so cluttered so fast?*

"Sen... e...ah?" Dan repeated. "Oh, Xenia! That's one of the Old Law things..."

"Yes! Yes, what does it say?" Phillip threw a bundle of clothes off a drawer in his closet. There it was. The book Adeline had given him—*The Old Laws: A Summary*— to which Dan had a copy. Adeline had put two copies in the mobile library.

"Let me check my notes," Dan said. Phillip heard some shuffling on the phone.

He flipped through the book, looking at the back first for an index... There it was!

Page 122...

"It's a big deal..." Dan said. "Like, a really big deal I think..."

Phillip flipped through the book. Page 122 didn't give him a definition. It was the start of an entire chapter labeled *'XENIA.'* He flipped forward to see how long the chapter was. It wasn't a chapter, it was a section of chapters... Taking up maybe a quarter of the large book ...

"Ah, here it is..." Dan said. "*'Xenia. Greek. The ancient concept of hospitality. In relation to the Old Laws, a general term that denotes the various responsibilities, expectations, and moral principles behind the guest-friendship and guest-host relationship. Specifically relating to material and nonmaterial benefits of the relationship. See also: moral reciprocity,'*" Dan quoted. "So, it's like, giving people a place to stay and eat and stuff..."

"There's a guy. At my house. He was sleeping on my porch. Asking for food!"

"No. Way." Dan replied, sounding more awake.

"I told him I'm not the owner, but he's convinced I am," Phillip explained. "There's tents outside too, by the bushes. But he says those are... *rattlers...*? Northmen maybe... Does that mean anything to you?"

"Noooooo," Dan responded. "You say they set up tents? Your family's going to notice that..."

"Yeah, no kidding... Dan, one more question. What happens if you break or violate the Old Laws? What happens if I tell these people to leave?"

"That's... unclear," Dan said. "I don't think it's official. But there's stories in the book Adeline gave us about people losing favor and their reputations. The Fae don't like it. There's also something about it strengthening the 'Hearth Bond', and helping establish 'homestead.' Hmm," Dan said something under his breath. "Did this guy show you something? Something you would call his '*Proof of reputation...*?'"

"I don't think... Wait, yes! He should be a little book with glowing symbols on it and notes!"

"That must be it. That's supposed to tell you that he's not a *creep.*"

"I don't know if that does me any good. Creep or not he's still here and..." Phillip looked out the window. "Dan, I need to call you back," He hung up the phone and ran down stairs as fast as he could, almost as he ran to the porch.

"Mr. Bertrand!" He said in a half whisper.

"Bert," Bertrand corrected. He was sitting and smoking a long pipe now. It gave off purple and pink fumes, sometimes forming images of stars or circles as it dissipated.

"Bert. You need to hide, I just noticed my uncle is up and about, and if he sees you here, I think there's going to be trouble." Uncle Jeff got up early on Sunday, aunt Elaine said so, and she mentioned the night before he might want to take the family out to church and breakfast. Which meant he was going to come and wake up Phillip. He was hoping he would just call him, but he suspected he would walk over...

"Hide?" Bertrand asked. Phillip lifted his arm and guided him up.

"Yeah, maybe the barn. No. How about inside. I have food inside the kitchen. You can go to my room. Just stay out of sight."

Bertrand seemed confused by these orders as Phillip tried to lead him inside. He moved over to the edge of the porch and peaked at the family house.

"Ah," he said in a small voice. "I get it now. You're the only one here in the Know, aren't ya'?" He looked at Phillip and slapped his leg, not waiting for an answer. "You make sense now. Well, you've gotten yourself into a complicated set of circumstances."

"Yes, which is why I need you to," he stopped talking, as he noticed uncle Jeff grabbing his shoes at the door of the family home. "I need you to hide."

"Hide?" Bertrand repeated. "Nonsense. I think I have just the thing. I know it's indecent to show thanks before you've received anything but I think you'll forgive me. Now, where is it...?" He tucked his pipe behind his ear, which continued to smoke as he bent down and retrieved an ugly brown duffle bag. Bertrand opened a side of the bag and mumbled to himself as he looked for something. Throwing out tin pots and articles of clothing that moved on their own. "I'm sure I had it in here..." He said, as he pulled out jars of glowing liquid and mechanical spiders which crawled away and a violin which floated instead of falling to the ground. "Ah! Here she is. Here she is!"

He was holding a stone statue of a large naked woman, her eyes closed in laughter. "A beauty, isn't she?" Bertrand said. He got up and put the pipe back in his mouth. Stomping his foot, a brimmed hat on the ground leapt onto his head.

"What are you doing?" Phillip asked in a rush. "What are you going to do?"

"Not to worry, master Phillip," Bertrand said, saluting Phillip. "I'm experienced, you have nothing to worry about. There should barely be any damage at all..."

And then he walked off the porch.

Not down the stairs, he went right for the side, and stepped over the railing as if it wasn't there before going around the house.

Phillip followed, wondering if he should demand that Bertrand stop what he was doing or asking what was going on, but never committing to one and saying nothing. Bertrand had gotten a shovel from somewhere and was pacing back on forth by the side of them home. Picking up clumps of dirt and giving them a sniff and a taste. "No, no. Not quite..." he said, spitting out some dirt and grass. He took another clump of dirt and said, "yes, this is it. Perfect!" And then drove the shovel into the ground.

"What are you doing?!" Phillip asked.

"I'm a little rusty, so I might need to work up to it..." Bertrand answered, as if that explained anything. He was done digging a small hole, and with the utmost of care, he lifted the tiny statue into the hole. Then looked at the sun and threw some dirt into the air before grinding it into his neck and eating some.

"What...?" Phillip began.

But before he could get out the words Bertrand took off his coat and yelled "Tak ya!" And went into a ridiculous pose, his arms jetting into the air.

"Mah! Ka! Noh!" He yelled. Bertrand adopted different poses, and started hopping, almost casually, around the half-buried stone statue. He took off his shirt while he was doing this, and then a shoe, and wasn't stopping there... "Toh Ma! Bertrand. Toh Ma!"

Two men had appeared, walking from the direction of the tents. They were both tall. One a pale man with long blond hair, the other a black man with equally long braided hair. They were both wearing rough tweed suits.

"*Go-han morgun*," the blond one said to Phillip with a pat to his chest. The black man repeated him. Phillip just waved back. The two men then looked at Bertrand, who had not stopped dancing.

"Was is dis?" The blond man asked, and Phillip knew it was a question.

Bertrand responded in a language Phillip didn't recognize. The conversation sounded casual, but Bertrand never stopped moving. "Taka sout?" Bertrand said.

"Taka sout...?" The blond man repeated, and then looked at his companion, who nodded.

The leaped forward so suddenly Phillip jumped and took a step back.

They joined Bertrand around the stone statue, continuing to jump in the air and land with loud yells and yips. They pulled off their ties and threw off their shoes just as Bertrand had done. There was no coordination between the three. The dance moves and the yelling seemed to be made up on the spot. The only constant was that all three were pulling off their clothes as they circled. "Tah! Mo ya!" Bertrand yelled. "Nah ha!" The blond man answered back while his companion howled like a wolf. Stripping off their undershirts, revealing both were covered in dark tattoos and blue paint.

Phillip just stood there. Speechless and too shocked to speak.

Fortinbras has come to watch the men dance, looking as confused as Phillip felt.

This was it. This was how the Fairchild's were going to find out...

His family. His uncle!

"Try to quiet down," he told the three dancing men, who ignored him. He ran around the house. As he feared, he saw his uncle making his way to the Dollhouse, the family dogs in tow. Rosencrantz walked ahead of uncle Jeff, Guildenstern slightly behind.

Phillip didn't know what to do, so he tried to act casual. He climbed to the porch and tried to look like he just noticed his uncle. He waived and his uncle waved back. He went out to meet him, best to keep him away from the house as much as possible.

"You're up early," his uncle said to him.

"Fortinbras had to go out to pee." Phillip lied back. "There's also this crow that keeps waking me up..." he elaborated, the second part was actually the truth. He bent down and began to pet Rosencrantz, which successfully stopped his uncle from walking forward.

"Maddie keeps saying the birds aren't acting right. Maybe they're spooked by all the construction in town, or in the house?" Uncle Jeff replied. "How's the dog doing?"

"Fortinbras? Just fine. I think he's really well trained. He probably had an owner somewhere," Phillip said in an attempt to distract his uncle. When he saw that it didn't work, he pointed back to the Fairchild house. "How are the repairs going?"

"Bad. Not as bad as we feared. But bad," his uncle replied. "The guest rooms and bathrooms are completely torn up, but the downstairs is fine. It's a good thing we're all on such an early schedule or this would be a burden. Steve and Harrison want to move to the Dollhouse with you. I keep telling them there's no room..."

A loud yelp came from behind the dollhouse.

"Did you hear that?" Uncle Jeff said. "Do you smell that? That fruity smell?" He started walking toward the dollhouse again.

Phillip scrambled. "Um, how's Maddie doing? Is she still having nightmares?" But uncle Jeff was making his way to the house now. A scowl on his face as he tilted his nose up in the air, looking for the smell.

What was he going to do? How long could he keep this up? His uncle would eventually notice the tents and Bertrand anyway. Should he act surprised? Lie? What lie would make sense? But how could he come clean? Tell the family about the Farm, about how Bertrand expected to stay here because of ancient magical laws? Have a sit-down conversation at the dinner table as he handed Steve and Harrison jars of liquid lightning as proof... What would they say? What would they do? His brain tried to imagine possibilities but he always came to the same conclusion, the family would spoil it somehow...

"Uncle Jeff..." He started.

He looked over at his uncle and stopped talking.

His uncle was distorted ahead of him.

Like he was bobbing on a boat and Phillip was on the shore. He looked around and noticed the rest of the landscape was following suit. The Fairchild house, the Dollhouse, the barns, all shaking and bobbing like ships at sea.

It was disorienting and hurt Phillip's eyes to look at...

The ground shook. A slow vibration that was building in his legs and hummed in his ears, like a train coming closer. He was losing his footing.

An earthquake? Did King's Hill get earthquakes?

The shaking grew faster, more violent.

There was a sound in the distance, like something heavy being dropped. And the shaking stopped, followed immediately by the largest and most dramatic wave yet. It felt like an elevator dropping.

It stopped.

He opened his eyes, he was on the ground.

Guildenstern was whining. Rosencrantz had his tail between his legs.

The world had returned to normal.

"Everything okay?" His uncle said ahead of him. He was on his feet. A look of confusion and worry on his face. His hands in his pockets.

He had not noticed anything... This had to do with Bertrand and those two men and whatever they were doing with that stone statue. But what had happened...?

"I'm fine," he said back to his uncle. "Just tripped over Rose. She's okay too."

"Tripped...?" He said as if still confused and looked like he was going to say more but instead turned toward the Dollhouse.

Bertrand was there, in front of the porch. He was mostly dressed again, and cleaning his shovel, which he folded up as if it was a piece of paper and put into his pocket.

Uncle Jeff froze. Bertrand didn't look up as he put back on his shoes. His pipe in his mouth.

"Uncle Jeff..." Phillip started again.

"There that smell is again," uncle Jeff interrupted. "Can you smell it? It's like fruit. Smells familiar..."

He walked right past Bertrand up the stairs of the porch.

Past the pile of magical objects,

Past the floating violin and the pants that wanted to walk on their own...
Phillip just stood there. What had Bertrand done?

Fortinbras had come around the house and was unsuccessfully trying to play with Rosencrantz.

Phillip walked up to Bertrand, who was now picking up and re-packing his things on the porch. He put away his pipe in his hat.

"What did you do...?" Phillip asked in the lowest voice he could.

Bertrand answered with a yawn. "Isn't it obvious?"

The two men he had danced with were walking back to the tents. They were holding their suits and had not bothered to get redressed. "Hey oh!" They yelped as they waved to Bertrand, who waved back.

"Now if you don't mind," Bertrand said as he walked into the home. "I think I'll take you up on that offer of food."

Phillip followed him into the home a second later. His uncle was in the kitchen. Bertrand walked into the living room.

The couches were different...

There was a white cloth tarp thrown over a piece of furniture that was not there before. Bertrand threw the cloth away, revealing a long antique couch, and sat himself down, taking off his shoes.

"What did you do?" Phillip repeated in a whisper. "Manipulate my uncle's brain for he couldn't see you? Where did this couch come from?"

"What did you say?" His uncle said from the next room.

"Oh, just talking to the dog," Phillip replied.

"Your uncle's brain?" Bertrand said with a weak laugh. "Oh, heavens and teacher no. I don't fuss with any of that. You know, I just..." Bertrand interrupted himself with a yawn. "Shored up the lines a bit, old place like this bound to have stuff tucked away. I'm here, what's happening over there is none of my business. It's your home, you'll have to tell me. Like..." Bertrand put his fists together then separating them with a snapping sound before laying down on the couch, his head on his bag, and closing his eyes.

"Phillip?" His uncle called.

"Yeah?" He answered, still looking at Phillip.

"Can't find the smell. Really familiar too," his uncle came into the living room. "I came over to tell you your aunt wants to go to church and breakfast, did I tell you that already? Steve and Harrison finally have a day off, you get to see them try to not move too much at church."

"Thanks uncle Jeff," Phillip said. Staring without blinking at his uncle in order to avoid looking at Bertrand, who was on the new old couch less than two feet away. "I'll get ready."

Bertrand was starting to snore just as uncle Jeff left the house.

Phillip poked him a few times on the shoulder. He didn't want to wake him, but he needed more answers. But Bertrand was in a deep sleep, his eyes covered by his hat. He didn't wake no matter how loud Phillip said his name or how hard he shook him.

He needed to get ready. He would need to spend the days with the Fairchild family. That would be expected. He saw no other option but to leave Bertrand here...

Walking back towards the stairs he noticed the furniture wasn't the only thing that had changed.

The wallpaper was different, so was the crown molding.

It was older and more worn. The fireplace was larger, and there was a painting of a young woman dressed in yellow holding a glass orb. There were dozens of small differences. One window was now stained glass. The banister smooth brass instead of wood. There were carpets in one room now, and almost empty bookshelves lined the hallway. There was a door under the stairs where there hadn't been before...

What had Bertrand done...? He thought over and over again uselessly.

He needed to get ready. He desperately tried to find an excuse in his mind to stay home. Maybe he could play sick... But no, that might affect his ability to go to the Farm. Nothing would do. He needed to get ready.

Phillip looked at his phone and saw about a dozen new messages from Dan.

'Whats going on??', 'I read its customary to offer drinks' 'you should offer drinks!' 'is everything okay?' 'Dont offer too much, they can take what you offer but its rude to offer too much' 'Can I call??'

Phillip called Dan, he picked after one ring.

"What's happening?!" Dan said in a rush.

"Dan, you will not believe what just happened..."

— o —

Dan *did* believe what happened, and demanded to come over as soon as possible.

"This doesn't make any sense at all! Why would there be new paintings! Why didn't your uncle notice any differences!" he said.

"I don't know, there's a ton of new stuff. Everything's a little different," Phillip responded as he walked around the house. "It's covered in dust and spider webs, like it's old." He went upstairs, and was shocked at what he saw. "Dan, there's another staircase up here now! It's really tiny, built into the wall! It goes up to a... a door. It's locked though." Phillip gave the door a few more pushes. It was shorter and thinner than average. Phillip would have to duck to walk through... If he could open it, that was.

"Phil," Dan said flatly, "I *need* to come over..."

But he couldn't. The family was expecting him. He had already said to them he needed to take a shower, that only gave him so much time, and come to think of it, he *did* need to take a shower.

A thought occurred to him. What if the bathroom had changed too? It turned into an antique china room or a closet, and he couldn't take a shower.

This would be a huge problem. He almost jogged to the upstairs bathroom, trying to remember how it looked for he could register any changes. *Was the tile white and black or white and grey?*

He opened the door. Which he was sure was white and not blue before...

It was the same.

As far as he could tell nothing was different. Which was unexciting, but still a relief.

He didn't have much time anyway, and took a shower as fast as possible, still looking around to see any change. Did the pipes always whine like that when he turned them on? Was that small painting of a sail ship always there?

He stopped the shower when it occurred to him that he should really be writing all this down. Still wet he went to his room, grabbed his pink notebook, and wrote down everything he could until his aunt Elaine messaged him to ask if he was getting ready. He threw everything that was important to him in the closet, which didn't lock but it felt safer there than being in the room... Which also only locked from the inside. He decided to bring some of his most important items—his Shepherd notes, his lashing glove and pocket knife, his pink notebook—with him. He went downstairs and found Bertrand still sleeping and snoring. There was no way to kick or force him out that Phillip could find, and it was probably a bad idea to do that anyway. He didn't understand the magical laws of Xenia but from what he could gather Bertrand, when he was a guest, would not be a danger to him... *Hopefully.* Not knowing what else to do he left a note in front of Bertrand. *'Went out with my family. Be back soon.'* And with a great deal of hesitation wrote, *'food and drink in the kitchen.'*

Should he lock the door with Bertrand inside? *That didn't seem right...* he thought, but found that the decision was made for him, as the door had changed. The lock was different. A large circular brass thing with a bigger rounder keyhole. *That could be a problem.* How would his family be able to lock the door from now on?

Fortinbras did like Bertrand, if that was any judge of character, he even sat in front of the couch Bertrand was on when Phillip walked out the door.

It didn't feel right walking away from the house, but that's what he did.

"Philly cheeeeese!" He heard Steve or Harrison, who couldn't tell which, say from inside the house before he went in. The family was all energetic, well dressed, and in mostly good-moods. Matthew was on the verge of cracking up or crying, his face suggesting that he was trying to decide which one was more appropriate. "Looking good, Philly cheese," Harrison said. "I wish I could clean up so nice," Steve continued. "It's probably because he has his own place," Harrison finished.

Maddie was the only one who was not energetic.

"Why are you bringing your bag?" Maddie asked Phillip.

"I'm vain," Phillip explained. "It goes with the outfit..."

Maddie rolled her eyes, which he noticed had dark circles under them.

"Maddie hasn't been sleeping," Harrison explained as he ruffled Maddie's hair why she swatted at him, "Woke up this morning because she thought there was an earthquake..."

"Shut up..." Maddie shouted.

"Harrison, stop bugging your sister," aunt Elaine ordered. "And Steve, get Matthew's bags and stroller in the car like I asked."

The church was right outside of the main strip of downtown. It looked like somebody had built a wooden country church on top of an old style brick and stone one. A wooden steeple built on stone archways and a tile roof. *'CHURCH of CHRIST the SAVIOR and TEACHER'* it said in front. "It's nondenominational," uncle Jeff explained. "Oldest church in town. Moved from another location brick by brick." Phillip was surprised when a man in green robes at the front of the church, who looked ancient with a long white beard, conducted the mass in a different language. Latin, uncle Jeff explained... Not having much experience with this, Phillip wondered if this was unusual. Phillip forgot to ask when it ended. His aunt and uncle got into conversations while everybody else under the age of eighteen went outside to the courtyard to play and talk. Steve and Harrison put on their red caps as soon as they went outside, and pressured Phillip to do the same.

'Did you leave Bert at the house,' Dan asked by message.

'Couldnt think of what else to do' Phillip responded.

'Thats best' Dan answered back. *'reading as fast as I can. Can I come over??'*

Conversation turned to his aunt and uncle questioning about the program he had joined. Phillip and Dan had already thought about how to answer these questions. Be vague, change the subject, talk about people, and a couple made up stories they both memorized. He told them about Emily, Andy, and Pieter. When they asked what he's studying, he told them he mostly spent time with other learners, going to different lectures, which was true enough. Maddie squinted her eyes during the entire conversation.

"You must have met Mr. Roach? The math teacher, he's the head there," Maddie said.

Sensing a trap, Phillip replied. "Can't say I have met him, you say he's around...?"

Maddie just squinted her eyes harder.

King's Hill was a pleasant place on Sunday, the weather was nice too, but Phillip found himself distracted as they walked the shop lined streets back to the car. *What was happening at home?* He thought, had Bertrand burnt it down in some ritual? Killed the dogs? Stolen everything the Fairchild family owned and left...?

Maddie was also trying to corner him and ask pointed questions. He found he could avoid her by asking Steve and Harrison something about the Crimson Harts or uncle Jeff anything about the town.

Messages came in from Dan.

'Srry.' One first said.

'I came over. Hard time finding place.'

'Phil, what happened to your house!!!'

'????'

'I'm here now'

Phillips stomach spun and tighten into a knot. *'What happened to the house!'* Phillip messaged back, *'explain!'* He sent.

But Dan didn't answer back.

The entire way home he just looked out the window, searching trails of smoke or some other evidence that the Fairchild ranch had burnt to the ground.

He didn't find any. And when they turned into the house driveway, he found that it was still there. No burning, no army of looters walking away with their stuff.

"You okay there, Phillip?" His uncle asked.

"Oh, yeah, just distracted," he answered as everybody got out of the car and brought things in, a considerable task with a baby in tow. "Hey, I'm going to get dressed out of these clothes. I'll be right back."

It was an almost impossible task trying to walk at a normal speed and seem casual. The house was still here. Same as always. Maybe Dan had come over and then left? This was proven wrong as soon as Phillip got closer to the house. Dan's bike lay on the ground in front of the Dollhouse.

Phillip heard music. It was the men who had set up the tents. They were playing something rhythmic, with drums and a flute. He could also see through the trees that they had started a fire. A large fire. There had to be at least five people around it. Phillip walked around the home. "Dan?!" He yelled as loud as he felt safe. "Dan?!"

He looked right and noticed something else. The barn.

The barn was... *different.*

No, it was new! There were two new barns where there hadn't been any before.

One tall and made out of thick stone and wood, an old roof that overhung the building and was supported by thick stone pillars. The other was low and wooden, with a roof that looked half-thatched, half-tile. Both buildings were surrounded by a thicket of trees and bushes. They looked old. Nature reclaiming them both. How had he not noticed these this morning...? He had been so distracted with Bertrand and what happened with his uncle and getting ready he hadn't noticed. A small hill he was sure was new.

Fortinbras wagged his tail and met Phillip on the porch. "Have you seen Dan, Fortinbras?" Phillip asked.

Bertrand was still sleeping on the new couch. Phillip ran upstairs, checking the bathroom, the master bedroom. His room. Nothing. He checked his phone again. No new messages. He sent one to Dan instead. *'Back home. Where are you???'*

Just when he was about to call Dan he looked out the window.

Dan was by the tree-line, he was standing next to the fire the men had built.

Relieved and breathing normally for the first time since the message, Phillip ran downstairs and outside. "There you are!" He yelled.

Dan turned around, he was holding a small thin drum, and was beating it, almost in line with the rhythm of the music. "Phil!" He said. ``Thank God you're back, I didn't see you come up. I thought I was at the wrong place, but then I saw Fortinbras on the deck and... Phil! What happened here?" Dan handed his small drum to another man Phillip hadn't seen before but who could have been the brother of the blond man he had seen earlier. There were now six people at the little camp, and three tents. An old man with an eye patch slept under a tree, a woman played the flute while another danced in a long skirt. The man Phillip had seen earlier... still not completely clothed.

"I'll explain everything," Phillip said, as he walked back toward the house. Phillip told Dan everything he could remember, out of order. Dan listened without questioning until the end.

"But where did your family's home go?" Dan asked.

"What do you mean, it's right there..." Phillip pointed to the Dollhouse. "It's just different, and now there's new barns..."

"No, I mean the bigger home!" Dan said. "Where did it go?"

Phillip didn't know how to answer that. And with a sudden jolt of comprehension asked Dan a question. "Dan, look behind me, do you see the big home? Do you see the car?" He asked.

Dan took a second to answer. "No... they're gone."

"Dan! I see them, I came home in the car, the rest of my family is in the house!" Phillip said in a rush. "You can't see the big house or the family cars just like my uncle couldn't see Bertrand! But you can see the new barns. Dan can you see the old barns, the one I got the bike out of?"

"No, everything is gone," Dan said. "Phil! This. Is. *The most* incredible thing. But where...? Why is this...?" He laughed. "What if I want to go to your family house?"

"I don't know. I really don't know anything. We should talk to Andy and Emily..." Phillip said.

"Good idea,' Dan said, distracted. "Phil, there's more. look..." Dan went into his backpack and retrieved the small black orbit ball from his bag. "I didn't mention it, but I brought my orbit ball over earlier. Thing is, it didn't work. I mean, it acted just like a normal ball. Doesn't work at my house either. But now..." Dan gave the ball a little toss, it circled Phillip before returning back to Dan. "It works now!" He said, and as if to make the point harder, he threw the ball hard to his side. It flew away and circled the entire Dollhouse before coming back to the place where it had been thrown. "I'm getting really good at it..." Fortinbras had come off the porch, deciding that the ball was something to be interested in.

"I need to wake Bertrand, ask him what he did with that statue thing..." Phillip said.

Dan went back into his backpack and retrieved bundles of paper and a book. "Took notes. Waking him is considered rude. I just happened to read that. Look, it's right here," he opened the large book to a tab he had set. "Frequent travelers sometimes travel overnight, walk for days at a time without sleeping.

It's called something but I can't remember what... It's a branch of magic tied to... deferment... or something, of pain and stuff. They can walk for days but eventually they need to make up the sleep they... the book uses the word 'promised', their bodies," he handed Phillip the book, "There's also something else I noticed... Do you have anywhere I can put this down, a table maybe?"

Phillip brought Dan inside. Being careful not to wake Bertrand. "Everything is different!" Dan said as they walked in. Phillip brought him to what was a back dining or living room. There was a table in there now, and a cabinet filled with fine china and some other items made of brass Phillip didn't recognize. Dan threw his bundles of papers on the table.

"Did you find anything that explains even a little of what all this means?" Phillip asked.

"What does what mean?" A voice said behind him. It was Maddie.

Phillip turned around and tried to recover from the surprise. Dan started talking but Phillip didn't hear him. "Just wondering about the... meaning of life," Phillip said.

"Who were you talking to?" Maddie asked in her usual pointed way.

"What's going on?" Dan said at the same time.

Phillip turned his head between Dan and Maddie, realization hitting him.

"Oh, just talking to Forty..." Phillip said to Maddie.

"You're talking to Fortinbras?" Maddie responded.

"What are you talking about?" Dan asked. "What are you looking at?"

Dan looked down the hallway, not seeing Maddie. The same way Maddie couldn't see him.

"I'll explain later," Phillip said in a low voice to Dan, but facing Maddie.

"Explain what later?" Maddie asked, and then furrowed her brow and looked around "Do you hear music?"

"I... do not," Phillip answered. "but I do need to get myself dressed so if you don't mind..." Phillip grabbed Maddie's shoulder to steer her toward the door, but as soon as he did, something happened.

The house... shifted.

It was not loud or dizzying or disorienting. It felt natural and easy, like reversing a jacket.

The walls changed again. Gone were the bookshelves. The portrait of the women in the yellow dress. The banister had changed. Phillip noticed dozens of small changes as his head darted around the room. The house was back to what it had been before, except Bertrand and the new couch were still in the living room, he turned around. Dan was still there too, his face confused.

"What's wrong with you?" Maddie said, looking up at his face.

"Where are you going?" Dan said at the same time.

Maddie screamed and Dan jumped. They looked each other right in the eyes.

"When did you get in here?!" Maddie yelled.

Dan didn't answer, but looked at Phillip.

"Dan just came over, Maddie, didn't you notice?" Phillip lied.

"Stop gaslighting me!" Maddie said. "No, he wasn't I was just in that room there's no way..."

"Gaslighting...?" Phillip repeated.

"It's a movie thing!" Maddie yelled as an explanation.

"Sorry I scared you, Maggie," Dan said.

"Maddie!" Maddie corrected.

"Yeah, sorry," Dan continued, and then walked into the hallway, but then stopped and looked around, at the walls and the furniture and over the fireplace. "Huh," he said, before catching Phillip's eyes again. The house had changed back for him too. But Maddie still hadn't noticed the snoring man sleeping on the couch...

"I do need to get dressed, Dan's just here to drop off something from the program, I forgot it," Phillip said, but then realized Maddie would probably follow up with a question and decided to change the subject. "Do you think it would be okay with your mom if Dan came over for dinner?"

This almost worked, it stopped Maddie in her tracks and caught her off guard for a second, "I don't know, I'll ask..." She said, but not to be deterred she immediately followed with, "he was *not* in that room. And I *do* hear music... and that bird. And I wasn't dreaming there was an earthquake. Why don't you just tell me...?"

"Maddie, I do really have to get dressed and Dan reminded me that I'm missing some homework I have to do so if you don't mind..." Phillip said as fast as he could, gently guiding Maddie to the door.

"Phil...? We could just..." Dan started.

"Maddie!" He heard aunt Elaine yell in the distance.

Maddie looked annoyed and went on the porch, "I'm over here mom!" She yelled back.

Aunt Elaine yelled something incomprehensible. Maddie said "What?!" a couple times before groaning and walking back to her house. "I'll be right back," she said to Phillip in the tone of a parent who was telling their child she hadn't forgotten they had broken the rules.

"Bye Maddie," Dan said with a wave, which Maddie returned with a suspicious look. "Phil..." He said when she was gone, "we could just..."

"Dan, tell me," Phillip interrupted. "Look out the window. Do you see the big house now? The other barns."

Dan looked out the windows. "Yeah!" he yelled, but then looked at the sleeping Bertrand and whispered. "It's there. I see everything again. Man, this is weird."

"It happened when I touched Maddie's shoulder..." Phillip explained.

And then something occurred to him, and he walked over and touched Dan's shoulder.

No change.

"Touch the couch," Dan said.

Phillip did so. Again, no change. Impulsively, he touched Bertrand as light as he could on the shoulder...

The room shifted again, a small turning, a little flip... and the room was changed.

The painting was back on the larger fireplace. Dan looked around, noticing the change too. He laughed and then clapped his mouth shut when he looked at Bertrand, who shifted a little on the couch. Dan looked out the window again.

"What do you see?" Phillip asked.

Dan moved from window to window. "Everything. The house. The new barns. Everything..." Dan answered.

But the mystery couldn't be solved now.

Phillip and Dan experimented, with Phillip touching random objects in the room in different sequences. He touched Bertrand's shoulder again, but there was no change. They did this until his family called him and Dan announced that he should really be getting home with the promise from Phillip that he would message him with any changes, anything at all. "You sure you can get home?" Phillip asked.

"I got here fine," Dan answered. "When I follow the same path it's easy..."

Phillip desperately wanted to continue exploring the Dollhouse, maybe go over to the new barns. Try to talk to the men and women who had set up camp. But he couldn't avoid going back to the Fairchild's home and having dinner. What would he do when night came around and he had to sleep? Should he try to feed Bertrand? He already offered him food and drink in the kitchen.

The question answered itself, as evening came Bertrand was just as asleep. The men and women of the camp were louder, the music faster. The flame in the middle of camp had grown taller, it swirled and danced in line with the music, sometimes changing its own color. Turning itself into an image of a dancing woman. *FaeFlame.*

The yellow bird was back on the porch, seemingly unbothered by any changes. Phillip grabbed the seeds he placed by the door, and went to feed him.

CHAPTER 23

Grabbing Mist

The Dollhouse wasn't done changing.

Phillip came back from dinner and movie at the Fairchild house to find the kitchen was different. It was larger, almost twice as large. The appliances missing or replaced with doors. There was a thick stone raised fireplace affixed with metal where the oven had been, a small wooden door where the fridge was. It was covered in cobwebs and dust.

He took one look at the kitchen and then ran to get his pink notebook. Dan had messaged him that he should record what was happening in there, and that drawings would be a nice touch. "I'll add anything to the list," Dan said on the phone. The "list" was the endless shared list of things they didn't understand that Dan was compiling.

But he had nothing for Dan, as when he came back to the kitchen it had reverted back to the one he was used to.

He entered and re-entered the home a dozen times. Closed his eyes, opened them.

Spun around. Nothing.

The new kitchen was gone, for now.

This happened several more times. Phillip didn't know whether it was the fact that he could spend some time in the house without thinking about the Fairchild family or if night had anything to do with it, but he was sure these things were happening more when the sun set. The house creaked and moaned more than it ever had before. At one-point Phillip was sure there were a dozen men climbing up the stairs. But found nothing when he investigated.

The men and women camping outside played music almost all night. Rhythmic drumming and flutes and sometimes singing. The multi-colored flame dimmer as the night went on but still dancing.

For these reasons, among many, he got a terrible night's sleep.

At least, he thought, *my bed hadn't disappeared.*

Dan was messaging him throughout the night with various random thoughts or things he had discovered. *'Can't find anything on Ramblers, u sure you got that right?'* *'You should offer people drinks. The book says it's important to offer people drinks.'*

He sat in bed with most of his clothes on, it felt odd getting comfortable given the circumstances.

Phillip played with his lashing glove. It was a great purchase, in Phillip's opinion. He managed to repair the split drawers with it.

Dan had left his orbit ball there too, which proved hours of fun. He found that when it bounced against a wall it traveled back on its own orbit. He drew a circle mid-air with his sky chalk and tried to throw the ball so it would skirt the edges.

It felt like magic. Like *doing* magic. And Phillip couldn't get enough of it. He had a moment of clarity around three or four A.M., and laughed at the strange events and circumstances he was surrounded in. *It was all so incredible*, so *wonderful, even the bad and stressful stuff*, he thought, and resolved to not worry so much...

He awoke to the sound of a shower, surprised initially that he had fallen asleep, and that sunlight was streaming through the windows. The orbit ball was still making little circles above him where he left it, he remembered wondering how long it would last in the air, he must have fallen asleep.

He leaped off the bed and put on his shoes. Taking one look outside at the tents. They were finally quiet. The flame at the center of the camp now just a plume of barely visible white smoke, wafting into the air at sharp unnatural angles.

Phillip went to the upstairs bathroom he wasn't there. Bertrand must be using the downstairs bathroom, but he could have sworn that wasn't working. But he was wrong. The sound of rushing water wasn't coming from the master bathroom, it was coming from the hallway closet... Which had a stream of water vapor coming out of the bottom of the door...

He heard an ugly sound inside.

Was Bertrand... singing?

The door swung open in a flurry of steam and sound. Bertrand came out, yawning and singing at the same time. Drying his hair with a small towel, the rest of him covered by a bathrobe two sizes too small.

"Morning," Bertrand said, closing the door behind him and walking away toward the kitchen. "Had to wash the road off me."

"No problem," Phillip answered. Going to the door Bertrand had closed and opening it, it was a closet. A small closet. Filled to the brim with forgotten old clothing and boxes from the Fairchild family. Phillip opened and closed the door eight more times, just to be sure.

"Mr. Bertrand...?" Phillip began.

"Bert," Bertrand corrected in the other room.

"Mr. Bert," Phillip said, following Bertrand into the kitchen. "Could you tell me...?"

Phillip stopped. The kitchen had changed again. Bertrand was wiping dust away from the raised fireplace. 'WORTHINGTON FINE CUSTOM COOKING HEARTHS.' It said on the side.

Phillip went to the door which had replaced the fridge. It was raised off the ground about six-inches. He opened and found a room, a room far too large to be accommodated by the space he was in. The room was covered wall to wall in shelves. It was chilly in here, the light provided by a vine with glowing flowers, which opened and grew brighter as Phillip walked in. One side of the room was covered in ice. In fact, Phillip saw, it was snowing lightly.

A pantry, Phillip concluded.

"What were you hoping to ask me?" Bertrand said through a yawn in a weak voice.

Phillip closed the door to the pantry. "I was hoping you could tell me what you did yesterday..." Bertrand was sitting at the table, which was also new, he had put what looked like a mangled soup can in front of him that was emitting flames, on top he had a pan he had put eggs and meat in. "Why is the house different?" Phillip continued.

"Isn't it obvious?" Bertrand said eating right out of the pan. "I just, you know. Snap. Poof," he said with a flourish of his hands.

"Could you explain what 'snap' and 'poof' mean...?"

"I just... took the... tucked stuff and" Bertrand's mouth was full, and his voice going in and out, he sounded drunk, or half-asleep. He finished his food and began walking back to the living room. "Couldn't be simpler... Just made the separation... Cleaner. It was wasting away, you know. Unmanaged and forgotten. Surprised it didn't collapse completely," he looked out the window. "Made choices like that. It's a sad thing. Losing and being lost... God, I miss what was lost. I threw it away, Master Phillip. Threw it all away. Had to. No choice. That's not true, dammit, it's not true at all. It was my choice, would make it again. But God do I hate it..." He looked at Phillip, barely registering he was there. Bertrand got up and walked back to the living room.... Have to live with what I am, what I've done, what the world is. That's what wise men do... I sometimes wonder if... my own vanity... I lied to myself, you see... Master Phillip, knew I was lying and did it anyway..." He dropped back on the couch. "Wonderful old house..." He said, barely able to form the words, before falling over and laying down.

Phillip ran over. "Bertrand!?" He said, giving him a shake. He was snoring again... "Bertrand!?"

It was no use. Bertrand was asleep again. Phillip looked down and saw that the small bath robe wasn't even trying to do its job of concealing Bertrand. "Jeeeez," Phillip said and looked away, going upstairs to get the small extra blanket. He carefully put it over Bertrand, who immediately grabbed it and spun on the couch into a more comfortable position.

The kitchen remained changed this time. Which was inconvenient, as most of Phillip's food was in the other kitchen. He opened some cabinets and found one filled to the brim with colorful bottles. Mostly wine and liquor. *'Offer drinks'* he remembered Dan said, and decided to take out two of the bottles. He put one in front of Bertrand under the note he wrote yesterday. He put on his shoes and—with Fortinbras in tow—went to the camp in the woods.

There were seven people outside the tents, some talking, some patching cloths. A barefoot woman in a red dress was asleep in a precarious position in a tree on a low branch.

When the men Phillip had seen yesterday saw him, they leaped up and spoke in what Phillip took as a greeting. They seemed thrilled to see him.

"I thought you might, uh, like a drink," Phillip said, handing them the clear bottle.

The blond man took the bottle and looked so thankful to Phillip that he thought he might cry. "Yeeesss! Yis," he said with a cheer, holding the bottle up to applause and yells from the other campers. He hugged Phillip, and patted him on the back, he was joined by two or three others, included another woman who tried to guide him into the camp.

"Oh, no, not right now, have to go," he said to them, motioning that he had to go. They nodded and seemed to understand.

Phillip got ready as fast as he could. He fed Fortinbras and left some food for the yellow bird and the crow. Excited to meet Dan at the Farm and tell Andy, Emily, and Haystacks what had happened.

———— ○ ————

"I've never heard of anything like that..." Emily said.

Dan had gotten there first and already started telling the story. Meeting with Andy and Emily in Haystacks' stable had become a morning routine. So much so that Haystacks and Henry had set up a raised platform with a table, chairs, and a good helping of snacks and tea.

"Sounds like a split home," Andy said with a full mouth.

"It is most certainly a split," Haystacks said.

"But that doesn't make sense... You can't just make a split on another person's property," Emily continued. "The principles of homestead..."

"Can somebody explain that...?" Phillip interrupted, frustrated, but then felt bad and gave Emily and apologetic look.

"What's a split?" Dan added more specifically.

"We mean he Folded the house..." Emily explained.

"I don't think this... Bertrand fellow did that..." Haystacks continued. "It was clearly already Folded. You can't fold a crafted object. he just opened it back up. Only thing that makes sense. Heck if I know how though."

The group was met by confused and blank looks by Dan and Phillip.

Andy was the first to realize what was happening. "I thought we explained Folds to you?"

"Assume we're dumb," Phillip replied.

"Done," Andy said.

"... what's a split home...? Explain the Fold thing again."

"Ummm," Andy said, unsure of what to say in a most un-Andy-ish way. "I don't know how to explain it, I don't remember learning it…"

"Imagine this table is a bit of land," Emily went forward, "and you're a teacup, you travel on this table on day," she moved the teacup on the table as if it was talking. "And the table gets used to you. But then another teacup comes by and starts sitting on the table. Most of the time the table will change what it's used to, or the teacups will come in conflict. But sometimes, rarely, the table will fold itself. Accommodating both teacups…"

"Emily, I love you like a sister, but that was a terrible explanation," Andy said.

"Well if you think you can do better…" Emily retorted.

"I do not," Andy replied.

"So, a Fold, it's like… another world…" Dan ventured.

"No, no, no. It's a *fold*, Daniel," Emily said, as if it explained everything.

"It's like a square of cloth," Andy said putting the end of her long black over-shirt on the table. "Stretchy cloth. You can fold it on itself and then it stretches back to its original shape. Same everything, just two layers now."

"Now that," Haystacks added. "Is a terrible explanation. I should know I just used that same metaphor."

"You'll get used to it," Emily added. "We all grew up with this, it's like explaining what down and up is. It becomes obvious in time."

"What we are confused about," Haystacks continued, "is how this traveler of yours was able to split the Fold back open. And it's clearly an old fold. You shouldn't be able to do that on another person's land, let alone a house built by a human. I've never heard of anybody being able to do that… Do you think Bertrand could be… is it possible he's an Inheritor? I've never heard of him." Haystacks now seemed very grave.

"Not possible," Andy said. "My family… would have noticed…"

"What's an Inheritor?" Phillip said, remembering that he heard 'inheritors' mentioned before.

"What about King's Hill…?" Dan asked at the same time.

"The Mundafold town, what about it?" Andy replied.

"That's just the thing, it's not on the maps I have in Knoxville…" Dan said. "It doesn't exist unless I'm there. Does that mean it exists only in the Primafold…?"

"No… well… huh, that *is* weird," Andy said. "I thought it was the biggest Mundafold entrance to the Farm… but if it's not on the Mundafold maps… but nobody there knows about the Primafold. I don't know what that could mean… Phillip, I want to come over to your house. Emily too. Maybe meet Bertrand."

"Sure," Phillip said. "My family already knows about you guys. Not that you can do magic or anything. They think we're in a special educational program."

"Hah! Full Privilege is great," Andy said. "By why not just tell them…?"

"What is an Inheritor, by the way? Phillip interrupted.

"Tough question." Haystacks answered. "The Inheritors are people, all humans. They have Inherited the right to make and collapse folds... at will. And a lot of other things..."

"That sounds like what Bertrand did!" Dan said.

"Yes, it does," Haystacks said as Andy shook her head. "Very powerful people, the Inheritors, as you can imagine. Sometimes it takes generations to create a strong fold, or get rid of one. They can do it in moments. Some don't believe they have any real power, at least not in the way most understand them. And almost everybody disagrees on how they got this power or how they pass it along," he said, uncharacteristically grave. "Most people think the Pauls are Inheritors. I do..."

A thought occurred to Phillip. "When that General Waltzrigg guy was talking to the Pauls, he mentioned their... friends, and asked point blank if they were 'choosing a successor.' Were they talking about other Inheritors? The ones they're not letting in?" The conversation made more sense. "Is... that what the Farm is, some sort of *contest* to see who gets to be a successor to the Pauls?"

Haystacks looked at Phillip as if his son was just learning to walk and he couldn't be prouder. "That's what a lot of people think. That's why a lot of people are here. Why the Wallmen stand being treated like hired guards and bureaucrats. Nobody knows what the Pauls are doing, why they are removing restrictions which will certainly put them in conflict with every great power. Why they've invited almost everybody under the sun, from banished unFae to Shadowkin to Choicers like you..."

"And why..." Andy said, "so many people and beings are trying to get into the place. Some of which are succeeding..."

"Andy, that was told to us in confidence..." Emily whispered.

"And I'm telling it to the rest of the Welcoming Committee *in confidence,*" Andy replied.

"Is that why everybody is here?" Phillip asked. "To try to inherit something...?"

"I'm here to stretch my legs. See what can be done and what's happening," Haystacks replied. "Been needing a vacation anyway."

"My family sent my brother and me to observe," Andy said.

"Mine too," Emily said.

"... and everybody is waiting for the Farm's purpose to reveal itself," Phillip continued. Everybody in the room nodded except for Dan, Henry, Buttercup, and Dryrot. "But you said things are getting in that shouldn't?"

Nobody answered right away, but Andy was nodding her head.

"There have been infiltrations," Emily answered. "Everybody has heard about them. All minor, nothing dangerous, don't worry. But it shouldn't be possible. They've been purifying the Farm practically every day... The Pauls and most of the top staff are gone most of the time. Patching holes. And something is happening in the Swamp... A highFea maybe. Some small Fea named Tutana has been ascended to Queen level and is calling the Swamp her dominion. But we shouldn't be talking about this..."

"Yes, we *should*, because I've recruited them into my special project. The informal and secret part of the Welcoming Committee," she paused for dramatic effect. "I call it the *Unwelcoming Committee*. Charged with figuring out why things are sneaking into the Farm."

"Sounds fun," Phillip said.

"I'm in! Sounds important," Dan said.

Emily shook her head back and forth while drinking tea, but was smiling.

"If we're being serious about security here, I think I have some advice," Phillip said. "Check the white fence that surrounds the place, Dan and I were able to jump it easy..."

<hr />

Morning tea ended abruptly as Emily and Andy realized they were running late.

They were told to buy a few books to understand Folds and Emily suggested to Phillip that, since he is living in a split home now, he should really invest in a good housekeeping book. "Split homes are very difficult to maintain. Never lived in one myself, but that is what I've heard," she said.

Andy didn't say much more about the Unwelcoming Committee. There wasn't much more to say, seeing as she just recently made it up. She did take the time to give Dan and Phillip titles though. 'Jr. High Inquisitor' and 'Assistant Executioner' respectively.

Before morning tea ended Phillip was able to ask a couple more questions.

The 'Ramblers', Phillip was told, were likely Northmen or Faroekin, they traveled with different rules than most Primafold travelers. They mostly kept to themselves, and never took too much, ethically they tried to leave the land the same or better then when they found it. It was also hard to evict them from land, even given Homestead rules.

Phillip reminded himself to read up more on the 'Homestead Rules.'

"They will almost never speak anything besides new Faroese," Emily explained. "Every Faroekin is paid a stipend to maintain the purity of the language and keep it alive. That's what makes it so useful formalized magic systems like NEKSS."

And Phillip wrote down a few more things to look up.

Haystacks class was cancelled... again. This time with a conflict involving an infestation of fish or something. But he continued giving Dan and Phillip private lessons, without any success.

Dan and Phillip suffered through another dismal Circles Class. This one involved a game where the class was divided in two. One side of the room trying to make bright red grass grow with circles to promote sunlight and prevent pests, the other side trying to get green grass to do the same, until one side of the room took over the other. The classroom was a madhouse of laughs and yells and declarations that "it's not fair!" as Miss Julie refereed. Unfortunately, Dan and

Phillip were on the same team, and caused their side of the classroom to lose as their circles did nothing to help. Thamus was particularly disappointed, but decided to channel that disappointment into some useful advice, "maybe you shouldn't play games right now..." He said before Miss Julie hushed him.

Dan had signed them up for a class he heard was going to be great but was only held on 'clear nights.' It was called 'Mist-Gathering' and Dan said it was, "what those guys were doing next to those blue doors.

They found themselves on the first night of Farm time on the grass next to one the larger lakes and an ancient looking wooden shack. Some lamps were set up around boxes and a stage. A sign instructed them to 'TAKE A CLOAK.'

Two dozen people sat around for almost an hour in dark black cloaks with pointed with tilted pointed hoods, talking only in whispers because another sign said in angry lettering 'DO NOT SPEAK LOUDLY!'

A bell rang out. It was so low and soft that Phillip almost thought he imagined it.

A man walked out of the wooden shack. He was so tall he had to duck past the doorway and so thin he almost looked sickly. He was bald, he had no eyebrows above almost white eyes. He smiled and nodded to the crowd, and put up his hand when they started to clap or murmur. Grabbing a round amber lantern attached to a stick, he walked away from the crowd into the tall grass, which parted for him.

The crowd took this as an instruction to follow. The ground was wet. Water seeped into Phillip's shoes as he walked. They came to clearing where the tall bald man had stopped, by lanterns sticking out of the ground. When everybody had arrived, and surrounded him in a half circle he gestured with his hands that had long boney fingers as if he was pushing the crowd lower.

Sit down? On the wet ground? People around Dan and Phillip were as confused by these orders as they were.

The crowd registered surprise at around the same time. As they bent down to sit their black cloak grew rigid in the back, changed shape, until when they were in a sitting position it was as if they were sitting on a wooden chair that didn't exist.

"This is cool," Phillip whispered to Dan.

The bald man heard him and put a finger to his mouth for the entire crowd. Nothing more than total silence would do.

The lamp went dark. The bald man sat down himself.

They waited, for how long it was hard to say, but his eyes were able to adjust to the darkness. Thick fog began filling the clearing, until it was difficult to see people just fifteen yards away.

The bald man got up. Slowly and smoothly but given that there had been no movement it felt dramatic. He walked towards the crowd and rolled up the sleeves of his cloak. He spun his fingers and hands around in front of him as if he was tying long strings together. He closed his eyes, sometimes shifting or jerking in one direction or another. He looked like a bad mime in the middle of an act.

He stopped moving. Opened his eyes. Smiled to the crowd, and pulled.

The fog was yanked out of the air. As if it was a blanket put in front of Phillip's face. As if it was a curtain yanked from a window. The bald man pulled and gathered the fog to himself, the fog itself bundling up in front of him. It did this until the fog around the crowd had disappeared completely. The bald man held a large bundle of fog, which looked more like impossible thin cloth. He took out a small bag and began shoving the fog into it until it disappeared from sight.

"My name is Elias Fogsmith," he said in a dry voice that was almost a whisper but was at easy to hear. "I keep the old naming rules, obviously. My family have been gatherers since as far back as we can trace, before the true King Shepherd forced everybody to have last names. I am a Housemaster of *'Loyal Brother and Sisterhood of Gatherers'*. And while I have always been supportive of women joining my trade I must admit the name was better before," a few chuckles across the crowd. The fog was rolling in again. Elias snapped his fingers, the lantern on the stick hopped over to his hand and relit itself. "Follow me," he said, walking deeper into the marsh. Sitting up was as easy as sitting down, the dark cloak losing its rigidity when Phillip got up.

"Gathering is one of the oldest disciplines you're likely to encounter," Elias said as they walked. "Almost everybody can learn how to do it, but it takes a lifetime to do it well. In a few weeks most of you will be able to grab clouds, which are easier to grab than mist or fog but harder to gather, or smoke, which is a good learning tool and useful in the home. But it takes years to learn how to grab and wrangle a storm cloud, or even a little rain cloud..."

"I thought those were gathered with kites," a man interrupted.

"Yes, which is a fair deal more difficult than what we are going to do tonight. But if we did not take the time to learn it half the usable land just west of the frontier line would go barren in a month," Elias continued. "Has anybody here seen a traveling storm show? Especially one around Shikaakwa?" Some people nodded or raised their hands. "The Native discipline of gathering is different than what I am able to teach you. It is more about hunting, and snaring. Which can make what you are gathering angry, but they have different methods of control. I am not a purist, as much as I might look like one. There are advantages and disadvantages to both methods. Now, line up at the lake..."

They did what he said, and as soon as they were there, thick tendrils of fog came from the lake, dozens of them, passed the crowd of students. Phillip gave an exploratory poke to the tendril, which felt like nothing.

"You do not gather with your hands," Elias said. "Mist is harder to gather than most others. But it is a fine learning tool. You gather with your whole self. Gatherers have a reputation for being more *mystically* inclined than most. I will tell you that this is true. It is hard to do this for long without feeling the pull of the old beliefs..."

He walked over, right to where Phillip and Dan were standing. He put his hand into the closest tendril of fog. "When you go to pick up a heavy bucket of water. You know you will fail if you try to grip the side with one hand and lift straight up. It is intuitive. You understand you must grab the handle, or the lip, or use two hands and grab the bottom of the bucket. It is the same with mist and cloud and smoke," his hand was waving inside the tendril of fog flowing back and forth as if the fog was a current and the hand a passive passenger. "You must intuit the mist. Understand where it can be grabbed and where it is slippery. This is a matter of mindset. You must work with the mist. Put your hands in the mist now," the crowd did so, lining up along the tendrils. "This mist has already been gathered by me. It is accustomed to being gathered. This will make it easier."

Phillip put his hands in the fog. It didn't feel like anything. Maybe a little wet.

"A good gatherer can feel the shape of the mist for miles on a quiet day. I don't expect you to do that," Elias continued. "I want you to start thinking of the mist as a single object, I want you to explore where it's tight and where it's loose and frayed."

Phillip and Dan followed the instructions. He was trying to feel the fog, or the mist, or whatever, but it didn't feel like anything. Maybe a little cooler in spots, and little wetter in others, by nothing that felt like an object. Elias would tell them, "imagine your fingers are attached to strings spreading as far as the mist goes. Feel the weight of those strings. Know when they are taunt," Phillip felt no strings, no matter how hard he imagined. He could tell Dan was having the same difficulty. "Makes the strings a part of you. Put more of yourself in the mist. You have to want it desperately, but you cannot try too hard to get it. Just like dating," he said to small snorts of laughter. "Good, good. Now when you are ready, when it feels right. I want you to pull."

Phillip and Dan did so, with everybody else. They moved their hands in and out of the fog. No success, but nobody else was having any success either. That was until, about fifteen minutes in, a girl declared, "I did it!" Everybody looked over and the girl became embarrassed "sorry I yelled" she said. Her tendril of mist now slightly misshapen. "Nothing to apologize for," Elias said with a warm smile.

Nobody was able to do what Elias had done. A few succeeded, but not many. The best in the class—the girl who succeeded first—was only able to pull the tendril a few inches out of its natural path.

"What a waste of time," said an older teenager after the class was over. He was one of the ones that had failed. Phillip noticed he was wearing a white uniform under his black cloak. "Old disciplines are always trying to be so mysterious. Keeps their market share safe. Close to a scam, really," he was talking loud enough for Elias to hear.

"Place your cloaks back in the boxes. If you are interested in the discipline, take a complementary smoke-tail candle you can practice with at home," Elias said, pointing to a small box by the shack. "They are graciously proved by the *Brother and Sisterhood of Gatherers,* free of charge." Phillip and Dan went to the box and retrieved two long white candles. "I greatly hope to see you all again when we do this again," and without another word walked back into the shack.

"That was awesome," Dan said, still feeling he needed to whisper.

"Yeah, it was," Phillip said, loud enough for the white uniformed teenager to hear.

CHAPTER
24
Independence Eve

Haystacks had Dan and Phillip complete two more deliveries the next day. The packages were larger this time, and had to be loaded carefully. Some of the packages shifted a little, as if there was an animal inside.

"No need to worry. Just some prototypes I've been working on," Haystacks assured them.

The banker they delivered too in Chadwick Cove was always happy to see them.

They were paid the same amount both times. "Maybe we should start talking about making this a more permanent thing, since I'm abusing your time anyway," Haystacks said.

They found the process of delivering packaged for Haystacks just as exciting the second time as it was the first. Dan and Phillip had been exploring with the bikes as much as possible, but not near the Fairchild house as the bikes looked different and he didn't want to have to explain anything. Few paths accommodated the bikes special gears, and the ones that did were so twisting it was hard to keep up speed. Dan had started the project of making maps of paths they could use the bikes on. They couldn't get enough of the bikes going in and coming out of the bell, which worked anywhere, not just in the Primafold, Dan noted.

Dan wanted to spend as much time at the Dollhouse as possible. He found the whole thing amazing. Shifting Dan from one side of the house, which they started calling 'Folds', was getting easier. Phillip just had to touch Dan and something else from the other Fold. Sometimes they had to walk. Dan loved the kitchen most of all. He even brought food to put in the pantry. "We should clean the place, see what we can do here," Dan said. "It's a perfect clubhouse for the 'Farm learning society,'" he said, and they set themselves to the task of cleaning.

"Farm learning society?'" Phillip repeated.

"Yeah, I dissolved the last club because it served its purpose, sorry I forgot to tell you," Dan explained. "Tell me if you come up with a better name."

Bertrand was almost never awake, except when he got up briefly and mumbled incoherently. At some point he was awake enough to get dressed in striped pajamas and drink the bottle Phillip had left him.

Phillip began thinking Bertrand was deliberately avoiding him.

The Ramblers—or the Faroekin—kept to themselves. At one point they were joined by another tent, they had also put bright streamers of small flags from the ground to the tree. The FaeFlame fire lit up the field all night, the flame figures dancing almost until morning.

The Fairchild family sometimes mentioned the music, or the smell of burning fire. Especially Maddie, whose sleep schedule was worse than ever. "Must be some kids in the woods," aunt Elaine said. "Is there anybody we can call?" Maddie was skulking around the Dollhouse more than ever.

"We got you a hat," Steve said in the morning at breakfast.

"A hat?" Phillip asked.

"Yep sir." Harrison answered, and threw him bright red, white, and blue affixed with two dangling blue and red fuzzy balls which floated over it which looked like fireworks. And just then Phillip remembered that it was July 3rd. He would have to spend time with the Fairchild family, he couldn't go to the Farm or teach the class tomorrow.

He put on his hat, which caused Matthew to burst out laughing.

"King's Hill does the crap out of Independence Eve," Steve said.

"The *crap* out of it," Harrison repeated.

"Harry, Steven. Don't cuss in front of your baby brother," aunt Elaine ordered.

"'Crap' is not a cuss word, mom," Steve argued.

"It's a baby cuss word, perfect for Matthew," Harrison argued further.

"No baby cuss words at the table," Uncle Jeff said before leaving for work.

'Independence Eve' was what King's Hill called Independence Day. It was held on the 4th and didn't seem to proceed anything. Why there was a difference none of the family could explain. It just was. He told Aunt Kath about it when he got on the phone with her. "That whole town is wacky," she said. "I'm sorry I couldn't be there..."

"No, it's cool," Phillip answered honestly. "King's Hill is actually pretty cool."

"You seem like you're doing well." Aunt Kath responded in a distracted way.

"Everything going well in California?" Phillip asked, sensing some hesitation in her voice. "Are people not as attractive as they say?"

"Oh no, super-hot, don't worry," Aunt Kath responded. "The course is great. I'm just getting worn out..."

He told Dan he couldn't come back to the Farm on Wednesday when he arrived at Haystacks' stable. Before anybody else got there "Don't you know?" Dan said. "The Farm is closed tomorrow. For something they call 'Independence Eve', which is almost the same as July 4th, as far as I can tell," Dan handed him the week's schedule, and sure enough, Wednesday and Thursday were off with the note *'ALL INDEPENDENCE EVE CELEBRATIONS TO BE HELD IN THE CAMPS. *Please keep brawling to a minimum.'*

"Independence Eve is Primafold July 4th," Phillip said, catching on. "I wonder why King's Hill celebrates it...?"

"The mystery deepens," Dan said. "And what's the difference?"

"The difference is," Andy said as she walked into the stable with Emily in tow. Both were wearing what looked like colonial era dresses and hats, "everything!" She said with a flourish. "But really, it's not that different, except the Primafold dresses up more."

"So, the Union of Washington, it's the same as the US government?" Phillip asked.

"Basically, yes." Andy said. "But no, it's half of it."

"Somewhat different history." Emily said at the same time.

"Totally different," Andy continued.

"The Primafold Union of Washington split from Britannia the same time the Mundafold colonies split from Great Britain," Emily explained. "They were more connected back then..."

"And it's a shame they split away at all," Haystacks said, fiddling with something at his table above them. "Perfectly good colonies before that. This should be a national day of mourning..."

"We bought you and Henry a hat," Andy said, and held up a colonial hat with Red, White and Blue ribbons on top.

"Well I've never turned down a hat." Haystacks said, jumping down and grabbing the hat "I guess I'm a traitor now. Fortunately, I'm also a fan of fireworks."

"What do you two plan to do on Independence Eve?" Andy asked Phillip and Dan.

"Big family dinner with my cousins, fireworks in Knoxville," Dan responded.

"Going to hang out with family in King's Hill," Phillip added.

"Well we," Andy said, not waiting for Phillip to finish, "are going to cruise over with Pieter to King's Hill..."

"Really?" Phillip said in surprise.

"Sure. I told Pieter about King's Hill not being on the map, and he was interested. He's sick of the Camps anyway," Andy replied. "I think he's in trouble with some South American Muki, which is weird because I thought they only hung out in caves..."

"That is a common prejudice," Haystacks said, adjusting his new hat in a mirror, trying to make it work with his ears.

"... Anyway, Pieter heard about it, and found a path right into King's Hill, he's bringing that whole trailer of his," Andy finished.

"That sounds great!" Phillip said. "I might need to hang out with my family throughout the night though."

"Of course, it is important to spend time with family," Emily said wisely.

"We'll get you away from that nonsense, don't worry," Andy contradicted. "If I'm shirking my responsibilities for this, I want to force everybody else to do it too."

"I thought you said Tadaaki was handling everything and he didn't need you," Emily said.

"No, yeah. I'm sure he's fine. He's busy at it right now," Andy evaded. "Reliable chap he is, he'll be fine. Which reminds me!" Andy yelled before Emily could follow up. "We have something for the special investigation branch of the Unwelcoming Committee! Phillargo, you should have really been on top of this..."

"What is it?" Dan asked.

"We'll show you!" Andy said, and beckoned them out the door. Leading them passed the hole they were building the new lake in and into the woods.

"Why don't you just tell us? Why all the mystery all the time?" Phillip asked as they walked past a group of small goats with softly glowing horns.

"I'm disappointed in you, Phillargo. Where's your sense of drama?" Andy replied, smoothing her dress. "Does your soul lack poetry?"

"I was born without soul poetry, sadly," Phillip answered. "Now where are we going?"

He knew as soon as they got there.

They reached a part of the woods that looked devastated by strong winds. Almost all the trees were down, and the ones that still stood were stripped of bark and leaves. The ground looked churned and beaten, as if it was boiled. And then Phillip noticed something else, lines of ground were different from the others, different patches of different colored soil. It looked like an earthquake had shifted the position of the land...

There were no animals here. No birds chirped. Even the sky seemed grayer.

"What happened...?" Dan asked.

"Another infiltration, last night," Andy answered. "This is not the only place, too. There's a dozen more sites like these. See the land there, the lighter earth, it's from outside the Farm. Got shifted right past the barrier... *While* outside time was shifted downward relative to us! That shouldn't be possible. Some composited creatures got in, Fae-made, we think. A few of the Wallmen got hurt..."

"We don't know how this happened, but..." Emily started.

"... but we can't deny the barrier is compromised," Andy interrupted.

"... which also shouldn't be possible. Even a weaker barrier should be able to keep this out..." Emily added.

"... that's why we think there's somebody behind this..." Andy concluded gravely. "Somebody inside the Farm. Poking holes in the barrier. It's getting worse. And the Wallmen just keep blaming inadequate purification. They won't consider something they consider impossible, that the strongest barrier any of them has ever seen can't keep out some Fae rats..."

"Willum and a few other officers are arguing what we are saying," Emily said, apparently trying to be fair to the Wallmen as a group. "If there's an infiltration like this, there must be an *infiltrator*."

"Is this why the Pauls and most of the head staff are gone?" Phillip asked.

"Nobody knows what they are doing, or who's in charge right now," Emily replied. "But yes, that's the best guess."

Phillip looked back at the barren trees and churned earth, it looked devastating.

"So," Andy continued, "hotdogs and burgers?"

"Sorry...?" Phillip asked.

"Hotdogs and burgers," Andy repeated. "Real ones. That's what people in the Mundafold eat on Independence Eve, right?"

"Yes," Phillip answered. "That's exclusively what people eat. Maybe barbeque chicken. Also, popcorn, corn corn too. Anything barbequed, really. A lot of people have pie, too..."

"I think I'm going to have a hotdog," Andy said. "I've never had a Mundafold hotdog. We have hotdogs in the Primafold. Duh, we're not savages. But they're different."

"Don't build up your excitement too much, Andy," Emily advised with a smile. "It will be the boxed cereal disappointment all over again..."

"All I'm saying is that if the box says it 'tastes like a shooting star' then it should taste like something other than a dry marshmallow," Andy said righteously. "The Mundafold must have terrible anti-fraud laws..."

They laughed and talked their way back to stable. Phillip and Dan suggestion foods Andy might like more, Andy countering with foods from the Primafold which she acted shocked they hadn't tried. As they jumped over a particularly large felled tree—which was hard to do for the girls in their colonial dresses—Phillip tried to imagine what animal or force was capable of doing this and wondered what this meant for the Farm as a whole.

———— o ————

Phillip woke the morning of July 4th to a bang.

Steve and Harrison had let off what sounded like small cannon. A firework shot off into the air and exploded just above the Dollhouse. Phillip looked out the window and noticed his usual morning crow had been scared away. "Sorry about that, Philly cheese," Steve said with a wide smile, Harrison waving at him. "Just wanted to make sure they were good."

The explosion had not waked Bertrand—but then again, nothing did—at least when Phillip was around. At some point the day before Bertrand had set himself up a cloth half-tent in the living room with the couch inside it, and lit what looked like faeFlame in the fireplace, in front of which he hung a string with his underwear and socks. A small pot of stew or chili bubbled in the fireplace.

Aunt Elaine was already yelling at Steve and Harrison when he got to the house, "you know your sister needs sleep!?" He heard her say as he went in for breakfast. Maddie was already up, wearing blue and red glasses shaped like stars and looking so tired she was almost falling into her bowl of oatmeal.

"Bad night's sleep?" Phillip asked. "Nightmares?"

"I don't have...!" She said back, but apparently thought better of it and didn't continue.

Uncle Phil came to the kitchen wearing shorts and a t-shirt, which looked so unnatural on him that Phillip thought Fortinbras might wear them better.

"Steven, Harrison," he said. "You ready to go stake a spot?"

"Do we have to...?" Harrison whined.

"Condition for me letting you drive. Chores for the family," uncle Jeff said, when he noticed Phillip's confused look, he said. "Viewing field for fireworks gets crowded, these two go ahead in the truck and stake a spot."

"Indentured labor is what it is..." Steve said.

"If you don't like it you can have your own kids to indenture and make them do all the work," uncle Jeff said back.

Aunt Kath called him twice before the family was done packing for the day into town. Like they day before, Phillip could tell she wasn't quite herself. Still joking, still laughing, still high-energy. But Phillip could detect an edge in her voice. She was uncharacteristically apologetic that she couldn't be there, and even opened up that she wasn't sure if going out to California was a good idea. Two subjects he would have jumped on a few weeks earlier. He felt guilty for that... and just asked "Is the program not what you expected...?" To which Aunt Kath replied, sincerely it seemed, "No, it's fantastic..."

She asked Phillip a lot of questions about his non-existent program. She was especially interested in King's Hill University. "Do you like the campus?" "Does it seem like a good student body?" "It's very highly rated, you know... Tier One research university..." Phillip answered as best he could. He made a note to himself to learn a little bit about the University, at least enough to sell the lie.

Somebody called him during the conversation, it was Dan.

He rushed Aunt Kath off the phone and answered.

"Dan? What's going on?"

"Phil, It's Daniel," he said pointlessly, sounding like he was in a wind tunnel. "Are you still at your family's home?"

"Yeah, why?"

"Well you see..." Dan sounded out of breath, "I usually do things with my mom and cousins on the 4th; but just this morning she got a call from a client and they want her to push a few things to production level or something by tomorrow, which she says is about twenty hours of work. She's an illustrator, did I ever tell you that? Anyway, she's really excited about it because this project will pay her more than she usually makes all year but she has to work all day. She asked me if that was okay and I asked her if it was cool if I hung out with my friend Phil instead of my cousins and she said 'yes!' So, do you think it's okay if I come over?"

"That's great Dan! Let me ask…"

"Of course, he can come over!" aunt Elaine said. "Tell him he can stay over for the night if his mom is busy," Aunt Elaine even called Dan's mother. They clearly got along on the phone, and Phillip wondered how it was possible that she could talk about addresses with a woman in Knoxville, Tennessee without realizing that they were in different states… He suspected 'Privilege' has something to do with it. He wondered what would happen if Dan's mother tried to drive to the Fairchild house. *Where would she end up?*

Plans were made, and Dan arrived at the house less than fifteen minutes later. Already packed to stay the night.

"What building is your program in at KHU?" Maddie asked as they were loading Matthew's diaper bag, food bag, and stroller into the car.

"Oh, it moves around," Phillip evaded.

"It's in the science building," Dan answered at the same time. "The memorial… science library… building."

"Hmmm," Maddie answered sarcastically. "Haven't heard of that. Memorial to whom…?"

"To… *scientists*," Dan answered as Phillip gave him a look. "The *dead* ones."

"Madelyn, get your brother in the car seat, could you?" Aunt Elaine ordered.

"Phil, I can't take this," Dan whispered as Maddie retrieved her brother. "Let's just tell her…"

"Not today," Phillip interrupted. "We'll talk about it later…"

Downtown King's Hill was more crowded than he thought possible. Every corner was covered in caravel tent or food buses or some kind of entertainment. Uncle Jeff parked in the alley next to his downtown office, which wasn't too far from the main strip.

"I recognize some of these stores, Phil, I've been in them," Dan whispered to Phillip, Maddie overheard them and gave them an inquisitive look, undoubtedly wondering why it was unusual to have been to stores in your own town…

There were almost as many booths and activities and small bands as there were people, and there were thousands of people. Most of them dressed up the most obnoxious red, white, and blue clothing they could find. Uncle Jeff had put on something that looked like a lab coat made out of the American flag, with an Uncle Sam top hat to match. Even Matthew was dressed up. Phillip felt underdressed in his firework hat.

They spent some time looking at the booths, especially the ones where stuffed animals could be one. "Don't do that one," Dan said to Phillip. "Always avoid the ones with only big prizes, those are scams, impossible to win."

"I think I got this," Phillip replied, putting down two-dollars at a booth and being handed a bowling ball attached to a rope. "So, I just swing it and knock down all the pins, right?" He asked the fundamentally uninterested man with far too-few teeth for his age, he said, "can't swing, just drop." Phillip dropped the ball, hit the first pin, and three others fell with it. "Too bad, better luck next time," the toothless man said without looking up. "One more time, I got this," Phillip said to Dan, putting down another two-dollars.

He lost. And then lost another six times. Each time feeling, he was closer than the last.

But on the ninth try something miraculous happened. All the pins went down.

"Yes!" Phillip yelled.

"Look at that, we have a winner," the toothless man said in the least enthusiastic voice Phillip had ever heard, as he rang a bell. "Pick a prize, pick a prize."

"Uh, that one, I guess," Phillip said, pointing to the stuffed bear half his size with a unicorn horn and a rainbow horsetail and stuffed tongue sticking out of its mouth.

"Congratulations, Phil," Dan said.

"Thanks Dan, it's nice to be recognized."

"Question, would you pay almost twenty dollars for that?" Dan asked.

"Probably not, why...? Ahhhhh," Phillip said as Dan laughed. "Don't be a jerk. It's a war trophy. It shall hang on my mantle..."

"A war trophy you have to carry for the rest of the day," Dan said.

"Don't be jealous of my glory."

Maddie's eyes went wide as she saw what he won. "Where did you get that?!"

"Won it," Phillip answered. "Do you want...?"

"Hey!" Dan interrupted, but he wasn't looking at Phillip. He was looking down the street and waving to two figures wearing colonial clothes. Andy and Emily.

"Good, I was wondering how we would find them!" Phillip said to his family. "These are my friends. I mean other students, from the KHU program..."

Emily met them with a customary bow. She was wearing one of the firework baseball hats Steve and Harrison had given Phillip, and it couldn't look less natural on her. Andy had procured a hotdog, three hotdogs actually. "*Not* a disappointment," she said with a full mouth.

"Let me take a picture!" Dan said. "I promised my mom I would."

There was some confusion coming from Andy and Emily on how to pose with a person who was holding the camera at themselves. "Maddie, get in the picture," Phillip said, seeing her look of suspicion at the newcomers.

"Maddie?" Emily said. "Your cousin Maddie! Well it's very nice to meet your young lady," she said with her customary bow of the head. Andy shook her hand, putting a hotdog in her mouth to do it. "Nice ta meet ya,'' she said, almost keeping food inside her mouth when she did.

"It is so nice to finally meet the people Phillip has talked about so much," Aunt Elaine said. "We were starting to think you didn't exist."

"I am almost certain I exist," Andy joked, then looked at Matthew. "And who is this?" She said in a baby voice. Matthew cracked up in his stroller as Andy bent down. "It looks like Uncle Sam but he's far too tiny," Matthew acted as if this was the funniest thing he had ever heard.

"Andy, you have mustard on your glasses, here," Emily said, handing Andy a napkin.

"Where'd you get those dresses?" Maddie asked Emily.

"I was able to use the one I had last year, with a few adjustments," she answered.

"You dress up every year?" Maddie asked.

"Yes..." Emily said, sounding like she was confused by the question.

"Tradition where we come from," Andy answered.

"Where are you...?" Maddie started.

"There you are!" Steve broke with Harrison through the crowd, somehow sounding louder than everybody else, which included a band. "Who are...?" Harrison asked, stopping when he caught sight of Emily. "Hi..." Harrison said in a voice Phillip had never heard him use.

"These are Phillip's friends from the program," aunt Elaine explained. "This is Andy, and this is Emily. Andy, Emily, these are my sons..."

"Steven. And Harry..." Harrison interrupted, his voice noticeably deeper.

"Steve," Steve corrected.

"I like your dress... *dresses*." Harrison said, continuing to talk in a lower voice. "Really got in the spirit of the thing, huh? Patriotism is cool," He tried to lean his hand against a pole, but missed completely, almost falling before deciding to cross his arms.

"Yes, it is," Steve agreed, looking from Emily to Harrison, clearly embarrassed for his brother. Phillip saw Andy roll her eyes.

Phillip was able to separate from the family with the aid of uncle Jeff, who told them where the truck was parked when they wanted to meet back up. "Steve and Harrison parked by the founder's statue, in the field. If you don't know where that is just ask. The fireworks are shot from the river. Keep your phone on you..."

"Your family seems lovely," Emily said when they were walking away, following Andy.

"Lovely-ish. Does that Harrison cousin of yours always have his mouth open like that...?" Andy said.

"Andy! Enough," Emily said reproachfully. "Phillip, where did you get the stuffed animal?"

"Oh, I won it. At one of the booths," Phillip said, handing it to her "... you can have it if you want..."

"Thank you!" She said graciously but gave the ugly bear a look "But I cannot accept, my space is limited as it is and I do not want to take away proof of your accomplishment."

"Yeah, it's ugly and kinda stupid," Phillip said, his face going hot for some reason. "And now I have to carry it for the rest of the day. It's stupid. Where are we going by-the-way?"

"To Pieter, he parked around here. We haven't told you yet!" Andy replied. "There's little bits of Primafold tucked all around here! Never seen anything like it…"

They went through the crowd, through an alleyway between two old brick buildings, climbed through a hole in a fence, and found Pieter. He was parked with a chrome trailer which had massive wooden wagon wheels in an almost impossibly out-of-place patch of forest overlooking the distant river. He was manning a fire he had set at the center of chairs and logs. He was also wearing a colonial era costume, complete with high socks a tri-pointed hat.

"My friends, I have made food!" He yelled as they approached.

"Already got food. Mundafold hot dogs," Andy announced.

"What's so special about those?" He asked.

"Best food ever. My life has peaked," she explained.

"Nobody else has eaten, Pieter," Emily added. Then pointed to Andy. "Just this one."

"No regrets. YOLO." Andy answered.

"Yo-low?" Pieter asked.

"Mundafold slang Andy read about."

"Ah. Good man, good man," Pieter congratulated. "Well for all of you who aren't pigs, I have a real treat. Traditional turkey meat pie and some even more traditional Pease pudding. All family recipes, you're welcome."

"Thank you, Pieter, that's very kind," Emily said.

"See how welcoming I am?" Pieter said "I even welcomed these two a few days ago, just ask them."

"It's true," Dan confirmed.

"We were thoroughly welcomed," Phillip added.

"It's almost as if I belong on some kind of welcoming… *organization* or something." Pieter said.

Emily looked stricken. Andy answered first. "As a secret member of the Unwelcoming Committee, that would be a conflict of interest. Speaking of, what did you learn?"

"Shouldn't have asked. I'm ashamed to say I've found nothing. Well, not exactly nothing," Pieter replied. "Everybody knows something. Most of it made up."

"You've failed us, Pieter," Andy said.

"I know," He replied.

"Good thing you have food," Andy added.

The food was excellent. It was apparently a tradition in the Primafold to cook traditional American meals on Independence Eve. Phillip had heard of none of them, but was more than happy to try. He suspected Pieter was a pretty good cook, or that Primafold food was just better.

Pieter taught them a wooden board game called Chant. It involved three boards, one shared in the center, and two for each player. It managed to be both simple and complex. Pieces were placed on the personal board and then could be transferred to the *'Arena'* board, which was supported by the pieces on the personal board, which formed *'chant lines'* and *'chant circles.'* "You should play with Andy, she's better than me," Pieter told Dan and Phillip, who were playing each other. "That's my brother's game, not mine," Andy replied, but watched and gave frustrated advice to Dan or Phillip as they played.

They watched a parade of boats go down the river, each adjourned with decorations. Pieter told the story of how he managed to get away from the South American Muki, "Wanted to take one of my fingers for a bit there, pay them in bones they said," he said, "But we worked it out, good guys really... Emily don't look so disappointed in me, it hurts my feelings..."

"I am not... *disappointed* in you," Emily said defensively. "But since you brought it up a person of your talents could be doing so much more with your time than gambling with..."

"Aleandra," came a voice so out of tune with the mood of the camp that it stopped everybody from talking. "Sister."

The only person who didn't look surprised to see Tadaaki standing there— in formal clothing complete with a sword—was Andy.

"Yes?" Andy said back in a neutral voice, her head tilted upwards.

Tadaaki looked livid, but his voice didn't match. "I think you know we are supposed to be somewhere right now. That there are responsibilities we should be attending to," he looked down at Andy's empty mug and used plate. "Do you think this is the best use of our time? Emily, Pieter, My apologies for interrupting..."

"Oh, it's okay..." Emily said.

"No problem, buddy," Pieter said, looking awkward.

"It is Independence Eve, and I decided to spend it here," Andy answered. "I had the utmost confidence in my brother to handle things while I was away."

Tadaaki paused and looked at her, clearly restraining himself. "I know what you're doing. *You* know that I know what you're doing..."

"Really? You know what I'm doing?" Andy said, standing up. "Then tell me what I'm doing. Say it out loud!"

Tadaaki gathered himself. "Is this the best time to revisit these issues? When we have so much on us, so much at stake?"

"I've done nothing wrong!"

"... you are spending time... here! Wasting away having food and drink in the Mundafold!"

"There is something going on with this town, I thought it might be important!"

"No. You didn't," Tadaaki said. "You wanted to get away and indulge yourself. The same petulant, selfish child we..."

"How dare you!" Andy screamed, the air crackling with energy. The pot on the fire boiling over. "Just because I don't follow the Rurik..."

"We should speak outside the camp," Tadaaki interrupted.

Andy and Tadaaki left the camp. Fighting louder as they went. The fight growing more personal, with more name-calling.

They could still be heard somewhere on the other side of the trailer. Saying something about the Pauls now... Phillip tried not to listen, but they had left the camp quiet in their wake.

"Emily..." Pieter said. "These are Primafold trees, if I'm not mistaken, flowering ones. I know it's late in the year now but perhaps they could be persuaded to bloom, maybe even sing a little... I think Dan and Phil here would like that..."

"Ah! Yes," Emily responded, catching on to something Pieter was saying.

She produced a small flute from her sleeve. Played three notes, and then started humming. It didn't seem to come to her after a while, but emanating from the air itself. It was a simple repeating rhythm. Her and Pieter were looking up at the tree, Dan and Phillip followed their eyes. The trees were blooming large pink and white flowers.

Thousands were blooming, one after another in a chain reaction. When Emily stopped humming it, the flowers themselves took up the tone. One would sing, and the one next to it would start, and then another. Blooming and closing. It was both disorganized and harmonious.

Beautiful.

And it drowned out the sound of Tadaaki and Andy fighting.

Feeling lightheaded for at least three different reasons, Phillip laughed, and found that the sound of his laugh carried from flower to flower, mixing with the humming and ringing before dying out like an echo.

'Enchantment," Pieter explained. Playing with his blond black hair. "Real live enchantment. Don't call it anything else but magic. Emily here is one of the most talented Enchantresses here in the States."

"Thank you," she said with a blush. "But no, I'm not..."

"Phil, Dan. I'm telling the truth," Pieter continued. "Her father is not bad either. She's been surrounded by professional Enchantresses and Lullabyists her whole life..."

"You should teach a class," Dan suggested.

Emily blushed all the deeper. "Enchantment doesn't lend itself well to a classroom setting. Apprenticeships are better..."

The flower blooming was traveling from tree to tree now. Dan seemed caught between trying to take a picture or record the experience in his pink notebook, in the end he decided to do both at the same time, struggling to hold his mug while he did it.

"You both have the same book?" Pieter said suddenly, as if it was a revelation.

"We found them," Phillip answered.

"Anything special about them?" Pieter asked. "Do they do anything?"

"A little. We don't know, to be honest..." Phillip answered, and then followed up with. "Is there a restroom around here?"

"The one in the van is broken right now, invited the wrong people over for dinner last night, and that's all I'll say about that..." Pieter told him. "But if you go that way, passed the tree line, there's a few of those portable Mundafold bathrooms, unless I've confused portable torture chambers with bathrooms, it would be easy enough..."

"Thanks," Phillip said, heading off in the opposite direction Andy and Tadaaki had gone.

"Check out the sofa trees why you're near there!" Pieter yelled, but was drowned out by the singing flowers. *Does he say 'sofa trees?'* Phillip asked himself, *I must have misheard him.*

The flowers had spread from tree to tree, and even caused other plants to act differently. Would the people of King's Hill notice this? They hadn't noticed the patches of Primafold scattered throughout the town. Or had they? Was it all normal to them? Maybe it worked like the bag and its contents. Forgettable when it wasn't in view...

Phillip found he wasn't following the path Pieter had suggested to the bathrooms.

He walked up to what Pieter had screamed about, he had not misheard him.

They were dozens of sofas, put into a tree.

"The sofa trees," Phillip said, and not being able to resist, climbed one of the massive branches which swept low to the ground. Dozens of different kinds of furniture, wooden chairs, two-person sofas with flower patterns, armchairs and ottomans. Some looked tied with thin ropes, others supported by branches grown around the sofa, some even looked like the tree had grown into them. There was a good view of the river and the setting sun from higher in the tree. "Sofa trees," Phillip repeated in amazement.

A giggle, or more of a snort, came from behind him. "Pretty neat, right?" Andy said.

She was sitting on a long sofa which didn't seem to have nearly enough support. Her arms were crossed and her legs were underneath her. Even with glasses on, he could tell her eyes were red. He wondered how she got up here in a dress.

"Sorry," he said.

"What are you sorry about?" She asked.

"I didn't mean to follow you..." He answered. "I was just trying to find the restroom."

"So naturally you climbed a tree."

"Well I figured, if someone put a bunch of sofas up in a tree there's a good chance there's a bathroom up here too..."

Andy laughed. "Try the armchair out. It's cozy," she said

Phillip jumped into the green armchair, which faced Andy. He nodded his approval at the coziness of the armchair. Andy's eyes were much redder than he thought.

"Sorry," he said again in spite of himself.

"Why do you keep apologizing...?"

"I mean about... what happened."

"You mean my brother yelling at me and embarrassing me...?"

"Well, actually I was thinking about those nasty hotdogs you were eating, probably come back later," Phillip said.

Andy snorted again. "They *were* nasty hotdogs, made me feel greasy. Still loved them..."

"If you don't mind me asking," Phillip said. "Is your brother... kind of a jerk?"

"An argument could be made..." Andy said with a smile but it left her face as she continued. "No, he's not a jerk. He's the... responsible and respectable one. Rurik family traditions demand a lot. He has to be responsible because I'm not. He spends half his life covering for me... like tonight. I think I'm the jerk... then we fight and make each other feel bad..."

"You think he feels bad?"

"I know it. Tadaaki is a wuss when it comes to suppressing bad feelings," Andy said.

"So, your families sent you here..." Phillip said. "They sent you two on some sort of mission. And your family, or families, are... rich."

"No, not rich. Well, yes. Rich..." Andy said. "But it's more accurate to say they're important. Emily's family is *rich*. And yes, they sent us here on a sort of a mission. Though nobody knows what's going on so there's no real objectives. Tonight, we were supposed to stay in the Farm, and here I am, playing around like it's a vacation... Dang, now I feel bad again."

Phillip didn't know how to respond to this. He suspected he was saying all the wrong things.

"Andy..." He started, hoping something would come to him, "you know, we... Dan and I, I mean... owe you a lot. We owe you everything, actually. We wouldn't have been able to do anything without you advocating for us. I know it's not your family's mission or anything but... and I know we're arguably more of a burden than anything else, but what you've done for us. It matters, it means a lot," Phillip cleared his throat, feeling stupid and awkward. "In fact, I'm starting to suspect we accidentally tricked you into thinking we're more valuable than we are..."

Andy's eyes grew a little wetter again.

"Like I said, don't let anything we do for you go to your head. You're just pawns. Oh, and you definitely tricked us," Andy said in a joking tone, wiping her eyes again. "Can't figure you out, actually. For instance, I can't tell if you're the wild one or the responsible one..."

"Can't figure that out myself. I used to think I was the responsible one. Always did chores, never had to be told to brush my teeth... But ever since this Farm stuff happened, I'm surprising myself. I keep stressing Dan out. I don't know if he's told you, but that whole generator lab thing was more my fault than his..."

"Oh, I know that, Rickshaun's been gossiping. I love gossip, by the way. Nothing personal," Andy said. "Has it always been that way between you and Dan...?"

"Always?" Phillip repeated. "No, I just met Dan just before I met you..."

"Really?" Andy said, surprised. "I thought you've been friends for years. You two seem so close."

"Yeah?" Phillip responded. "I guess magical Farms have a way of accelerating friendship…"

"That's what they say," Andy said wisely. "Do you have many Mundafold friends?"

A pop and a snap echoed in the distance with a flash of light. The fireworks were starting on the river. Phillip got off his green armchair and joined Andy on the large sofa for he was facing the right way. "Not really," he answered. "I mean, I'm friendly with a lot of people. I used to have more friends, but then my parents died and things got weird… How about you, how long have you known Emily?" Blue and green fireworks lit up the tree, followed a moment later by soft pops.

"More than half my life now. She's my only *real* friend," Andy said. "One thing about being born into an important family, they have a lot of control over your social groups. I've been receiving visitors since I was six-years-old. People trying to get close to the Kanamori or Rurik family. Other families surrounding Tadaaki with girls early," she said with a roll of her eyes. "Emily's family, the Morris family. The dad's a financial success. He grew up poor, and he's a bit of a… *climber* now. Came over to my house and gave Emily instructions to get close to me. She felt so guilty about what she was doing she confessed to me less than an hour, even cried about it. I knew, of course, I was used to it. Nothing offensive about it," Andy laughed at the memory. "We've been best friends ever since."

Phillip laughed with Andy at this. This seemed typical of both of them.

He noticed something on the branch. "Speaking of Emily, there's one of her singing flowers…"

The flowers hummed and sometimes added the sound of fireworks to their song. "Such pretty magic…" Andy whispered. "I wish I learned some pretty magic. I don't even think this tree grows flowers. Emily is so good at that. All I know is gross old German boy-magic…"

"I don't even know that…"

"What are you talking about? You and Dan made lighting!"

"That's true," Phillip said in a distracted voice, not wanting to go into it.

They were silent then, not wanting to distract from the sound and sight of the fireworks, or the enchanted flowers which opened and closed and echoed their sound.

The fireworks show lasted a long time. So long that it was still going on when Phillip was able to find his family, on the bed of the truck Steve and Harrison had parked earlier.

Aunt Elaine was glad Phillip was back, and even more glad he had brought his friends with him.

"Sit down, sit down. We have too much food!" She said over the blasts, trying to comfort Matthew, who seemed undecided on whether he should be interested or terrified by the firework show.

Andy, Emily, and Pieter stayed for the show. Pieter got along with Steve and Harrison, but then Phillip was starting to suspect that Pieter got along with most everybody. Andy and Emily played with the baby and talked to Maddie, who did nothing but ask probing questions, which Andy expertly deflected.

"Maddie!" Phillip interrupted her, and held up the stuffed unicorn bear. "Do you want this?"

Maddie's eyes went wide. She reached for the ugly bear "You sure?" She said, and when Phillip nodded, she grabbed it. "Thanks!"

His friends, with the exception of Dan, left soon after. The show ended and they were left with the tedious process of packing up and getting home. Dan would be spending the night, it was determined. He had spoken to his mother three times on the phone to arrange it. The day had tired everybody out, and the road home seemed particularly long.

Everybody had eaten at the fair. Dinner at the Fairchild house was more of a snack-fest. With heavier food being heated in the microwave. Because of Matthews early schedule, Steve and Harrison's morning practice, and Maddie's homework, Dan and Phillip were able to retire to the Dollhouse without much fuss. "And they don't bother you at all at the house?" Dan asked.

"Mostly no." Phillip answered. "Except Maddie."

"Whoa!" Dan yelled and pointed.

On the grass in front of the Dollhouse. Dozens of massive figures now sat. Silent and still. Illuminated only by the moon and stars.

"Buffalo!" Phillip said. "What are buffalo doing here...?"

"Bison," Dan corrected. "Buffalo are only in Asia and Africa. This is an American bison. But whoa!"

The Ramblers were playing music again. Neither bothered nor particularly interested in the small herd of buffalo—or bison—right outside their little camp.

"They seem docile," Phillip said. The bison were relaxed. The same could not be said for Fortinbras, who sat as guard on the deck, his head darting from bison to bison. The only sign he saw Phillip that his tail began to wag.

Dan noticed something else.

"Phillip can you look up?" Dan said. "Tell me what you see..."

Phillip did so, and saw stars.

But not just stars. He could see the entire milky way.

Stars so numerous they looked like clouds. Some stars flickered and he was sure he could see that some had colors now. Yellow and light red and blue. Familiar constellations now were more colorful. Orion's belt was blue. He could see every star clearly, even under the lamp of the porch, even with the full or almost full moon.

"I would have noticed this before," he said to Dan. "Why can we see so many stars?"

"Is this how stars look in the Primafold? Does this have something to do with your split house?" Dan asked himself.

"I don't know... maybe Bertrand is up, let's ask him."

But Bertrand wasn't up. For that matter, he wasn't in the living room, or in the kitchen, or anywhere else in the house.

Phillip found a note on the coffee table in fine handwriting he was surprised belonged to Bertrand.

> To a most gracious host,
>
> Thank you for the great kindnesses you have shown me, but I must depart. Please forgive me for this rudeness.
>
> I am aware it is indecent for a guest to make a show of the reciprocal presents given to a host, but considering I have had the great honor of being your first guest I made an exception. I have left you a guest book and signed it with my name...

Phillip looked on the table, a large leather book was there with 'GUESTBOOK' burnt onto the cover. Phillip opened it to the first page. 'Bertrand J. Bertrand' signed his name, next to it a series of glowing symbols and stamps.

> I have also left you some odds and ends I no longer had a use for. There are some seeds in the kitchen. A purifying houseplant that was hard to travel with, and some old memory cloth. I do warn you, the memory cloth has stored light, sun, and wind in it; but do not activate the wind unless you want it to blow itself halfway to China. I've made that mistake many times.

Phillip walked around the house. Found the jar of multi-colored seeds, found some food. Found a large houseplant in the hallway, and then found a large folded up cloth with old rusted dials attached to it. Phillip spun the one that had a symbol of the sun on it. The cloth brightened as if it was outside, spilling light and warmth all over the room. Phillip quickly turned the knob back.

"What was that?!" Dan asked. Phillip didn't answer, and instead read the rest of the note.

> I cannot thank you enough for my kindness. With great gratitude,

231

Bertrand J. Bertrand.

P.S. – I don't like telling another man what to do, but I would not suggest kinning with those bison. Made that mistake too. Downright clingy, bison are, and make difficult house pets.

CHAPTER
25

The Monster in the Lake

Phillip was disappointed that Bertrand had left.

But he had to admit the house was now a much more relaxing place.

"I still think he's weird," Dan said. "This memory cloth is cool though…"

Dan had turned one of the dials on the cloth without meaning to, it turned out to be the *'Stored Wind'* dial and they spent the better part of an hour trying to peel the memory cloth off the ceiling, held in place by strong winds that weren't there.

Neither of them felt like sleeping after that. They decided to take some books and snacks to the porch and relax there. The combination of the full moon and the usually bright stars illuminated the porch so much they found they didn't need light. They could even read and take notes with no problem. "What do you think is special about these seeds?" Phillip asked, looking at the large glass jar.

"Maybe they're just for snacking. Like trail mix…" Dan suggested.

"I don't think so," Phillip said, taking off the metal cap of the jar. "Nothing's just trail mix here. Maybe it's…"

Phillip stopped talking as the seeds in the jar lurched for his face.

"Ah!" he yelped, dropping the jar.

The seeds ran out of the jar like hundreds or insects. They jumped off the porch and went into the grass. They had grown little legs made of vine to walk on. Fortinbras jumped to his feet. He had been watching the bison faithfully and was caught completely off guard by this change in potential dangers. He did manage a weak bark or two, before backing up and falling down the first step of the porch.

Phillip recovered, grabbed the jar and the lid and closed it. Three seeds were still inside. The stood at the bottom of the jar and seemed confused when they pressed against the sides. The hundreds of other seeds had disappeared into the grass.

Dan snorted. "Oh my God!" he said. "What is *that* going to do?"

Phillip looked at the despondent seeds left in the jar. "Heck if I know. Plant themselves?" Phillip said. "Maybe became evil vines that kill the Fairchild family, or lift their house off the foundation...? Put it on the question list."

Dan and Phillip made some effort to follow the seeds into the grass. Fortinbras, to make up for his cowardice moments before, insisted on keeping guard. They wove through the sleeping bison. But found none of the seeds. They went looking in the Ramblers' camp. Their hands were grabbed and they were invited to dance by the fire. The woman in the red dress spinning by the flame, the flame spinning with her.

They seemed perpetually in a good mood. They handed Dan and Phillip drinks and offered them to sit or play games. They initiated conversations with Dan and Phillip, the fact that they were speaking a different language and neither of them could understand them didn't seem to deter them in the slightest. Dan was kissed on the cheek by the woman who then winked and joined the dancing at the fire. This left Dan silent and blushing.

Later in the night, Dan reported to Phillip that the upstairs bathroom had changed.

It was larger now. With more wood instead of tile. The shower bath had been replaced with a bathtub that was taller than it was wide, like a barrel, and shaped like the number '8.' "Bad news Dan," Phillip said, looking at the toilet, which had some ropes next to it, "Primafold toilet, the ropes are back..."

"Ahhhh maaaan," Dan said. "How do we get the other bathroom back?"

"Don't know, sometimes when I walk around the house in a certain way, things change back."

But the bathroom didn't change for the rest of the night. Dan used the one next to the master bedroom. "Worst case-scenario. *All* your bathrooms change, and I have to get used to the ropes," Phillip didn't like the ropes any more than Dan but had to admit they were effective...

They woke up early the next morning, "we can make up sleep at the Farm," Dan said. "I want to explore this place a little more. Check out those new barns..."

That's exactly what they did, but they found the new barns - while clearly in a state of disrepair, the large one missing a chunk out of its roof—were locked tight with thick doors, with the same locks Phillip saw on the Dollhouse. "Maybe we can get a ladder, go through that hole up there..." Dan suggested, looking at his watch. "But I don't think we have time..."

Phillip could see the Dollhouse, the new barns, and the larger newer Fairchild house at the same time. He could see two things at once, so long as they didn't overlap. But Dan could only see one or the other. "I see a fence over there, where the bison moved, do you see it?" he asked Dan. "No," Dan replied "I wonder what would happen if I tried to climb it."

Turns out, when Dan was with Phillip, the fence appeared for Dan, along with the rest of the 'old' Fairchild property, but then Dan couldn't see the new barn. Or the patches of forest... "This is wild. Really, really wild," Dan said.

Dan had to leave not long after. "My mom pulled an all-nighter with the project," Dan explained. "She says she wants to go out, eat as many pancakes as is humanly possible to celebrate, and 'crash for the next two days'," he quoted.

He didn't see Dan again until they were back at the Farm. Phillip, as usual, was the last to arrive for morning coffee. "Check out the schedule for the week," Dan said, handing him a piece of paper.

"Wow," Phillip said, reading it. "That's amazing. This starts today?"

"Yep," Dan confirmed.

Farm days were expanding. There would now be at least eighteen-Farm-days and seventeen Farm-nights each day. All with only a single hour-long break at noon. Even Sunday, usually saved for purification, had Farm-Days. Phillip added it up...

"So, if we go every day this week, that's... what? One hundred twenty days! Something like that?" Phillip said. "I'm going to get old. I'm going to forget my family. I'm going to forget all the math I learned in school!"

"It's not *time-time*, remember," Emily said. "It's *work-time*..."

"Maybe you should take notes, like Daniel, for you don't make a fool of yourself," Andy suggested in a sweet voice. "The Wallmen are in a tizzy about the compression," Andy added. "They say they need more purification time. Captain Karo has been complaining to anyone that could listen. I think he's afraid if something happens, he will be blamed..."

"Willum is one of the ones who is concerned," Emily said. "He was there during one of the breaches, he said none of the older men have ever seen a barrier this strong be penetrated..."

"That's because of the agent. The enemy agent. The *infiltrator*," Andy said, looking at Haystacks, who seemed confused. "Sorry, special investigation for the Unwelcoming Committee. Which is a secret branch of the Welcoming Committee. Which I shouldn't be telling you about... Phillargo, you check out Haystacks? Is he trustworthy...?"

"Super trustworthy," Phillip affirmed. "Don't know about Henry though," Henry looked towards them, and spit out a seed he was chewing.

"Where is herb-stamping class?" Dan asked, looking up from his notebook. "Sorry I interrupted. It says on the schedule its location has been changed but doesn't say where."

"What's an 'urb'?" Haystacks asked, and then looked at the schedule. "Oh, for bloody sake. 'HER-bah!' It has a bloody 'H' in it!"

When Dan and Phillip asked about why the stars were so bright all of a sudden, or why they could suddenly see them during the day at Phillip's house, they were met with confusion. "I don't think the stars changed..." Andy said.

'Herb-stamping' turned out to be a fun workshop.

Dan and Phillip were able to do what the rest of the class did. This was because machines did all the magical work, and all they had to do was operate them. They would take plants. Place them on certain sheets of paper, and use a large wooden and metal device to 'stamp' the plant into the paper. If it was done right, the plant would look almost like a drawing on paper. The herb could then be stored and retrieved at leisure.

"A good stamping can last fifteen to twenty years and still be retrievable, depending on the subject," the teacher said. It was impossible to tell her size underneath multiple layers of clothes and overalls. She looked like someone who would be sleeping at an abandoned bus stop, but spoke with clarity and confidence. She even shut down a few of the white-uniformed 'Brick and Hammer Academy' students, who were teasing other Choicers in the class. They had the same sneering attitude as their teacher, Antony Müller. Apparently, 'herb-stamping' was another profession dominated by Choicers...

Dan and Phillip had stamped a half-dozen plants each. Which they carried like trophies for the rest of the day.

It felt good to do magic. Antony Müller couldn't take that from them.

Haystacks class was delayed again. "I'm starting to think there's a conspiracy against me," he said. "At least I get to teach you two. Your mice are coming along well. Dan, good job resewing it. Phillip, your mouse's head is a little lopsided, I think you overdid it with the stuffing."

"Is that why he only walks in circles?" Phillip asked.

"More likely it's the orientation logike splines," Haystacks answered.

"When it works, I never know what I'm doing right, what I did differently."

Haystacks laughed. "Puppetcrafter trade secret," he said. "No matter how good you get you're going to feel the same way."

Unfortunately, Dan and Phillip's classes were never cancelled

And they were garnering far less respect each time.

The class was growing restless, and smaller. The exercises they had created together were failing to grab interest. Antony Müller was mocking them more opening. Every class seemed longer and more stressful than the last.

But any humiliation of teaching was wiped away soon after by the greater humiliations they suffered in Circles Class. They were further behind now the class was getting more advanced. lucky for them, Thamus offered to be their study buddy, or to cheat for them... whatever they needed.

He did find he slept better in Haystacks stable than in the Dollhouse. The Dollhouse felt open and exposed in a way the Farm didn't. There were odd sounds at night at the Dollhouse. He woke up at least three times a night thinking there was something in the house, or in the closet, or just outside the window.

Fortinbras felt it too. The dog had gotten into the habit of whining in the middle of the night, while looking at the window or at the closed bedroom door.

Probably just picking up on my energy, Phillip would think, before turning on the light and looking at his pink notebook until sunrise.

The responsibilities of Dan and Phillip had in the Welcoming Committee—what little they were—started to wane, as the influx of new visitors to the Farm started to stabilize.

Still, there were quite a few requests for information, and a fair number of people complaining. They met the runaway Davis again, who had procured a good-sized treehouse for herself. Her hair had seemed to grow five times as long, or maybe she was wearing it differently...? There was something distinctly different about her, which Phillip couldn't put his finger on. The Farm will do that to you, he supposed.

Phillip didn't mind the jobs at all. He even liked them. Made him feel like he was something other than a charity case.

Except when they were involved getting up before dawn.

It was foggy Farm morning, it would be the last morning of that day, when Dan and Phillip were tasked with delivering study materials to several Choicer families with young children. They had split up the work to save time. It was tedious but felt productive.

Dawn was the calmest time in the Farm. Almost nothing moved except the fog.

Phillip attempted to grab the fog as he walked. Occasionally, he thought he succeeded, thought he could feel the shape of it like Elias said, but the fog didn't come away from the air when he pulled. It was just a draft. He tried to remember the various mental and physical exercises. *You must really want it, but not be desperate...*

"Could never justify looking so silly. But then again, I've always been vain," came a calm voice to Phillip's left.

Phillip jumped. On the shoreline of one of a small lake sat a man in a folding chair, his bare feet submerged partially in the water.

It was Paul. *Old* Paul.

"Sorry if I disturbed you," Phillip said, seeing three fishing poles Old Paul had cast into the water. "I didn't know you were back..."

"Disturb me? Not at all. I find fishing boring anyway. I was hoping a distraction would show up. Come and join me. I have another chair," he said, pointing to an empty wooden stool. "Trying to gather the fog?"

"Oh, yeah," Phillip responded, making his way to the stool. The ground was wet, and water leaked into his shoes. Old Paul had set up where there was at least an inch of water. Phillip took off his shoes and socks like Paul, placing them on a stone that sat between them. There was a glass bowl on the stone, filled with white sand. "Just some salt. I was collecting some moonlight before the sun took over," Old Paul explained. Phillip tried to make himself comfortable with his feet submerged in cold water. Old Paul seemed comfortable. "Just got back," Old Paul continued. "Errands, you see... decided I should relax and have myself a fish."

"Where did you go...?" Phillip asked, not sure if he should.

"Just errands," Old Paul said. "I trust everything is going smoothly?"

"Well..." Phillip started, not knowing how to answer, "there's these breaches. A whole bunch of trees fell down, and..."

"Shhh," Old Paul interrupted. Looking up. His tight pointed beard looking up with him. "You hear that?"

Phillip tried to listen. "No," he said.

"Exactly. *Nothing*," Old Paul said. Phillip thought for moment Old Paul was telling him to be quiet, but he continued. "No bugs. No little curious little fae or wood sprites picking my pocket, no wandering shadows. Nothing. Dawn is silent time, Phillip, not a Nothing time. Do You know what this means, Phillip Montgomery?" Phillip shook his head. Old Paul was staring straight ahead. "It means there's a predator about. A great big monster. Maybe even in this lake... Maybe watching right now. Maybe saying the same thing about us... you play chess, Phillip?"

Phillip was caught off guard. "I know how to play," he answered. "But no, I don't play much."

"I'm terrible at chess," Old Paul said. "And I hate losing. Whenever I see my opponent has the upper hand I have a hard time not just flipping over the board and punching my opponent in the face. Who wins then?" He looked straight at Phillip, his eyes like spotlights. "The right answer is, it depends. It depends on what the real game is..."

"The... monster you talked about...?" Phillip said, going back. "Is it dangerous, to the Farm? To the people in it...? Is that what we're talking about right now?"

"The Farm is something... that threatens a lot of people," Old Paul answered. "Many want to join it, or stop others from joining it, or steal it. Danger, yes. There's danger anywhere when Man is concerned. Especially when *Anywhere* is concerned..."

"*Anywhere*, sir?" Phillip asked.

"Anywhere," Old Paul repeated. "Where we are now. The home of the Farm. *Anywhere*," He repeated, as if it explained everything. "Now let me ask you a question, Phillip Montgomery. I'll even let you ask a personal question in return..."

"Okay," Phillip said, unsure.

"When you and your friend did that little stunt out in the field, when you *made* the lightning. Why did you take a drink of that liquid before pouring it...?"

Phillip was embarrassed to be put on the spot. His notes were terrible from that evening, and he wasn't in his right mind. Was Old Paul trying to find if he was a fraud? And how did he know about that part of it? He started talking, hoping the answer would come to him. "Well, we were thinking. Dan mentioned something about Sunday school. And it's... it's like Circles Class. When you want to keep the thieving termite out of a circle... But also, when you want to keep stuff in a circle... The drink was the thing that connected everything in the circle to us. And when it was inside our stomachs, we were connected to everything... or something... I can check my notes..."

Old Paul just looked at Phillip, he was smiling. "Circles Class, eh? Useful. Now go ahead, ask me a question. Anything you want."

Phillip was relieved, and the first question that came to his head, something he had been wondering about. "You and... *Big* Paul. If you don't mind me asking. What's your relationship?"

Old Paul chuckled. "I wish I could answer that question simple enough to be understood. But... I suppose you could say our relationship is defined by a mutual hatred and distrust and bound together by an even greater agreement and a more desperate need." He laughed. "I'm proud of you, Phillip Montgomery, you've found a question that makes me uncomfortable. Now let me return the favor, how is your teaching going?"

"Not... great," Phillip said, unable to commit to lying. "I have to ask, why did you have me and Dan teach that..."

"... before we go down this road, Phillip, let me ask you..." Old Paul interrupted. "If teaching this class was a precondition for being invited to the Farm and gaining Privilege here, would you do it."

"Yes," Phillip answered. *Absolutely, yes,* he thought.

"Let's leave it at that right now, okay?" Old Paul said.

"Okay," Phillip agreed. Looking off at the lake.

"Plus, hearing that you're having a hard time teaching was the only thing that's keeping Rickshaun from banging down my door every evening. He's still steaming over you blowing up his lab, you know," Old Paul laughed at this. "The man holds a grudge like a child..."

A bell rang on one of the fishing lines.

"Here she is!" Old Paul yelled. "Phillip, grab the line on the right!"

Phillip did what he said without asking. When he picked up the line, it pulled him almost into the water until he planted his bare feet in the ground. "Hah! Haaaa! That's it!" Old Paul yelled. "Keep pulling, keep pulling! Bring the line in tighter. We have her now!"

He spun the handle on the rod as best he could, trying to resist the urge to let go.

He noticed the poll and the string were glowing blue. The brighter it was, the more pressure.

Old Paul struggled to his right. "Too old for this," he heard him whisper.

What was on both lines, Phillip wondered, but didn't have to wonder for long.

A fish broke the surface.

It was the size of a car, with bright orange and white coloring. It looked like a giant koi.

The lines weren't attached to hooks, they were attached to netting that looked like a spider web. "We got her now, Phillip!" Old Paul yelled, spinning the handle.

They were able to pull it to shore with an enormous amount of physical effort.

"Now the hard part." Old Paul said when the giant koi was within ten feet, he threw Phillip a shiny wooden stick. "Here, you take the sword, I'll bang the gong."

"Sword...?" Phillip looked at the shiny black stick. It had a handle on one side. It was a short sword... "I don't think I should..."

"Hurry up we don't have much time. Get closer! Get closer." Old Paul yelled and began banging a gong with a stick rhythmically.

Again, Phillip followed his instructions, and approached the giant koi, staying away from its mouth. It flopped on the ground, but only weakly. Old Paul continued to bang the gong.

Something was coming out of the fish's back.

Long... *things.*

They were as transparent as ghosts and glowed a faint white and blue. They looked like multi-headed worms thicker than Phillip's leg. They popped out of the giant koi like parasites.

"That's it Phillip, don't cut them too soon, wait to see past their tendrils..." Old Paul said. "But you might want to unsheathe the sword now... Get ready!"

Not knowing what else to do, he took the sword out of the scabbard. The blade was as transparent as the creatures coming out of the Koi. It looked like a reflection, with almost no weight...

"There's the body of them. Cut, boy! Cut!" Old Paul ordered.

Phillip swung the blade like a baseball bat at the body of one of the worms. Staying as far away as his arms would let him. The blade cut through the worm as it screeched like old car brakes. It died and turned into smoke. "Keep going, keep going. They'll get used to the sound soon!" Old Paul ordered.

Phillip leaped from worm to worm. Cutting them as fast as he could. Sometimes skipping awkwardly around the fish, and leaping to get where he couldn't reach, until he couldn't see any more. The giant koi jerked and spasmed as if it was in enormous pain...

"Just one left," Old Paul said, and began to bang the gong slower.

Another worm came out, larger than the rest. Phillip waited until he could see the body, and sliced the worm straight through. The worm screeched, so loud he thought the entire Farm would hear, and vanished.

The giant koi seemed to relax, as much as Phillip could tell...

"That should do it. Thank you, Phillip," Old Paul put down the gong, and pulled a small lever at the bottom of both the polls. The string and net snapped, and evaporated as fast as the worm creatures.

"Sir, what were those?" Phillip asked, still holding the sword at the ready.

Old Paul approached the giant koi and placed his hand gently on the top of it. "Sorry, old girl," He said, then looked at Phillip. "Her name is Big Betsy. Every Farm should have a Big Betsy, I figured... And those things, they were just some nasty creatures that got in because I'm not doing my job right. The creatures in the Farm are taking the brunt of these breeches. The innocent are always the first to suffer," Old Paul closed his eyes. "Now I sound more like myself... Well, thank you, Phillip, for your assistance. Feel free to keep that old blade there. It's traveled long enough for me. Ghost blades can be useful on things that aren't quite as real as you and me."

"Are you sure?" Phillip said, looking down at the strange blade.

"Least I can do, and I won't monopolize any more of your time either. Daniel is probably wondering where you are." Old Paul's mood had changed, he almost looked as unreal as the blade, standing on the water.

"Oh, no sir. This has been fun. Really!" Phillip said.

"And are you? *Having fun?* At the Farm?" Old Paul said, still distant. A slow unnatural wave came to the giant koi and picked her up, bringing her gently back into the lake. Old Paul comforting her.

"Yes!" Phillip answered.

"Good. Good," Old Paul said back. "If I could teach one thing it would be to teach the tremendous importance of fun. Men are built on fun, you know? Now go back to your friends, Phillip Montgomery, have some fun today, on my behalf."

"Yes sir, I will," Phillip said.

"And one more thing," Old Paul said. He put his hand up in the air, and grabbed some lake mist as smoothly and as easily as if he picked up a coat. "Try not to spook the mist with desperation. It doesn't like that. Paradoxically though, it will respond to genuine need. There are so many parts of ourselves that stay hidden until we *need* them. Really need them."

He threw the bundle of mist at Phillip. It floated in the air like soup bubbled. Phillip reached out to grab, convinced he would be able to, and for a moment he thought he was able to slow it down, to rest it in his hand, But the mist dropped away, and vanished. "Keep at it, Phillip," Old Paul continued. "And don't forget to have fun."

"I will, sir," Phillip repeated with a genuine smile.

He was soaked and didn't bother to put back on his shoes as he went back to the stable, stopping sometimes to look at the ghost blade. Thinking about how he would tell the story of what happened this morning.

The following weeks were both calmest and busiest they had at the Farm.

Dan and Phillip took every course and class and workshop they could, understanding almost nothing. Their shared list of questions was not just uselessly large but now *comically* and uselessly large. Dan had taken up the responsibility of separating them by category, and making an index. "Do you think I should keep all the Alchemy questions under 'Willastic' magic or 'Older Crafts...?'" Dan asked Phillip. "And what about Pathmaking...?"

Tales of breaches at the barrier had died down. Dan and Phillip faced no major disasters, or confrontations, or embarrassments.

Not any more than they were used to, anyway...

They made no progress on the hunt for the infiltrator, or *infiltrators*. Andy was annoyed they weren't showing enough interest, and to appease her, Phillip and Haystacks set up an 'investigation area' in the stable. Complete with all the evidence they had... which was almost nothing. The only difficulty keeping Buttercup's cubs from swatting at the pin-board or biting their shoelaces when they talked about theories.

"I should come over to your house," Andy said. "All of us! Emily and Pieter too..."

"That would be great!" Phillip said. "I want more people to see what happened to the house."

"Is it like a dinner party?" Emily asked.

"It can be," Phillip answered. "I can order pizza..."

Andy lit up at the idea of trying Mundafold pizza. It was another delicacy she could never get away with trying in the Primafold. Dan was enthusiastic as well. "Maybe the Ramblers will still be there. They're fun."

Aunt Elaine thought it was a great idea when he got home. "I would love for your friends to come over... They're so nice, especially that Emily Morris girl..." She said, then whispered, "You might not want to tell Harrison that Emily is coming over, I think he's smitten and won't leave you alone," she winked at him. "Don't make any firm plans until tomorrow..."

"Why?" he asked.

"No real reason," Aunt Elaine said, looking at her phone. "Your uncle just got home with Maddie. And I just remembered he put his toolbox in the Dollhouse, do you mind getting it for him?"

"Sure," Phillip said. He was trying to find a reason to go over there anyway.

When he approached the porch, he noticed the yellow bird was on the railing. Waiting for more food, and that Fortinbras was on his feet. He didn't look afraid, or even nervous... more like unsure. Fortinbras wagged his tail, but it was far less enthusiastic than usual. He looked over to the Ramblers, the camp was quiet, they usually took naps this time of day.

He had the oddest feeling that the door had been opened. *It had*, he thought, *uncle Jeff had come into the house when I was gone*... but for some reason that didn't shake the odd feeling that overtook him.

The house felt... *opened*. Maybe *exposed* was the right word.

He approached the house slower than usual. Walked in, and immediately realized a problem, what if uncle Jeff had left the toolbox in the Mundafold kitchen, and he couldn't get into it right now.

"Ahhhh!" A figure shrieked in a high voice behind him.

Phillip spun and jumped back as fast as he could, put his hands over his head, grabbed his bag for protection. A laughter had taken over the room. Phillip looked at the creature.

"Oh God dangit..." He said, his stomach going back to its normal resting place. "I hate you."

Aunt Kath stood at the center of the room. Laughing herself breathless.

"Everybody said I shouldn't... do it," she said, unable to stop laughing. "That it was mean. But I convinced them..."

"When did you get back!?" Phillip practically shouted. Joining her laughing and giving her a hug. He wasn't expecting Aunt Kath back for another week.

"Program ended a few days early..." Aunt Kath said. "Changed my ticket. Your uncle just picked me up. Thought it would be fun to surprise you. And I was right, it was fun."

"Ah, that's right, I hate you now," Phillip said.

"There's so much to talk about! You need to tell me I look tan and healthy. Also, did we officially adopt the dog...?" She said, pointing to Fortinbras, who was wagging his tail.

His heart was still beating hard from the shock. It also just occurred to him that, in a world like the Primafold, there were a lot more reasons to be skittish, and he probably overreacted to Aunt Kath's scare.

"I think he adopted us," Phillip said.

"You're going to classes at the University, we have a new dog, a house," Aunt Kath said. "We're really setting up shop here in King's Hill."

CHAPTER
26
Dinner Party

Dan usually saved all his deepest thoughts for after midnight.

And usually shared them with Phillip as soon as he had them.

"Wait," Dan said on the phone. 'In the Primafold house, where does the water come from? When you flush the Primafold toilet, where does everything go? Does it use the Mundafold plumbing?"

"That's a… *really* good point," Phillip admitted, rubbing his eyes. He had fallen asleep in his clothes again while studying. He was careful not to talk too loudly, as he was no longer alone in the house. "I wonder if we could test that. But I think the water is Primafold water…"

They talked a little more about magical plumbing, Dan concluding that since the Primafold can make mail appear to a mailbox in a closet, plumbing must really be spectacular. "It's crazy that your aunt is back." Dan said, changing the subject. "I was reading the Old Laws book about receiving guests for dinner, there's a whole bunch of stuff you have to do… I'm supposed to give you a small gift, depending on our relationship. Do you consider us business partners…?"

The *'Secrets to Good Housekeeping'* book had proved invaluable in understanding the Primafold version of the house. There wasn't much in there about split homes, but there was plenty in there that explained how to prevent parasitic infections, non-purified energies, and unwelcomed hauntings. How to manage faeFlame in the home—which was really just a matter of setting clear guidelines and not showing fear—and how to make mutually beneficial deals with local spiders. There was a whole section on creating a good *'Magical Ecosystem'* for the home.

Some of the advice was less logical than others.

The sections dealing with sealing and purifying a home especially. He didn't understand why it was a good idea to have a 'New sapling' in a hallway, or why it had to be gathered in 'fair-grown woods at night.' There was a whole section on houseplant maintenance that made no sense at all. Which was unfortunate, seeing as the plant Bertrand had given him had grown a whole foot since he left, and he could really use some advice on that front...

He was learning to get the version of the rooms he wanted, with a decent rate of success. Go up the stairs, touch nothing else, end up in the Mundafold bathroom... Look out the window at the new old stone barn, end up in the Primafold kitchen. It worked most of the time...

He noticed Fortinbras seemed to be in whatever part of the fold he wanted to. But wasn't sharing his secrets with Phillip.

Dan had found lamps scattered around the Primafold Dollhouse. There were more objects scattered around the home every time they looked. The lamps looked like a combination of a light bulb and an oil lamp. "FaeFlame lamps," Dan said. "I'm sure of it. I wonder if we could ask Henry and Haystacks how they adapted those light bulb lamps back at the stable," Phillip put them around the home.

The Primafold home was darker than the other one. He had taken to carrying a flashlight everywhere he went. The 'Memory cloth' Bertrand had left as a guest present had proved useful here. Phillip kept it in the upstairs Primafold bathroom. Spinning the knob for sunlight made the room feel like it was outdoors. They discovered a knob for moonlight too.

Training the faeFlame lamps was difficult, the lamps were old and dusty, and flame complained as much as it could, sometimes it tried to jump out and find another resting place. "You put the lamps exactly where they are in the Mundafold house," Dan noticed a few days later. "I don't think you intended to do that... *Spooky*. Is that what 'convergence' means...?"

The book told him how to manage a large faeFlame like a fireplace. He spent money, more money than he wanted, on a faeFlame tinderbox and managing tools, which allowed him to start the faeFlame, and more importantly, turn it off. *Almost* off. *Resting* was a better word when talking about faeFlame.

FaeFlame could run on anything, he learned concentrated moon gleam, sunlight, wood, certain kinds of stones, even memories. It was especially fond of candy, he found.

Phillip was starting to get used to this. The hardest part now was managing Aunt Kath.

She asked a lot of questions, especially about the 'program' he was in, and Phillip's normal excuses didn't work as well on her as it did with the Fairchild family. She asked almost as many questions as Maddie did. A few times she cornered Dan with questions, who did not hold lies well and bumbled his responses, which Aunt Kath was too polite to call him on.

Fortinbras loved Aunt Kath. This had less to do with personality and more to do with the fact that she gave him snacks whenever she saw him. "You're going to make him fat and spoiled," Phillip said. "Did the same thing to get you to like me and you turned out fine," she responded.

She was especially curious about King's Hill University. "How do you like it?" "Is it a good campus?" She asked several times. "It's a big research University, you know..." she said, as if trying to convince him.

Phillip looked up all the information he could about the University and tried to fill out the lies he was telling about the 'program.' He wished Adeline or Sarah could be called on for help, but they had gone missing with most of the staff at Crownshead...

"Lots to talk about," she continued to insist, though when Phillip pressed her about it, she just repeated herself, "we have to catch up." Her time in California had been eventful, filled with a flurry of odd characters and weird teachers.

Aunt Kath was also excited about the dinner party he planned. Thrilled to meet the friends he had talked about and she had only seen in one picture that Dan took on July 4th...

They had set the dinner party for Thursday when most of the Fairchild family was going away to the neighboring town, Gardenvale, something to do with Steve and Harrison's training... they wouldn't be home until the following afternoon. Only Maddie was staying home, to be watched by Aunt Kath.

Pieter was coming too and providing the transportation to get to the Fairchild property. "Good about finding my way between the Mundafold and Primafold. Plus, I have a real car. I think your Mundafold family would be surprised if we came up in a puppet carriage. What should I bring, food-wise?" He asked. "I think we are ordering pizza," Phillip answered. "But you can get that in the Primafold!" Pieter complained. "Andy's kind-of dead set on it now," Phillip answered.

Phillip awoke to rain the day of the dinner party. But when he got out of the bathroom, he noticed it was bright and sunny. *That cleared up fast*, he thought, but a moment later he walked into the hallway and he noticed that the rain was still going strong...

It was raining in the Primafold, and not in the Mundafold.

This had never happened before, he didn't think it was possible given what he learned.

He didn't know how to deal with this, except to try to make sure he stayed in the Mundafold version of the house as best as he could. Outside the Ramblers stayed up in their tents, the fire smoking. Phillip's eyes registered a kind of double vision. He could see the rain and clouds, but it didn't make him wet. The wind didn't blow his shirt.

He ran into Maddie on the way out, who looked like she was trying to listen to something faint. Lightning crashed in the distance, they both looked instinctively at the sky.

Maddie looked at Phillip, her eyes both wide and accusatory. "You heard...!" She got out, but Phillip was able to mount his bike and leave before she finished the question.

He was having a hard time justifying to Aunt Kath why he should go to class on bike, and why he never seemed interested in taking Aunt Kath along. "I won't embarrass you, I promise," she said. "I'm super groovy. I promise. I'll be super cool and hip..."

He laughed it off, and the conversation usually ended there.

Emily, Andy, and Pieter arrived in Pieter's car, which was a model and make Phillip didn't recognize. They arrived in the Mundafold, but he noticed their car was wet, and they all held umbrellas and rain jackets as they approached the house. Phillip and Dan met them on the porch of the Dollhouse.

"Cloud-herding season," Pieter said. "I thought it was late in the year for that..."

"It is," Emily confirmed. "It must be very dry down south right now."

"Phillargo!" Andy yelled. "We've brought gifts!"

Maddie and Fortinbras joined them on the porch. Pieter handed Phillip a big pot of something spicy, "it's a potato dish, thought it would pair well with pizza," he said.

Emily and Andy gave him a small potted plant that could fit in his palm. "We're cheap so we chipped in and got this, it's supposed to smell like good memories when it blooms," Andy whispered to him. "But I don't know anything about that..."

"Why did you bring Phillip a plant?" Maddie asked, who had appeared out of nowhere.

Andy took a second to answer. "Ancient... Japanese studying tradition..."

"I... don't think it is..." Maddie said.

"But it very well could be," Andy added.

Maddie, not to be deterred, said, "... and why did you all bring umbrellas..."

"You must be Maddie, Phillip's cousin..." Pieter said. "That's a very good question, Maddie. You ever here the phrase, 'luck follows the prepared?' You probably haven't because I think only my dad says it..."

"I like you, Maddie, properly inquisitive" Andy said. "We should hang out more."

Aunt Kath came out on the porch a moment later.

"And you must be Katherine Smith, Phillip's aunt, it is a great pleasure to finally meet you," Pieter said, wiping his hand on his jacket before taking Aunt Kath's hand like an old French lord. "I'm Pieter Vanderleer. This is Ms. Emily Morris, and we call the small one in the glasses Andy..."

"Nice to meet you all!" Aunt Kath said, laughing at Pieter's manners. "The pizza is already ordered, I think I ordered too much. Phillip all you have to do is tip. We'll get out of your hair for you can study..."

"Oh, Ms. Smith no, don't leave. Didn't Phillip tell you?" Pieter said. "These study sessions are really just an excuse to hang-out, we don't get any work done. It's all a lie. We'd love to have you for dinner."

Aunt Kath thanked them but insisted she had plans of her own with Maddie.

"You didn't tell me your aunt was so... um... *young*, Phillip." Pieter whispered before walking into the house.

"So, what are you studying?" Maddie asked in a mockingly casual tone.

"Didn't Phillip tell you? Magic, of course," Pieter said.

Maddie stopped dead in her tracks, so did Phillip.

"... specifically," Pieter continued. "Finding scientific justifications for ridiculous magician stuff. You take a question like 'How can a man turn into a bird?' and the team that comes up with the best scientific evidence, given 'real' scientific principles, wins. There's also a part where you get to ask other teams questions. There's a prize if you win. Nothing big. 'Whatif debates' they call them. It's dumb, but I have to say it's fun."

"Oh..." Maddie said.

Pieter winked at Phillip.

Aunt Kath and Pieter kept conversations so well it was almost difficult for the others to join in. Pieter, though, clearly practiced, always brought the conversation back to the group. Emily was delightful, but like Dan, squirmed a little when it came time to lie. Unlike Pieter, who lied so easily it was almost offensive. Even Maddie had dropped her pointed questioning and was enjoying herself. Maddie and Andy talked about Fortinbras and the general subjects of pets for at least thirty minutes. "Parents won't let me get pets," Andy reported. "Unless you count the crab I almost didn't kill and those little guys in the garden..."

"What little guys?" Maddie asked.

Andy paused for a moment. "Chipmunks..." She said.

Phillip noticed Pieter was a little too comfortable touching Aunt Kath's hands. Is he flirting with Aunt Kath? Why is he flirting so much? Phillip wondered, *he can't be much older than me...* and that stunt he pulled with the magic conversation!

"Andy..." He managed to whisper.

"Yeah?" she said.

"You ever have fantasies of hurting Pieter?" Phillip asked.

"God yes. You should see my dairy, psycho stuff in there. I have drawings," she said, and they both laughed.

"Tell me..." She asked the group. "Is this meat on top made out of real animals...?"

"I think so," Phillip answered.

"Oh, now I feel bad," she said, but took another bite. "But I love Munda... *pizza* so much... better than hot dogs..."

Aunt Kath and Maddie did end up leaving a little while after they ate pizza. Dan had to leave for home a little while later. "My mom doesn't like me to ride when it gets too dark," he said.

"Let's get a look at this house," Pieter said when they were gone. "What fold are we in?"

"This is how the house looked before Bertrand came," Phillip explained. "Did you see the Ramblers when you came in?"

"No," Emily confirmed for the group.

"Okay, everybody gets up." Phillip ordered. "Grab my shoulder, let's walk through the hallway and come back..." They did so, slowly. Andy remarking how stupid they looked, Emily shushing her. Phillip tapped the faeFlame lamp he kept in the Mundafold closet.

"It worked!" Emily declared. "I see the travelers now! Oh, there are a lot of them aren't there?"

"I've met a lot of Ramblers but never camped with them, that might be fun." Pieter said, then pointed to the painting of the girl in the yellow dress. "Who do you think she is...?"

"Dan and I think she might be a relative of the Fairchild family," Phillip answered. "If it's true the house was built this way and whoever owned the house likely owned both folds and the Fairchild family has owned this land forever. Or maybe it's just a painting of a lady."

They explored every part of the house which was different. Pieter liked the kitchen the most. "There's some good old stuff in here. It works fine. They don't build them like this anymore!" He said.

Emily was able to tell him that some of the objects on the shelves were "Old astrological equipment, I think. *Skyworking* equipment. I don't know how any of it works though," she was also able to identify the plant Bertrand had left. "I think this is a sunleaf tree! You must have made a good impression as host, Phillip. It's a type of cave dwelling *prunas* tree. Very useful in dark cold climates if you know how to take care of it." She then proceeded to tell Phillip exactly what to do if he wanted it to grow up 'happy and healthy.' "I'm not boring you, am I?"

"It's impossible for me to get bored," he said, feeling stupid the moment it came out of his mouth. Emily laughed. No, *giggled.*

"What's behind the locked door up here?" Pieter asked. "Attic?"

"Don't know," Phillip answered, happy for the interruption. "Can't find a key anywhere. Can't force it open either, same with the closet downstairs. It opened once, when Bertrand was here."

"This would drive me mad," Pieter said, anything could be behind there... Money, a great big pile of skulls, old Fireday decorations..."

They spent a long time exploring the home. Trying to switch between the Mundafold and Primafold version. Andy wandered into Phillip's room. "So, this is Phillargo's room, is it?" She said loud enough for him to hear her from the hallway. "But why does he need so many pictures of half-dressed women!? A dozen would do the job, this is just excessive..."

"Aleandra! Leave his room at once!" Emily said, but Phillip got the distinct impression she was trying to suppress a smile.

"I like variety!" Phillip yelled back, proud at himself for not blushing at Andy's joke.

"I wish I was telling the truth, that place is boring, just clothes and bags," Andy said as she walked back into the hallway.

"I have a magical bag and crayons hidden in the closet. Also, a mounted deer head."

"I'm going to scrutinize your washroom," Andy said.

"They must have been talented or wealthy, to afford this much, out here near the frontier," Pieter said.

They had to leave soon after. Emily and Andy had to get back to Crownshead, the entrance points were harder to manage late at night. Pieter cryptically said that there were some debts he had to take care of in the Camps. They waved goodbye to Aunt Kath on the porch, the car a little too wet and muddy to be explained by the clear Mundafold evening. He noticed the stars were just as bright, even though he was sure he was in the Mundafold. He noticed he could, if he looked hard enough, see the stars shining through the clouds.

Dan would want to know about that... he needed to remember to tell him.

"Have fun?" Aunt Kath asked as he went into the main Fairchild house.

"Tons of fun," Phillip confirmed. "But Pieter was right, we didn't end up getting any work done."

"Ah, Pieter," Aunt Kath said. "He's a dangerous one, isn't he? Know the type. I love your friends, if that's not too uncool to say," Aunt Kath said. "They're all so interesting. And nice."

"Yeah, I like them a lot." Phillip said. "Emily's dad is super rich, she knows a lot about agriculture..."

"And that Andy girl, she's really cool," Aunt Kath said, looking straight at Phillip's face.

"Really cool," Phillip confirmed.

"I'm just happy you're making friends," Aunt Kath continued. "There's a lot I need to talk to you about..."

"You keep saying that, but you never follow up," Phillip said.

Aunt Kath took a moment to answer. "Alright, but here's a condition. Think about what I say. Don't answer right away. I want an honest response..."

"Well now I'm really curious."

"I've been offered a scholarship in a graduate course at King's Hill University..." Aunt Kath said, letting the words sink in before continuing. "The program went well at Berkeley, and Professor Lewis wrote me a recommendation letter. They contacted me! I'm not trying to brag, I didn't even consider KHU until they offered me the scholarship... It's a top tier university..."

"That's great news!" Phillip said. "Why didn't you tell me sooner?"

"Because it, well if I take the scholarship..." Aunt Kath continued immediately, "it would mean moving to King's Hill for a little while. A year-and-half at least. Maybe more. It means you going to school here."

"Ah," Phillip said, the implication hitting him. "Still, it's great..."

"I don't want you to answer right away... I want you to think about it," Aunt Kath interrupted. "Be honest with yourself on how you feel. This would be a big change... I spoke to my sister and Jeff about it. They want us to stay in the Dollhouse, they love the idea... So, that's part of the deal. Think it over!"

"I will... ferment my thoughts," Phillip said.

"Chocolate syrup is in the fridge!" Maddie yelled from the other room.

"Awesome!" Aunt Kath yelled back. And then whispered to Phillip. "Maddie's been having some sleeping problems. I wasn't supposed to give her any late snacks. But I, you know, *did*. Don't tell my sister!"

———————— o ————————

He was able to get away to sleep in the Dollhouse. "All my stuff is over there, it would be a pain to bring it over," he said. "I have Fortinbras, I won't be lonely," he assured her. Aunt Kath and Maddie had changed into robes while they ate ice cream. They were planning to "do their toes next" and that Phillip was welcome to join them.

A full scholarship to King's Hill University.

Was this, again, an example of the 'Privilege' he was granted. Aunt Kath getting a sudden opportunity in the town where he had discovered the Farm? Out of nowhere...? Perhaps it was just a coincidence, but he didn't think so.

Did he want to stay in King's Hill? He certainly didn't want to leave the Farm. But Dan was in Knoxville and he was able to attend. Did he really want to leave Maine for that long? The home of almost every memory he had...? Bad and good. His school, the familiar shops, his parents' graves...

He would go anywhere to be closer to the Farm. He knew this. And he desperately wanted to support Aunt Kath, she had been delayed enough, to say nothing of the financial benefits of being offered a scholarship and house to stay in...

But he would be lying to himself if he said it didn't feel complicated.

He was so introspective he didn't notice until he was almost back at the Dollhouse.

The *feeling* was back.

The feeling that the house was opened-up. Exposed.

Fortinbras was likewise acting nervous. Though it was possible he was just picking up on Phillip's feelings. A kind of tingling played at the back of Phillip's neck.

He turned on and left on more lights than were necessary. Even lit a few of the faeFlame lamps, which burned freshly cut holly plants he had spent too much money on earlier in the week.

It didn't work, the feeling stayed with him.

He found himself turning around and looking behind him. Opening doors and then making sure they were sealed tight. Fortinbras took a defensive posture, standing close to Phillip's legs, even as he brushed his teeth. He checked the whole house a second time for open windows or doors. Nothing. Fortinbras looked out the windows and whined, "stop making me nervous," he said to the dog.

I just have the creeps, he told himself. He was just reading how unhygienic houses can create bad feelings... he needed to work harder to clean it like the book said. That was it. And Fortinbras was probably just missing Aunt Kath, he had grown attached.

But the reassuring thoughts had no impact on how he felt.

He sat in bed with the lights on. Listening to the house creak and moan as it set in for the night. Listening to Fortinbras softly whine and look out the window.

CHAPTER 27

The Night Raid

Fortinbras barked. A nervous, shallow bark.

Phillip woke up. Not realizing for a moment that he had been asleep and finding it difficult to adjust to reality.

It was dark, the lights had gone out and only starlight illuminated the room. Fortinbras had crawled onto the bed. He was whining and shaking. Every part of him nervous.

"What's wrong Fort…?" he started, but stopped when he noticed it…

"Ah!" He yelped and pushed himself into the wall.

Red-eyes.

Massive, bright red eyes.

Luminous, almost glowing. Staring straight at Phillip. And they were attached to a body. A body that took up most of the room.

The red-eyed stag stood, almost twice as tall as Phillip, in the center of the room.

It was still. Still like a stone, but vibrating with a living energy.

"What… do you want?" Phillip said. When he spoke, vapor appeared in front of his face. He could see his breath. It was freezing in the room.

The red-eyed stag lifted its head at Phillip's words. Then turned and looked toward the doorway, and then back at Phillip.

"I… don't understand," Phillip said. Was it trying to tell him something? The air was biting cold and he was starting to shiver.

The red-eyed stag turned and walked toward the window. When Phillip was sure it would run into the wall, nothing happened. The red-eyed stag blended into the wallpaper, part of its body becoming two-dimensional—*or maybe it was always two-dimensional*—and then switching back in a way that hurt Phillip's eyes.

It walked through the window like it wasn't there.

It was on the roof. It jumped. Phillip made no attempt to look where it went from there.

He jumped up. Put on his shoes. Grabbed his bag. Picked up the wood handled pocket knife. Picked up the ghost blade sword Old Paul had given him. Picking up his phone, it wasn't working...

The air was still cold. Colder, even.

Frost had collected on the windows, and it was growing thicker.

He looked around and noticed for the first time that his bedroom had changed. The wallpaper and lights were different. So was the door. There was a ladder opposite the bed that led to what looked like a loft where the ceiling of the closet should be...

And he noticed how bad he felt.

A feeling like thousands of pinpricks invaded his feet and his spine and neck. *It's cold*, he thought. But he knew this had nothing to do with the cold. The feeling cut much deeper than cold. It felt like he was being hurt, like he was being touched and he couldn't do anything about it... His brain yelled *'fight!'* and *'run!'* and *'stop this!'*

But he couldn't run anywhere, and how would he fight...?

Fortinbras followed Phillip in adopting a defensive posture.

He looked out the window. It had begun to snow outside.

No, not snow. What fell outside the window an ugly grey and black and bright red. It looked like old embers falling from the sky.

The Ramblers were out of their tent. Looking at the ashy substance falling from the sky. *Maybe they know what's happening*, Phillip thought, I should go out there to see. But really he just felt the need to be around other people.

He wanted to get to them as fast as possible, something in his mind made it hard to move.

He opened his door and walked into the hallway.

It was a mistake.

There were figures in the hallway. Dark. Dark like they were holes in space. There were four or five, he couldn't tell. He froze in place. No two were alike. The tallest almost scraping the ceiling.

They were almost human shaped, but too thin and too tall.

Their heads long and misshapen. Their whole bodies misshapen, kept into place by tight wrapping. Belts maybe. They had eyes, gleaming little eyes, too many of them, set low in their heads.

Phillip didn't move, neither did Fortinbras. He didn't think he could even if he wanted to.

The dark figures, whose arms and fingers and shoulders came to points tipped over objects on the shelf. One was scratching the walls. Small ones which looked like infants with elongated limbs and giant heads were sniffing the floor like animals. They moved with odd, unnatural motions, only sometimes obeying gravity.

Fortinbras growled.

Every dark figure stopped moving. Then turned its head toward Phillip. Dead, gleaming, dark eyes looked at Phillip. The things were still.

He backed up.

The black figures moved forward as if they were one.

He grabbed Fortinbras's collar and pulled him back into the room as fast as he could. He slammed the door. The door had changed with the room, but he found a heavy latch and slammed it down. He grabbed the entire dresser table and dragged it in front of the door. He swore under his breath and stepped back.

Fortinbras barked once, but Phillip shushed him and he was quiet.

He waited.

He heard scratching. The light at the bottom of the door went dark. Something like the sound of thousands of insects filled his ears, and he saw at the bottom of the door fingers and what looked like loose scraps of ripped black cloth make its way into the room. The doorknob jiggled. "Crap crap crap crap crap!" He said, having no idea what to do.

Snap! Bang!

Phillip let out a short yell as splinters and paint shot toward his face.

A black spike, like an enormous nail, shot through the door and made it almost halfway across the room.

Crack! Bang! Snap! Bang!

The giant spike went through the door, and the wall next to it. Six more spikes in rapid succession. Leaving circle holes in the wall, letting in small streams of light.

Then it stopped.

A moment passed, he saw those eyes look through the holes...

Then the arms starting coming through.

Some were the size of children's arms but with long fingers. Some looked man-sized but had those infants sized arms for fingers. The largest was easily as long as Phillip was tall. They went into the room slowly, sliding through the holes like snakes, and then began to feel the walls.

Looking for the doorknob, Phillip realized in terror.

He didn't wait a moment longer. He opened the window, which was almost sealed due to the ice, and climbed onto the roof, putting Fortinbras in front of him first. The grey red ash stung his eyes.

Crack! Bang! He heard behind him. The figures were getting impatient.

He ran to the edge of the roof. Dragging a confused and scared Fortinbras by his collar. It was a good fifteen feet drop from here, but he didn't see how he had a choice. But then he noticed three Ramblers were approaching the house. They were looking up at Phillip, calling to him. They were all holding weapons.

Moving to the edge of the roof, they understood he needed help, and went up to the porch and stretched their hands out. Fortinbras resisted, but he was able to grab him and holding his collar, lifted him down to the Ramblers outstretched arms. Phillip climbed down the water gutter, almost falling but helped the Ramblers.

"There's something in the house! A bunch of somethings!" Phillip yelled. The Ramblers furrowed their brows, but followed where Phillip pointed. They seemed to understand him, as the entire group backed up from the house when they heard breaking and crashing emanating from the room above.

Phillip resisted the urge to run for the other house, or run off the property together. He was safer with the Ramblers, he knew this.

Aunt Kath! Maddie! He thought suddenly. God, he hoped they were okay...

The black figures began to come out of the upstairs window. They were almost liquid they were so flexible. The tallest one stood on the roof. Three of the smallest climbed higher. Going to the corner of the roofs, they tucked their feet and arms into themselves. They opened massive angular mouths to the sky.

They began to wail.

It was one of the worst sounds Phillip had ever heard. Screeching and howling, he felt it in his bones. The failing ash was disturbed in the air, and it felt like it got colder.

The blond rambler, not looking away from the Dollhouse, handed Phillip a silver ax before he took out his own. Phillip grabbed it, and realized that he left the ghost blade sword up in his room... Would that have done any good? These creatures looked more real.

Black figures climbed off the roof, the Ramblers seemed determined to stand their ground. They were joined by two others. The black figures moved slow. At one constant speed.

A woman screamed back at camp.

The all turned around,

"Ah!" yelled one of Ramblers near Phillip.

One of the black figures had moved forward so fast it caught him by surprise. It grabbed both his hands above his head. He dropped his sword to the ground.

Phillip and the other Ramblers raised their weapons, but the black figure held a spike to the man's throat and looked at them. Both passive and dead and utterly threatening. The black thing shook a little back and forth. The Ramblers stopped, fearing the figure would stab the man if they moved closer.

Phillip tried to watch, but the other black figures were getting closer...

It held the man with two arms, and sniffed his face, though Phillip couldn't see a nose. With two other arms it reached inside his jacket, pulled out his pockets... like he was being mugged.

The Rambler kicked at his attacker. The black figure barely moved but seemed confused for a moment.

One of its arms turned into a spike.

"No!" Phillip yelled, a moment too late.

The black figure stabbed the man in his stomach twice. The black spike of an arm going through all the way to the other side.

Fortinbras barked wildly and ran to the black figure.

Not knowing what he was doing Phillip ran to the figure and raised the small silver ax. With a scream to push away the fear he drove the ax as hard as he could into the creator's neck.

At first it was as if the creature didn't notice. It turned its head slowly to look at Phillip.

The howling wails on the roof intensified. The black figure dropped the Rambler to the ground, who landed with a thud. Phillip pulled the ax out of its neck and drove it home again and again as Fortinbras bit at its legs.

The creature moved slowly, it was as if Phillip wasn't doing anything.

It raised its spiked arm.

The other rambler got to it first. Swinging their swords and axes and spears much more effectively than Phillip. One Rambler breathed fire, but it stopped with a sputter and he seemed confused.

They managed to force it to the ground, but it still moved, making no sounds. Finally, the two Ramblers who had brought spears forced them through the creature into the ground.

The creature was pinned, for now. But was working its way back up the spears. Looking straight at Phillip as if the Ramblers weren't there...

The other creators!

Phillip looked for them. They had walked around them. Some, and there was more than Phillip thought, were in the house. Throwing furniture out the door. There were others at the Rambler's camp, cutting through tents and overturning bags. They had no care for their companion pinned to the ground.

The Ramblers moved with their weapons at the blond man's orders to intercept them.

"No!" Phillip said to the Ramblers at the last moment. "No," he tried to tell them again. "They won't attack you if you don't attack them, I think. They're looking for something..."

The blond man looked into Phillip's eyes and seemed to register what he was saying. He yelled something to the other Ramblers, who stopped moving but held their weapons to the ready. Fortinbras was still biting the black creature pinned to the ground.

More creatures came. Some of them approached close and sniffed and then went away. There was crashing in the house, something like glass breaking. They were moving faster now, more aggressively. They weren't attacking, but how long would that last?

He desperately tried to get his paralyzed mind in motion.

They needed help. They needed a bigger weapon or somewhere to hide until they went away. *Think! Phillip, think!* But all he thought about was what was happening at the large house, were Aunt Kath and Maddie safe...? Maybe they were safe in the Mundafold...?

The Mundafold...

He was in the Primafold side of the home now... they probably couldn't even see the big home.

And what was a fold? A fold was a stretching, it was geometry. *Local Isolated Space.* Something partially defined by a barrier. He had just read this...

He didn't need a place to hide or a bigger weapon. He needed a barrier. He needed to keep the *'Thieving Termite'* out...

He needed a circle!

But how? He thought, and the answer came to him. He reached inside his bag, took out his sky chalk. He had more in the bag, his lashing glove, the pocket knife, the... orbit ball.

Remembering what Dan and him had done a few days before with the ball. An idea struck him. Would this work? He didn't have time to question it...

He put on his lashing glove. Tested the sky chalk in the air to make sure it worked.

He lashed the button so that it stuck in the on position. Putting the ball next to the sky chalk dispenser, he pressed them together and did the motion with the glove. The sky chalk was lashed to the ball.

Phillip ran to where Dan had stood just a few days before, leaving a trail of white chalk in his wake.

The black figures began to take notice of him. They turned their terrible heads and dropped what they were doing to move toward Phillip. The Ramblers noticed Phillip moved away and yelled in confusion in what Phillip took as 'stay close.'

He didn't have time to explain. He drew a tight circle around himself, drew a line around the circle. Drew a triangle.

The black figures were getting closer. Fortinbras was in front of Phillip growling. "Good boy." He said. He moved into the best position he could. And with every bit of strength he could muster, he threw the orbit ball attached to the sky chalk to his right. It floated away above the ground until it was out of sight. The chalk marking its path. It was impossible to see where it went, the ash falling from the sky had intensified and blocked his vision. The air was so cold Phillip's lungs hurt in his chest.

Please work, please work! Phillip begged.

The blond rambler moved to a defensive position around Phillip, followed by one of his larger friends. He was still confused, but seemed willing to go with Phillip.

The figures got closer. And Closer. Some were crawling. Others stood taller, almost ten feet tall...

Just when Phillip was sure he had failed. He heard the sound he was listening for, the scratching sound of the sky chalk. "Yes!" He yelled, and looked to his right, just in time to catch the orbit ball.

It had formed a near perfect circle around the house and the property, hovering a few feet above the ground. A circle Phillip completed. Drawing an intersecting line that connected the small circle to the big one.

He needed to seal it! *But he couldn't...*

The nearest black figure was within ten yards now. It's eyes on Phillip.

"Blond guy! Blond guy!" He yelled to the rambler. "We need to seal this circle. Seal the circle! Do you understand?" Phillip clapped his hand and then pressed them down, pantomiming the motion. "Clap, clap, stamp! Clap clap stamp!"

Comprehension lit in the Rambler's eyes.

"Ah hah!" He yelled triumphantly. "Clump clump Stuump!" And copied Phillip's motions. "Clamp Clump Stuump!"

The other rambler joined him, they dropped their weapons. They beat their chests hard. Yelled something incompressible, and drove their hands into the ground.

The rush of wind was so intense and sudden it was as if explosion had gone off.

But it wasn't just wind. It was the ash. It was pushed out of the center of the circle so violently it felt like it would take Phillip with it. Cold like icicles and staining his clothes red and gray as it passed.

The wailing on the top of the roof cut out. They sounded like they were being drowned before they fell off the roof.

The tallest black creature took a few more unsteady steps toward Phillip before falling to the ground as if it was a puppet whose strings were cut one by one.

The rest of the Ramblers, realizing what was happening, moved into the circle. The creatures outside the circle retreated into the woods, going with the cloud of ash.

And just like that. It was over. The Ramblers were silent. There was no more wailing.

The cold had left with the ash...

Silence was broken only when the woman in the red dress ran with a scream to the rambler who had been stabbed. The other Ramblers covered his wounds, and held his hand as blood came out of his mouth. He was beginning to shake. The woman sobbing and chanting over him.

Phillip just watched, breathing hard, unable to move.

CHAPTER
28

Special Circumstances
Investigator

The Rambler who was stabbed didn't die.

The other Ramblers pressed on his wounds on the grass, an old woman with twigs in her hair and wearing too many jackets came from the Rambler camp. Phillip didn't remember seeing her but the other Ramblers moved aside. She rubbed her hands together, and placed them on the Ramblers wounds. He spasmed in pain, but then relaxed. The old woman said something in what Phillip guessed was New-Faroese, the men picked up their injured companion and brought him to the porch.

At least he knew Aunt Kath and Maddie were okay. He saw the living room light go on at the larger home, he could see Aunt Kath through the window. She was turning on lights. Holding a blanket. In the kitchen. He could see Maddie on the couch.

Phillip stood, watching Aunt Kath, paralyzed in the small circle. Not knowing if he could leave the safety of it. Not knowing if he wanted to move at all.

The decision was made for him. The blond rambler came up to Phillip and hugged him with such strength Phillip was picked up the ground and placed outside the circle.

"Aha! Aha! Cramp cramp stuump!" the blond man repeated as if it was a joke. Other joined him in patting and hugging Phillip. One man shoved a bottle into Phillip's hands and he took a drink without thinking about it, happy to find that the liquid was just water. He didn't realize until now how dry his mouth was... They were petting Fortinbras, who seemed to enjoy the attention.

He didn't think any of the Ramblers were left in the camp. They were all on the porch now, or starting a new fire right outside it. Phillip invited them in the best he could. There was more of them than he thought. Some of the Ramblers were doing small magics, placing their hands in the air and leaving trails of fire vapor. They talked amongst each other and seemed to be experimenting. They lit their palms the saw way he saw Emily did, emitting a soft glow.

Phillip pieced together what they were doing. Magic didn't work right when the creatures were here. But his orbit ball had worked, and his skychalk... but his phone didn't...

He got the phone out. It was working now. It was 3:33am.

He messaged Dan, the only person he could... *'my house was attacked. im okay.'*

The Ramblers seemed to be coming back to their usual, boisterous selves. One of them had even begun playing a flute. They didn't adapt well to being inside, they even looked a little unnatural. But the furniture and had already been turned over and the walls scratched so what harm could be done? Every room of the house was the Primafold version for him now. Phillip grabbed drinks from the cupboard, handed them at random to the Ramblers, who cheered at the sight.

He didn't have much food, he couldn't get to the Mundafold refrigerator right now, and all he had was what Dan had left here... some jerky and cheese snack packs. But then he noticed Pieter had left his pot here. And brought that out to the living room. He delivered food and drink to the injured man and the woman in the red dress outside. Her eyes were wet but she was smiling. The man was relaxed but sweating. The old women with too many jackets sat on the rocking chair and smoked.

The Ramblers were helping clean up, picking up the furniture and sweeping the floor as if being attacked by horrifying black figures was no more noteworthy the picking up after a messy house pet. One of the older men beckoned the others to sign Phillip's new guestbook. Raising the bottles to Phillip as they did so.

The blond man was retelling the story to the other Ramblers, who were also there but listened intently. He pointed to Phillip and said "Noooo!" While doing an impression Phillip swinging the ax. "Cramp Cramp Stuump!" He said, telling the rest. Fortinbras sat next to him as if he was listening. Phillip thought the dog liked it when the blond man pointed to him and imitated growling while patting him on the head.

Just when Phillip was wondering what to do next, Dan called.

"What happened?!" Dan said before Phillip could say hello. Phillip tried to explain as best he could. His thoughts were unorganized and he felt tired. Dan was silent on the phone as he spoke.

"Who should I contact? Should we go to the Farm?" Phillip asked.

"Don't worry, I snuck out of the house. I'm on that now," Dan said.

Wallmen arrived at the Dollhouse less than two hours later. Dan had gone to the Camps, found Pieter, who had contacted Emily and Andy, who had contacted the Wallmen. They came on four carriages pulled by puppet horses, but they stopped before entering.

"Do we have permission to enter?" A middle-aged Wallmen woman said behind the glowing circle of chalk. She wore the Wallmen uniform but it with a brimmed hat.

"Oh... yes. Come in," Phillip said.

"My name is Lieutenant Morana Singh," she said, shaking Phillip's hand. "I'm a special circumstances investigator for the Wallmen. You are Phillip Montgomery, am I correct?" Phillip nodded, Morana Singh managed to sound both comforting and aggressively efficient. "We technically have no grants or permissions to operate in this area, but let's worry about that later, shall we? I need you to tell me what happened here..."

Phillip did so, leaving nothing out he could remember. He even told her about the prickling feeling he had the night before. The other Wallmen got to work without being ordered. Some of them were wearing glass and wood visors, and put what looked like large wooden cameras on tripods. They threw sticks into the air, they cracked and buzzed, and then spilled the outside with light. There were Wallmen wearing full masks, standing guard over the fallen black creatures with large glass and metal guns.

"You think they were looking for something?" Morana Singh said. "Do you have any idea what?"

"No," Phillip said. "I mean, there's a lot of stuff in the house I don't know about..."

"... you said the small ones on the roof fell off when you made the circle," Morana Singh said. "Why do they have swords in them?" She asked, pointing to the small bodies around the house.

"I think the Ramblers did that afterward," Phillip answered. "Probably wanted to make sure they stayed down..."

Morana nodded. "Steffens," she said to a passing Wallmen. "We have Faroekin here, make sure we have a translator, and try to get them to stop cleaning before we are able to make a recording."

More people arrived. Dr. Bartly amongst them. "Where is the injured one?" He asked Phillip, who pointed to the porch. He was accompanied by two others, a boy and girl, in white hats and outfits who looked younger than Phillip and held medical supplies. Dr. Bartly sat next to the injured man, he took off his wide brimmed hat and spun it in the air, it stayed there, got larger, and emitted soft light over Dr. Bartly. "Who treated these wounds?" He asked the woman in the red dress, who stared back at him without understanding.

"There was a woman, she had twigs in her hair," Phillip said. "Older woman. She was just out here..." Dr. Bartly nodded as if it wasn't important and continued his inspection. He spoke to the girl and boy with him, he seemed to be instructing them as they looked over his shoulder.

Phillip had heard nothing from Dan since their last call.

"This home is folded, is it not?" Morana asked. Phillip nodded. "And the residents in the accompany home, they are not in the Know, are they? You are a Choicer, am I correct? Have you always been aware of the Primafold?"

"Yes," Phillip answered, looking at the wooden cameras on tripods, which spin around slowly and made loud clicking sounds, releasing a trail of shining tape behind it. "I mean no. Yes, to the first questions. I didn't know the Primafold existed until about a month ago..."

"Good morning, Mr. Phillip Montgomery," came a mocking voice. Captain Karo had arrived, with his own group of Wallmen. He didn't ask permission before walking under the chalk line.

"Good Morning, Captain," Morana Singh said. "I am in the middle of conducting an interview, if you do not mind, I would like..."

"An interview. Good," Captain Karo said. "Has the Privileged Phillip Montgomery here told you that he has been at the center of one disaster after another?"

"I have not asked him yet," Morana Singh said calmly. "If you would give me some time, I'm sure we will get to it. This is *my* specialty, after all."

"That's just the thing, Lieutenant. I believe this investigation belongs on my side," Captain Karo said. "Let me guess what happened here. Non-local geography pressed itself into the home, and brought these creatures in with it...?"

"The description of this event matches that," Morana Singh said carefully. "Red embers or ash fell from the sky, there were significant changes in temperature. Normal energy flows were disrupted... are you saying you have experience with this, Captain?"

"Some," Karo said, lacing his words with irony while he looked at Phillip. "And how did you stop this? With this circle?"

"Ye," Phillip answered, defiant to Karo's implied accusations. "Made it with skychalk and an orbit ball..."

"And what did you use to define the circle?" Morana Singh asked, taking the questioning back from Karo.

"I... uh... put myself in the small circle. Then drew a transference to the big one..." Phillip said, not quite understanding her question.

"You used yourself?" Karo said as if he couldn't believe it.

"And then you sealed it?" Morana asked, just as calm as before.

"Uh... No. I'm not very good at sealing. That was done by the Ramblers. The blond one with long hair and one of his friends..."

"So, your story is, you're able to define a circle with *yourself*, but you're not able to... 'seal' it?" Karo said, looking at Morana Singh.

"That is a highly unusual, Mr. Montgomery," Morana said to Phillip, managing to sound understanding and compassionate rather than accusatory.

"It is absurd!" Karo said.

"And yet here we are, in a circle with immobilized creatures. A circle he made and the Faroekin sealed," Morana Singh. "I believe they will collaborate this story, as odd as it sounds."

"What's so odd about it?" Phillip said, feeling defensive. "We do that in circles class all the time..."

"I have been around the world, Mr. Montgomery," Morana Singh answered. "In my entire life, I have met maybe five or six people who can define a sanctuary circle like this without a physical anchor or strong reference. Every single one of them is more than twice my age, with years of hard study underneath them."

Phillip didn't know how to answer that. His hand went for the pink notebook, which he just realized was in his bag.

"Lieutenant Singh?" Came a voice from the grass.

"Yes, Steffens?" Morana answered back.

"Sorry to interrupt," Steffens continued. "We need you to take a look at this. The Doctor too, if Mr. Bartly is done..."

They walked over to the tall collapsed black creature. Nobody said anything when Phillip followed behind. Dr. Bartly and the two kids in white followed along, wiping blood off their hands. Several Wallmen in brimmed hats and face masks surrounded the creature. In the daylight it didn't look so much like a creature as a thing. All cloth and leather bindings to give it its ugly shape. Only its eyes looked like something that used to be living.

"Do it," Steffens said to another Wallmen.

The Wallmen in the mask cut a leather strap and pulled away the black cloth from the creature's chest.

Almost every person in the circle backed up and gasped. One young Wallmen made a retching sound. Morana Singh was the only one not to react.

There wasn't a body underneath the impossibly dark cloth. There were... organs. Strung together by strings and glass tubes. There were full animals sewed into each other, squirrels and rats and small mammals, they looked alive and breathing but half-decayed. Dozens of eyes and teeth and claws. There were bugs, too. And maggots. Crawling amongst the organs, nesting in the living creatures...

Phillip looked away, feeling as if he was going to throw up. Captain Karo had put a cloth up to his mouth. The two kids with Dr. Bartly cried and held their stomachs. Dr. Bartly himself looked furious.

"Captain Karo," Morana Singh said, just as even and calm but her voice laced with something dangerous. "You say you've dealt with these... composites, before?"

"No," Captain Karo said, losing any sarcasm he had in his voice. He looked almost as mad as Dr. Bartly. "The breaches brought in some infected animals, some forbidden lowerFae and unFae, nothing close to this..."

"Do you know anybody *capable* of producing this?" Morana continued. "Somebody *willing* to do something like this."

Karo took a second to answer. "We know of somebody who might be capable, who has a history of illegal experimentation..."

"We found some evidence they've been here for a while," Steffens said. "At least a few weeks, maybe. We found a sort of nest in the woods..."

Morana nodded, deep in thought, not taking her eyes off the horrible sight in front of them.

Phillip lingered on Steffens words. *These things were in the woods for a week!*

"These creatures need to be put out of their misery!" Dr. Bartly said. "I won't stand for them suffering a moment longer!"

"Steffens, have you made a full recording?" Morana asked.

Steffens looked as if the blood had left his body. He looked at the man behind the moving tripod camera thing, who nodded back, "just got done, Lieutenant."

"Then please, Doctor, by all means, end these poor things," Morana said. "Steffens, help if you can..."

Dr. Bartly was already moving forward. With the help of the two kids he circled the creature. The girl handed him a small vial of copper liquid. The boy circled it and did odd hand motions. Both had tears in their eyes. Dr. Bartly nodded to the boy and he backed up, then threw the vial onto the creature.

It erupted in flames so bright and hot it looked like the sun. The flames not leaving a clear circle around the creature. The creature gave one screaming howl of pain before burning so completely it was as if it evaporated, the smoke collapsing into itself and disappearing.

The creature was gone. A hole in the ground six inches deep burnt black.

Dr. Bartly and the kids went immediately to the next creature. And then the next, until they were gone and the yard was covered in perfectly circular charred holes.

"Captain," Morana continued. "If you say this is more a matter of your department, I believe you. But it seems to me that none of us have all the facts, and given that my specialty is investigations, I would greatly appreciate it if you allowed me to offer my services..."

Captain Karo took a moment to answer. "That would be... greatly appreciated."

"Good," Morana said. "Mr. Montgomery, some of the Wallmen here are going to do their best to strengthen the homestead barrier here. I am not going to lie, I do not know if such a thing will be effective..."

"Thank you," Phillip said.

"Captain, I think it would be prudent to stage some of your men on or near the property. If Mr. Montgomery here does not object..."

"No, I don't," Phillip said, eager to regain some sense of safety.

"We will," Captain Karo confirmed.

"Good. Captain Karo, I'm going to go to the Major and report on what happened here in person," Morana said. Karo's eyes went wide. "Would you like to join me?"

"Yes," He said. "I think that would be for the best."

"Good," she said, and turned to Phillip. "Here is my card with my information. I will probably want to speak to you again. Please be available."

"I will. Thank you," he said back.

Morana left with Karo, leaving the Wallmen behind to finish the job. The purification squad worked around the property, they took the liberty of cleaning away Phillip's circle. Then did something with bells, and small incense burners attached to chains.

Phillip watched without seeing them. sitting on the porch, His mind racing and then going blank. He de-lashed the orbit ball from his skychalk, and absentmindedly played with it, staring straight ahead. The sun had just risen above the tree line.

Some of the Ramblers, the blond one among them, came onto the porch and looked at Phillip. They were smiling and seemed happy. Without a word the blond man handed Phillip something wrapped in blue cloth.

Phillip took it and unwrapped the cloth. It was a silver ax.

"Are you, giving this to me?" Phillip asked, looking up. The blond man seemed to understand and nodded with a smile. "Thank you," Phillip continued, not wanting to turn them down.

They cheered.

An older rambler who was clearly drunk sat next to Phillip while they handed him a drink. He pushed up Phillip's sleeve and put an ink soaked wooden spike next to his arm.

They were going to give him a tattoo.

"No! Uh, not right now," Phillip yelled to him when he realized what they were doing. Did they really think he wanted to tattoo himself right now?! The blond rambler politely waved the older man away. And then gave Phillip one last pat on the shoulders, before joining his friends at the new fire.

Two days. Two different weapons he had collected.

Maybe I should start a collection, he thought with a smile. But then it occurred to him, *maybe being a part of this world meant he needed to...*

The Ramblers left soon after.

Apparently, being attacked at night by horrific monsters made of living animals was a sign for them that the party was over. They packed up faster than Phillip would have thought possible, got rid of the fire pits, and walked away. The camp was unspoiled. It looked like they planted a tree where the fire was. It was almost like they were never here.

The injured man was even walking. Stiffer than the others, covered in bandages, using the woman in the red dress as support, he seemed happier than the rest of the Ramblers combined.

It was surprising—given how rambunctious the Ramblers were—how effectively they cleaned up. The only evidence they were here the presents they left for Phillip around the house. There was a half-dozen mugs, some made of metal, others wood. There was a small hand drum and flute. In the kitchen, they left some hanging meat half the size of Phillip. They left dozens of notes and symbols—all incomprehensible—in Phillip's guestbook.

But even with the Ramblers help cleaning up, The Primafold version of the home looked like a mess. It looked like hundreds of knives were dragged across the floor and walls. Some of the old wallpaper was loose. There was broken glass in a lot of the windows. It looked like one of the creatures was climbing on the ceiling. The door was broken on the side, and sitting at an odd angle.

The meat reminded him too much of the creatures, so with a great amount of effort, he got the meat into the pantry. He looked down at himself and noticed he was filthy, still covered in the ash.

The only bathroom available to him was the Primafold one with the tall wooden bath. It would have to do. He cleaned himself as best he could. The water stayed warm. He used some cleansing stones he stole from the bathroom at the Farm to get the ash off.

He gave Fortinbras a bath outside after him. Which the dog didn't like at all.

Dan had not contacted him back in hours, he wondered what was going on. Was Dan at the Farm? In which case his phone would be wrapped. That would be an explanation. He half expected Dan to come riding up on his bike when the Wallmen were here...

It was an easy thing to lose himself in thought. He sat on the bed, glad that he felt clean but his mind sending him back to the feelings a few hours before. It should feel good that he was safe now, he should feel relieved. The events of the night before didn't feel real, like it never really happened, but also that safe *now* was a lie.

Feeling safe was something not to be trusted.

He stared blankly at the rounded sharp holes in the wall, imagining again the spiked arms piercing through them. There were bits of splinters still on the ground. Scratches on the wall, holes and rips in some of his clothing. He moved his furniture back in place earlier but that was the only thing he felt like doing at the moment.

His room was different. A new ladder led up to a loft, there were new doors and wallpaper. But oddly, he had total access to all his things, his clothes and bed. He would explore that later. He wondered if the massive holes in the wall would also be in the Mundafold version of the home. That would be hard to explain to Aunt Kath and Fairchild family...

He went over to the Fairchild home to check on Aunt Kath and Maddie.

They were both asleep in the living room, he tried to sneak back out.

"You're up early," he heard Aunt Kath say. It was nice to hear her voice.

"Sorry, came over for a snack. Bad night's sleep," he answered, which was technically not a lie.

"Cool," She yawned and got up, walking passed Phillip into the kitchen. "I need to pee."

"Well that's the kitchen," he told her.

"I know!" She said, then whispered "Maddie had a bad night too. Nightmares. She was delirious. Said she heard something, and that she was cold. But she didn't have a fever. Gave her a few more blankets and she went to sleep. She threw them off ten minutes later..."

"We should let her sleep then," Phillip said. "I'll go back now."

"When do you leave for your program?" Aunt Kath asked.

"I was actually thinking about taking the day off. Or at least half the day," Phillip said.

"Cool. Let's go to a movie if you're skipping school..."

Phillip's phone rang. It was Dan.

"Here he is now asking about it. I need to take this," He told his Aunt, and walked out of the home towered the Dollhouse. The purification squad was still working around the property.

"Dan?" He answered. "What's going on?"

"Phil?" Dan said. "They said they sent people over, are you okay?" And then without waiting for an answer he continued. "They've been questioning us all night, Phil. They've been asking about everything. Phil, it's terrible. I don't know what I'm going to tell my mom... Andy and Emily are furious. Pieter disappeared. Andy said Tadaaki are contacting their parents, but I don't know..."

"Dan, slow down, what happened."

"Haystacks!" Dan said breathless. "The Wallmen arrested Haystacks!"

———— o ————

He left for the Farm less than fifteen minutes later.

"I thought you were going to stay home..." Aunt Kath asked.

"Just remembered I have some things I wanted to do. I'll keep my phone on me!" He yelled, already going for the door on his bike.

He took the Many-League Bike to the Farm, hoping it would speed him up. But the turns were so numerous it hardly helped.

"What do you mean, arrested?!" Phillip had yelled back at Dan on the phone.

"I mean he was taken into custody!" Dan said. "Him and Henry. Phil, he wasn't in the Farm, they arrested him in Godwick's Cove. Not by the Wallmen, by 'local authorities.' Something to do with what happened at your house. The Wallmen told me when they were questioning me. They asked me if I did any deliveries, and I said yes. They asked me what was in the packages, and told the truth and said no. Then they showed me pictures of that banker guy..."

"Mr. McKroft."

"... right! They showed me pictures of him and asked me what my relationship was," Dan took a breath. "Andy and Emily said they would contact their parents... the Pauls and Adeline are gone again... Phil, what do you think is going on here...?"

They agreed to meet at their usual entrance to the Farm. Dan said his mother didn't even realize he was gone, and that he was lucky he didn't get into trouble.

Phillip rode his bike all the way through the Camps. Impulsively, he checked on the campsite Dan and him had set up next to Pieter's trailer. It was gone. An empty spot already being taken over by a neighboring camper. *Why had Pieter disappeared?*

He didn't have time to wonder, he needed to meet Dan.

The entrance felt more abandoned than usual.

"Phil!" Dan yelled when he saw him. "The Wallmen are tearing apart the stable."

Half the contents of the stable, including the furniture inside Dan and Phillip's stall, was outside the door. Buttercup the bear was in a cage, miserable, her cubs in a cage next to her.

Willum was leading the effort, giving orders to other Wallmen.

They were stopped before they could walk inside.

"You kids can't be here," Willum said, and Phillip decided he really hated his stupid face.

"You really think Haystacks had anything to do with what's happening in the Farm?" Phillip said. "What happened at my house!"

Willum looked conflicted for a moment. "Come over here, really quick," he led them away from the other Wallmen. "Look, I get he's your friend. The Wallmen are just running an investigation. We have no ability to arrest or make charges unless we're given that authority. This is all."

"He's a good person," Dan said. "He didn't do anything wrong."

"He's friends with the Pauls, they trust him," Phillip added.

"Look!" Willum said again. "I know you *like* him. Lots of people *like* Haystacks. But people are not always what they seem. And I'm sorry, but that's especially true for Imps. Gremlins, I mean," he looked over at the other Wallmen and then spoke lower. "You two were delivery packages for him. Do you have any idea who Mr. McKroft is...?"

Dan and Phillip shared confused looks.

"... yeah, you don't, do you?" Willum almost looked guilty for continuing. "Did your friend Haystacks tell you that he was banished from Britannia? That he can't step foot in any European Primafold nation? Did he tell you why? Illegal puppetcrafting experiments. We don't know what but there's a good chance he was playing around with biomancy puppets. *Living* puppets. Like those things that attacked your home, Phillip..."

Dan and Phillip were quiet. He didn't know how to answer. Willum wasn't done.

"... I bet Haystacks didn't tell you his brother and half his family and friends are connected to radical gremmish supremacy movements... that there's a least two dozen different Federal and City-State investigations into to him..." Willum said. "And this Henry fellow. I don't even know where to start! What Haystacks must have over a guy like that to get him to work for him, I don't know."

"He's a good person..." Dan insisted again, but in a smaller voice.

Willum looked down at Dan and Phillip's faces, he seemed to feel guilty. "*People* are... complicated. They can be multiple things at once. Gremlins more so. I know they put on clothes and adopt accents just like people, but they're not. Their good mimics, but their minds work a lot different than ours. They're more like Fae..." He continued before Phillip had a chance to answer him. "You can't be here. Don't worry, I'll make sure none of them hurt any of your things... I promise."

Neither of them had any idea what to say, so they left.

"We need to get to Crownshead," Phillip said to Dan, they were already walking in the right direction. "See if we can contact the Pauls. Maybe Adeline... Where's Emily and Andy?"

"They went to the high-camp," Dan explained. "They are trying to contact their parents. They're mad about Haystacks too..."

Crownshead was empty today. Like the rest of the Farm, it felt like. Empty and dreary.

"We should split up," Phillip said. "Save some time."

"Oh, that reminds me. Here," Dan said, grabbing something out of his bag. It was an old grey walkie-talkie. "It was going to be a surprise I had Haystacks help me. I found something at the market. Little red bulbs that act like they're right next to each other no matter how far apart they are. They're good for things... but anyway. Haystacks helped me work them into the antenna. Well, he did all the work. But it was my idea. He also got rid of the Mundafold battery and... a bunch of other things. It's purified, so it won't get infected. And since the little red bulbs are tied to the signal now..."

"...we can hear each other wherever we are Primafold or not..." Phillip interrupted.

"Right," Dan confirmed.

Phillip gave it a test, pressing the button and hearing his voice on the other.

"Dan, this is really, really cool," Phillip said. Wishing he could feel more excited. "Great idea."

"Thanks," Dan said in a distracted voice.

"We're going to get Haystacks back, and thank him for this," Phillip said.

Dan nodded, and they split up.

Crownshead was less intimidating now that they had been there a few times. But there was still an air of foreboding here. The place felt old, and Phillip always felt like an intruder, being watched by the walls.

Dan said he didn't feel that way but agreed that the place was "creepy."

The place was empty. Every room.

Phillip took to calling out for people "Adeline?!" He yelled. "Anybody here?!"

The only living thing he saw was Bo'jo the mandrill. He wasn't wearing a mask this time, he was sitting on an armchair, a pile of fruit around him, enjoying the lit fireplace. "Sorry about the yelling," he said to the monkey, and continued to search.

A sound of shuffling, or doors slamming behind him.

"Hello?" he said as he turned around, catching sight of some grey and white hair before it went around the hallway. He followed. "Hello?"

The sounds were now behind him. In the large room to the right. File cabinets opened and closed. He saw behind a glass display of bones a small figure, who knew instantly who she was. The old women they met they first day at Crownshead.

The one who told them to pick up the key...

"I need help," Phillip said, walking around the display. The old woman was gone.

Behind him there was more clattering. He looked up and saw the old women behind a bookshelf a level above him. Mumbling something to herself. Books flew off the shelves.

"Your... *Crownshead*, aren't you? *Lady* Crownshead. That's what the Pauls said," he said to the woman. She was no longer behind the bookshelf. She was cleaning a fish tank in an adjacent room. "The Pauls said you liked to... play pranks. But I need your help right now."

The sound of glass cleaning disappeared. The woman was in the hallway behind him, cleaning the floors with an old electric vacuum.

Phillip spoke louder "I think the Farm's in danger!"

The vacuum shut off. Phillip stayed where he was, afraid to move closer and lose her.

"The Farm is in danger," he repeated. "And somebody has been arrested that shouldn't have been. And I think it has something to do with what happened at my house. And... I don't know what else! I want to help, but I don't know how. I think we need to get in contact with the Pauls! If you have any idea how to contact them..."

"File on the desk," The old woman said from the hallway.

"What...?"

"Wooden file. On the desk. Pick it up," she said.

It took a second to find, it was thin and made completely out of wood. There was a stamp on the front that said. 'WALLMEN EYES ONLY.'

"What am I supposed to...?" Phillip began to ask.

"Read it," the old woman said. She was right in front of Phillip now, she looked worse than she had before. She was just as old but she looked more tired. Her hair was a mess. She had bruises and black eye, and was leaning on a cane. "Read it," she repeated.

Phillip found a seam on the side and opened it.

There were hundreds of papers inside. Some typed, some handwritten. Transcripts of conversations. Papers labeled 'Evidence' and 'Findings.' There were pictures too. Of locations in the Farm he recognized and some he didn't. One of a dead horse. The pictures looked normal, until Phillip moved them from side to side and realized they were three-dimensional.

There were pictures of him in here. Of Dan and Haystacks. Of Andy and Pieter and Emily. Pictures taken when he was going about his day. Laughing at morning tea. Going to class... There were timetables for each of them, listing their location and what they were doing.

This was an investigation file for the Wallmen.

"What am I supposed to do...?" Phillip said.

"Read. It," the old woman interrupted. "Stupid boy."

"And this will help me...?" He asked desperately.

The old woman was walking away, and then was suddenly behind him.

"Read. It," she repeated again. "But promise. Tell no one of it now. No one. Promise!"

Phillip paused. "Why...?"

"Tell. No one! Promise."

"I... promise," Phillip said.

"Phil, Phil?" Dan's voice blasted through the walkie talkie, making Phillip jump. "I can't find anybody, have you found anything? Over."

Phillip took the walkie talkie off his belt. The old woman was looking at him. "Uh, no Dan, I didn't find anything..."

The old woman looked satisfied, she nodded to him, and limped slowly towards a dark doorway. "Read it. Trust. No one. Consider. *Everyone*. Show. No one..." she said, her voice echoing over-and-over again.

Just when Phillip was about to ask the old woman another question, Dan came on the Walkie Talkie. "Phil?" He said. "You have to say 'over' when you're 'over', or I don't know when I can speak. Over."

"Sorry Dan," He said, putting the wooden file into his bag, making sure it was concealed "Over."

CHAPTER 29

The Unwelcoming Committee

At first it seemed the only big difference between the 'Camp' and the 'High Camp' was one of scale. The differences became more apparent as they walked on.

The Camp was cramped, wild, organic, messy. The High-Camp was orderly, quiet, punctuated by gardens and streams and high faeFlame street lamps. Everything was larger. The tents were sometimes the size of mansions. Multiple stories, some even had balconies. The trails through the High-Camp could almost be called roads.

Emily and Andy shared a property and a tent on a wide piece of land they claimed with a gate, an *actual* iron and stone gate. "This is it, I think," Dan said, looking at his map. At the center, surrounded by tall bamboo, was a large low tent so angular it looked like a massive block of granite.

There were guards around the property, all wearing cloth masks. Some had those glass wood guns Phillip had seen the Wallmen carry, others carried glass spears, or short swords. Dan and Phillip were approached by them when they got close to the property.

"They are with us. Let them in," came a measured, mildly accented voice behind the guards.

Tadaaki waved Dan and Phillip in. They thanked him awkwardly.

"Dan, Phillargo. Good to see you," he said politely.

"*Phillip*," Phillip corrected.

Tadaaki looked confused for a moment, and then embarrassed said, "I thought that was your name..."

"No, It's fine. Andy calls me that," Phillip said, realizing that telling her brother his name was 'Phillargo' seemed like exactly Andy's sense-of-humor. "She called me a bunch of names at first but then settled on that..."

"I suppose there's only so much you can do with the name 'Phillip,'" Tadaaki added.

"My cousins call me 'Philly Cheese'"

"I don't get it..." Tadaaki said.

"Neither do I," Phillip admitted, suddenly realizing 'Phillargo' made even less sense...

Tadaaki was being friendlier than at any other time in their relationship, which Phillip realized wasn't quite fair, as they had never really interacted in any length. He wondered if he should dislike Tadaaki for Andy's sake, and then instantly felt guilty that he was thinking about such petty things at a time like this.

"There they are!" Emily called from the wide room inside the tent, from the inside it was indistinguishable from a luxurious modern home, rooms separated by simple white cloth separators and rugs. "Daniel! Phillip! we're so glad you're alright. We didn't get any word if you were injured, we couldn't believe it when we heard you were attacked."

"Is it true that they destroyed the creatures that attacked you?" Tadaaki asked.

"Yes," Phillip answered. "Dr. Bartly demanded it. Said they had to be 'put out of their misery.'"

"Shame," Tadaaki said. "They might have been able to clear Haystacks..."

"How?" Dan asked.

"The bodies of those creatures will contain some mark of their creator," Tadaaki answered. "If it's not Haystacks..."

"It's not," Phillip insisted.

"... If it's not Haystacks," Tadaaki repeated. "It will show somewhere. I know they made a recording, perhaps that will be enough..."

There was something about Tadaaki's attitude that was grating to Phillip.

"There was another breach this morning," Emily said to them. "We just learned about it. From what we hear it's the largest yet. I'm told they moved everybody out of one of the family holdings."

"It's true," said two voices at once. Andy had walked into the room, interrupting her brother. She was wearing what looked like a light business suit mixed with a classic Japanese kimono. A female version of the one Tadaaki usually wore. Her hair was styled and she wasn't wearing her glasses. Phillip had never seen her so formal.

"It's true," Tadaaki continued. "A lake has been ruined. Everything in it was killed. Some migrating trees were injured. A half dozen Wallmen are being treated for injuries. One bright spot in all this the Wallmen can no longer deny this is purification issue. *Somebody* is doing this. The good Captain Karo is laying the groundwork to shift blame to the Pauls. It will play nicely into what a lot of people think about the danger of the Farm."

"Did they see the same things that attacked Phillip's house?" Dan asked.

"Doesn't sound like it," Andy said. "The only creatures are some infected animals, the..."

"... the damage is caused primarily by non-local geography being shoved into the barrier," Tadaaki finished, which clearly annoyed Andy.

"That's what Karo said happened at my house!" Phillip said. "It's why magic didn't work right. There was gray red ash falling from the sky..."

"Who would want to damage the Farm?" Dan asked.

"We don't think the *infiltrator*—and whoever they're working with—is trying to damage the Farm," Emily explained. "We think they are trying to get in..."

"This has to have something to do with Waltzrigg," Phillip said, repeating something he had said before when they were looking at the 'suspects' list at Haystacks' stable. "He practically threatened to do just that. He said the Pauls had insulted their friends... and something about 'Grannies.'"

Phillip touched his bag, thinking about the wooden file inside, almost revealing it to his friends. Stopping only because the old women of Crownshead said not to. But why listen to her? She was known to lie, to "play pranks."

"I doubt any Granny tribe could do something like this," Tadaaki said. "I'm more likely to believe it's another Inheritor. But even *that* violates what I thought was possible..."

Phillip thought about what Adeline had said when she came to the Fairchild house, *'The combined might of the Inheritors couldn't break in...'* He had dismissed it at the time, just another thing he didn't understand...

"I've contacted my parents,'" Andy said after a pause. "They said they couldn't get either of the families involved," Andy said with contempt. "They are willing to send resources. We will have to hire investigators and lawyers privately."

Tadaaki did not seem surprised by this news. He turned to Emily. "Which will take time. For now. Haystacks is at the hands of the local authorities of Chadwick Cove and the Wallmen..."

"And *us*..." Andy added. She put her arms to her side and snapped her fingers. The formal outfit she was wearing went rigid, and then split apart from a seam that wasn't there. She walked out of the outfit like she was walking out of a door. She was wearing her usual Andy attire now. An open long light jacket, shorts, and a band t-shirt that said *'OLD MEDICINE HUNT,'* with a picture of grungy looking men and one gremlin with instruments.

She put on her glasses and looked relieved to be out of the outfit, which crumpled to the floor behind her. She kicked off her shoes into the pile.

"Perhaps if we want to get dressed, we can find a more appropriate place than the common area?" Tadaaki said, and Phillip thought he gestured to him when he said it.

"What can we do for Haystacks?" Dan asked, overriding Tadaaki.

"The Wallmen are spending a significant amount of time focused on us," Emily said.

"Emily is being nice. They're focused on you two," Andy added.

"Karo is convinced you are in some way responsible for what is happening," Tadaaki said.

"Nothing new there..." Phillip said, again thinking of the file in his bag.

"Maybe we should just talk to them more, answer all the questions they want," Dan said. "We have nothing to hide, they can look at everything..."

"They don't think that way," Andy said.

"The more you give them, the more they have to work with to build a conspiracy..." Tadaaki said. "Men like Karo are not professional investigators. They are trained to act on incomplete information. His hounds are trained to your scent... he's going to keep going until he thinks he has something. I think his current theory is that you two are unwitting pawns in a Haystacks centered conspiracy..."

"Does anybody know what was in those packages we delivered?" Dan asked the room. "The Wallmen kept asking me that. A bunch of questions about Mr. McKroft too... and they showed me a bunch of photos of other gremlins and asked me if I knew them..."

"Mr. McKroft has some sympathies with gremmish-liberation groups. Nothing spectacular, as far as I can tell," Tadaaki said. "I don't know what else Haystacks is involved in."

"... but we are almost certain what's happening to the Farm has nothing to do with radical gremmish-rights stuff," Andy finished.

"What happened to Pieter?" Phillip blurted out, wanting to change the subject.

"Pieter's disappearance is... not surprising," Andy said.

"Pieter is exactly the kind of person you would expect him to be, and not a pebble better," Emily added in the voice that was both cold and angry and utterly out of place for her.

"His dad... probably ordered him back when things got weird here," Andy said, sounding diplomatic. Emily didn't answer, but Phillip noticed her jaw was a little stiffer.

"So, what do we do?" Phillip asked, changing the subject again, eager for anything he could do.

"Right now, you go about your normal business," Tadaaki said. "The Wallmen are watching you. You need to be as boring and routine as possible. Give them nothing to go on. Remember, they are a private group here, they have no more authority than my guards outside. You have Privilege here at the Farm. They cannot stop you..."

"And then what...?" Phillip asked, unsatisfied.

"...my brother thinks it will become clear to them that you and Dan are dead ends," Andy said. "Maybe they will start devoting attention elsewhere. I have a different plan."

"What's that?" Phillip asked.

"The Unwelcoming Committee," Andy answered. "No jokes. We force Karo and the Wallmen to look elsewhere, we help expose the truth," she sounded resolute. "Because I think he's right about two things. The breaches are not just an external force trying to barge in. They have an anchor in the Farm."

"The infiltrator..." Dan said, not as a question.

"Yes..." Tadaaki continued, "but not just anybody. The simplest and most likely explanation is also the most disturbing..."

"The infiltrator," Andy interrupted back. "has, in all likelihood, been trusted with at least a half-Privilege by the Pauls. Which means..."

"... we're not just looking for an *infiltrator*," Tadaaki continued, "we're looking for a liar and a traitor..."

It proved impossible to go about 'business as usual.'

There was something about knowing you were being watched that made it impossible to act normally. Phillip found himself overcompensating for invisible observers. Acting normal proved difficult, it was like he forgot how. *Do I take out my book like this? Do I usually nod to Dan when we talk? How casual should I act, given the circumstances?*

"What about the mounted deer?" Dan asked as they head back to Haystacks' stable.

"The red-eyed stag?" Phillip responded, distracted. "It's gone. After it woke me up it didn't come back to its mount. I told the Singh detective woman about it, I hope that's okay..."

"No, I would have done that too," Dan responded. "It's a good thing I left everything at your house. Do you think it was trying to protect you? How did the detective woman respond to it?"

"Come to think of it, she didn't really react to it. Maybe things like the stag are normal here...?"

"I'll put it on the list," Dan said. Phillip was amused that Dan was still thinking about growing their 'question list.' He wished he had as much faith as Dan that things would eventually return to normal.

There were two Wallmen waiting at the stable, the rest of them had gone.

"Phillip Montgomery and Daniel Castellanos," the tall man said as they approached.

"Yes," Phillip answered, but knew the statement was not a question.

"We have a few more things to ask you," he said. He didn't look like a soldier. He was tall and thin and balding with a combover. He looked like someone who collected taxes or filed insurance claims... "Do you have the registry of creatures for this stable?"

"Registry? No, I don't know... why?" Phillip answered.

"Come with us," the tall man said. The other shorter, younger man following and taking notes. He brought them to the front of the stable, where dozens of cages were stacked on each other.

"You have been here for several weeks. Do you notice any animals missing? Any that aren't here?" He asked them.

"I don't know," Phillip answered honestly.

"It's hard to tell." Dan said. "Animals would come and go. I didn't even know they were here officially, or anything."

The tall man wrote down their answers, he looked like he was surprising a yawn. "Thank you, we will speak again soon," he said, and walked off.

"Wait," Phillip said. "Are you going to leave the animals like this? Who's going to take care of the stables?"

"That's not a Wallmen issue," he said, not sounding defensive in the slightest.

He walked away. Phillip and Dan were left at the stable. The Wallmen had made a mess of it. Half the contents were piled outside. They noticed Willum had kept his promise. Their things in the last stall were rearranged, but still in the stable.

"You know where Haystacks keeps the food?" Phillip asked rhetorically.

"Yeah," Dan answered, already walking there.

"I think I'm going to get Buttercup and her cubs out of the cage first. She seems the most agitated," Phillip said.

"You sure we should do that?" Dan said back. "What if the animals, without Haystacks here, start eating each other."

"Nah, that won't happen," Phillip explained. "Haystacks kinned with some of them. Others are here conditionally. Kinning is tied to a place as much as it is to a person. It's context sensitive, I think. Otherwise the animals would go at it every time Haystacks taught a class. I read about it."

Phillip released Buttercup's cubs before he released her. She was only really worried about her cubs, anyway. She was more protective now, guarding them and not letting them wander until Dan came out with their meal, artificial fish filled with compressed meat and false bones for they took a while eating them.

Phillip and Dan had been in the stable long enough to know Haystacks and Henry's routine by heart. "Have many days have we spent here. Farm time, I mean?" Phillip asked, trying to do the math. "Around one-twenty," Dan answered, as he scooped hay into a bin. "That many?" Phillip said, surprised.

They couldn't get up to the rafter easily, so had to settle with bringing Haystacks' stuff back inside. It took most of the day, and they missed every class and workshop they had scheduled.

"Why does Haystacks run a stable?" Phillip asked, when they had finally taken the time to eat. He enjoyed the physical work. He was able to stop thinking about what bothered him, about Haystacks and the attack, about the folder that he still hadn't looked at.

"He told me. Advanced puppet crafting needs to take inspiration from the real things," Dan answered. "Not just inspiration. The puppet master needs to know things about them. Especially if you're doing anything autonomous. Remember the mice we made." And with that Dan took his puppet mouse out of his bag, wound it up, and put it in front of him as he ate.

Phillip wasn't looking at the puppet mouse. He was looking at the smaller animals, who were just settling down after the odd day they had. He was thinking about Haystacks taking care of them, feeding them, petting them. And he thought about the horrible insides of those creatures. The living animals that made them up...

"Haystacks didn't do anything wrong," Phillip said.

"I know he wasn't responsible for the attack on your house," Dan replied.

"But you think he did *something*...?" Phillip said, sounding angrier than he wanted.

"I had a cousin, used to be like a big brother to me," Dan said. "Coolest guy ever. We played games. He protected me and stuff. But he stopped hanging around. Later I learned my parents made him stop coming over, he was involved in things they didn't like. He listened to them. He still sends me presents on my birthday..."

"What's the point?"

"... thing is, it's like my dad said when I asked him about my cousin. People can be what you think they are, and also be who you can't imagine them being... or something," Dan continued. "Point is. I don't think Haystacks meant any harm, but we don't know everything about him. What he's involved in or what it all means. The Wallmen weren't lying, he was kicked out of the entire continent! And what were in those packages, Phil? We could have been doing something illegal, we never questioned it because it was Haystacks..."

Phillip took a second to answer. "You sound like Willum." he said, regretting the accusation the second it came out of his mouth. "Sorry. It's just. We have to trust somebody..."

"I know..." Dan said, guilt lacing his words.

They didn't talk for a while.

"I'm going to get cleaned up," Dan said. "Maybe get my clothes cleaned..."

"Don't forget your toilet paper," Phillip said to lighten the mood.

"You know, I still hate them, but I'm getting used to those ropes," Dan said.

"That's disgusting," Phillip responded, and they shared a laugh before Dan left.

Phillip admitted to himself that he was happy to be alone. This gave him time to think. With a far-too-casual look around him to see if any obvious Wallmen spies were lurking about, he went back into the stable. Being alone gave him time to look at the file.

Their investigation area had been torn-apart by the Wallmen. All the notes and papers in a pile. *Good*, Phillip thought, *if they Wallmen knew we were investigating the infiltrator, maybe they wouldn't suspect them.*

Was that why Lady Crownshead had given him the file? Because the Wallmen were useless, focused on the wrong things? *Where had she even gotten it?* He looked at the wooden cover, opened it again. There were more papers and pictures in it then was possible. Like his pink notebook, it went on-and-on.

He took out his picture, attached to dozens of papers. The first was a list of his movements. He had been watched, since he got Privilege, and even before. The newest entry listed him at the *'STABLE. Cleaning and feeding animals'*

It said that he was with Dan...

The file was still being updated!

It recorded Dan's list of movements, even mentioned that he was going to the bathhouse.

The question echoed again in his head, why had Lady Crownshead given this to him? He said it over-and-over, his mind not producing a suitable answer.

There was a good possibility this was a prank. Like the key trick which had sent them into the meeting with Waltzrigg. He wanted to tell Dan about this, tell Andy, ask Emily and even Tadaaki what they thought...

But he didn't. Because there was another possibility.

The file was important. And so was the reason she had given it to *him*.

It if was a prank, it might not matter, but if it wasn't... then what the Crownshead woman said to him was important. *"Trust. No One. Consider. Every One."* Her words played again in his mind as he looked at reports on Andy, Haystacks, Pieter, Adeline, Sarah...

A flood of implications followed the possibility that this was not a prank.

It meant Lady Crownshead knew something, and was unable, or unwilling, to say so...

Phillip couldn't even guess why this would be.

But it was the next thought he had— the much bigger implication—that made his stomach drop.

Lady Crownshead had given him a file because he was close to the infiltrator. Because the infiltrator was one of the pictures in this file...

Consider. Everyone.

The possibility was sickening, but on some level, he knew it was there from the first moment she had shown him the file. Maybe Dan was right, how well did he know anybody here...? He didn't understand magic, or the politics of this world, or the ways people thought... Dan was right, there were too many assumptions he was making. He wrote down everything he could he could think of...

"Phil? Phil?!" Dan called when he walked into the stable. Phillip jumped.

"Up here, Dan," he gathered up the papers, threw them back in the file. "Just looking around," he needed a place to look at the file where he wasn't being watched, where Dan couldn't walk in or wonder where he had gone. Where he could spread out. "I was thinking about going home early today..."

"I remembered when I was in the bathhouse!" Dan said. "There's one class we can't skip..."

Phillip didn't register what Dan meant a few seconds.

He groaned when realization hit him.

"Can't we miss one?" Phillip said.

"They told us to do what we normally do..." Dan said.

Phillip signed. "Do we have a lesson plan...?"

"From last week. The history lesson," Dan replied.

"Right, Siberian Willastic traditions..." Phillip said, wanting nothing more than to bail on the whole thing. There were too many important things to do "Let's get this over with. Then I'm going back home."

The one benefit of staying in the Farm was that he was able to get some sleep without worrying about wasting time.

The file's existence in his bag was torture.

He itched to pick it back up. He hated every distraction. Eating was a waste of time, making small talk with a vendor required heroic effort.

The class they taught, when it rolled around again, was the worst yet. Time always went slow when they were teaching, but now it practically stood still. So much so Phillip considered in all seriousness if the classroom was its own pocket of Farm-time.

The class was more crowded this time. Still much smaller than when the class started, but larger than average. There were five young Wallmen who were sitting at the back, making no attempt to take notes.

Emily or Andy were missing this class, as was the support they gave them. Phillip found himself missing the distractions Andy often provided, or the lightened tone Pieter brought about every time he talked. Phillip noticed Antony Müller was on the attack more than ever. He questioned every part of the lesson, interrupted, made rude comments laced with sarcasm.

On top of everything, Phillip had a headache. He felt sick to his stomach. He felt tired.

"…in your opinion teacher, does the Siberian model of *will* more accurate…? Or is this just a run-around?" Müller interrupted Dan as he went through the history lesson. "Not that I am complaining, teacher, you make history come alive."

Phillip rubbed his eyes—they wouldn't stay focused—resisting the urge to say what he wanted to Müller.

"It's… important, to have an understanding of what the traditions are," Dan responded. "For that we can…"

"And it was understanding these traditions that allowed you to accomplish the impossible…?" Müller continued.

"Well… it's not the…" Dan stuttered. Phillip's head was throbbing now.

"Forgive me for interrupting but this is all…" Müller started.

"Look!" Phillip barked at Müller. "We don't know, okay!"

The classroom went quiet, including Müller, who was still sneering but the expression was mixed with confusion. Every eye was on Phillip, including Dan's, communicating his horror at Phillip's outburst.

Phillip turned to the class, tried to calm down. "We don't know," he repeated. "We don't know everything. Why we were able to do what we did that night, it's still a bit of a mystery…"

"Then how…?" Müller began.

Phillip interrupted. "What do you think the answer is going to be?! You're going to come into this classroom and we provide you a formula and then you walk out of here shooting lightning out of your eyeballs? I don't know… but I don't think it works that way. If you could learn it like that way people would have done it by now... this is different."

"And what to the accusation that the whole thing is mystic fraud?" Müller said.

"I would say that you're all here for a reason," Phillip answered. "Not just in this classroom, but at the Farm. I think you know the Pauls can-do things others can't. Maybe it's not what they say it is, but you know it's there..."

Katie Caster raised her hand. She was by far the most enthusiastic student, and possibly the only sincere one. She made Phillip feel bad about wasting class time. Phillip looked at her, which she took as permission to talk. "Can you describe what it felt like when you made the circle? Was it systemic, or more of an emotional-cognitive ritual?"

"Oh..." Phillip answered, surprised to get a question like that after his speech. "Uh... we didn't succeed the first few times we drew the circle. We changed it each time, but I don't think that mattered as much as... Well, Dan had this idea that you make a ritual more real by doing it. It's a combination of meaningless symbols and repetition, or ritual, and it combines to make the symbols *real*..."

"I think I learned that in Sunday school..." Katie interrupted.

"Exactly!" Dan said enthusiastically.

"... yes. So, to answer your question. I would say it's more of a ritual. But the symbols matter," Phillip continued. "All for the purpose of... changing, I guess is the right word... changing you into a person who can do it, who can make lighting," Phillip didn't know he was going to say that until it came, but found that it rang true.

"Neat!" Katie said. "Do you mind... I hate to change your plans, Siberian magic is very interesting, but do you mind if we go through how you made the circle? Step-by-step?"

Dan and Phillip looked at each other. "Sure," they said at the same time.

The effect on the class was tremendous. Gone was the mixture of boredom and confusion, the whole class was engaged now. Katie Caster most of all, who asked the most questions, even offering some of her own thoughts and theories, which were added to or debated by the other students. Müller—while he didn't interact—stayed quiet for the rest of the class.

Phillip felt less like a lecturer or fraud under attack and more like head of team, tasked with solving a mystery. It felt so much better, Phillip could even see himself enjoying this class, looking forward to it.

"You should have done that day one," Dan said, looking as relieved as Phillip felt.

———— o ————

The good feeling from how the class ended up didn't last long.

The weight of the file in his bag, the reality of Haystacks imprisonment came rushing back as soon as Dan and Phillip were walking back to the stable.

"I'm going to go home," he told Dan. "I left some things hanging when you told me Haystacks was arrested. I need to get back."

"You can leave now, but you can't get back in until the break…"

"I know," Phillip said. "But I can't wait."

He took the Many-League bike back. Wanting to get home as fast as he had gone to the Farm. He still found the ride excruciating. The file in his bag felt like it weighed a hundred pounds. It was all he could think about. The same questions and counter-questions, worries and doubts playing again-and-again in his head.

"Welcome back," his Aunt Kath said when he checked in with her. "Get that thing done you wanted to get done?"

"Yes," he said, acting as tired as he could. "Actually, I'm a little tired and I'm still not feeling great, so I think I'm going to take a nap," and managed to leave for the Dollhouse with the promise that he would be back for lunch.

He took the first long breath in recent memory when he was back in his room.

Stealing tape, a staple gun, and construction paper, he covered some of the holes in his wall and door as best he could. It was ugly, but at least a little less distracting.

He threw his bag on the bed. And took out the file.

He took out the pictures, the individual packets tied to each one of them, putting his own picture aside. He needed to lay out everything, be methodical. Be careful. He took the tape and hung pictures on his wall. He put up Dan, Haystacks and Henry, Andy, Pieter, Emily, Tadaaki. There were pictures of people he didn't recognize, he didn't know if these were suspects or not but put them on wall anyway, writing questions marks in skychalk next to them.

He laid the notes out on the floor ahead of him.

If he was right, the infiltrator was in here somewhere.

If the cryptic words of Lady Crownshead meant anything, it was possible the infiltrator was somebody he knew, somebody close to him. Tadaaki had said almost that, the infiltrator was a 'liar and a traitor'… Did that count Tadaaki out as a suspect?

Maybe the Wallmen were right, he let himself consider, maybe Haystacks was responsible for something. Dan was right, what were in those packages…? Andy and her brother were from an 'important' family. They were clearly here on a mission of some kind. Andy even said so! He knew nothing about Adeline or Sarah. Pieter was acting suspicious… and the only thing he really knew about Emily was that she was rich and polite. They were all trying to get something out of the Farm…

He looked at the picture of Dan.

Dan, who had run into him the evening after he found the bag, who had led him to the Farm, who had been there the whole time.

Instantly friendly Daniel.

He grabbed his pink notebook to take notes, the action taking him long enough to realize none of this made sense. Not a bit of it. You could build a conspiracy off anything, just like Andy said. It's what Karo had done to him. He had to admit, for the first time, that he had to look odd from Karo's perspective. Showing up suddenly, sneaking in, blowing up the lab, doing something in a field and gaining Privilege. It sounded ridiculous even to him.

Sitting on the floor, he looked up at the pictures, at the notes that accompanied them. Fortinbras joined him looking at the board. He looked down at reports and correspondence. *'No Criminal History', 'No Earning History,'* it said concerning Dan. *'Inconsistent Behavior in suspects. External Influence is suspected,'* it said on a report titled *'PROFILE MAKEUP.'* His eyes glanced over all of it.

He wasn't the right person for this job. Lady Crownshead had trusted the wrong person. She was a fool, or maybe just a prankster. He would tell his friends about it. Their opinion was better. He would go back on break...

Getting up to go to the bathroom, Phillip took one last look at the pictures of people and places on the wall. So, distracted he put his messenger bag back on, and so tired he left it there. Feeling further away from an answer then he had before.

He nearly slipped and tripped when he walked backwards toward the door.

It was a book he had slipped on. A thin one. It was one of the children's books he found by the creek. The ones with the girl who wore a pink witch's hat and matching dress. But it was different this time... gone was the incomprehensible writing, it was in English now. *'PENNY PINK HAT and the MONSTERS WHO COULD NOT LEARN BALLET'* it said on the cover.

"Weird," Phillip said, picking up the book. The whole thing was in English, and he recognized the cover. It *had* changed. He noticed when he turned the book from side-to-side, that the image had depth to it, just like the pictures in the file. He opened the first page. An illustration of three monsters—all wearing a tutu and ballet shoes—was paired with simple text:

A Valley sat not too far away
On which were three monsters
Who could not learn ballet

The biggest was clumsy
The smallest was green
The one in the middle unlucky
and mean

The next page featured the girl in the pink witch hat.

Penny Pink Hat Followed the sound
To find the three monsters prone
on the ground

They Cried and they Whined
and they moaned and they hissed
Ignoring the girl who had
come to their midst

"What's Wrong?" Penny said with
a tip of her hat
Causing three monsters to jump like
Three cats

"We Can't do Ballet" Said one,
When his pride had recovered
Saying it sad not
forgetting to Blubber

The girl, Penny, considered them for a moment, and then stuck her hand in the air. *Why was it in English now?* Phillip wondered. Was it because of the house? Maybe the books were only meant to be read in the Primafold...

"I'll Solve the Problem" she said with delight
Hoping to share her magical might

At Once she noticed what were
The problems
And determined to tackle each right at the bottom

The green monster
Who was the size of twig
Was wearing shoes at least
Eight-sizes too big

The mean one had a problem worse
Than his shoes
He was trapped at the waist by a great big tutu
It was old and it was tattered and it was ugly
And it was loose
It made him as mad as a fat mother moose

The biggest monster the most obvious yet
The could have seen this problem
even if she slept

His hair was long, and messy, and wavy
Blocking his eyes

Like a river of gravy.

Phillip skipped ahead, piecing together the rest of the story. Penny gave the monsters various magical gifts and spells to fix their problems they couldn't see. A potion to shrink the shoes, a spell to mend the tutu, and magical comb to fix the one monster's hair.

They were happy for a while, but learned they still couldn't do ballet.

Penny was confused. She consulted with a talking stuffed animal out of her bag— a bear with a baby face— who told her the monsters still needed to practice.

Penny followed the advice and inspired the monsters, who were able to do just one good pirouette by the end. Penny left the monsters, who were now happily practicing ballet.

And so Penny left at the end of the day
Leaving the monsters, who were learning Ballet.

"Weird," Phillip said again, taking the book with him, along with everything else, on his way to the bathroom. "Put it on the list."

The distraction didn't last a minute. He was no closer to solving the problem. No closer to helping Haystacks in any way. His head was pounding worse than ever. Maybe he needed to get some medicine...

"I saw you..." A voice shot behind him.

"Ah!" He screamed in surprise. It was Maddie, who was as surprised by his reaction as he was by her. "Jeez, Maddie," he said. He was jumpier now than he was before the attack.

"I didn't mean to sneak up on you," she said, sounding angry rather than apologetic.

"It's fine, I was just going to the bathroom..."

"You didn't take the old bike this morning. I saw you," she said. His head was pounding, throbbing with his heartbeat. "You were on a different bike, which is gone now...

"Not now Maddie," he said, rubbing his pounding head.

"... Also, you're in different clothes..."

"Not now Maddie!" He yelled. His eyes going blurry his head hurt so much.

Maddie froze in place. Her eyes drifted around, seemingly embarrassed, she looked tired and frustrated. *And why shouldn't she be?*

"Sorry, Maddie..." he said, trying to calm down.

"You have one of those books..." She continued in a slower voice. "Where did they come from and why...?"

Phillip stopped listening. He looked down at the book when she mentioned it. Saw the monsters on the cover. The monsters who needed Penny Pink Hat to see their problems...

It hit him like a cold wave.

He combed the hair off his forehead with his hands.

He grabbed his bag, put his hand in it. His hand grabbing nothing. *Nothing.*

He looked up and stared at the wall, seeing nothing ahead of him.

Why shouldn't she be? He repeated in his head. The words of Lady Crownshead bouncing again in his mind. It felt like the floor was giving away. Like he was failing. His headache is the only thing keeping him here in the house. Maddie had stopped talking, noticing he wasn't listening.

He looked at her, and something about his look caused her to take a step back. Her eyes were exhausted. She looked more tired than him.

"Maddie, I'm sorry," he said, and ran back to his room. Only just noticing that the house and reverted back to its Mundafold version.

He looked at the pictures on the wall, looked at the notes and pictures on the floor. Fortinbras stared at him like Maddie had. He went through his pink notebook, finding notes he wrote weeks ago. *There it was*, he thought to himself...

It was all there...

He checked his messenger bag again to make sure. *Gone,* he thought.

The headache gave way to a feeling in his throat and stomach.

He threw everything he might need in his bag, and ran back outside, Maddie was still standing in the hallway.

"Maddie, I'm so sorry," he said as he passed. "Can you tell Aunt Kath I forgot something at the school, thanks!" and left before she could answer.

He didn't bother getting the old bike, he would run to the end of the driveway and use the Many-League Bike. He messaged Dan on the way. He had to do this right...

'Dan get everybody in the stable I need to talk about something.'

'Talk about wat?' Dan answered back.

'Have to say it in person,' Phillip said.

He had to do this right. he was sure he was right.

The ride back to the Farm felt like a dream. Like it wasn't real. His mind going over and over the same facts. He even looked down at his pink notebook, to confirm them all again. He was surprised when he got to the Farm, realizing he didn't remember traveling there...

It was break now, he could get back in.

He was out of breath when he got to the stable. So much so he had to lean against and fence to recover. Was everybody inside already? *He had to do this right...*

Walking inside. The group, Tadaaki included, was already talking amongst themselves

Talking to the Pauls.

Big Paul and Old Paul were inside the stable.

Old Paul in a hat and traveling clothes. Big Paul sitting down, petting Buttercup. The stable went silent when Phillip went in.

"The Pauls are back," Phillip said. "I mean, you're back. Sir. I mean Sirs."

"Yes, we are," Old Paul said. "Lady Kanamori and Lady Morris were just filling us in about this terrible situation with Haystacks, we're not bothering anything, are we?"

"No... not at all," Phillip replied, recovering from the shock. "It's good that you're here."

Phillip went to the end of the room, he was being watched, the conversation didn't continue.

"We have been looking into what has been happening in the Farm," he said, holding up the notes, "Trying to figure out who's behind it. We call it the Unwelcoming Committee."

Big Paul chuckled, Andy and Tadaaki seemed embarrassed.

Now was the time to say it! Just say it. "When I went to Crownshead to find somebody the woman who gave us the key that got us in the meeting with Waltzrigg, the old woman, Lady Crownshead, she gave me this..." He held up the wooden file. "It's an investigation folder made by the Wallmen..."

"She gave you that? Why...?" Dan started.

"That sounds like her," Old Paul said. "And what did you learn, Phillip?"

"She told me not to tell me to tell others about the file," Phillip said, answering Dan's unsaid question. "Now I know why..."

"And why is that..." Big Paul asked.

"I think I found the infiltrator," Phillip said.

Every eye in the room widened, except for the Pauls and Buttercup's.

"And who is that...?" Old Paul asked.

"I am," Phillip answered, a breath of relief coming out with the words. "*I'm* the infiltrator!"

CHAPTER 30

The Infiltrator

Phillip expected more of a response.

There were no gasps, no fainting, nobody dropped anything. Every eye in the room stared at him, even Buttercup and her cubs, but beyond some furrowed brows, there was little in the way of reaction...

"I'm the infiltrator..." Phillip repeated, looking from face to face.

"Phil, that doesn't make sense," Dan said.

"I don't think that... I agree with Daniel. That does not follow the facts," Emily agreed.

"You can't be the infiltrator," Andy added.

"... we are looking for somebody deliberate..." Tadaaki finished.

"That's what I'm trying to say...!" Phillip started.

"So!" Old Paul yelled to the group. Every single person in the room went silent and looked at him. He stroked his beard and looked straight at Phillip. "You figured it out. Good for you!"

This time there was a reaction. Emily gasped. Both Andy and Dan went silent in shock. Tadaaki hand went to his sword, as if instinct was registering a threat. Phillip's stomach dropped. *He was right, it was true...*

"That's impossible. We know Phillip," Emily said.

"He's not..." Andy started.

"I'm right. You knew?" Phillip said. "Why did you...?"

"I would be happy to answer any questions you might have," Old Paul said. "But right now, I'm much more interested in hearing from you. Why do you think you are this infiltrator?"

All eyes were on him again. Phillip tried to organize his thoughts. He planned on what to say on the ride over, but Old Paul's declaration had thrown him off. He didn't know where to start anymore. "I figured it out at my house. There was this book I slipped on and it all occurred to me, we've been writing a diary and..."

"Why don't you slow down," Big Paul said, just as calm as he was before. "Start at the beginning."

Phillip took a breath and continued, trying to keep the emotion out of his voice. "I realized in the hallway at my house, I yelled at Maddie..."

"Maddie?" Old Paul asked.

"Phillip's cousin," Emily answered.

"Yeah..." Phillip said. "I yelled at her. I had a headache and... she doesn't know about any of this, the Farm I mean, but she's suspicious. She knows something is going on. And it hit me in the hallway how weird I've been acting! Dan, you said it to me ten times, why not just tell Maddie?! She can't sleep, she's being driven mad! And I never answered you... The truth is I didn't have an answer. I never even thought about it, I just excused it away. That's not like me! Why was I working so hard to keep it a secret from Maddie...?"

"You said it would be too complicated right now..." Dan offered.

"Right! I blew it off," Phillip continued. "Maddie can't sleep, she's doubting her own sanity... telling her about everything would be simpler. It was *mean* not to. I realized this in the hallway when she pushed too hard, what was I doing? And then I realized for some reason, I don't know why, that when I was around Maddie it felt like it did when I was forgetting about the bag... Like it did when we jumped the fence of the Farm. Like I was on autopilot..."

"What does this have to do with anything..." Andy said, sounding defensive on Phillip's behalf.

"... Because it made me realize... It made me think about where else it felt weird... There was this book, a children's book I was reading, about these monsters learning ballet."

"Are you speaking of the Penny Pink Hat books?" Big Paul said.

"Good books, those," Old Paul added.

"Yes, those. Well anyway, it wasn't the point of the book, but each of the monsters had problems they couldn't see, they were blind to them. And it just made me realize, it hit me like a rock, what I was missing. I'm the thieving termite!"

"Thieving termite?" Big Paul asked.

"It's an educational aid, a doll. Used in Circles class," Emily explained. "The thieving termite shows how foreign power structures can be stolen from and snuck into barriers..."

"Yes, yes! And that's me. I'm being used. To sneak stuff into the Farm, to weaken the seal!" Phillip said.

"That's not how barriers work, Phillip," Tadaaki said. "It's not as simple as Circles Class, if it was that easy to take down a barrier, all of them would be..."

"Let the infiltrator talk," Big Paul said, his voice laden with sarcasm. "Then we can argue with him that he's innocent."

Phillip organized his thoughts the best he could. "Look, the reason I mentioned Maddie and the fence was because... Well, they were clearly manipulating me. The bag didn't want to be noticed, so I forgot about it, had to fight it. The fence didn't want to be jumped, so it made me think about other things, made me *not want* to jump it..."

He took a breath, he needed to explain this well. He needed to think.... when Lady Crownshead gave me the file. She told me to 'consider everyone.' I didn't know what she meant. And I did consider everyone. I was suspicious of everybody. Too suspicious. Every time I would focus on any one of you it all made sense. And then when I started thinking about what I was missing, it was all clear. My thoughts were being manipulated, around myself. I took out the files. I put my own aside. But that's not all! I put a ton of reports aside that have nothing to do with me! I didn't even realize I was doing it. It's just like the fence. Whatever is happening to me wants me to avoid certain subjects... *I'm the thing it wants to avoid*! That's what the Crownshead lady was trying to tell me. Consider Everyone! She meant *me*. But if she said it outright, I would have ignored her."

The Pauls were as unbothered as ever, but his friends had gone silent, no longer arguing with him. Waiting for him to finish. "It felt just like when I was forgetting about the bag. Like when I couldn't even think about jumping the fence. There were little moments of clarity, but then they went away and everything made too much sense. The only reason my mind is trying to avoid thinking about myself and the infiltrator is because there's something there... I checked my notebook. We... Dan and I have been writing a diary for we can compare notes. Mine didn't make sense. When I realized what was going on, I remembered doing things I never wrote down... And I think when you realize something, when you think about it directly, it doesn't work well."

"Why do you think you're able to say these things now?" Big Paul asked.

"Because..." Phillip started. He had to tell them their secret, but it wasn't just his secret. He looked to Dan. "I... have this notebook, I found it. And I don't know why but it makes it so I can do things. Like remembering the contents of the bag I found the notebook in... or jump the fence. But only if I realize what's happening. Sometimes I have to write in it, or be touching it..."

"Is that why you are holding that pink thing now?" Big Paul followed up.

"Yes," Phillip answered. "It usually works if it's in my bag, but not always..."

"I have one too," Dan confessed. "We both found them individually."

"I was wondering why you two had a matching set..." Andy said.

"There's more," Phillip said. "The timelines! That's one of the files hid from myself. It was the timeline of events the Wallmen had put together. When I realized it was happening it was the first thing I looked at, and checked my notes. The first major breach in the Farm was the night the exact hour I accepted the invitation into the Farm. It's just gotten worse from then on... especially after I found the cat."

"The cat? Is this the cat you saw on our ride back from the delivery?" Dan asked.

"Same one! Gindersnaps the cat. Gingersnaps the cat. *Little tabby Gingersnaps*," Phillip said in an old woman's voice. "I didn't tell you I got a phone call asking me to find a cat. And then I found the cat! I thought it was just a coincidence, or something to do with magic. But now... Andy!"

"What...?" She said, surprised he yelled her name.

"You said in your Mindworking class. Mind viruses can travel with strong visual imagery and sounds. Well what if somebody called you, told you the name of a cat and a description, and then you found that cat for real... That would work, right?"

"Well, yes. As an introduction method for a virus. But it would convey no information by itself," Andy said.

"... But there's more. I found the cat. I found it and brought it into the Farm. Hoping to find its owner. And then she got away, but before that she slipped out of her collar. I put the collar in my bag, walked away, and didn't think about Gingersnaps again until right after I yelled at Maddie. Didn't mention her in my diary, didn't think about her at all... Just like the bag! Just like the fence! Just like all the files I was ignoring! You don't realize, I'm not a forgetful person with stuff like this..."

"What happened to the collar?" Old Paul said. Big Paul had taken a stick playing with the hay.

"I lost it, gone from my bag. Never took it out," Phillip admitted. "At least when I finally remembered it, it was gone from my bag... it's just like the Old Laws book says. The Xenia chapters. Inviting somebody in makes you vulnerable to them. You invited me to the Farm, gave me Privilege. And then something else had me sneak in... whatever it is. I think I'm the one who broke the seal! Captain Karo is right..."

"Phillip," Old Paul interrupted. Grave and serious.

"Yes?" Phillip asked.

"Put down everything you're holding," Old Paul said, he was standing and turned away. "Walk toward me. Stand in front of me."

Phillip had no idea what to expect but did what Old Paul said. Dropping his things to the ground he walked forward, his heart beating hard for some reason. He stopped in front of Old Paul, who turned around and stared in his eyes. He stomped his foot twice on the ground, and then bent down and picked up some hay. Andy, Emily, Tadaaki, and Dan stared at him, and looked down at his feet. "Keep looking at me!" Old Paul said to Phillip.

He walked over to Phillip, staring straight into his eyes. Old Paul's gray eyes like spotlights, seeing right through his, burning the back of his skull. It made his knees look up.

Old Paul grabbed a loose thread of hair from Phillip's head. Yanked it off "Ow!" Phillip yelled, more confused than angry.

Old Paul ignored him. He looked at the hair with great interest, held up the hay next to it. Dropped both to the ground. Then bent down and examined them.

He signed, got up, and looked back at Phillip. The intensity in his eyes gone. "Well Phillip, I hate to disappoint you, but I don't think you're the infiltrator."

A weakness, like Phillip just stopped running, hit him.

It was exhausting, he had tried so hard to explain. But what did he really know? The Pauls knew magic, he couldn't even do the tasks in a simple circles class. He was tired. He was still weak from the fight at his house. His mind jumped to conclusions, and he came in here and embarrassed himself... Which also meant the infiltrator was still out there. He had wasted so much of everybody's time! But who was it? Pieter going missing was suspicious... Maybe Haystacks *was* involved...

"Maybe..." Phillip started.

"Whoa," Andy said under her breath. Emily gasped again. All his friends had tensed up. He looked at them, but nobody looked back, they were all looking at the floor. He followed their eyes, but there was nothing to look at...

"What...?" Phillip asked, nervous, but hardly feeling it. He was so tired...

"Daniel," Big Paul said, still sitting. "Please retrieve Mr. Phillip's things for him."

Dan did so. Handing Phillip his bag. He looked as confused as Phillip felt. "What's going on...?" He asked, angry now. Dan handed him his pink notebook.

The moment he touched it, his exhaustion doubled. He felt sick to his stomach. His headache came back.

"Sorry to put you through that, my boy," Old Paul said, but he was smiling.

"Why...?" Phillip rubbed his eyes.

"Look down," Big Paul said, and Phillip did so.

There was a circle there, a glowing copper circle. And Phillip was the center. The edges surrounded by ruff, scribbling lines.

Before Phillip could ask Old Paul continued. "We caught it in the act. Phillip. The circle you are standing in is a measurement tool. It measures you, Phillip. And what it measured this time was cognitive and emotional changes. You see this here, Phillip. This is you before you put down your things, your notebook. And this here, you see when the lines get all wild, that's when I told you that you weren't the infiltrator. It goes wild. I made you weak Phillip, sorry to do that without asking. Whatever's infecting your mind went on a rampage. It seized on the opportunity to change the narrative. In your weakened state, it was easy."

"What does this mean?" Phillip asked, looking down.

"It means your case is made," Big Paul said. "It means you're the infiltrator."

Silence met Big Paul's statement.

For the third time since he walked in the room, Phillip felt sick.

Before anybody started talking again, Big Paul got up. Reached into his breast pocket. The action keeping everybody quiet. He took out a small strip of cloth, and a silver tag.

"Gingersnaps' collar!" Phillip yelled. "Where did you...?"

"We found it," Big Paul said.

"...in the Work-Time Engine room. Dropped right into the water," Old Paul said. "I believe you took a tour there just before we found it..."

Phillip almost threw up. He needed to sit down. He was used to things affecting his memory, but how much control did this... *infection* have over him? Could it make him take out a collar and drop it? Do things he didn't realize? Was it really that powerful?

Every eye, again, was on Phillip. All except Andy's, who was looking at the Pauls. "This still doesn't make sense!" She said. "So, what if he's infected with something? That's still not enough to breach a barrier like this..."

"... not nearly enough," Tadaaki added, looking in the same direction as his sister.

"You would be absolutely right, Lady Kanamori..." Old Paul added, in a pleasant voice. "But there are a few facts you do not know. Phillip, you have done a wonderful job piecing this all together. I have to say, you've really gotten a lot out of Circle's Class, I will have to give my compliments to Miss Julie."

He cleared his throat and continued. "Ordinarily, it would not be enough to weaken a strong barrier like this. Unless..."

"Unless," Big Paul interrupted. "We left ourselves more open. Made the barrier porous by design..."

Tadaaki looked away from Phillip, and stared at the Pauls shocked. "Why would you do something like that? What purpose does that serve?"

"That's not an easy question to answer," Old Paul said. "It would require a base of knowledge you simply do not have. If I had to describe it, I would call it... *recruitment.*"

"Or a draft," Big Paul added, Old Paul giving him a look.

"... Surely as the, what do you call yourself, Welcoming Committee? You noticed how many Choicers are here, how many odd people?" Old Paul said. "We did this by design. Made the Farm discoverable. Sprinkled the world with... let's call them gifts. The intention, an open invitation. Spiced with intrigue and mystery..."

Dan Phillip looked at each with wide eyes. Dan looking down at his notebook. The bag. The mailbox. The stag. The notebooks...

"You used allurements to... *recruit* to the Farm?" Emily asked. "Why not simply invite people under proper conditions?"

"Well, my dear, we do have a good reason for that, but it's a little hard to explain." Old Paul said. "You could say I was trying to abide by the letter of some agreements we're bound by, while trying to undermine their spirit..."

"It means," Big Paul said, looking at Old Paul, "that as clever as we thought we were being. Our actions weren't only discovered, but anticipated. Which confirms certain suspicious about which one of our... *friends* is really sponsoring Waltzrigg..."

"What it means," Old Paul repeated, and looked right at Phillip, "is that I'm bad at chess."

"Waltzrigg?" Phillip said, ignoring Old Paul's last comment. "He *is* behind this. Is he responsible for me being *infected*, or whatever?"

"Ultimately, yes. I think he's responsible. But also, no," Old Paul said. "What happened to you is too archaic and subtle. This reeks of Granny magic. I know he's been flirting with some northern tribes. Probably hired a few for this... Phillip, do you have any more memories of encounters, things being given to you, especially gifts?"

Phillip looked back, grabbing his pink notebook tighter. "There was a woman in a bookstore who recommended I buy a Mindworking book before I knew what Mindworking was... There was also a woman on the street who said she was kicked out of the Farm..."

"That could be something..." Old Paul said, rubbing his chin like it was only of academic interest. "My guess is Fat Barta—if she is behind this—was planting bait and seeds everywhere. That's how I'd do it... Phillip here was just the unlucky worm that got bit..."

"Why would any Granny tribe help the Waltzrigg or the Sturmjägers...?" Emily asked.

"Treasure. Protection. Rights to land. Entertainment. Revenge. Could be anything..." Old Paul answered. "But Fat Barta is not the focus here. Waltzrigg is a bit player but let's treat him as the focus. I think he intends to move soon."

"What does he intend to do next?" Phillip asked, embarrassed by how desperate he sounded. "What should I do next? You know I'm the problem, you can fix things, right?"

"What Waltzrigg intends to do, I believe," Big Paul said, "is penetrate the Farm. I believe he intends to steal from us. But more importantly, I believe he intends to harm the Farm, and kill a great deal of people in it..."

"Nobody would stand for that..." Tadaaki started.

"Which is why," Old Paul said, "we think he intends to do it in such a way that it looks like an accident. One caused by my foolishness and disdain for safety..."

"What we are doing here is unpopular," Big Paul continued. "Admittingly dangerous. We lowered or removed all common restrictions. Most people just went about what they did before. But it was only a matter of time before somebody did something dangerous and stupid."

"Waltzrigg was sent here as information scout. But also—we believe—a *saboteur*," Old Paul said. "If he could not argue for his clients being invited to the Farm, his goal was to hurt it. To embarrass us. There's already rumors that we're starting to wander. Getting innocent people killed would hurt our reputations."

"We need to evacuate the Farm," Tadaaki said. "Get people out of the Camps..."

"I'm afraid that won't work," Old Paul said.

"Why not?" Tadaaki said.

"Because the Farm," Big Paul answered. "Is *Anywhere*."

"It's *in* Anywhere, we meant," Old Paul corrected.

This had an effect on everybody but Dan and Phillip, who were confused.

"It's true than..." Emily said. "What they say about the Inheritors... *Anywhere* is a... *real* physical thing, a place, not just metaphor? And the keys to Anywhere reside with you?"

"Ms. Morris, I wish it were that simple. But for the sake of understanding, yes, Anywhere is very real. And you are all standing in it, right now. The Farm is just part of it," Old Paul confirmed. "Anywhere possesses incredible qualities.

Qualities which have been ruthlessly exploited by Waltzrigg, or more accurately, those who hired him."

"Like the fact that, since Anywhere is anywhere. Everybody who touched it, or passed through it, still carries it with them," Big Paul added.

"Which means…" Old Paul continued, "that if Waltzrigg is successful what we think he is trying to do, being outside the Farm won't matter. The reaction will affect you as if you are next to it. Because you are."

"Reaction…?" Tadaaki asked in an aggressive voice.

"Didn't we say?" Old Paul turned to him. "The breaches the Wallmen are dealing with are the least of the problem. Something has seized hold of the Work-Time engine. Temporal geometry is fluctuating, we can barely control it any longer. We think he intends to cause a temporal oscillating reaction."

Emily went white. Big Paul looked ashamed. Tadaaki looked angry.

"You did this," Tadaaki said. "You set up a system this dangerous and…"

"Tadaaki…" Andy said. "There's no point…"

"What does that mean?" Dan asked.

"It means." Tadaaki said. "That if Waltzrigg is successful. It will pull the Farm apart, and the people in it. And the people outside of it!"

"Yes," Old Paul said. Calm and still. "It will affect the Mundafold too. The effects would be devastating. It would probably shake loose and snap closed most of the Undertrails this side of the country…"

Phillip felt as if the room was spinning. This was all his fault. People were in danger, real danger!

"What about my family? My family's house. My aunts. My cousins…?" Phillip asked. "Will it affect them?"

Big Paul finally looked up to meet somebody's eyes. "It might," he said. "It is hard to say the level of connection. The intensity of the reaction Waltzrigg will employ… but yes, it's possible…"

Dan's eyes went wider than they already were. Phillip couldn't answer, he couldn't look up. "This is all my fault…"

"I admire that ego of yours, Mr. Phillip," Old Paul said. "To make yourself responsible for the actions of reprehensible man at the tail end of centuries of shared history and conflict, amazing! And there's certainly something admirable about taking ownership of a problem. But that can get excessive…"

"What can we do? What can I do?" Phillip asked, looking from Paul to Paul.

"My boy," Old Paul said. "I thought you would never ask…"

CHAPTER 31

Always Be Prepared

Old Paul snapped his fingers, and the world slid away.

The stable, Buttercup and her cubs, the hay on the ground, slid behind them like it was on an enormous treadmill. They flew across the Farm so fast Phillip couldn't make out anything but flashes of green and blue blurs.

It felt motionless. The world was the thing that was moving.

"Ah!" Andy yelled, as they all grabbed whatever was next to them to balance. Which proved to be nothing.

The world stopped.

They were in a large room, as large as the stable.

It looked like a library and study had been combined with a laboratory and kitchen. Metal instruments spun and swirled, a fireplace cracked in between leather sofas.

"Anywhere does have its advantages," Old Paul said. Nobody but him and Big Paul had gotten their balance back. "Can't go doing that all the time. Else people will be on to us."

Lady Crownshead was in the room. She was holding a tray of teacups. She looked more injured than ever. Her eye was patched.

"I told you," she said to Old Paul. Her voice both weak and stern. "I told you about him and you didn't listen. I told you and you didn't listen. I tried to keep the boy out. Tried to hurt him..."

"I know. It was a noble effort, my dear," Old Paul said. He sat her down, poured a cup of tea, and handed it to her. "I will promise, next time Lady Crownshead, that I will listen. But right now, you will have to believe me that this boy is still under my protection, and I will not remove Privilege from him now. He is on our side, my Lady."

"I. Am aware!" Lady Crownshead yelled, and Phillip thought he felt the room move. "I was the one who. Led him. To truth. You did not know. I did!"

"We know you did," Big Paul said. "Please do not exert yourself. You are going to need your strength for what is to come."

"Lady Crownshead... I'm sorry," Phillip said. "I didn't mean to. I'm going to try to make it right. Whatever I can do..."

"Arrogant," Lady Crownshead said with a laugh.

"Not such a bad quality in the young. Now relax," Old Paul said.

"Wait. Does that mean that she was responsible for us going to the meeting after we used that key?" Dan asked.

"Yes," Lady Crownshead said, a certain amount of glee in her voice. "To get. You. Kicked out. Also, made you meet the liar with the bottles..."

"That McMann guy?!" Dan asked. "That was you too."

Lady Crownshead laughed, almost hysterically but she didn't have the energy. "Yes. Yes. Get you oiled. Send you somewhere dangerous. Get you. Kicked out. Worked! Then didn't... *still* funny..." The memory of tricking them seemed to please and relax her more than the tea.

"Phillip, Daniel, the rest of you. We need to plan, time is against us," Old Paul said.

"Wait," Big Paul interrupted, he looked almost angry. "Only Phillip has agreed to do anything..."

"We don't have time for this," Old Paul argued.

"Does everybody here agree to take on this task?" Big Paul said to the group, ignoring Old Paul. "And the danger that likely goes with it?"

"I do," Phillip said immediately.

"Yes." Dan said at the same time, nodding to Phillip.

Andy, Emily, and Tadaaki all said "I do," after that.

"Do you want to ask anybody else's permission if we want to save their lives?" Old Paul asked Big Paul. "No? Good, then I'll continue," he turned back to the group. "Right now, at this very moment, we are protected..." He looked around, as if waiting for somebody to respond. "On what, you ask? I'll tell you. On Waltzrigg's greed. He has his finger on the trigger, but he doesn't know we know that. He's looking for a bigger payout. A *better* target."

"Which is why it's imperative." Big Paul added. "That we do not give him any reason to think that we are onto him, until it is too late. We will stay out of the Farm with the executive staff..."

"Stay out of the Farm...?" Emily repeated. "What do you mean?"

"Show them," Old Paul said to Big Paul.

Big Paul signed. Then closed his eyes.

His entire body shook, his arms went wild. He looked like a balloon that was deflating.

On the chair, in Big Paul's place was a Big Paul shaped scarecrow or dummy. Complete with Big Paul clothes...

"A doll?" Emily said. "Where are you right now?"

Old Paul was snapping his fingers at the Big Paul dummy. "Don't go too far out, come back. Come back," the dummy shook again, gaining back some substance little by little. And Big Paul was back, looking like a normal human being, with the exception of his arm, which was still made of cloth and hay. "To answer your question, Ms. Morris, I am right now outside the Farm, with the executive staff, Adeline and Sarah included, trying to contain some of the damage done to the barrier. People will be hurt if we don't. If we leave in any real sense, Waltzrigg will be on to us. Which is why you five need to act for us."

"Ms. Morris, Lady Kanamori, Lord Rurik," Big Paul said, still trying to get his arm back to its normal by shaking it, "you need to stay in the Farm. We doubt Waltzrigg intends to die, and we think we've figured out how he's going to avoid killing himself and those who work for him. You are going to protect everybody in the Farm and in the Camps, you can..."

"We can discuss what is to be done with them later..." Old Paul interrupted, "right now, we need to get Phillip and Daniel on their way. You two have the most important job..."

The words caught in Phillip's ears. *The most important job?*

"I'm sorry," Phillip blurted out. "I want to help any way I can. I'll do anything. But you should know..." He swallowed. "I'm not very useful. I can't do any magic."

"Then you're going to have to be especially clever," Big Paul said.

"There is no other way, Phillip. It has to be *you*," Old Paul said. "You are the center of this. You are the anchor. It's unfortunate. But that is where we are. It doesn't get to be another way because you wish it was so," Old Paul let out a long breath. "Being the problem gives you an advantage. You can also be the solution."

"What do you mean?" Phillip asked.

"I mean," Big Paul continued, "that if you follow the path of the first breach, you can reseal it. We gain back control over the barrier. End of story."

"How do we do that?" Dan asked.

"Exactly what we said. Lady Crownshead, the map," Old Paul continued, Lady Crownshead pointed to the table in front of her. Old Paul picked up a folded map, and handed it to Dan. "It means Phillip travels the path of the one who made him an anchor. Through the first breach, into the Farm, and back to Crownshead. Drop some seals along the way, and presto! Just like a zipper. The breach is sealed, the barrier will purify itself."

Dan was looking at the map. Big Paul had gotten up, went to a table which had on it beakers and bottles, some with boiling liquid in them lit by open flames. "We thought we might have to do something like this. Here," he said, and handed Phillip what looked like long railroad spikes. "Drive these into the ground at certain points. We made them earlier, they should do well to seal the breach..."

"Then all you have to do is come to Crownshead," Old Paul said, and he handed Phillip and Dan each and small doll, each dressed like one of the Pauls. "Activate these, by cracking them in half. We'll hear it and come here. That will be enough to give us back control."

"This path is from King's Hill," Dan said, still looking at the map. "Some of it's over water! How do we get down the river?"

"Do you have a boat?" Old Paul asked.

"I have a... blow up raft..." Dan replied.

"Now you're thinking!" Old Paul said. "Which reminds me. The path you have to take there, it takes you two right through the Swamp. Which ordinarily wouldn't be much of a problem, but at this moment there's a small-time Fae there, named Tutana. She's been building coalitions and offering favors, absorbing as much as she can. I think she thinks she can make a go at it. Become a real local power. Waltzrigg probably has something to do with that, he at least bribed her to ignore him. She might be a problem..."

"How do we deal with that?" Dan said, sounding more nervous.

"Do *not* deal with it by offering service. Take these coins," Old Paul responded. Handing Dan a small leather bag. "Travelers tokens. Golden ones. Should buy her off if she's making a fuss about you passing. She has no right to stop you, don't let her imply that she does. And under no circumstances offer her your voice or name or a single bone in your body! Even a finger."

"You might need to break through a few paths. And you most certainly need to break through the last archway. That will be closed on the breach. It needs to be opened again, forcefully," Big Paul continued. He put on a mask and took off a boiling pot of blue liquid and then poured some into a jar. "I brewed some of this up earlier. I expected to use it myself. It rips apart most barriers. Since you are the anchor, Phillip, and you have Privilege, you can blow past the arch... It's just about the most powerful barrier breaker you are likely to encounter... Well, we call it a barrier, really, it's an *exciterent*. Makes everything more energetic, until it breaks. Do not let it near fire, especially faeFlame."

He handed Phillip the jar. Which was warm but not hot despite the bubbling liquid inside. "Do I, spray it, pour it on stuff?"

"No, it needs to work through a medium. Let me show you," Big Paul took back the jar, grabbed a teaspoon, open the jar and carefully dipped the spoon in the blue substance. The spoon came out blue. Not like it was covered in blue paint, but like it *was* blue.

Big Paul held up the spoon for everybody to see, and then threw it at the door.

The door exploded open. Coming of the hinges and flying away.

Dan and Phillip jumped.

"Enough to worry about!" Lady Crownshead said. "Do not. Make a mess!"

"Sorry, Lady Crownshead," Big Paul said, turning back to Dan and Phillip. "Coat something in it. Fling it at whatever barrier you want to not be there anymore. Fae don't like it either, if it comes to that. But I wouldn't recommend it..."

"Will it work on BB's," Phillip said, having an idea. "BB's for a BB-gun? I think my cousins have some old ones, I saw them in the barn."

"Yes, it should. Good idea," Old Paul said.

"The plan is..." Big Paul said. "Go from Phillip's home. Follow the path, place the spikes where I marked the map. Go through the Swamp. Break through the gate to the Farm. Head to Crownshead. Wake the dolls..."

"Problem solved. Simple as that," Old Paul finished. "Get it?"

THE FARM FROM ANYWHERE

Dan and Phillip, their hands full. Nodded to each other. "We think so," they said together.

"I will go with Daniel and Phillip," Tadaaki said. "Their task is too important. They could use help."

"Unfortunately, no. We need you here," Old Paul said. "What we have to do to protect the Farm is too advanced. You are only one of a few people who can do what we are going to ask."

"My sister will do it, the Wallmen," Tadaaki started.

"We need Privilege for this, and there's not enough time," Old Paul said.

"Simply extend Farm time then," Tadaaki argued.

"We cannot," Old Paul said with an air finality. "Waltzrigg's group has control of the Work-Time engine, they benefit from it working. It accelerates their plans. We are canceling Farm time from here on out. It might tip off Waltzrigg, but it's the only thing we can do."

"There's another reason you can't go with them," Big Paul added, looking at Old Paul. "Daniel and Phillip are the only ones who possess those incredible notebooks. There is more subtle protection on the Farm than just the barrier. We do not have time to go into it, but I am almost certain the only people able to follow this path, beyond me and him are the possessors of those notebooks. Everybody else would be a burden."

More questions than he knew what to do with invaded Phillip's brain, but he didn't announce any of them. Lady Crownshead spoke first.

"They need. To go," she said, wheezing a little. "Hour grows late. He's coming. He's close..."

The room was quiet for a beat. Nobody looking away from Lady Crownshead.

"Our hand is forced," Big Paul said. "Phillip, Daniel. You need to go. Are you ready?"

Phillip tried to organize his thoughts. It was all happening too fast. "We think so," he said, not thinking so at all.

"Do everything you can. I believe in you both," Old Paul said. "If you don't think you can do something, shut yourselves up. You're wrong. Think about me. I'm older and wiser than you both. You both have incredible talents. You wouldn't be in this room if you didn't..."

"Thank you," Phillip replied, meaning it. "I just have one more question..."

"And what is that?" Old Paul said.

"Haystacks?" Phillip asked, his question clear.

Everybody turned to Old Paul.

"I'm glad you asked. That question doesn't make me feel like a complete failure!" Old Paul said. "The benefit of being not-exactly-here right now is that I'm an exceptional multitasker. We pulled in a few favors. Haystacks and Henry are still being investigated, *Federally*, I might add, but are being released for the time being."

There was a collective sigh of relief in the room. Emily laughed. Andy said "yes!"

Their situation was almost as bad, but at least they did right by Haystacks.

"Good luck, Phillargo. Danny-boy," Andy said. "I haven't come up with a good nickname for you yet, Dan, so be extra careful."

"'Phillargo' is not that great a nickname either," Phillip told her.

"*Extra* careful," Emily repeated, looking more emotional than anybody, which made Phillip more nervous than anything.

Even Tadaaki patted them on shoulders for encouragement. It was horribly awkward, and he seemed to regret it immediately after he did it, but it was a nice gesture.

"Time to go," Old Paul said. "Lots for everybody to do."

It was time to go, Phillip repeated in his head, *there was a lot to do*, and they didn't have much time to do it.

"I took the mailbox home when Bertrand was sleeping at your house," Dan said to Phillip as they walked out. "Do you think we will need...?"

"Bertrand?" Big Paul asked, his voice sounded surprised.

They turned around.

Old Paul was looking at him again with that penetrating glare. "By any chance," he said. "Are you referring to Bertrand *J. Bertrand*?"

"Yes," Phillip said, surprised. "He slept at my house. He's a traveler. Do you know him?" And then another thought hit him. "Oh, God. He's not involved in this, is he?"

Old Paul and Big Paul shared a look. "I wouldn't... think so..." Old Paul said, rubbing his chin. "I guess I didn't know him as good as I thought. I could have sworn he had a funeral a little while back..."

"It has no bearing on tonight," Big Paul said. "Phillip, Daniel. It's time."

Dan and Phillip said goodbye again. Which felt very grave and significant and made him more nervous. They were on their bikes and going back home in less than twenty minutes. Dan was going over the plan, and then going over it again. Phillip shocked that everything was moving so fast. He didn't know who the infiltrator was a few hours ago, and now they were on a mission to stop Waltzrigg. It was too much to process.

"The Pauls know Bertrand, huh," Dan said, his nervousness clear in the way he babbled and changed subjects. "Crazy. What do you think they meant about the funeral?"

"Don't know," Phillip said, thinking about nothing but what they had ahead of them. "But like Big Paul said. It's a mystery for another time..."

<hr/>

Dan decided he needed to go home first.

"I have a few things to get. I'll be right back to your house as soon as I can," Dan told him. "We'll both lie to our moms—my mom and your aunt, I mean—I'll say I'm going over to your house—which is true, I guess—and you say you're going over to mine."

"Sounds like a good idea," Phillip said, sounding a little vacant, even to his ears.

"Hey Phil..."

"Yeah?"

"How dangerous do you think this is going to be, really?" Dan asked.

"I... don't know," Phillip answered, it was the only question he was thinking about too. "I think it might be a little dangerous, at least..." He thought about what he could encounter.

What there was to encounter that he didn't even know about.

What would happen if he ran into Waltzrigg? But he knew the answer to that...

Waltzrigg would hurt him. Maybe *kill* him. Waltzrigg hurt people for a living. Waltzrigg was trying to hurt people now. He wasn't just a guy that liked ice-cream and gave advice, he was an enemy, and a killer.

"But we have to do it, don't we?" Dan said, saying it more to himself than to Phillip.

"I think... yeah, we have to do this." Phillip said.

"Thought so," Dan said, nodding and looking ahead. "Hey, good job figuring out you were the infiltrator, by the way. That was cool. Really surprising. But run ideas by me next time... I'm your best friend now. And don't say I'm not, no other friend found magic with you. Don't care how great they are..."

Phillip smiled, he guessed it was true. "I don't have great friends back home. Friendly friends. School friends. Don't hang out with many people..."

"See what I'm saying? *Best* friends, like I said," Dan continued, he turned on the road. "Don't go without me. I'll be right back. Sneak out if I have to. Do you think we should bring the stag head mount thing...?" But he was out of earshot before Phillip could say 'no.'

Phillip was back at the Fairchild Ranch less than twenty minutes after he left.

He looked at the watch Haystacks had altered for him. Even when the Pauls ended Farm time, there was still a distortion. Something to do with when Phillip came in and when Phillip left.

The Dollhouse was empty—which was a relief—except for Fortinbras. "Sorry I left in a rush, boy," he said to the dog, who accepted his apology immediately.

He needed to talk to Maddie, tell her the truth, but he didn't have the time now... he needed to get ready. The Dollhouse was behaving well. He didn't need to work hard to get to one version or another.

"Thanks," he said to the house, as he threw what he wanted to bring on the bed.

He got dressed in his most comfortable pair of jeans. He put the wooden knife on the bed, the orbit ball, which already came in handy once, the skychalk, the lashing glove, the ghost blade sword, the walkie talkie. He went to the barn and found the BB-gun and found the BB's near them. He went to the bathroom to get the memory cloth Bertrand had left. He read sunlight could repeal night Fae... *that was useful, right?*

God, he thought, *I'm getting like Dan.* He was going to need his backpack...

As if summoned by his thoughts, Dan knocked at the door and called for Phillip.

"I hope I brought enough. Do you get the BB-gun?" Dan asked, walking in and putting no less than three duffle bags on the floor.

"Yes," Phillip said. "What did you bring...?"

"I think we should coat the BB's and stuff in the blue stuff beforehand." Dan said, ignoring Phillip. "I brought a hammer for the spikes but do you think we should bring two hammers in case I lose it? I brought the boat, too. I have a pump... I figure we can abandon it once we're done with it."

"That's a lot of stuff..." Phillip mentioned.

"Well you know they say 'always be prepared.' Scout's motto..."

"Did you bring the Boy Scout's manual too?"

"I've never been a boy scout, I just know the motto..."

They went up to Phillip's room and got ready. Phillip put the BB's on the floor. He took out a ladle. The idea being that he was going to dip the metal balls in the blue substance, and then bring the ladle with them in case they needed to throw it.

"Oh, good do mine too," Dan said, and handed him a box. Phillip shook it, they didn't sound like BB's. He opened it up, and a row of shining gold bullets looked up at him.

"Dan, are these real...? Did you bring a *real* gun?!" Phillip asked, looking at Dan's bag.

"I didn't have a BB-gun," Dan said, as if defending himself. "It's only a twenty-two..."

"Here I am going out there with a miniature BB-gun, and you with that," Phillip said. "I'll look like an idiot."

"My dad's military, Phil," Dan said. "I have access. This is a farmhouse, right? There's probably a real gun around here somewhere."

"I'm not going to look for a real gun right now," Phillip said, taking the bullets out of the box, and then dipping the ends in the blue bubbling liquid. Looking at the rifle on the bed. "How do you load these things?"

"There's a magazine tube... here I'll show you."

They checked and double checked their walkie talkies. Put on different clothes–Dan had brought changes – they wanted to be comfortable but covered. Dan thought it was a great idea to bring the memory cloth. "I can think of a million uses for that!" But surprisingly, Dan was ambivalent about bringing the ghost blade sword. "It doesn't cut anything but see-through worms. See, it goes right through the bed. Where's that ax the Ramblers gave you?"

This was a good argument, and Phillip decided to bring his ax.

It was right after the argument on how many flashlights to bring–Dan thought five, including headlamps, was far too few. And during Dan's third attempt to rearrange his things, Phillip said "I need to go talk to my Aunt, will you be ready to leave after that?"

"Sure. Definitely. Maybe not, though…" Dan replied. "I'm starting to think I'm bringing too much face camo paint…"

Maddie and Aunt Kath were up when he got over. Maddie was watching TV.

"There you are," Aunt Kath said in the kitchen. "How's it going with your friend over there?"

"Just fine, just fine," Phillip said, wondering what Aunt Kath was making. She only knew how to make a few meals and there were far too many ingredients out. "I'm actually going to go over to his house for a bit. We're finishing a project. Dan's obsessed with it. He's kind of neurotic, but he does most of the work so I don't complain…"

"Exploiting other people for personal gain, I dig it," she said back, looking for something in the cabinet. Phillip was a little disappointed that she didn't argue with him about going over to Dan's. That she didn't turn around to talk to him. He had so much to say to her, but he couldn't say it now. If he made it back…

If he made it back.

Because there was that possibility, wasn't there? And then what would Aunt Kath do? How would it be explained? He would disrupt her life more than he already had.

"You okay there? You look shell shocked or something," Aunt Kath said.

"Huh? Oh, just tired. Hey…" He said to her, but she still was busy finding things in the cupboard and reading labels. "Hey, look at me real quick."

Aunt Kath was surprised by the tone, Phillip moved in closer. "I have given it a huge amount of thought, so I don't want you to argue with me," he said. "I really think you should take that opportunity at King's Hill University. It would be stupid not to…"

Aunt Kath smiled. "Really? But what about…?"

"Pfft. No excuses. Maine will still be there, probably, when you're done," he said back. "Plus, we get to avoid Maine winter, that's worth it in itself. Honestly, we can't let an opportunity like this pass us up. No more delays," he gave her a hug, which surprised her. "See, we hugged on it, now it's official. Do it."

She took a minute to answer, and was smiling when she did. "Okay, I'll get the ball rolling. But I want you to think about it more. I want you to check out the schools here. I think it also gets cold here, so don't expect an easy winter… but cool, let's do this thing!"

"Good. Do it though. No matter what. Cool?" Phillip.

"Cool," She said. "You should come back, I'm trying to make something. It's an experiment. We are going to watch movies until she Maddie falls asleep. I'm seeing how much I can ruin that poor girl before my sister gets back, it's a challenge. I'm making brownies too."

"Sounds fun," Phillip responded, meaning it. "But I do have to go…"

"Shame. Have fun," she said, turned around again.

"Will do," Phillip said, backing out. "Later"

"Bye."

"Love you, Aunt Kath."

She laughed but didn't turn around. "Love you too, Kiddo. Be careful."

"I'll try," he said.

And he walked out of the room. He grabbed the door to leave but then he remembered he had one more thing to do.

Maddie was sitting by the TV, books open in front of her.

"Watcha watching?" He asked her.

"Don't know, doing work," she said, without looking up.

"So, hey, Maddie..." he said, ignoring her answer.

"What...?" she started, looking up. "What's wrong with you? You look weird..."

"Yeah...?" he said. "It's probably because I have a lot ahead of me right now. I just wanted to say... Sorry, Maddie. About everything. I wasn't acting like myself, and there's a good reason for that but still, sorry."

"Sorry... for what?" she said. That suspicious look of hers back on her face.

"About gassing you out... I mean."

It took a second for her to realize what he meant. "'*Gaslighting!*'" She corrected.

"Right, right. Gaslamping," he said back. Maddie roller her eyes. "About all the stuff that's been happening around here. About all the magic."

The word hit her like a slap. She looked up, shocked. Then she looked suspicious, then confused.

Just when she looked like she was about to speak again, Phillip whispered "I have to do something important right now. But later we can talk. And Maddie, if... if I don't come back for a few days. There's some stuff in my closet you might be interested in. Be careful! And... tell everybody I love them, okay, Maddie?"

She sputtered out "okay," in a small voice.

He left before she could follow up. The sound of Aunt Kath in the kitchen the last sound he got from the Fairchild house.

Dan was on the porch, waiting for Phillip.

Looking still and grave in a way Dan never did.

"We ready to do this thing?" Phillip asked, trying to convey confidence.

"Yeah," Dan said, meeting Phillip's eyes. "Let's do this thing."

CHAPTER 32
The S.S. Plan-B

Fortinbras protected the house.

Because that was the thing that had to be done. Because Fortinbras was a loyal dog. Because Fortinbras was a good dog. He had wandered for a long time. It was the only thing he could remember. But now he intended to do right by the place he found.

There were dangers. So many dangers. Big dangers. Smelly dangers. The loud dangers. Dangers that ran from him and climbed trees or went into holes or cheated and flew. He knew how to handle most of them. Boy was so calm and strong, he left the dangers up to him. Because Fortinbras was an important dog. Because Fortinbras was good dog.

But now Fortinbras was scared himself.

Because boy was scared.

And because Fortinbras was a smart dog, that meant Fortinbras should be scared too.

Boy was leaving again. Fortinbras knew because boy always brought things with him. Boy was always bringing things with him. Boy must have a good reason for this, but what it was Fortinbras did not know...

The only thing to do was to go with Boy.

"No, Forty, boy. *Stay*," Boy barked at him. This was to be expected.

Fortinbras was the only one capable of protecting the territory they had won. Boy needed him there. Fortinbras knew this.

But *now* was different. Now Boy was in danger. He should go with Boy now. Territory was unimportant. Boy would see... Fortinbras should go...

"Fortinbras. No," Boy barked again in a way that made Fortinbras dip his head. Boy came to Fortinbras. "Look, buddy. You can't come right now. Stay here. Protect the house, okay. Protect Maddie, she might come over and we don't know if it's safe yet. Stay," and then Boy gave Fortinbras food. Because Boy was a good Boy. Because Boy was kind.

And because Boy was a Boy who could speak. Almost speak. Fortinbras always knew what Boy meant. Boy thought the territory was important. So, Fortinbras thought it was important to. Boy wanted to protect the other. Fortinbras would. Because Fortinbras was loyal.

But he was not happy about it. He sat on the coolest spot in the territory, where he knew the shade would last. Whining as he watched Boy go.

Feeling in the core of his being that if he didn't go, Boy would not return.

Because he was a smart dog, he knew this was true.

━━━━━ ○ ━━━━━

Dan had labeled the mission *'Operation: Farm Rescue.'* But he admitted he wasn't too happy with this and was open to suggestions.

Fortinbras had made a fuss at them leaving—more than he usually did—which just served to make Phillip more nervous. Phillip locked down on these feelings as best as he could. They had a plan. It was as simple as could be expected. *This was no more dangerous than deciding to sneak into the Farm*, he told himself.

The special gears on the Many-League Bikes were almost completely useless where they were going. Too many turns. Too many trips through and around the Mundafold.

This worked out fine, as they had to make frequent stops to study the map.

"It's the Primafold entrance to the river," Dan said. "But I think we need to go through that old dockyard or whatever it is to get there." They got off their bikes and stored them back in their bells, putting them in their pockets.

They climbed over an old fence and through another broken one. Walked around large abandoned warehouses with broken windows. Dan led them back into the woods.

A small tree, barely taller than Phillip, walked in front of their path.

"I think we're in the Primafold," Phillip said, studying the duplicated map. "We need to enter the river there. Which means we need to put in a spike... yeah, right over there. Look, the Pauls marked the rock on the map."

Dan took out a spike and a hammer, they had split the spikes among them, in case one of them dropped their bag. "Is this good?" Dan asked, placing the spike on the ground.

"I think that's it. Yeah, that's it. Do it," Phillip replied.

Dan drove the hammer home.

The moment Dan made contact with the spike the earth shook. It sounded like the ground—the entire earth beneath them—was an enormous gong that Dan was banging, and they were just ants on the surface. It vibrated their very being.

"Keep going!" Phillip yelled, holding his ears uselessly to the sound. "Get it over with."

Dan hit the spike again and again, wincing as he did so.

Birds flew away. The trees that could move did so. The water of the river disturbed. Each time Dan did it the vibrations became softer, more muted. When he finished, hitting the spike made almost no sound at all.

Phillip adjusted his jaw and rubbed his ears.

"So, we're going to be noticed whenever we do that..." Phillip said.

"No kidding," Dan replied, picking up the duffle bag. "Help me with the boat. I only have a hand pump. It will go quicker if we switch off."

Phillip put together the plastic oars as Dan laid the inflatable boat on the ground. "You sure that's big enough?" Phillip asked.

"It's the only one I had," Dan answered, finding the plug.

It took ten minutes of pumping to realize something was wrong.

"It should be getting bigger than that by now," Phillip said. "Maybe there's a leak." He moved his hands over the boat.

"Doesn't have a leak," Dan said, panting. "Just used it!"

Phillip moved his hands over the boat until he found what he was looking for. He held the boat up and showed Dan. A six-inch-long gash on the bottom.

"Alright," Dan said, he stopped pumping. "Maybe it has a leak..."

Phillip tried to think. "You have duct-tape, right? Maybe I can use my lashing glove too... oh. Wait," he said, as he noticed the bottom side of the had dozens of rips in it.

"I'm starting to think my cat got too it," Dan said. "Maybe we can find a store. Buy a new one."

"I can go back to the Fairchild house. They might have something," Phillip said. "Do we have time for that?" He looked around for a solution. Was there a boat they could borrow? Something to float on?

They didn't have time for this.

"Hey, Phil," Dan said in a distracted voice. He was looking up a tree. "You have that pocket knife, right?" He pushed the tree back and forth. "And the lashing glove? How good can that knife cut? How much can we bind with that glove...? It's instantaneous, right?"

"Yes, makes your mouth feel dry. But yeah," Phillip answered, and looked up the tree, then around. "What are you think..." And then it hit him... *Would that work?* Did they have time? Did they have another choice? "Yes, the lashing glove can bind really big things. Dan, you're a genius!"

They set to work at once.

A pile of old downed trees and trash providing most of the material they would need. Phillip took his sky chalk and drew, on Dan's instructions a wide rectangle on the ground by the river. "We need to plan ahead, Dan. Build some rails first so it's easier to move into the water," he said. "Do we just build a bed? Is that enough?"

"No, we need the thickest logs on the bottom. And then the medium logs connecting them. And then the bed we will lay the thinnest ones the other way. At least I think that's how it goes," Dan said. "And I say we build it right in the water, it won't float away. And saves time. Can your lashing glove do that?"

"Think so. Good idea." Phillip said. "There's a down tree over there. Pretty big. Let's use that."

They found the downed tree. Twelve-inches thick at least. "We should have, I don't know, maybe three lengths of ten feet for the bottom layer. Is that too big?"

"Cool." Phillip said, but he was concentrating hard on the pocket knife. He didn't want to know what would happen if he accidentally touched his skin with it. "So, right in the middle. We can always make it smaller."

Holding his wrist with the knife in it, he turned his head in case there were splinters. He carved a small cut into the top of the downed tree.

Crack!

The cut traveled all the way through the tree. A perfect cut. Phillip used his own feet to estimate ten-feet, and did it again. Crack!

The tree fell away. He made a perfect log. "Awesome," Dan said.

Phillip made two more cuts, to get two more logs. And then used the knife to rid the logs of branches. "Alight," Phillip said, satisfied. "Now how do we move them...?"

Moving them was pure physical labor. They didn't have a solution for that. They could be manhandled from one side but they had to be rolled and dragged. Both Phillip and Daniel were out of breath by the time they got to the river. "Wait..." Phillip said. "We should have the crossbars before we put them in the water, it will be easier." Dan, too out of breath to answer, just nodded.

They found hundreds of branches and small trees which they dragged to the river. Phillip cutting some to make them easier to move. They found lumber, real processed lumber, rotting next to the building they had passed. "This is perfect for the cross-supports," Dan said, and they carried them back. The wood staining their clothes and hands.

Phillip took off his shoes and his pants to get into the water. He didn't like dark water, but he couldn't avoid it. He turned around and noticed Dan had changed too.

"You brought a bathing suit?!" Phillip said.

"Under my clothes," Dan said defensively. "Came in handy, didn't it?"

They rolled the logs into the water. "Let's do all three at once," Phillip said, putting the lashing glove on. "I'll pre-cut the lumber. What do you think, seven-feet each? Six?" They went into the knee-deep water with the logs and the newly cut cross-supports.

Dan held the logs while Phillip worked. The three logs were hard to wrangle... He put one of the cross-supports over all three, at the end. "Hold them still. I just need to make sure the angle is not too far off."

Phillip went to the one of the logs, and lashed with his glove the lumber to the log.

Silver lines appeared and disappeared.

It stuck perfectly, like it was meant to be there. Phillip lashed the log on the end next, and then the one in the middle. Even with only one cross support, it held together fine. Phillip added another, and then another. Until he was ready for the bed logs.

Dan tied the logs with a length of rope to a tree on the side, while Phillip cut branches off the bed logs they had found. "I'll cut them more when they are on the thing," Phillip said.

Phillip was in the water, and then a thought occurred to him. "I have an idea," Phillip said, and ran to his backpack. Taking out the memory cloth and showing it to Dan, making a point to hold up the third dial. "Great idea!" Dan said. "We should build that before the bed though..."

This turned out to be the hardest task yet. They found two more logs of suitable width and they made what looked like a ladder. This was Dan's idea. "It doesn't need to be that tall..." Dan said. They crossed the ladder with thinner bars, which Dan tied to the memory cloth with rope. "Be sure it's facing the right way," Phillip instructed. "It only goes one way..."

They were careful not to get the cloth wet as they put it on the middle log. It took both of them to lift it up. The ladder-pole straddled the middle log. Phillip lashed it in place. It stood. Not satisfied that it had enough support, and took some of the smaller cuts of wood to support it at angles. lashing it to the main frame. "I'll tie some rope to it too," Dan said.

The only thing left was the bed frame. Which was easy to place. Phillip doing the lashing, making sure to lash each log to the log next to it and below. Dan took the knife, and was cutting them to the right length.

After Dan had placed some support ropes on the mast, they were done. Dan laughed, and stood on it. He even jumped a couple times.

Phillip thought he might be prouder of this than of anything he had ever done.

Floating in the water was— in Phillip's opinion— a perfect wooden raft.

Over ten feet long and six feet wide.

Complete with a mast and memory-cloth sail.

"What should we call her?" Dan asked, as satisfied as Phillip.

"The Plan-B," Phillip answered.

Dan laughed. "The S.S. Plan-B. I like it. What does 'S.S.' stand for?"

"Sailing Ship," Phillip answered.

"Oh," Dan said.

Phillip looked at his watch. "We need to go. It's going to get dark soon..."

They got dressed. Dan had brought a towel to dry with. They leaped on the boat, unsure at first. "Carry the guns now. We might need them..." Dan said, and he strapped the rifle to his back, checking the safety. Phillip put on his small BB-gun.

Phillip cut the rope. "Grab the pole I made you," he said, "We need to push into the river."

The S.S. Plan-B floated into the river like it knew where it was going. Phillip only had to push against a rock with his pole once to clear it of the bank, into the deeper water of the river, where they were pushed by the current. Dan picked up one of the oars to steer. "The inlet we need to get to is on the other side. About a mile away, maybe a little more..." Dan said.

"I think it's time to test the memory cloth," Phillip said. "Ready?"

"Ready." Dan confirmed, he had tied himself to the bed of the boat with some rope.

Phillip got up. Went up to the memory cloth. Grabbed the third dial, and turned.

He turned it faster than the wanted.

The memory cloth came alive. Pulling against the mast and the ropes it was attached to. The S.S. Plan-B shot forward and Phillip stumbled back, almost losing his footing. Dan took the oar and placed it in the water, learning in the moment how to steer.

The memory cloth held to the mast.

They were moving, fast—or at least *faster*—through the water.

Dan and Phillip laughed from the thrill of it. "Phil, we built a boat!" Dan yelled.

"I know!" Phillip said, congratulating them both with his tone. The buildings and trees and rocks of the shore passing them by.

The thrill couldn't last for long. They had work to do. An inlet to find.

"I think we are getting close..." Dan said, unsure. "Yeah, see that big boulder on the side. That's the inlet, right there..."

It was getting dark. Phillip didn't notice at first. Managing the memory cloth and steering and navigating taking up too much of his thoughts. But it was getting darker.

Darker far sooner than it should...

He looked at his watch. One of the hands was going forward too fast, another was left behind.

Wherever they were going, Mundafold time was diverging from it. Fireflies were lighting on the water, it grew foggier as they approached the inlet.

"Here," Dan said, and handed Phillip his head lamp. Which he turned on. "Maybe we should use the light from the memory cloth?" he suggested.

"That's sunlight," Phillip said. "Bothers some Fae. Shouldn't use that unless we need to."

Dan nodded, and they both looked forward. Phillip had grabbed his pole, and was looking for rocks. He dialed back the memory cloth, going as slow as possible without being taken back out by the light current.

The inlet was covered by a canopy of thick trees. It was night now, and they blocked any light from the stars, the mist doing the rest of the work.

Dan and Phillip were silent as the S.S. Plan-B went into the inlet, as they were engulfed by darkness and mist. The fireflies the only light they could see.

CHAPTER 33

The Queen of the Swamp

The moon broke through the clouds. Providing them some light.

Water spread around them in all directions, smooth when not covered in floating plants. There was no trace of a current anymore. They were surrounded on all sides by thick trees which had roots like massive spider legs. Phillip could see one of the trees moving from through the water, slow enough that it barely caused a disturbance.

"This is where the directions get tricky," Dan whispered, "it says follow the 'thickest path,' but that 'any path' will do... I guess this is it?"

Phillip looked down at the dark water, and moved closer to the center of the boat. "I'm just glad we're not in a small plastic boat right now..." he said. He thought he saw dozens of shining eyes look back at them in the water when he turned his light in any direction. But they submerged again when he looked for too long.

"I think we're getting close to the Swamp," Dan said, swallowing hard.

He saw up ahead some lights. Not fireflies. Stationary lights. He could hear music too.

He turned the wind on the memory-cloth down lower, turning it almost off as they approached.

There were buildings built on stilts, going into the sky as much as twenty or even fifty feet, getting thinner and bending and odd angles. FaeFlame was lit everywhere illuminated dozens of bridges that connected the buildings.

They were surrounded by music. Fast string music. People danced and drank on the pathways and in the lighted wooden buildings and in boats on the water. Phillip could only pick out one or two humans. They were the extreme minority here. Most were gremlins or something like gremlins. Some were too tall and thin and covered by cloaks. Ones that looked human turned out to be misshapen in some way, or possess antlers or horns or hooved-feet. Some wore masks. Some were naked.

One bridge was possessed entirely by transparent shadows which were vaguely human shaped. Shadowkin.

Things flew in the air, too large for fireflies, they laughed like children as they passed.

Animals walked on the pathways and swam in the water. Dan jumped as two alligators passed the S.S.-Plan B, both wearing masks made of bone over their eyes, which were painted in glowing symbols. "Were those alligators," Phillip said, not wanting to think about it. "I think they were crocodiles, longer snouts..." Dan replied in a hollow voice.

They could not stand out more. Still, nobody paid them much attention. Except for a canoe which pulled in next to them. A woman with fish scale skin and webbed hands and a wide lipless mouth offered them barbequed rats on sticks.

They declined as politely as best they could.

"We're close," Phillip whispered. "Just don't meet eye contact with anybody..."

The buildings thinned out. It started to get quiet again as they left the party behind them.

They were noticed. Children were walking along the pathways, following the boat with even steps.

There was something wrong about them.

They had wide smiles, and hungry, predators smile... massive black eyes and pale skin, walking far too smoothly for children. They pointed at the boat and whispered in each other's ears, laughing sometimes. Their voices were the only thing that seemed human about them. Their smiles widened and they followed faster. Dozens of them now, looking like they were about to pounce on the S.S. Plan-B at any moment.

Phillip turned the wind dial on the memory-cloth, the sail picked up, and they moved faster from the water, away from the party and black-eyed children. "Don't look at them," Phillip whispered to Dan, who was already following these instructions.

They jumped from the pathway to the trees. As easily as if they were monkeys. They stood on branches and watched the raft pass. Phillip tuned the dial more.

They finally passed them. Dozens of them still looked after the boat. Phillip could see their wide still grins from here... They were pointing at the raft. He could still hear their laughs, as close as if they were laughing right in his ear.

"I think this is why Andy told us not to go into the Swamp," Dan said when they were surrounded again only by water and trees. "I don't think I can handle this..."

"Let's just get through..."

The S.S. Plan-B slammed into something hard, and came to an abrupt halt.

Dan was sitting and slid forward. Phillip tripped, and grabbed the raft before he fell off, one leg falling into the water. His guiding stick fell in with a splash.

He pulled himself back on the boat. Dan was checking himself to see if anything was missing. The rifle was still on his back. He muttered, "What'd we...?"

"Was my party not to your liking...?" A sad, confused voice came from the trees. It was both soft and distant, but also felt like something whispered into his ears.

Dan and Phillip spun around, looking for the source of the voice. They couldn't find it.

"I asked..." The voice said again, this time the voice carried with it a pressure which pressed on their ears. The swamp trees were moving around them, walking on their roots and surrounding the raft. "Was my party... *unsatisfying* to you? Why did you leave? Why *would* you leave?"

Phillip gulped, and summed the courage to answer. "We... thought it looked great, really fun. But we have to do some stuff right now." He hated how scared he sounded. "Are you... Tatuna? Queen Tatuna, I mean."

The voice giggled.

The water in front of the swirled, out of the black water a head appeared.

He saw hair like seaweed, bright and the color of moonlight.

And then a smiling human-like face.

A face as tall as Phillip's entire body.

"Yes!" Tatuna said like a happy child. "I am the queen of the Swamp. I am Tatuna. You have heard of me? Have you come to seek me and my favors?"

She had a neck, and what looked like a shoulder under the water. But what had to be a massive body slid away the wrong angles. Her arms were coming out of the water. Too many arms. Of different shapes and sizes. Twirling the hanging branches absentmindedly like it was hair. One hand floated above the raft, and caressed the bed with finger the length of Phillip's leg. He knew, underneath the water, that Tatuna looked nothing like a person.

"Um... we, actually are just passing through..." Phillip said.

Queen Tatuna's face went sour. Sour like a child's face. She placed her cheek on the raft, causing it to rise on the other side.

She almost looked like tears were going to come to her eyes, but then her head lifted again. She looked angry, a petulant, unrestrained anger. The massive head began to dip back into the water. "We did not mean to offend!" Phillip said at once. Tatuna stopped. "We are new at this, and we sometimes... forget our manners..."

Tatuna stopped, looked Phillip in the eyes, and laughed again. Her voice was not inhibited or changed in any way by the fact that her mouth was now underwater. "All is forgiven," she said, any hint of anger gone. "Please tell me what I can do as your host to please you. But fair warning. A Queen's service does not come cheap."

Phillip's head spun. What should he say? "We... could use fair passage through the Swamp..." He said, but it sounded more like a question when it came out of his mouth.

"Such boring, small things to ask for," Tatuna said. "I am a Queen. I can give you *power*. I can give you *wealth*. I can give *love*, maybe. Or fun. Do you want treasures? I have treasures too... I can make your lives glorious. Delicious lives. You can laugh and never stop, if you want."

His tongue was caught again in his mouth. He had read about deal making with Fae. Turning down a Fae could be as dangerous as accepting something from them. He needed a way to placate her, a way not to offend her...

"There is something... you can help us with, if you want to," Phillip said, Tatuna giggled. "There are some men. One of them is named Waltzrigg. They have been staging themselves in the Swamp. They are trying to get into the Farm, to hurt the Farm..."

She looked offended at this. "Why do you say this? That they want to *hurt* the Farm?"

"Because it's... true..." Phillip said, and then it occurred to him. She wasn't asking who Waltzrigg was, or where they were, she asked about their motivation... "You've already spoken to them, haven't you...? They are already here, aren't they?"

Tatuna laughed, spinning her head around without moving her shoulders so that she looked at Phillip upside-down. "And what if I have?"

"I'm telling the truth. They intend to hurt the Farm. That will hurt the Swamp too..."

"Your kind are always saying things, most of it means little," Tatuna said, turning her head back. "What is true to you know is gone by the next morning. The Waltzrigg boy-man has given me gifts. Great gifts. Helped me become a Queen. He is my ally. What have you done for me?" A dangerous look flashed in her eyes.

"I..." Phillip didn't know how to answer. "I have no doubt that Waltzrigg helped you. He does that to help himself, he helped make you Queen, but did he say how long he expected you to actually *be* Queen," he tried his best to look Tatuna right in the eyes. "You need to believe me, Tatuna. We are here to save the Farm. Waltzrigg might have helped you become Queen... but we can help you stay Queen!"

Tatuna looked away from him. She looked bored. "I have promised to hold any man-person who follows this path..."

"Tatuna... If you can just... We have..." Phillip stuttered.

"Shhhhhh," she said to him, and put a massive finger up to his face. "I have promised to hold man-persons here. But I did not say for how long I would do so..." Her arms started submerging again into the water.

It took a second to register what she was saying.

"Thank you... Queen Tatuna," Phillip said. "We..."

"I can only give you a short head start," she said. The boat was moving again. Tatuna chin sunk below the water.

"Head start?" Dan said.

"Only a short one, I'm afraid. I have made promises. A long head start would be rude..." Tatuna said. "Now, I suggest you move. You are not rich in time. I like you two boys-men. Better than the ones I've met before. I very much hope my servants are not successful in devouring you."

Dan and Phillip didn't need more encouragement to get moving.

Phillip picked up the spare staff. Dan the oar. Phillip stood and spun the wind dial.

The S.S. Plan-B sped off.

Phillip managed a weak, "thank you" to Tatuna as she waved them away.

Dan turned back on his head-lamp and looked behind them.

"Do you see anything?!" Phillip yelled. The mast cracking under force of the memory cloth.

"No, I don't... oh. Yeah. yeah, I see something," Dan said, his voice going out.

Phillip turned around.

There were hundreds of... *somethings* in the water. Crocodiles, maybe... Phillip looked up to the canopy. Something was crawling there too... and some of the trees were moving. Making their path slimmer as they went. Almost touching the side of the raft.

The *somethings* were fifty yards away but getting closer.

There were eyes coming from the left and right. Coming closer to the path. What if one got too close? Should they shoot it?

"They're getting closer, Phil!" Dan yelled.

Phillip saw Dan was right. Something huge and slithering was twenty yards away. Ten. It was breaking the surface.

Phillip twisted the second dial of the memory cloth, as far as it would turn.

The cloth lit up like the sun. It burned Phillip's eyes and showered him in heat. It felt like his skin was melting. But it stopped the approaching creatures. Something screamed and turned away. Something else fell out of the trees. Even the trees themselves backed up from the light.

Phillip could barely see the light was so bright. It burnt the colors out of the world. The water and the trees seemed monochrome. But there were no creatures.

Dan was rubbing his eyes. "It worked!" He said.

But as soon as he said that something happened. The light grew dimmer. Not noticeably at first, but then it started to dim further, and fluctuate.

He had turned the dial too hard.

He had used all the sun stored in the cloth.

It was getting dimmer every second. Whatever was in the water and climbing through the trees began to feel comfortable enough to start approaching again.

"Let's go faster!" Dan yelled, and began paddling with his oar.

Phillip spin the wind dial on the memory cloth more. The cloth pulled on the ropes and the wood making them creak. "Faster!" Dan said. "They're getting closer!" Phillip spun the dial more and was almost thrown back by the force of the raft moving forward. The front of the raft caught in the water, and then dipped back before it evened out again.

"There it is!" Dan said. "There's the shore."

Phillip wasn't looking. He was looking behind him. The light from the memory cloth was almost out. The creatures were moving faster than ever. They would reach him soon.

He did the only thing he could think of. He dropped the staff. Took the BB-gun off his back. Pumped the handle. Aimed. And fired behind the raft.

The BB traveled through the air as if carried by a bolt of lightning. Sparks catching on the leaves of the trees and the water before it hit.

The water exploded as if a boulder had been thrown in. Lighting sparked on the waves.

Creatures screamed again, huge unnatural screams, and retreated. "Whoa," Dan said.

The light from the memory-cloth flickered out completely "Do it again!" Dan said.

Phillip fired another shot where he saw movement.

Lighting. Explosions. Screeching screams.

Dan turned the wind dial as far as it would go. The raft picked up. The wood whining.

Bam! Crack!

A rope hit Phillip's shoulder like a whip. At first, he thought the creatures had gotten close to the raft. I took a second to understand what was happening. Dan was looking forward in disbelief. Half the mast and the memory cloth had broken from the raft and flew into water. The memory cloth still pulling strips of wood with it as it left.

The raft slowed and came to a near halt.

Dan and Phillip were still for a moment. Then both at the same time picked up the oars and began to row as fast as they could.

They were going to be too slow. Whatever was in the water was moving fast. Phillip stopped rowing to fire BB's at the water. What would he do when they got too close?

"We need to jump!" Dan yelled. "We are close enough now!"

Phillip spun. The shore was twenty yards away, maybe more. But they would never make it rowing. Following Dan, he dropped his oar and jumped into the water.

He didn't go underwater. His feet hit ground. The water went up to his waist.

He jumped and ran as fast as he could. He had never felt so slow in his life. They were within fifteen yards...

Just when he was certain the creature would grab him or bite him and pull him over he hit land. Leaped so that he was on his stomach next to Dan, and then got up and went further on to shore.

They turned around just in time to see something like a horde of massive earthworms come out of the water and slam into the raft, reducing it instantly to splinters. Dan and Phillip crawled backwards as they were showered in bits of wood and dark water.

The creatures turned around. The water went still.

It took five minutes of panting on the ground before either of them felt like standing.

"Bye S.S. Plan-B," Dan said, neither of them had taken their eyes of the water yet. "She served us well..."

Phillip laughed, not quite knowing why. Dan joined him. He took out the map.

"Next spike goes right here," he said.

They were still out of breath, and soaked from the stomach down, but they took out the spike, both of them wrapping cloth around their ears before they drove it home.

The earth shook like a gong again, vibrations moved over the water. Shaking the whole world, less and less each time.

And then they were done.

"Two down. Two to go," Dan said.

"The broken arch should be over here," Phillip said.

They both walked slowly. Not talking any more than what was necessary. Both recovering from their trip through the Swamp. The broken arch was ahead of them, in a clearing between boulders. A stone pointed arch that looked like the entrance to a church, but without a building to support it. Broken and collapsed. There was a wooden door in the center.

"Here we are, Dan said. Both had taken off their guns. They knew what needed to be done next. Their instructions were clear "Are you ready?"

"Ready." Phillip said, *ready for this to be over...*

He pumped the BB-gun. Looked down the sights at the door. And pulled the trigger.

CHAPTER 34

The Blue Door

The door blew open as if they were shooting cannons. Leaving only a burnt mess of wood behind.

On the other side, they could see the sun and waves of grass.

"Let me reload before we go in," Phillip said, but he suspected that he had enough loaded already to last. He just wanted to be sure... Dan took the opportunity to re-arrange himself. Phillip took out the short silver ax, and hung it on a strap from his belt.

He never thought he would need to use it. Now he thought he would be lucky if he didn't...

The other side of the arch was a field.

"We're here again!" Dan said.

It was the field they walked on when they first jumped the fence to the Farm. Hills which rolled up and down like slow waves on the ocean covered in long blue-green grass. The archway was on a hill that for some reason didn't move like the others.

The sun was up, but setting. *Fast.* Phillip looked at his watch but couldn't understand what it told him. Every hand was fluctuating, going back and forth in irregular patterns. He understood why in less than a minute...

The sun set, and the moon shone above. But in less than a minute, the sun popped back over the opposite horizon, before running out of energy, turning around, and setting again. Crickets and frogs announced the short dusk and nightfall. Morning birds awoke and then grew silent every sunrise.

"What do you think is happening?" Dan asked.

"Don't know... The Pauls said Waltzrigg was messing with the work-time engine," Phillip answered, squinting as another sunrise caught him by surprise.

Dan had put on sunglasses. He was looking at the map.

"We are looking for a shortcut. There's another weird shaped boulder thing," Dan said. "Do you have the next spike?"

"Getting it now. Hand me the hammer." Phillip said, taking out a spike.

The waves of grass vibrated and stopped when they hammered the spike in. The archway behind them collapsed into a pile of rubble. When they stopped, the waving hills continued. The sun continued to set and rise.

They followed the rolling fields from landmark to landmark on their map. A large tree. Some ruins on stationary earth. A crow shaped boulder. A teapot shaped boulder. Boulders that looked like *'women's breasts.'*

"It actually says that?!" Phillip asked. "It's right here, the Pauls wrote it right here. I'm not making this up," Dan explained.

The setting and rising sun made it difficult to navigate. Phillip's eyes hurt from adjusting so much.

"Here we are," Dan said, when they reached the 'spiky pointy boulders.' Which were spikier and pointer than he expected, jutting into the sky seventy feet at least. "Right between there. There's a passage. After that it just says we can put the fourth spike 'anywhere in the central grounds.' That's all it says..."

There was another door. Smaller this time, almost perfectly square. Phillip tried to pull it and push it open. It didn't budge. He took the BB-gun off his back again, Dan took his rifle. They backed up and stood behind a rock.

"Fire in one. Two. Three. Fire!" Phillip said, and they both pulled their triggers.

Two sparks flew across the air and hit the door, the bullet traveling faster than the BB and hitting first. There was a burst of blue light.

When their eyes had adjusted and the smoke cleared, they noticed the door was still there. Cracked down the middle, but still there.

Phillip pumped the BB-gun, Dan pulled back the bolt of his rifle. "Again. One. Two. Three. Fire!"

Another burst of light. The crack was larger, but the door held.

"I thought the Pauls said this would work..." Phillip said. "Here, let me try something." He retrieved the ladle he was using to dip the BB's in the blue liquid. He went over to the door and placed the handle in the crack.

"Alright, aim at the ladle," Phillip said. Running back to Dan behind the rock. "One. Two. Three. Fire." They pulled their triggers again.

The rush of wind from the blast was so large it blew them backwards, even behind the rock. Dust and dust was thrown into the air.

Phillip got off the ground, coughing, and looked to the door.

It was open. Blasted away. Its frame was cracked and broken.

It opened up onto darkness. It was so dark their headlamps couldn't penetrate it. Even the sun which rose and set behind them couldn't beat it. Phillip put his hand in, it was cold. He put his foot in, and a smooth floor underneath him. "I guess we go in...?" He said.

Dan was tying twine to a thin tree outside the door. "Here, hold this," Dan said. "For we don't get separated," Phillip followed his instructions, but doubted the twine would do any good.

They turned on their headlamps to full brightness. And entered the doorway.

It was darker than Phillip had ever experienced. Darker than that cave tour he went on with his parents. The light coming in from the doorway didn't last. The headlamp couldn't penetrate it. They walked in ten steps, then twenty. Dan behind him. Both crouching and putting their hands forward. The floor felt smooth and hard, like marble.

"Phil! Phil!" Dan said behind him.

"What?" he asked.

"The door is gone. There's something wrong with the twine," he said.

Phillip turned around. The headlamp didn't penetrate the darkness far but it was enough to see what Dan was talking about. The twine was taunt behind them, but ended mid-air a few feet away. Phillip tugged on it. They walked forward a few steps and the twine followed like a tail.

It snapped. And fell to the ground. Phillip and Dan stared at it.

"The Pauls wouldn't have sent us in here if there wasn't a way through," Phillip said, trying to convince himself as fear boiled up inside him. "Grab the back of my shirt. We keep walking."

And that's what they did. First twenty steps. And then fifty more. And then fifty after that. Until Phillip thought they had made an enormous mistake, and that it was best to turn back now, maybe they could still make it back.

"Dan..." Phillip said.

Dan shushed him.

There were voices. Muffled voices. Like people talking in another room. Phillip listened hard. They sounded like they were in front of him, or just to his right.

With no other point of focus they walked toward the sound. Phillip didn't know if it was because he was listening as hard as he could or if he was getting closer, but the voices sounded louder.

Phillip ran face-first into a door.

A door!

"Dan!" he said, and turned around. Dan was still behind him but turned the other way, his hand was pressed against a wooden wall that wasn't there moment ago. There was a wall to their right, their left. A low ceiling. They were in a small room, or a wooden box barely big enough to accommodate them. Only lit by their headlamps.

Phillip pressed on the door, which had a seam down the middle. It opened with a creek. Light poured through. With a breath of relief Phillip pushed it open more and walked out. "Are we in a closet?" Dan asked.

Phillip looked around outside the door.

He ducked to the ground as soon as he saw it. Grabbing Dan's shirt and bringing him with him to the ground. Dan started to ask "wha...?" but Phillip caught his eyes and put his finger to his lips.

They were in a large, long room. There was glass separating different parts of the room.

On the other side of the glass, was *Waltzrigg.*

He gave orders in another language. There were dozens of men around him. He was dressed in simple brown and black clothing. Men around him carrying long rifles were dressed in a similar fashion.

"I am absolutely thrilled for your men that they are so happy, Lady Barta," Waltzrigg said.

"*Fat* Barta," a woman wearing furs and smoking a long pipe said to him. Her voice sounded like an asthmatic frog. Deep, cracking, but resonant.

"Excuse my rudeness. *Fat* Barta. My memory has never been good and it's not what it used to be," Waltzrigg corrected. "But as I was saying. I am thrilled for your men that they are happy, but I do worry. I am such a worrier, you will excuse me. That they are being tad too... *rambunctious*."

There were other men in the room. Coming in and out of doors on the side. They were in the cloud-gathering room! The one with the doors that opened into the air. Rough looking men in furs and leather went in and out of one door and into another. Carrying oil paintings and silverware and large wooden chests.

They were looting the place. They were looting the Farm.

Phillip heard something moving on the floor around the men. Maybe dogs. They made harsh clicking sounds as they walked...

"My boys know how to be quiet when they need to be," she said to Waltzrigg. "Oy!" She screamed to the men in furs. "Cut the racket! You're worrying our patron here."

"Yes Ma'am," a few of them said, while others chuckled.

"Greatly appreciated," Waltzrigg said. "Are you satisfied yet?"

Fat Barta shrugged and blew out a trail of smoke from her nose. "My needs grow in the taking. They are endless. Even so, I like to stay as humble as possible. Tell me when you need us to be done, and we will be done."

Dan and Phillip were stuck, crouched behind a table in the glass-lined room. The cabinet they had come out off shut with a click. Phillip looked at Waltzrigg, he didn't seem to notice.

"I do not think I have said how much I am enjoying our partnership," Waltzrigg said to Fat Barta. "So much so I almost didn't notice we were being watched..."

Waltzrigg turned fast on the spot. At looked right into Phillip's eyes.

Waltzrigg's men and Fat Barta turned to the glass-lined room. The men pointed their long wooden guns. A few fur cloaked men turned to see what was happening.

Phillip felt like he swallowed a golf ball. He ducked behind the desk but he knew it was too late. Waltzrigg had noticed them. Why had the Pauls sent them here?! They needed to get to the grounds for the last spike. It was useless being inside!

"Come on out now, interloper," Waltzrigg said. "I would like to meet and compliment the person who escaped my notice for so long."

Phillip didn't move. He looked around for anything that might help.

Dan was looking at the far corner. "Look," he whispered, and pointed.

There was a door there. One of the blue cloud-gathering doors, in front of it was a small chalkboard which said 'FARM proper' on it. "Do you think it leads to somewhere else?" Dan whispered. Phillip considered getting up and running for it.

"Too shy? Shame," Waltzrigg said. "Shame. So much is wasted on shyness. We will have to come in then..." He whistled. And the men with the guns opened fire. Bright copper light slammed into the glass. The room shook from the shots. The glass cracked, but held.

"Go to the door!" Phillip yelled. Dan was already moving for it. He grabbed the handle and pulled it open.

On the other side of the door, was *blue*. Clouds. Sky.

This was a cloud gathering door, Phillip thought, *of course it opened thousands of feet into the air!* The copper light didn't stop. The cracks of the strange guns continued. The glass broke a little more.

What do they do?

Phillip and Dan looked outside the door. They could see ground down below, through breaks in the clouds. Cold wind was blowing through the door, disturbing everything in the room not disturbed by the copper shots.

Dan was reaching in his backpack. He took out another long spike.

"Do you have any feathers?" He asked.

"Feathers?!" Phillip yelled back. Dan had gone mad. "Why would I have feathers?! Why do we need feathers?!"

"Because we need to put this into the ground. And I'm thinking we can throw it out of this door. But we need to make sure it lands spiky part down. To do that, it needs resistance on one side, because that's how *resistance* works, Phil! That's what makes an arrow fly straight! Get out your lashing glove, and find something we can attach to the spike!"

He looked around, but didn't find anything. Phillip put on his lashing glove, and ripped the bottom of his shirt. "Will this work?" he asked Dan.

"Don't know," Dan said, handing him the spike.

He used the lashing glove and attached two lengths of cloth to the fat end of the spike. Making a long tail. He looked at Dan, who was still crouching. The copper light and the bangs stopped.

Waltzrigg was looking in the room, through the cracked glass.

"It can't be!" Waltzrigg said in a happy voice. "I know these boys! Well it is a delight to meet you again. We just keep running into each other! But I hate to say it seems Paul was not entirely honest with me. You boys are clearly special."

Neither Dan or Phillip answered him. Waltzrigg turned to other people, three of them in gray cloaks and hoods, who wore masks from their noses down with blue paint coming down from the eyes. "I understand the Weepers are very talented in pulling down walls like this. Could I perhaps request your assistance...?"

"We are not here for that," one of them said, his eyes looked hateful at Waltzrigg, even from where Phillip stood.

"Of course, I would not want to press you," Waltzrigg said. "But I would be most appreciative."

The ones in the gray cloaks looked at one another, and then turned for the glass room.

Slam! Bang!

It sounded like an elephant had run into the glass. The glass cracked further still. The ceiling split and particles of stone fell on their heads.

Waltzrigg turned back to them. "I would like nothing more than to solve the mystery of you too. But I am afraid circumstances will not allow that..."

Slam! Bang!

Phillip tested the spike, he pulled on the cloth. The bond was strong.

"... Think of this as a gift I am giving you, if you can manage that..." Waltzrigg continued. "Most people do not know how they would act in a situation like this, when death is close and almost a certainty, they are forced to imagine."

Slam! Bang!

"... but you get to see firsthand who you are. You know yourselves, boys. More than others who live a hundred-and-fifty years and never get to experience what you have..."

Slam! Bang!

Stones and wood beams fell from the ceiling. Dan and Phillip ducked back under the table.

"... That is a privilege boy amongst privileges. Something, if you don't mind me saying, something worth dying for. Worry not, your short lives were not wasted..." Waltzrigg was pacing back and forth looking in the glass-lined room. His head was hunched now, like some beast of prey on a hunt. A tiger in a cage waiting for a meal.

There was no more time. With the ceiling falling in, Phillip ran to the open door.

"... what do you have there?" Waltzrigg asked.

Slam! Bang!

Phillip walked a little out of the door, there was a deck outside the door, not much larger than his foot. Phillip dropped the spike into the clouds.

"Stop for a moment," Waltzrigg said to the men in gray cloaks. "Now what did you do there?" He asked Phillip.

For the first time Phillip met his eyes. It wasn't an easy thing to do.

Fat Barta was staring at him too.

Nobody talked. Nothing happened for over ten seconds, which could have easily been an hour.

Just when Waltzrigg was opening his mouth to speak, they heard it.

Like an impossibly large drum had been hit in the distance, the sound traveled through the ground and into his bones. It lifted him off the ground and vibrated his eyes.

Like the earth was hit by an impossibly large hammer.

They had done it! They had placed the last spike.

Waltzrigg looked around, confused.

Fat Barta laughed like a toad. "I know this boy," she said, pointing to Phillip. "He's the bait I used…"

Waltzrigg stared at Phillip. "It can't be," he said, amazement and honest joy in his face. "Coincidences are amazing, aren't they?" And then he took something out of his breast pocket. A red vial of liquid. He threw it on the ground and crushed it under his feet while staring into Phillip's eyes.

Nothing happened. Waltzrigg looked around. Then closed his eyes, smiled and laughed.

"What was that, what does that mean?" Fat Barta asked, not sounding particularly interested in the answer as she relit here pipe.

"It means my connection to the engine has been severed. It means your hard work and patience has been lost," Waltzrigg said. "It means we're going to have to be a little more aggressive from here on out…"

He turned as if going to head out of the room. "Weepers. Men. Break down that room and kill those boys. We are moving to contingency. Kill anybody who sees you. Fat Barta, I hope that you follow the same rules."

Waltzrigg walked out of the room, half his men in tow.

Slam! Bang! The Weepers continued their assault on the glass-lined room.

The walls were buckling. Phillip ran to the cabinet, but it led nowhere. Just an empty cabinet. He took the BB-gun off his back and held it, expecting a fight.

Slam! Bang! The entire wall bent forward.

The men in the gray cloaks stopped whatever-it-was they were doing. The other men held up their rifles. Copper flashes, but this time they didn't stop at the glass, the pierced right through. Lines of copper hit the back wall, blasting the stone. Ricocheting around the room. Phillip thought he heard something speed past his ear.

Phillip ducked. Dan grabbed his shirt and they ran the only way he could, out the blue door. Phillip skidded to a halt, Dan half fell off the side of the small deck.

The doors slammed behind them.

Phillip got to his feet. The deck was only a little bit longer than Phillip's feet. He stood and pressed himself against the door.

"What now?!" Phillip yelled to Dan over the wind. Dan was looking down and appeared to be hyperventilating.

Something banged on the door. Were they men trying to get to them?

It banged again and again. Then suddenly stopped.

It was quiet on the small deck except for the howling wind.

Nothing happened. Dan and Phillip were grabbing whatever part of the door they could. Until Phillip noticed the blue door and deck was turning grey, and then black, and then… Nothing. The door, and the deck underneath them was burning… dissolving away into the air.

Like tissue paper over a flame.

CHAPTER 35

The Chant

Phillip pressed himself as hard as he could against the door.

He turned himself sideways to accommodate his backpack. When he shifted his hand on the doorframe, he dropped his BB-gun. It hit the end of the deck and fell. Phillip followed it, he lost sight of it in seconds, it was engulfed in clouds.

Patches of the wood door were dissolving around them, seemingly at random.

Dan had turned around the best he could. He was trying to open the door back up. When that didn't work, he tried banging on it. Phillip didn't want to move that much. He just looked down, looking for the BB-gun. The wind seemed to pick up as he did so, threatening to make him lose his balance. Or maybe he was just getting dizzy...

"What do we do?!" Dan screamed.

Phillip didn't answer, he was looking at a patch of wood dissolving beneath him. It was close to his foot now.

Dan was muttering curses under his breath, or maybe he was screaming them, he couldn't tell. A cloud passed over them. Phillip put up his hand as it blocked his vision. It felt cold and wet.

Phillip looked at his hands, it was hard to see them now, in the cloud. He made a fist, and opened them again. Felt the cloud in his palm...

"We're going to fall!" Phillip yelled.

"I know, don't you think I know?!" Dan screamed back.

"Listen! Listen!" Phillip said, pushing past the dryness in his mouth. "We are going to fall. We need to grab the clouds on the way down!"

"What?!" Dan said. "We can't...!"

"We! Have! To!" Phillip said. "Cloud gathers can do that all the time! It's on their stupid logo thing!"

"It's a crest, Phil!" Dan said desperately. "We can't. We've never..."

"Dan!" Phillip yelled again. "I don't have a better idea than this! I don't have anything. Do you?! Paul, Old Paul, he said something when I met him by the lake. We can do this when we really need it! He said that Dan, he said to trust him, that he trusted us. He's the most magical person we know...! I don't have a better idea, Dan! Do you?!"

Dan was silent. After a moment, he shook his head back and forth.

"Alight, we need to get ourselves ready! Tuck in your shirt, make sure you pack is on tight!" Phillip said, thinking of anything that seemed useful. Anything that felt like doing something. How long did they have? A minute? Two? "Take out your notebook!" He said, a thought occurred to him.

Dan looked at him confused, but carefully pulled it out of a pocket on the pack.

Phillip did the same. "Write down that we can do this! Write down that we are able to grab clouds! Draw a picture of yourself doing it!"

"Why...?!"

"Because the books are special, that's why!" Phillip said, the wind felt like it was picking up. "Because you read the same stuff I did! Declare intent! Declare intent. We keep reading about how important it is! Do it now!"

Dan and Phillip did so. The pages flying back and forth in the wind.

"Now write down something!" Phillip said. "Focus! Grab... no. Feel! Focus! Feel! Grab! In that order...! Focus! Feel! Grab!" Dan wrote it down as best he could, his handwriting was illegible, the paper flapping back and forth. "Just like what you said when we made lighting. We are going to make it a ceremony! Make it real! Repeat the chant until it's real, Dan! Focus! Feel! Grab! And remember Paul told us we can do this!"

They started to repeat the three words in unison. Screaming them louder than they had too to be heard.

Dan took his pink notebook and put it under his shirt and tucked it in his pants for that it was touching his skin. Phillip did the same. Maybe touching the pink notebook would help.

It helped before.

"Focus! Feel! Grab!" They yelled in unison.

Dan went into his pack one last time, and took out his bundle of rope. It was knotted and cut from when they built the S.S. Plan-B. Dan let a small length of rope fall into the clouds. He took one length and wrapped it around himself, going through his legs and around his shoulders before tying it as his stomach. He handed Phillip a different length of rope. Phillip tried to copy him the best he could. Dan took the two lengths and tied them together in what Phillip just learned was a double fisherman's knot. Dan was good at knots.

Now, tied together, if one of them succeeded, both might survive.

They nodded to each other. "Focus! Feel Grab!"

The door was dissolving quicker, or maybe it just felt that way. There would be no room to stand any second. Dan and Phillip screamed their chant louder.

Phillip slapped himself on the face. He didn't know why. It just felt appropriate.

"Focus! Feel! Grab!"

Should they jump now? Phillip wondered. *Would they be able to jump?*

Before he could answer the question, Dan fell.

A second later the rope that attached them pulled Phillip's stomach and he let go of the door.

He was falling. Head first into the clouds.

Putting his hands forward, he tried his best to grab anything. The wind making it hard to close his palm. *Focus! Feel! Grab! Focus! Feel! Grab!*

His arms flailed about. He tried his best to focus on the cloud. To feel anything. But the only thing he felt was the wind. He couldn't see anything except blurs of gray, he couldn't open his eyes much.

Focus! Feel! Grab! He thought, or maybe he yelled it, he couldn't tell.

He was still falling. Blurs of gray turned into blurs of blue and white.

They had passed through the first cloud.

He needed to catch the next one! He didn't know if there was going to be another. He grabbed and grabbed and grabbed. *Focus! Feel! Grab! Focus! Feel! Grab!*

Nothing. The clouds might as well be air.

He was going to die.

He was going to fall through the clouds, and he was going to hit the ground, and he was going to die.

How would it feel? He managed to wonder. *Confused blurry spinning and then... What? Blackness?* And what happened after that? Aunt Kath would notice he was missing, and then try to call him... And then organize a search, call the cops. Would they find a body? What would Aunt Kath do?!

"No!" He managed to scream, angry at the thought like it one of the creatures that attacked his house. "*Focus! Feel! Grab!*" He tried to yell, but the pressure from failing prevented his mouth from moving correctly. He grabbed again. Grabbed at nothing.

Aunt Kath would never get over the confusion and pain from this. What about Fortinbras? What about Dan's mom and dad? Why didn't he write Aunt Kath a letter before he went? Stupid! Stupid! Why didn't he realize how stupid he was being? What would Aunt Kath do now? And he thought about—of all the things he could be thinking about—the ice cooler she had forgotten to fill on their road trip...

His right arm went numb. And then his left.

Like he had been sleeping on them the wrong way. They felt like they didn't belong to him. Like they had grown too large. Like they were something attached to his shoulder.

He tried to open his eyes, and found that he could.

He was still in a cloud, it was still windy. He could open his eyes, but couldn't see anything...

The cloud broke into blue sky, and the ground below.

He was floating.

Phillip arms, above his head but not strained, were attached to clouds, wrapped around his wrist and forearm like blankets and stretching into the body of the cloud above. When he looked at it, he knew what he was feeling. He wasn't numb. It was like the nerves of his hands and his body were stretched into the clouds itself. He could move the cloud, manipulate it like a folded blanket.

He was floating...

He had done it!

"Dan?!" He screamed. "Dan?! Are you there?!" He didn't want to move too much, to look for the end of the rope that attached them.

"Here!" Phillip heard behind him, and despite himself he turned around.

Dan was floating there. Tied at the arms and the waste to cloud above him so that he was horizontal with the earth. He looked manic.

"Yeeeeessss!" He yelled to Phillip, who yelled right back with him, mixing it with laughter, but stopping suddenly every few seconds when one of them got nervous making so much sound.

They were descending. They broke through another cloud, then another.

Phillip saw the Farm. Saw Crownshead on the hill. Saw the silo building.

It was the most beautiful sight Phillip had ever witnessed.

The sun, which Phillip noticed was no longer setting and rising, looked perfect. The entire green world looked perfect.

They were getting closer to the ground now. The part of the cloud they had grabbed split away from the main body. It looked, and felt, like an elongated balloon above them. They were moving faster than Phillip thought... It was going to be a rough landing...

They were above trees, then above a field. One-hundred feet up. Fifty-feet. Twenty.

Phillip hit first, raising his feet just before he smacked into the ground, hurling him forward. He lost his grip on the cloud. And he skidded to stop.

Dan landed with thud. Scraping the ground, and skidded next to Phillip. He let go of his cloud too, it floated away to join Phillip's.

Phillip pressed his forehead into the earth. Nothing had ever felt so good. Nervous chuckles managed to escape both of them. They sat on the field, looking forward at the clouds floating away.

"I lost a shoe," Dan said blandly, looking at his feet. For some inexplicable reason this caused both of them to break out in laughter. "That was the *worst* thing that's ever happened to me..." Dan said. "Best thing too."

The laughter was short lived. Dan pointed to his right.

Captain Karo, followed by three other Wallmen, were heading straight for them.

CHAPTER
36
Solid Ground

"**We** still need to activate the Pauls doll-things," Phillip said, getting up shaking feet. It took a few tries. Trying to untie himself from the knot that Dan made, which proved impossible, so he took the end of the silver ax and cut the rope. He hadn't put the ax in his bag. It still hung from his belt. He was lucky it didn't fly away and land on them.

"Maybe we should tell him what's happening..." Dan suggested.

"Maybe, but..." Phillip said.

"Is this yours?" Captain Karo said to them.

He held up Phillip's BB-gun. It was bent. It looked half-melted, and the chamber for the BB's had exploded outward. Willum, and another Wallmen of similar age, was standing behind him.

"Yes," Phillip said, unable to forge the energy to lie.

"Can you explain to me why you felt it was necessary to explode it next to a cow-pasture?" Karo said. "Why are you both armed? What is...?"

"Captain Karo..." Phillip started.

"Do not interrupt me!" Karo said.

"Captain Karo! Listen!" Phillip yelled back. "Waltzrigg is here."

Captain Karo didn't answer, he acted as if Phillip said something nonsensical.

"Waltzrigg is here!" Phillip repeated. "He intends to hurt people. Hurt the Farm, he's responsible for..."

"Enough. Lies!" Karo barked. Willum and the other Wallmen looked distressed. "You are not very good at it..."

"We're telling the truth," Dan said, trying to stay calm.

They didn't have time for this, Phillip thought, *they had so much more to do and they couldn't spend their time trying to argue with Karo...* They needed to go. He helped Dan to his feet. The Wallmen behind Willum grabbed his sword.

"I don't care what Privileges you have. They stop short of you trying to injure people. Walking through here fully armed!" Captain Karo yelled. "You're going to come with..."

"Karo! Listen! You're right about me," Phillip said, Karo paused and closed his mouth. "I'm the infiltrator. This is all my fault!"

Karo was quiet then. The momentary look of shock in his face turned into a renewed angry contempt. "Waltzrigg used me," Phillip continued. "He got a Granny to... I don't know, *do something* to me. Sneak stuff past the barrier. They used me as an anchor. I didn't even know I was doing it. But because it was me the Pauls said *I* have to be the one that helps fix it. You need to listen to me. Waltzrigg is here. He's in the Farm right now. And he wants to hurt people. I think that's his whole goal here. Crownshead is being looted right now!"

The hard line of Captain Karo's mouth opened for the briefest of seconds before closing again. He looked at Phillip like he was a bug in a jar.

"I would listen to the boy, Captain," a voice said to their right.

It was Haystacks, walking toward them with a thick briefcase.

Dressed in a ruffled traveling suit. Henry was with him. Carrying several packages and suitcases, looking as nonchalant as ever.

"Haystacks!" Dan and Phillip yelled at the same time.

"Boys!" He said back, smiling. "Sorry if you had to fair for yourself at the stable. Got held up for a bit in Chadwick Cove..." Dan hugged him, Phillip joined in. Henry gave them both pats on the back. How he managed to do this with so much luggage Phillip wasn't sure. "I was just getting back when I saw some cloud riders and I thought I'd take a look. Don't get many of those in the city."

"That was us!" Dan said. "We fell out of a door."

"Waltzrigg was chasing us..." Phillip added.

"Waltzrigg? Chasing you? And by God boys why are you armed? And since when have you been able to ride clouds...?" Haystacks asked.

"There's not much time. We need to get back to Crownshead for..." Phillip started.

"I'm happy to see that you're back, Haystacks," Captain Karo interrupted, his bile and sarcasm back, as strong as ever. "I trust the formal investigation has cleared your name. I'm so happy the legal system can be trusted to not employ any anti-Imp bias."

"Oh, quite right Captain. Quite right. I have nothing to fear from the law when guided by *competent* investigators," Haystacks said, and continued before Karo could answer. "Like I said, Captain. You should believe them. It's too ridiculous of a story to make up. And the consequences of believing them far outweigh the consequences of failing too..."

"Sir," the young Wallmen behind Willum yelled, pointing to the edge of the woods.

Something moved fast out of the woods. Something on two legs, heading straight for them. It looked like a flightless bird, maybe three times the size of a chicken.

When it got closer, Phillip could see that it was a puppet. A puppet with shining claws and a sharp beak. It ran straight for them, it's eyeless face oriented toward them.

"Is that one of yours?" Karo asked Haystacks. The young Wallmen unsheathed a clear copper-glass sword. Willum took out some kind of handgun and put a wooden visor over his eyes. Captain Karo stood his ground.

"It is not," Haystacks said. "It looks like an old War-Puppet. A scout model, maybe."

"Those are illegal..." Karo said.

Just as he spoke, the puppet stopped, and then put its head into the air and gave two high pitched squawks.

"I think it found what it was looking for..." Haystacks said. Both him and Henry had dropped their suitcases. Henry looked to be assembling a pole in multiple sections he took out of his breast pocket.

"They belong to Waltzrigg!" Phillip yelled, remembering the scratching sound at Waltzrigg's feet in the cloud door room, the movement he saw but couldn't place.

Nobody turned away from the puppet, or said anything. The puppet gave out another high-pitched squawk into the air. "I suggest the young soldier there do something before it runs off," Haystacks said to Karo.

"Incapacitated it," Karo ordered Willum.

Willum adjusted something on the side of his wood and glass handgun. And then fired.

The shot was almost as loud as Dan's rifle. But it was a different kind of sound altogether. Hollower. Echoing. When whatever it fired hit the puppet, it exploded in a shower of copper light. Willum fired twice more. The puppet fell to the ground, its head still moving.

"Contact anybody. Tell whoever's close to come here," Captain Karo ordered.

The puppet gave out another sound, and then spasmed. It glowed white and sparked. It screamed as the white light got brighter, engulfing itself and turning into flame and liquid which burned a hole tight into the ground.

"It seems the owner of that thing knew it was illegal and decided to build a contingency if it got caught," Haystacks said.

There was a sound. A low rumble.

The rumble turned into something deeper. The sound was coming in through his feet. The ground shook so much that Phillip and Dan lost their footing and fell to their knees.

The burnt remains for the puppet glowed. The woods behind it parted. A split broke into the earth. From the part in the woods came a different landscape entirely.

Raised twenty feet in the air was a different chunk of land, red and brown clay, woods on the top of it, moving on its own, pushing the environment it displaced away is if it wasn't there.

"A breach!" Captain Karo yelled.

The small mountain of alien land was making its way toward them. Haystacks and Henry had no trouble standing but Dan and Phillip couldn't get to their feet. There was a different forest, and large red rocks on top of the moving land. Boulders fell off as it moved like a boat through water.

It slowed to a stop. The shaking stopped with it.

Everybody got to their feet, Haystacks helped Dan and Phillip up.

Henry was now holding a long spear.

Phillip took out his ax. Dan took his rifle off his back.

"Did you call for reinforcements...?" Captain Karo asked.

The wind picked up. Fog and mist fell from the landmass. Dark shapes fell with it.

More puppets. All the shapes of birds. Some trailing smoke.

No, not smoke. Mist. It floated behind them and dispersed into the air as they walked. The puppets ran from left to right. One made a straight line to them.

"Willum, shot to kill. Steffens, get rid of the mist!" Captain Karo ordered, taking out his own gun and long knife.

Steffens put away his short sword. Stuck out both his hands, and looked as if he was throwing something. He was snapping his fingers. The air exploded in front of him, clearing round sections of mist, but only for a few moments. Just long enough for Willum and Karo to fire at the puppets, who exploded in coppery blasts.

Steffens' snapping wasn't enough, the mist was overtaking them.

Phillip could hear the scratching hurried feet of the puppets around them.

One came in view as Steffens snapped his fingers in front of Dan, who opened fire. A blue bolt shot from the gun, hit the puppet, which was completely destroyed. This caught Captain Karo and the other Wallmen by surprise.

Another puppet got close. Henry pierced it with his spear to the ground.

It still wiggled and squawked. Phillip took his ax and swung at the puppet's neck. He hit it again and again, enough times to stop it from moving. The puppet glowed and began to burn and melt.

Henry took away his spear and threw it into the mist. Phillip couldn't see where it went but he heard a puppet scream. Henry held out his hand and the spear flew back to him. He threw it again.

Henry had taken off most of his shirt at some point, revealing a torso covered in crude tattoos, mostly shaped like spears. His corn cob pipe never left his mouth.

Steffens' snapping was now having almost no effect. He was out of breath. The mist was too thick. It sounded like there were hundreds of puppets around them.

"You boys need to get out of here," Haystacks said to them. He had put on a thick glove on one arm and on the other hand held a thin dagger.

"We can't leave..." Dan started.

"We'll be fine. You need to complete the mission the Pauls put you on," Haystacks said, he had put on his work glasses he always kept in his pocket. "End this, if you can. Be safe if you can't."

Captain Karo was looking around for puppets to shoot, but managed to glance at Dan and Phillip.

"Don't you dare leave!" Captain Karo said.

"Get out of here!" Willum interrupted, surprising Karo more than anybody. "You say the Pauls need you to do something. Go do it!"

Phillip got up and stood frozen, not wanting to leave Haystacks or Henry. Copper sparks lit the ground around them.

"We're being fired at!" Steffens yelled.

"Shields up. Steffens ignore the mist! Close ranks. Close ranks!" Karo ordered.

"Go!" Haystacks said to Dan and Phillip.

And they ran. Away from the invading landmass and the sound of puppets running and Karo yelling and guns going off. Copper light flashing from behind them as they went.

They ran far enough that they hit woods, and then the mist stopped. Until they could no longer hear the sounds of the puppets. Only the faint popping of guns, like fireworks in the distance. "I have a gun!" Dan yelled through strained breath. Limping on his shoeless foot. "Maybe I can help."

"No," Phillip said, taking all his resolve and courage to say so. "Haystacks is right, we need to finish this... *save the Farm*."

Phillip had never run so fast for so long in his entire life. But neither of them slowed their pace. Dan was wheezing but never slowed. They didn't know where they were heading. They followed what felt like the thickest trail.

A flash of white passed them through the trees.

He looked, and another set of eyes stared back at him, just as surprised as he was.

"Emily!" Phillip yelled, his chest hurting as he stopped.

"Phillip!" She called back. Andy was next to her. "Phillargo!" She yelled at the same time.

They were both wearing white flowing outfits, and were covered in what looked like dark paint. Symbols covered their skin and stained the white outfits.

"What are you doing here?" Andy asked.

"No time to explain," Phillip answered. "We need to get back to Crownshead, a safe room somewhere in Crownshead to activate the dolls... Where are you heading?"

"We are following signs of a breach," Emily said. "The Pauls have had us doing purification ceremonies since you left us. What...?"

"It's Waltzrigg, he breached the Farm. We thought we solved that problem with the spikes but I guess not..." Phillip started.

"Do you know a way back...? To Crownshead where we won't... be seen?" Dan said, out of breath.

"I believe we do..." Emily said.

"Yes," Andy said at the same time.

"Take us," Phillip said.

"What is that?" Emily said, pointing behind Dan and Phillip.

It was a puppet. Waltzrigg's puppets. Two of them.

"Dan!" Phillip yelled, getting his ax ready. Dan was lining up a shot.

He fired. Blue lighting hit the first puppet and the feet. Causing it to vanish in a flurry of white and blue light. The other one shot forward, and ran for them. "Dan!" Phillip yelled again when he didn't fire. Dan was reloading the gun. The puppet ran faster. Emily and Andy held up their hands. Dan pulled back the bolt of the rifle. Fired again, and hit the puppet right in the body. It exploded on the spot, less than ten feet from Phillip.

"I can't believe I hit it..." Dan said. "I'm a terrible shot, Phil."

"You seem to be doing okay," Phillip said. "Waltzrigg's war-puppets. We need to go."

"What in all blasted Hell was that?!" A voice screamed in the bushes.

They all turned towards the woods. Dan raised his rifle, Phillip his ax.

The bushes parted to reveal the red bearded face of man, and a mane of black hair. He looked from one of them to the other, his eyes landed on Phillip and Dan. He smiled.

"Oh no..." Phillip said under his breath.

"You?!" Rickshaun yelled, his smile widening.

"Mr. Rickshaun, we don't..." Phillip started.

"That's *mister* Rickshaun to you!" Rickshaun yelled back.

"That's what I said..."

"... *master* Rickshaun if you want to flatter me and avoid a small helping of pain." Rickshaun was tucking in his shirt. He looked disheveled, even flustered as he made his way for them.

"You don't understand, Mr. Rickshaun, we're on a mission for the..." Dan blurted out.

"I've been looking for you two. Not too hard, mind you. I am a busy man. Very arrogant of you boys to think I've spent all my time obsessing over you. But the thing is I could never find you. Like some force was keeping us apart." Rickshaun was close to Phillip now. Close enough to grab him.

"Mr. Rickshaun..." Emily said in a soft voice.

"Emily Morris? By god you've grown! How's your father getting along?"

"Ricky, what's going on?" Another woman's voice shot out of the woods before Emily was able to speak again.

"Nothing, just stay..." Rickshaun began to answer, but the bushes broke again, revealing bright red hair.

"Ms. Julie..?" Dan and Phillip said at the same time.

"Daniel? Phillip?" She said, coming out of the woods. Her clothes and hair were just as disheveled as Rickshaun's, Phillip noticed. She looked just as flustered...

Oh, Phillip thought, and couldn't keep the thought from his face, which he was sure Rickshaun noticed, as he was looking straight at Phillip's face.

"Look who I ran into!" Rickshaun said, patting Phillip and Dan on the shoulder.

Something moved in the woods to their left. Not like a person moving in the woods. Something smaller and faster. "Puppets...?" Dan said in whisper.

"We have to go," Phillip said.

"Now where do you think you're going off to?" Rickshaun said. "We need to chat. For instance, I'm curious why you're both armed."

"Mr. Rickshaun..." Phillip said, downed out by the fact that everybody in the woods had said the same thing at the same time, apart from Ms. Julie, who said "Ricky..."

"The Farm is in danger!" Dan yelled, and every face turned to him. Surprised for a moment he had attention. "The Farm is in danger because there's an infiltrator and it turned out that the infiltrator was Phillip but he didn't know it because he was used by General Waltzrigg and this granny lady named Fat Barta who just tried to kill us and if we don't get to Crownshead people might be hurt and there's probably an army of puppets and Waltzrigg's men just behind us!"

Then everybody was quiet, the only sound coming from Dan catching his breath.

Rickshaun grunted. "Damned fool story," he said.

Just when everybody was about to answer him, he grabbed the rifle out of Dan's hands. He spun and aimed it in one smooth motion.

Firing once, then twice into the woods.

The blue lighting sparks causing everybody to jump.

An unnatural scream came from the woods, followed by bright flashes and sparks. The puppets. Damaged and burning away.

"A damned fool story," Rickshaun repeated. "I might considerer not believing it if I thought you were clever enough to make it up." The screaming and burning continued. There were other sounds. Men, yelling in the woods. *Waltzrigg's soldiers?* "You better get going, do whatever the Pauls want you to do." Ms. Julie came and touched his arm. "What are you doing still standing there?!" He yelled at them. "And why do you have that fool look on your face?"

Phillip realized he hadn't spoken or moved. "We just... didn't expect to be believed right away..." He said.

Rickshaun grunted again. "You better start deciding what you want and not hesitate when you get it, or life's going to be doubly hard for you, fool that you are," he said. Again, there was the sound of voices and scuffling in the woods. Rickshaun handed the rifle back to Dan.

"Don't *you* need it?" Dan asked, who none-the-less grabbed it and reloaded.

"We can handle ourselves, dear," Ms. Julie said. At some point she had produced a small wood and glass handgun, which she handed to Rickshaun. "Go with them," Rickshaun whispered to her. "Shut your mouth and aim, Ricky," Ms. Julie answered in a most unteacher-y way. Taking out of her pocket a long, incredibly thin ceremonial knife, which she spun in her hand expertly.

Rickshaun chuckled, then immediately turned to them with exaggerated frown. "The hell you still doing here?" He said. "You the types that need to be yelled at to do anything?"

And then they turned and left.

All four of them. In the opposite direction and without another word. Phillip sensing a 'thank you' to Rickshaun would be inappropriate and unwelcomed. *Leaving more people behind*, Phillip thought.

They had to finish this fast.

"So, besides that, how's everything going well on your end?" Andy asked sarcastically.

"No big problems..." Phillip responded.

"Except we had to make a boat..." Dan said.

"... and Queen Tatuna tried to kill us..." Phillip added.

"... also, those creepy kids with black eyes..." Dan said.

"... then Waltzrigg made us jump out of the sky and we had to catch some clouds," Phillip said.

"... after that, the breach happened and the puppets started coming after us," Dan finished.

Emily and Andy were silent. They looked at each other and then back and Dan and Phillip. "I guess you'll fill us in on the way," Andy said, as they went deeper into the woods.

CHAPTER 37

Long Live the Farm

Like most ways around the Farm, the path they followed didn't make the slightest bit of sense.

They just ended up in different places. They went next to the lake so clear it looked almost like it wasn't filled with water at all, stone buildings at the bottom submerged in it. They passed a sculpture garden with moving sculptures. A field of corn stocks, except these corn stocks were at least forty feet tall and waved back and forth slowly as if they were underwater.

They started their trip at a slow jog, which dissolved into a trot. And then a fast walk.

"These stocks can't survive without constant enchantment reinforcement," Emily said offhandedly about the corn. "They have to be sung to at least once a day when they get to this size. It's very labor intensive, so they are usually harvested when they are a little younger."

"I hope Haystacks is safe," Dan said, almost to himself. "Rickshaun and Ms. Julie too."

"He will be," Andy said. "Gremlins are tough. He'll be fine."

Dan nodded, but didn't look convinced.

"What are you wearing?" Phillip asked.

"Nihon purification gowns. You won't believe what the Pauls had us do," Andy said. "Tadaaki is still doing it... He's at the border now..."

A familiar squawking shot off in the distance.

"They found us..." Dan said. They picked up their pace again. "How are they still tracking us? We're jumping all over the Farm..."

"We should find the door soon. It should be right around here," Andy said, adjusting her glasses as she looked at a small notebook. "Yes! Here's the door," she said, pointing to what looked like a cellar door.

She banged on it three times. And the door flew open a crack. Andy patted her body. "Does anybody have anything to offer?"

"Will a traveler's token do?" Dan asked.

"Yes! Perfect. Give one here," she said back. Dan handed her a large copper coin. A wrinkled hand shot out of the door. Andy placed the token and the hand went back in. The door slammed, and then opened again. A blast of cold air hit them. "Let's go," Andy said and walked in.

Dan and Emily followed, Phillip backed into the doorway. He tried to shut the door behind him but found that it did the job for him. Slamming shut and locking.

They were in some kind of cavern, sparkles of light reflected off crystals in the walls.

It was freezing, he could clearly see his breath ahead of him. Dan took his red jacket out of his bag and handed it to Emily, and then took another green wind-jacket and handed it to Andy.

"You brought two jackets?" Phillip said.

"One for you and one for me," Dan said, as if Phillip was stupid for saying anything. "I should have brought *four.*"

"I would let you have your jacket back," Andy said as she wrapped it around herself, "but you know, I want you to feel chivalrous. So I'm forced to keep it."

The cavern was massive.

There were sounds. Something like ticking clocks and wire being wound and springs being sprung. The walls were carved, into the shape of stone tubes with etches and designs on the side. Phillip touched them and found that they were warm.

"We are looking for a doorway. One with writing over the top..." Andy said.

"Is that it?" Dan said, pointing to a wall.

There was a carved stone archway, on the side were words, *'THOSE WHO SEEK SHALL BE GIVEN.'* The words were carved crudely, not following the design of the arch.

"No, wrong writing. Oh, there it is," Andy said, looking at the other side of the chamber. Another carved archway had words over the top. *'UNTIL WISDOM LIBERATES ALL,'* it said. These words looked more designed, more part of the archway. but were almost entirely scratched out...

Phillip decided he hated this place.

He felt like the carved stone tubes were moving in on him. The sounds grated on his nerves, and the light from the crystals always seemed to shine in his eyes when he wasn't looking. He had developed a stomach ache, he didn't know if it was the cold, but he felt like he could throw up on the spot if he didn't stop himself.

"Let's get out of here," he said, nobody argued. They were all feeling the same way.

The small door between the archway opened without the need for payment.

It led into a fire lit room. It was the library study the Pauls had brought them to before.

"Yes," Dan said under his breath.

Lady Crownshead sat on a sofa.

She looked worse. She didn't move. She couldn't even open her eyes.

Dan and Phillip didn't spare another second, they both reached into their bags and retrieved the dolls. They held them out in front of them and cracked them in half, the way they were told to do. Something inside them, like a glass vial, broke.

The dolls waved back and forth in their hands, they grew longer as they stretched themselves. Become adult size in a moment. The straw that made up their body became flesh.

In less than five seconds, the Pauls were standing in front of them.

"Excellent job! Excellent job both of you!" Old Paul said. "We're almost done now. How have you been holding up..."

"It's been..." Dan said.

"... Kind of, hard to explain..." Phillip added.

"We're fine," Dan said. "But Haystacks and Henry and Karo are in trouble. Rickshaun and MS. Julie too. We're ready for this to be over."

"It will be over soon, I promise," Old Paul said.

Big Paul went over to Lady Crownshead. He put his hand on her forehead. "I'm sorry, old girl," he said. "We did it to you again... I'm so sorry..."

"We need to pull this scab off, the faster the better," Old Paul said to big Paul.

Big Paul got up, only looking away from Lady Crownshead for a moment to give Old Paul a look of pure contempt. He clapped his hands and panel on the wall opened up on both sides of the room. The Pauls went to one each, and pulled the levels simultaneously.

The room shook.

"It's Waltzrigg!" Dan yelled.

"No, Daniel. We are just exposing the foundation," Old Paul explained. The room rotated, and sunk into itself. The walls with books disappeared, the windows went away. Red glowing pillars rose out of the floor in the center of the room.

"What's happening?" Phillip asked. The question reflected in everyone's face.

"Children," Old Paul said. "I need to tell you something. Something that might come in useful in a few moments. Or a few years. Or maybe never at all but one should never turn away an opportunity to learn something..."

Old Paul went to an umbrella stand, and picked up two large hammers out of it. He tossed one to Big Paul.

"The Farm is in *Anywhere*. But it also is *from* Anywhere. There's an important distinction there..." Old Paul continued. He walked up to the pillar. "Anywhere connects everything that it touches. It bends and ignores the law of space and time. Remember that, children. The Farm is not a collection of buildings, it is not a place. It is not *somewhere*. It is *Anywhere*."

Old Paul lifted his hammer, and drove it into the pillar.

The pillar cracked. The room shook.

Lady Crownshead screamed in pain.

Old Paul drove the hammer down again. Big Paul did the same.

Lady Crownshead screamed all the louder.

"What are you doing?!" Andy yelled. Emily put her hands up to her mouth. Dan and Phillip were too confused to say anything.

"I am doing right by those under our protection..." Big Paul said.

"That is why we are destroying the Farm," Old Paul said.

Their hammers came down. The room shook. Lady Crownshead howled again.

"The Farm is dead..." Big Paul said.

Old Paul destroyed what was left of a glowing pillar. "Long live the Farm..."

CHAPTER 38

One Last Task

Emily rushed to the sofa and grabbed Lady Crownshead's hands, trying to comfort her as she screamed.

"What do you mean, 'destroy the Farm?'" Andy said.

Old Paul hit another pillar. The world shook with it.

"It means exactly what I say it does," Old Paul said. "We are unraveling the Farm..."

"Then what was all this for!?" Phillip blurted out. "We nearly died! At least three times..."

Another glowing pillar collapsed. Phillip had to grab a table so he wouldn't fall.

"This was always the plan, Mr. Montgomery," Big Paul said. "You did well. We need to destroy the Farm, in order to save it. And more importantly, save everybody in it."

"But..." Andy stuttered, she seemed more upset than anybody, "You're gosh-dang inheritors for God's sake! We've purified the grounds! Throw up another barrier, kick anything out you don't like...! Isn't that the point of being Inheritors?" Andy said. She looked down and, her eyes darting from side to side, she was thinking of something. "Unless... what you had Emily and me do wasn't protection or purifications... It was getting ready for this!"

"That's why none of the ceremonies made sense..." Emily said, she held Lady Crownshead head to her chest.

"Yes and no," Old Paul said. "What you did will allow us to unravel the Farm. Your actions did purify. They established a clear borderline between the Farm and those in it..."

"We can save people this way," Big Paul added.

"Right. I can save people," Old Paul confirmed. "To answer your first question. Yes, 'The Pauls' are powerful. Big fish, but there are sharks out there... We can probably stop Waltzrigg. But we can't stop what's behind him. Not without it costing too much. If we let the people invited into the Farm be killed, we lose. If we let the Farm be stolen, or corrupted, we lose. This is the best win we can manage..." He said, looking at Phillip. "I was outmaneuvered. Simple as that. The only choices, win and lose everything, lose and lose everything, or flip over the gameboard... I was never very good at chess..."

There was only one and half pillars left. Books were flying off the shelves. Glass off tables.

"I'm sorry, Mr. Montgomery, Mr. Castellanos," Big Paul said, he slowed himself. "You hardly got to see anything here that was truly remarkable. And Anywhere *is* remarkable. It all ended too fast... people are going to be disappointed..."

"What were you doing here?" Emily asked on the sofa. "What was the point? Is it true that you were choosing successors?"

Old Paul and Big Paul didn't answer. They didn't swing their hammers anymore.

"Tell. Them," Lady Crownshead said in a weak voice.

Big Paul took a moment to answer. "The other Inheritors and us. We've been locked in a kind of stalemate for a... very long time."

"That's why nobody has made a claim on the Frontier," Andy said, a statement rather than a question.

"One of the reasons, yes." Big Paul continued. "The short answer is, our intention was to break some rules. Share what we agreed not to share. Break this unacceptable stalemate..."

"Throw some chaos into the system," Old Paul added. "See if we like what comes out on the other end. Do this by inviting people into Anywhere. Loosening all common restrictions. Asking people to share and follow the Old Laws..."

Old Paul continued to slam his hammer into the pillar.

Phillip didn't understand any of it. He felt hollow, burnt out.

The pillar came down. The shaking stopped, replaced by a pulsing under their feet. Like a heartbeat. Beating faster and faster. Old Paul looked at his hand, it was turning back into cloth.

"Everybody. You have done remarkably well. Your actions are going to save people. And hopefully do more than that," Old Paul said. "But we are not done yet... I need to ask more of you..."

This was too much. Phillip wanted to be done.

"We need to shake this old bird loose," Big Paul said. "Once it starts to unravel, people will be safe. But it needs a shove to do that."

"That's why Phillip, Daniel," Old Paul said, "we need you to destroy the work-time engine..."

"How...?" Phillip stammered. "How are we supposed to do that?!"

"Don't know..." Old Paul said, "That's your job to figure out... but I would suggest, do what you did to poor Rickshaun's lab. A little bit of lighting might just do the trick."

"We haven't been able to do that since the first time!" Phillip said.

"Just like you weren't able to grab clouds. Until you did," Big Paul said. "Do you expect to read the first time you pick up a book? Be good at everything without exposure and practice?"

The beating under their feet grew stronger. Dust was falling from the ceiling.

"It was downright entitled of you to think you could waltz in here and do whatever you want right away," Old Paul said. "That it would come easily. That there wouldn't be a struggle."

The beating was like a slamming now.

"We don't have time. We will lose connection to these dolls in moments," Big Paul said. "Boys, you two have so far shown a remarkable ability to use what you have. There's more magic in resourcefulness than there is in bottles of lighting. If something fails, do something else. Work the problem until it goes away!" Half his face was turning to cloth.

"Wait!" Dan said. "You said Anywhere connects everything it touches. That's how we got from Haystacks' stable to here, right? That's why we went from that hallway to the garden where you were meeting Haystacks. Does that mean we can make it to the generator room, right from here?"

"Hah! Yes, Daniel. Yes. She should be able to manage that," Old Paul said.

Lady Crownshead's hand went out, too weak to point. "Under. Newspaper."

Phillip picked up the newspaper, underneath was a large brass key. "Use. Anywhere. Red doors," Lady Crownshead said, then laughed like she had said something funny.

"There's nothing I can do that would make up for what we've done," Big Paul said. "You have all been remarkably brave. Thank you so much." And with Big Paul shriveled and turned back into a doll, still the size of a person, smoking when it hit the ground.

"If you don't trust yourself. Trust me," Old Paul said, his arms and one of his legs became cloth. "Good luck..."

And then they were gone. Emily gave out a short gasp.

They looked over and found that Lady Crownshead had vanished from the sofa.

The beating was becoming more intense. Like bombs going off in the distance.

Phillip looked at the key. Not knowing what to feel or what to do, and then realizing that was a lie.

He knew what to do. They weren't done yet. They needed to destroy the work-time engine. They were the only ones able to do it.

They needed help. Help to *destroy* the Farm...

Phillip looked to Emily and Andy, then at Dan. "Dan, do you have one of the jars of lighting?"

"Yes," Dan answered, and went through his bag.

Phillip smiled. "Of course, you do. You have the rest of the blue paint stuff too, the exciterant..."

"Have that too..." Dan confirmed.

"What are you thinking?" Andy asked.

"I'm thinking, if we lash the two jars together, and then break them at the same time, the blue exciterant would probably create a big reaction... Enough to destroy the engine, maybe..." Phillip said.

"We should go," Dan said.

Phillip put on his lashing glove, Dan handed him the jars and Phillip lashed them together.

"We're just doing this. No more questions?" Andy said.

"Do we have a choice?" Phillip asked, he looked at the key in his hand and then looked for a door to use it on.

"How do we know this is not a suicide mission?" Andy said. "The Pauls have never been straight with us..."

"Do you remember what you said to us?" Phillip said, a calm had set in to him. "That we need to pick somebody to trust?"

"You're paraphrasing..." Andy said.

"Got the gist of it." Phillip replied. There was a door on the far side of the room. He noticed it was red. "It was good advice then. Good advice now. I don't know anybody better to trust than the Pauls... except you two and Dan. Maybe Haystacks. We know Waltzrigg is a bad dude. The Pauls said this is the only way to save people..."

"It's the only good choice," Dan said/

"I agree," Emily said, she stood and looked more resolved than he had ever seen her.

"Dang," Andy said, adjusting her glasses for the lenses changed colors. "My own wisdom had been used against me. I'm promoting you both. You're now both grand generals and presidents of the Unwelcoming Committee. I hereby step down..."

"This is the proudest day of my life," Phillip said. "I wish my Aunt was here..."

"Where do we go? President?" Andy said.

"I'm thinking this door." Phillip said, pointing to the red door. The ground was no longer beating but vibrating under their feet.

Phillip put the brass key in the lock and turned.

————— o —————

The door led to darkness. Once they got past that, they ended up in what looked like a supply room of some kind. The walls were metal.

"Is this close to the engine?" Phillip asked.

"Looks like the area, but I don't know... we need to get outside the door..." Andy said.

"No, there is movement..." Emily said, her hand on the floor. "I can hear it. Men. A few of them..."

"Waltzrigg's men?" Dan asked.

"I can't tell," Emily said. "They are wearing heavy boots..."

"Do either of you know any way to get past them?" Phillip asked, whispering now.

Andy and Emily looked at each other. "You have been trained in combat magic," Emily suggested.

"My brother's better at that..." Andy said.

"But *you* know it too..." Emily said, unexpectedly pointed.

"These are trained men. Professionals. I don't think I can..." Andy said. "What about some enchantment? Something that makes them want to go somewhere else. Something subtle, like they heard a noise..."

"I don't know if I'm able to enchant people," Emily said.

"Actually, new idea," Andy said. "I'll work the mind stuff. You just do the delivery method. Here," She took out her skychalk, drew an almost perfect circle around herself. And then another around Emily. She connected the two circles with a line. "Do natural sounds, get it in their heads, I'll do the rest..."

Emily nodded. "Phillip, Daniel. We will need to stay here to do this. Walk around for a bit... I will try to listen to your footprints. We will try to make sure your path is clear. Will this work, Andy...?"

"I... think so," Andy said. "Just provide the delivery system, I'll make the men hear things in the other direction. Simple as that. Dan, Phillargo. You need to be as quiet as possible.

"Daniel, Phillip, are you ready?" Emily asked, she had taken out her flute.

"As ready as we'll ever be," Dan said, they had gotten to their feet and stood at the door.

"Emily, Andy, thank you for everything. Everything," Phillip said, not knowing why. "Don't worry, I won't let it go to my head."

"Go to your head?" Andy repeated. "What do you think? We helped you out of obligation? Because our parents told us to spy on you? We're like the bestest friends ever, Philargo, Danetia. How dare you discount that."

Phillip smiled. "Be safe," he said to them, and joined Dan at the door.

"You too," Emily said. And then put the flute to her mouth, which made sounds.

Sounds, not music. It sounded like clanking, like the hissing of pipes. Emily put the flute down and continued the sounds with her voice. She had her hand on the ground. Andy had closed her eyes, so had Emily. "Go now," Emily said.

The opened the door a crack and looked out. The hallways were clear.

Dan and Phillip crouched as they walked, stepping as lightly as possible. Dan had an easier time since he had only one shoe.

Voices around the corner. Speaking another language. Dan and Phillip jumped into a doorway, which wasn't thick enough to hide them. Just as the men attached to the voices were about to go around the corner. They stopped. Were quiet for a second, and then turned around. "Alight Andy and Emily," Phillip whispered under his breath.

The way to the engine was marked, so they didn't have to find their way. They snuck around corridors and through thin metal doors. They heard other men down other hallways, but they never encountered them.

They turned the corner, and Phillip saw something that made his heart sink.

War puppets. The same as the others. Eyeless birds with claws. Two of them.

Emily and Andy wouldn't be able to fool them...

The war puppets turned and looked straight at Dan and Phillip.

"Crap," Phillip said. "New plan. Run."

Dan and Phillip ran down the hallway. The war puppets squawked like mad and followed. Voices of people reacted to them. Men dressed in brown clothes appeared from everywhere, yelling orders to each other.

"Here! They are here!" A man yelled in accented English.

They were running as fast as they could. They made random turns. And ended up in a long hallway leading to a single door. The war puppets metal claws could be heard clicking behind them. Men fired guns just as they turned a corner.

Phillip tripped and fell to the ground. He looked in front of him. They weren't going to make it to the door before the men shot them...

He left the jar on the ground. "Dan! Dan!" He yelled. Dan looked at him but didn't answer. "Get your gun out!" Dan did so.

They ran down the hallway, *were they far enough?*

"Dan shot the jars! You need to shoot the jars," Phillip said, pointing down the long hallway, where he had left them. The war puppets turned into the hallway.

"We need those!" Dan said.

"We need to survive right now. Shot them!" Phillip said.

Dan turned around. The war puppets getting closer to the jars.

Dan fired, and missed... Sparks of blue lightning arced from wall to wall. The bullet lit the hallway where it landed.

He fired again and missed. The war puppets were almost next to the jar. Men in brown coats turned could be seen down the hallway.

"Just keep firing!" Phillip said. "Breath or something!"

"Let me concentrate!" Dan yelled back. He had crouched to one knee, he exhaled, and fired again.

He hit the jar.

Crack! Boom!

The explosion of light was enormous. It was so loud that it didn't register as sound. Lighting, as if it was coming down from the sky. Was striking in the middle of the hallway. Stringing the sides of the doors. Destroyed the puppets. Melted the walls and the ceiling and collapsed them...

Crack! Boom! The lighting went off again.

Dan and Phillip didn't stay to watch. They ran toward the metal door. As fast as they could.

Phillip pulled up the latch, and they went in.

It was the engine room.

The massive work-time engine stretching from far above them to the water below. "What now?" Dan asked, as he looked up at the pulsating machine.

"You heard the Pauls..." Phillip said, trying to think of another way. "We make lighting, right here..." Phillip said, and ran up a metal staircase. The higher the better, and least that's how it felt.

They both took out their skychalk, and their pink notebooks.

"What happens if we can't do it? Actually, what happens if we're successful!?" Dan said. "We blow it up, and blow ourselves up too..."

"I was thinking about that," Phillip said, opening his book to his notes about the Pauls circle. "Look, you were right the night we succeeded. This is all just a metaphor, just a bunch of symbols that are meaningless until we give them meaning. We make them real with the doing..."

"So...?" Dan asked.

"So, we don't actually need to be in the circle. But we do..." Phillip.

"We need a jar... some coins..." Dan said.

"We'll use some of your bullets as the coins." Phillip said, looking down at the water. "That's our jar right there..."

"Why do we think we will be successful this time? The second time we..." Dan asked.

"Because the second time!" Phillip interrupted, he took out the orbit ball and for the second time lashed it to the skychalk "We didn't follow our own rules! We were only thinking about Captain Karo. Out internal state didn't match the effect we were trying to achieve!"

Phillip threw the orbit ball and skychalk. It circled the engine and came back to him, leaving a perfect circle in its wake. He de-lashed the ball from the chalk. "And how do we get our internal state aligned?" Dan asked.

Dan and Phillip were filling out the circle. "Because..." Phillip said, reaching into his bag and taking out a bottle. "We're going to drink the last of our miracle juice. It's a placebo, but I think it will work," Phillip uncorked it and took one horrible swig before handing it to Dan.

Dan took it. "You say I over-pack..." and then he took a swig. He poured the rest into the water below. "What do you mean we will be in the circle?"

Phillip took his silver ax, took his orbit ball. He took the ax to his palm, and cut a painful line into the top of his left hand. He placed the bleeding cut on the orbit ball. And then handed the ax to Dan. "I mean a part of us will be in the circle..."

Dan understood immediately, looked away and winced as he cut his hand. Placing blood on the orbit ball. When he was done, Phillip tossed the ball so that I orbited the engine and stayed within the circle.

"Get your head straight, think of nothing else but what we want to achieve," Phillip said. "Make a chant if we need to, like we did when we rode the clouds."

Dan and Phillip completed the rest of the ceremony until they felt good about it. They dropped the bullets into the water below. "Think it'll work?" Dan asked.

"Has to," Phillip said. "We should leave…"

"Phil…" Dan said, looking up at the engine.

"Yeah…?"

"I'm really glad I ran into you," he said.

"Me too," Phillip said back.

A door flew open below them, and then another at ramp above them at the same time. Men in brown coats came storming in with war puppets at their feet.

"Dan, Phillip!" Andy yelled with Emily from the door above them. "Over here!"

They ran to Andy and Emily. Dan ahead of Phillip. The men yelled below and pointed at them. "Do not shoot!" one of them yelled. "Collapse the walkway!" another said. Just as he said it the walkway they were on began to vibrate violently. It broke in front of Phillip, and section falling to the water. "Be careful. Fools!" One of the brown-coated men said.

Dan had made it to the door, but the walkway behind him had collapsed. Phillip was separated behind the break. The war puppets were making their way up the stairs.

"Jump!" Andy yelled.

"Can't make it!" He yelled back, it was at least fifteen feet. He looked to his right and saw another door. "Leave! We'll meet back up," He took his walkie-talkie out of his bag and turned it on, Dan did the same,

Phillip ran to the door, and as he did so the walkway began to vibrate. He leaped just in time for the walkway to collapse beneath him. He held onto the door. Pulled the latch, and pulled it open, holding on to the sides, desperate not to fall. He went threw the door, and gave one last look at Emily, Andy, and Dan before running down the hallway.

He ran without any concern with where he was going. He just needed to get away, get some distance between him and the men. He needed a door outside. Where was a wooden door when he needed it?

As if to answer him, he went down a hallway that turned into stone and wood. He went through the first red door he saw. "Phil? Phil? Where are you? Over," The walkie talkie blurted on his side.

The red door led to another hallway. A carpeted one lit with bright lamps. He talked into his walkie-talkie, "I'm running," he managed to say. "Are you out?" he asked. "Over."

"We are by the portable schoolhouse, Circles Class. Tell me when you're out and we'll do it! Over," Dan said.

"Right! Over." He opened door after door. Why was this place such a maze!? He opened a yellow door that was half his size, and saw the best sight he had ever seen. Green grass, the silo in the distance, which he could barely see through low grabbing mist.

He ran out the door. Nothing had ever smelled so good as the grass underneath him. The yellow door dissolved behind him. The ground was pulsating. There were yells in the distance. It sounded like an avalanche.

"There you are," a voice said casually behind. An accented, aggressively casual voice.

Waltzrigg was accompanied by two men, Fat Barta, and war puppet at his side.

Phillip turned to run. "No, no, no..." Waltzrigg said, and it was as if Phillip ran into a net. The air was sucked out of his lungs, and he was turned around. "There won't be any more of that nonsense. I am far too old to run around like a child..."

He needed to do it now. He needed to tell Dan. He grabbed for his walkie talkie but Waltzrigg stomped his foot and a tendril of soil and earth wrapped itself around his arm like a whip and pulled his arm down. He heard what sounded like a snap. The walkie talkie fell at his feet. Phillip screamed at the pain.

"What is going on here?" Another voice said. It belonged to a figure in a white outfit who practically walked into one of Waltzrigg's men.

It was the teacher, Antony Müller. "General!" He said when he noticed Waltzrigg. "I am sorry, sir, I did not know you were here." He saluted, his hand to his chest. His eyes turned to Phillip. "Montgomery?" he said in confusion, his eyes traveling over the tendril of soil which trapped him.

He looked confused, and disturbed.

"Pleasure to meet you? I am always happy to meet fans," Waltzrigg said, forcing a handshake. "By the looks of it you are a teacher, am I correct. Education should be the ultimate goal of an advanced society, that's what I believe..."

"Yes," Müller said. "I teach at 'Brick and Hammer'... why...?" he started.

"I would love to talk about this all day. It is one of my great passions, but I'm afraid time is not on our side... Do you have students here?" Waltzrigg asked.

"Yes..." Müller replied.

"Good. I need you, without asking another question. To go make sure they are safe, as is your duty as a teacher and Sturmjäger," Waltzrigg said. "Very odd happenings here, good teacher, we must tell the higher ups about it as soon as we can. Will you stand with me and do that? But first, will you care to the safety of your wards?"

"Uh... yes sir. I will do that," he saluted again, and left, looking uneasy and giving one last look at Phillip.

Waltzrigg watched him go, he gave a pointed look to both of his men. They nodded to him and turned to follow Müller. Fat Barta lit her pipe again.

"Now, where were we?" Waltzrigg said, turning back to Phillip.

Phillip raised his free hand over his head, like he was surrendering. He tried to glance down without making it too obvious what he was doing. His foot inched toward the walkie-talkie. He forced every ounce of energy he had toward what he wanted to happen. Tried his best to ignore the pain in his arm. He closed his eyes. He had to make it right. *Please just make it right,* he thought, but pushed the thought aside. It was useless.

He looked back up at Waltzrigg. Then with his foot he pushed the button on the side of the Walkie-Talkie. He heard the static. "Dan! Now!" He yelled. And drove his raised hand downward to the ground. Imagining the lighting. The engine room...

Waltzrigg looked at him confused, Fat Barta looked up.

Nothing happened, until it did.

A pillar of light erupted behind the silo, reaching into the sky. Not like lightning, it was too straight and orderly. It lit the grounds and cleared away the mist.

The sound of an explosion came to them a second later.

They had done it!

The pillar disappeared. The ground stopped shaking for a moment, and then started again. Different this time. Like the ground was turning to liquid or shifting sand. The silo was shaking itself loose.

Waltzrigg only looked at Phillip.

"What does that mean?" Fat Barta said, as if the question only mildly interested her.

"It means..." Waltzrigg said, approaching Phillip. The tendril around his hand tightened. "That we should go," he was close enough to Phillip to touch him now. "It means we won... Not as clean a win as I hoped, but a win, nonetheless... Now, dear boy, I must ask. What have I done to offend you so...?" He stared straight into Phillip's eyes.

Phillip didn't know what to say, or if he should say anything at all. "You... attacked my house!" he yelled, wishing he just kept his mouth shut.

"Attacked your *house,* did you say?" Waltzrigg said. "Boy, I barely know who you are, let alone where you live. But why would I attack you? Our own anchor...? Hah! It seems this all just a big misunderstanding. Funny when those happen," he turned around and began walking away. "Fat Barta, be a dear and kill him for me, would you? I have no stomach for that sort of thing... and make it painful, for me, would you? Thanks."

He walked away without another word. His head low on his shoulders.

Fat Barta looked at Phillip, her pipe smoking. The tendril of soil around his arm loosened and Phillip tried to place his feet so he could run.

But Fat Barta raised her hand.

Phillip stopped, he stopped doing everything. He felt like he was going to hurl. Like every muscle in his body had gone tense. He felt... scared. More scared than he had ever felt in his life. He couldn't move. Could hardly breath. His mind screamed at him *Don't move! Danger! Don't move! Hide! Don't move!* All he could do was stare at Fat Barta as she approached him with her big furs and her dead white eye. He tried harder to move than he had ever tried anything. His body wouldn't let him. It convinced him to stay, he could only manage small jerks back and forth. He couldn't even speak.

"Phil! We did it. Where are you Phil? Over," Dan said on walkie talkie.

Fat Barta kicked it aside. She walked up to Phillip and grabbed his face, and looked at him as if he was a not-too-particularly interesting insect. She turned his cheek to the right, and then to the left and blew smoke in his face.

Something attacked her. Grabbed her jacket and pulled on it.

Fat Barta turned, annoyed but not concerned.

The attacker was a dog.

It was Fortinbras.

He growled and pulled with all his might at her jacket. Fat Barta didn't budge. She held up her hand and Fortinbras whined. He let go of her jacket, and fell to the ground, curling into a ball. It took everything Phillip had left to say "No!" But almost nothing came out.

Fat Barta turned back to him. Grabbed his cheek. She whistled. And something crawled onto her back. It was an orange tabby cat. It was Gingersnaps. The cat stared at him with Fat Barta.

She took one long fingernail, and cut his cheek under his eye.

The blood felt cold on his skin.

The ground underneath them was becoming more unstable, he could feel it shifting.

"Thanks for helping my cat..." She said with a smile, her voice deep and grating.

She gave him a wink with her dead eye. Let go of his face, turned on the spot.

And walked away.

Phillip collapsed to the ground when she left. Looking at Fat Barta go, the cat Gingersnaps still on her shoulder. The horrible feeling in his stomach leaving with her.

CHAPTER 39

Unraveling

Phillip crawled over to Fortinbras, he was breathing, but he wasn't recovering as fast as Phillip, he was still curled into a ball. "Forty, how did you get in here?!" He yelled to the dog as he patted his head. "You stupid, very good boy!"

He picked up the walkie talkie with his good hand. The ground was shifting so violently it was bouncing away.

"Dan? I'm over here near the silo! Far side, I think..." Phillip said. "Over."

"We're close, we'll come to you! Over," Dan said back immediately.

The silo was shaking itself loose. One of the stone tubes that made up the building fell to the ground, but Phillip didn't hear a crash. Instead it went to its side and rolled away.

Trees moved too, not like the moving trees on their roots, but like the ground underneath them was moving. Fortinbras looked up at him just as a river changed its course in front of them, moved closer to them. and then away. Animals ran around in a panic.

Great herds of wooden chests moved across the grounds of their own volition. Buildings moved and were broken apart as they did so.

The sky was going wild again. The sun rose, moved across the sky and set so rapidly it left a streak of light across the sky. It felt like dusk and nightfall and morning all at once.

"Phillip!" Andy yelled behind him.

Emily and Dan followed her. Phillip got to his feet the best they could.

"We are going to try to find Haystacks and Henry," Dan said. Then looked at his arm. "What happened to you?" Emily touched his shoulders and looked him over.

"I'll explain later. Forty followed us to the Farm," Phillip said, pointing to the dog, who had gotten to his feet but didn't like what was going on around him at all.

"Let's move now. Try to find the place where you left him..." Andy said. Dan led the way, Phillip was too exhausted to try to navigate.

The shifting ground made it hard to travel. Phillip found himself bumping into Dan. Emily and Andy moved away and had to run back to them. Entire chunks of the landscape were moving around like boats on water. Nothing was firm to the ground anymore. It was a miracle they could walk at all. They had to jump over a fence which appeared in front of them like a snake. Dan had to hold Fortinbras as Phillip couldn't use his arm.

Phillip released it would be impossible to find where they had left Haystacks and Henry. But just as he thought this a building appeared ahead of them.

Haystacks' stable! In front of it, and a patch of ground that for whatever reason didn't shift away. Haystacks was on the ground. Dan and Phillip ran with Fortinbras to where he lay. Andy and Emily followed behind.

"Haystacks!" They called. He waved back to them. He was injured. His arm looked mangled and broken. There burn marks on his clothes. Henry was giving him first aid.

"Boys!" He said with a cough. "You survived!"

"So did you!" Dan said back. Buttercup came over and gave Dan lick to the face. Fortinbras was not happy with Buttercup, and kept to Phillip's feet.

"Barley, those twats are lucky I'm not a few decades younger," Haystacks said, smoke was rising from his skin. He held up the birdlike heads of one of the war puppets. "Got myself a war trophy. Not bad craftsmanship, I have to admit..."

"Did everybody else survive?" Phillip asked.

"When I left them, they were alive. Wallmen are not bad fighters, I'll give them that. We retreated not long after you..." He grimaced in pain as Henry applied a bandage. "Left...us..." He said. He looked like he was getting thinner. Even losing some height. Is this what happened to gremlins when they got injured? He saw the concern in their eyes and said "I'll be fine, boys..."

"Phillip!" Emily yelled, and he looked behind them. Emily and Andy were still approaching the stable, but as fast as they moved their legs they couldn't get any closer.

What was happening? Phillip looked to his right and saw Tadaaki. Also dressed in white, with his sword unsheathed. "Tadaaki?" Phillip said. Tadaaki was able to move closer to Emily and Andy but none of them were able to move closer to the stable.

"What's happening?" Phillip said, turning back to Dan. He noticed he was just as close to Dan and Fortinbras, but they were now ten feet from Haystacks. Dust was rising from the ground.

"This is how it works!" Andy realized, getting farther away. "That's why Tadaaki is closer to me!"

"What?!" Dan yelled, looking back and forth from Andy to Haystacks. They couldn't get closer to Haystacks, no matter how hard they tried.

"It's pulling everything apart. Pushing everything out of the Farm!" She was almost too far to hear now. Dust was rising from the ground. "It's pushing everything to their own entrance points...!"

"Boys! We are not going to be able to talk for long," Haystacks said. "I want you to know I didn't have you do anything illegal. I'm a complicated Imp, I'll admit that. But I would never..."

"We know, Haystacks." Dan said, still trying to get closer. He was twenty feet away now...

Haystacks looked satisfied. He collapsed onto the ground. Henry put his hand on his head.

"Haystacks!" Phillip yelled. He looked like he was still breathing. He was too far away to tell now. And the dust being kicked up obscured his view.

Nobody was around them anymore, it was just Dan, Fortinbras and Phillip.

Phillip crouched down and grabbed Fortinbras's collar with his good arm. He hid his eyes from the dust and smoke. Dan crouched next to him. Sounds like mountains crashing into each other were all around them. With his eyes closed it felt like he was on a raft in rough seas. The light in the sky grew more intense. A wailing echoed in the distance. The sun rose and fell and rose and fell in long arcs, so fast it was a streak of light across the sky. It was night and day and morning and evening all at once.

And then it was over.

He looked up. The sun was above the horizon. Stationary.

The dust was clearing. The ground was still.

They were in the fairgrounds. Tents and poles were half buried in churned earth. It looked like the place had been scraped clean. Upended firepits smiled in piles around them.

They were the only ones around, Phillip sat on the ground. Dan did the same. They didn't talk for a very long time... The pain in Phillip's arm was growing greater.

"Hey look." Dan said on the ground next to him. "My shoe."

Sure enough, Dan's missing shoe was in front of them, along with a broken BB-gun, Phillip's backpack. The memory cloth, still attached part of the mast, and a few books they brought with them to Haystacks' stable.

Dan put back on his shoe. "Much better..." He said.

CHAPTER 40

The Farm from Anywhere

The Farm, and the Camps around it, was gone.

Only a stretch of ugly, burnt earth remained.

Where everybody was, Phillip didn't know. Pushed to their entrance points like Andy said they would, he guessed.

They walked back to Fairchild's Ranch. They couldn't ride their bikes, not with Phillip's arm and Fortinbras in tow. The path had changed, too. A few shortcuts that were there before were no longer present. "Phil, what if I can't get back to Tennessee? What if the only thing connecting the two places was the Farm...?" Dan asked.

"We have the Many-League bikes..." Phillip answered. "We'll find a way back."

Phillip didn't know what time it was. It could be early morning or late afternoon. "It's late afternoon," Dan said. "That's west..." Pointing to the sun.

"Oh... duh," Phillip said. He didn't have the hands to reach for his phone.

It was a long walk, but it felt oddly cleansing. They didn't talk for most of it.

What they had just done already didn't feel real. Even Fortinbras was tired by the time they got back to the Fairchild house. Phillip looked over at the main house, light was in the windows. Jeff and Elaine's cars were still gone.

They went straight to the Dollhouse. Threw all their bags on the deck, and sat on the rocking chairs. Staring blankly into the distance. Fortinbras sat with them.

"You guys weren't gone long," Aunt Kath said walking around the deck. "Oh God, what happened to you?!" She yelled.

"We fell down a hill we were riding on..." Phillip said, the lie coming easily. He got off the seat and approached Aunt Kath, and gave her a single armed hug, which she seemed confused by. "I think I messed up my arm... my life flashed before my eyes. I'm just really glad to see you." He said, trying to pass it off as a joke.

"You need to tell me these things!" Aunt Kath said, looking at his arm, and then his face, and then his arm again. "That must have been a hell of a fall, you both fell at the same time?"

"Same time, yeah..." Phillip said. "Luckily, we both grabbed on to something on the way down, could have been a lot worse..."

━━━━ o ━━━━

Aunt Kath still agreed that Dan could stay over, but said it would be boring for him since she was going to take Phillip to the 24-hour emergency clinic. Dan was all too happy to go.

Phillip had not broken his arm. It was badly strained. though,

The doctor, a stern looking man with a suspicious air, asked him "Where did you get these bruises? It looks like something grabbed you..."

"Must have happened when I was falling..." Phillip said. Maddie looked at him just as suspiciously as the doctor, but apparently didn't feel like it was the right time to press the point. *Oh yeah*, he thought, *I agreed to tell Maddie stuff...*

After getting cleaned up, he gave Phillip a sling and gave him instructions to ice it a few times a day. Aunt Kath seemed relieved that he had not broken his arm, though this seemed like more of a pain. They put disinfectant and bandages on his dozens of cuts. The one on his cheek continued to bleed.

"What bikes were you riding? You didn't take any bikes when you left," Maddie whispered to Dan and Phillip when Aunt Kath went to get food at the vending machine.

"Oh, we took the magical bikes," Phillip said casually. "The ones that come out of the bell in our pockets and can go really fast..."

This got Maddie stuttering until Aunt Kath came back. Dan looked confused too.

"I feel like pizza," Aunt Kath said, "Does anybody else feel like pizza? I know we just had pizza but I feel like it again. Phillip, can you make it to the car by yourself, or are you going to fall again?"

"I was thinking about it, get some workers comp," Phillip responded.

"Good thinking," she said back. "I'm pretty sure that's how it works."

Dan was completely fixated on whether or not he could get back home. He barely enjoyed the pizza when they got back to the Fairchild house. Phillip, on the other, was in such a state of relief that he didn't think anything in the world could bother him. Or maybe that was just the pain medications...

"I hope Haystacks is okay..." Dan said. "And how do we contact Andy and Emily to see if they're okay?"

This was concerning, Phillip thought with a full mouth of pizza, "I'm guessing they'll contact us. We can't call them..." Phillip said. "And Haystacks said he would be fine... I'm sure he's fine..."

Maddie didn't question him for the remainder of the evening. She did look at him when she thought he didn't know about it. He would tell her everything, but he just wanted one night to relax... He could use a whole week, in fact.

"What you said, before you left..." Aunt Kath said to him when he was alone. "Were you serious about that?"

"About you taking the scholarship thing? Yeah," he said. But without the Farm nearby, how did he feel about being in King's Hill?

Didn't matter, he concluded, this was for Aunt Kath...

"Alright. Cool," Aunt Kath said. "Well I called, just to see how much of a hassle it would be to change schools. If this screws up your school, I wasn't going to do it. But it turns out that Adeline woman already got you processed in their system. It's basically all set up..."

"Huh," Phillip said. "*That's* convenient."

Was this Privilege? Still working to accommodate his choices?

If his Farm privilege was still intact, what did that mean now that the Farm was gone?

Just another question for the list...

Both Dan and Phillip decided that it was best to try to get back to Tennessee tomorrow rather than tonight, but that didn't stop Dan from worrying...

The went to the Dollhouse to find a sound. A ringing upstairs, like a small bell.

"Is that the mailbox?" Phillip asked.

"Can't be... I took that home..." Dan answered.

They walked to Phillip's room, which still had holes in the wall from the attack, which reminded him that he hadn't told Dan what Waltzrigg had said to him...

If Waltzrigg wasn't responsible for that... Who was? Fat Barta, she certainly didn't do what Waltzrigg wanted all the time.

And thank God for that, he thought.

The ringing was coming from the closet.

It was, in fact, the square blue mailbox. Its flag was up.

"I took that home... I'm sure of it..." Dan said.

"That is the least weird thing that's happened to us..." Phillip said. "Well, let's open it."

Dan opened the box, inside was letter. On the front, in crude handwriting, it said:

Daniel Castellanos
and
Phillip Montgomery

"Open it, open it!" Phillip said, eager to see what it said.

It was a letter, written in equally crude handwriting.

Daniel, Phillip,

I do not have the words to thank you for what you done for us, and even if I did, I lack the sentimentally to honestly share my feelings in such a way.

Suffice it to say, there are a great number of people who are alive now because of your efforts. You have prevented a truly dark person from exploiting the Farm. You deserve every award, every honor I can think of.

But instead I can only give you something small. Advice.

Leave. *Get out. Get as far from the happenings of the Farm as you can, and never look back.*

I know this statement must burn in your head, but I assure you it's the advice of sane man, who knows what is out there. Who knows what waits just outside.

You have been exposed, boys.

Of all my many sins I hate myself the most for this. There are dangers in the world and now you're open for them. I cannot protect you from all of them, or even some of them.

I know how you feel. I know what things youth does with the idea of danger. But please believe me when I say that what Anywhere can take from you is so much greater than what it can give you.

You are amazing people. I ask you to focus on what is important. Protect yourself and the ones you Love.

With great gratitude,

Paul

P.S. – Haystacks and Henry are fine.

"Huh…" Dan said.

"What do you think he means here?" Phillip asked. "What does he mean 'run?' Does he mean stop studying magic? Bury all the stuff we found? Or literally leave where we are…?"

"Well, I guess it's awesome that Haystacks is okay."

"Would it have killed him to be clearer?" Phillip said, re-reading the letter.

"And which Paul do you think this is?" Dan added.

"Right!? Good question."

The box rang again. The flag went back up.

Dan and Phillip went to grab the handle at the same time.

It was another letter. On the front, in eloquent handwriting, it said:

Phillip & Daniel

"Who's this from?" Dan asked, and almost cut himself opening it:

Phillip, Daniel,

You did it! I never doubted you for a second you wonderful kids you. Though I will admit you made me a little nervous when we saw you were held up by Tatuna.

But you handled it! You did it! You brave adventurers you. You heroes.

I know you were disappointed the Farm had to be destroyed. It was for the best, boys, it really was. But let me tell you not to despair. There's so much more out there. There's a lifetime of new horizons for you boys.

Do not give up. No matter what.

You both are too talented for that. It would be a waste. Don't listen to those who tell you that you don't belong, or that it doesn't belong to you, or that it's too dangerous, or that you simply don't have the skill.

You know more about the world now, boys. It's the basic law of discovery. Knowledge doesn't shrink. It's part of you now. You need to be true to it. True to what you know.

Be your own compass, and your own guides. Set sail straight for what you want. Let nothing hold you back. Explore every dark corner. Pull every thread. Be bold. Push through the struggle!

You'll get there, boys, I promise. And when you do, I'll be right there with you.

I'll look forward to meeting you again.

And do be careful who you tell what to. Knowing is a powerful thing.

Gratefully and sincerely,

PAUL

P.S. – Your friends are fine. They might not know where you live anymore though, you might want to contact them through the mail or the wire line.

"Huh..." Phillip said. "That's some *contradictory* advice," he said, holding the letters side-by-side. "Which one do you think we should follow?"

"Don't play games, Phil," Dan said, grabbing the second letter. "You know exactly which one were going to follow..."

Phillip laughed. "Yeah, I guess I do..."

"I mean, what does Paul expect us to do? Sit around, knowing there's all this out there? Just sit there thinking about it? What if I get a girlfriend and I really like her and one day I want to tell her about the Farm and she thinks I'm crazy and breaks up with me and then I never get to find out what our kids would look like...?"

"Solid reasoning," Phillip said.

"Yeah, it is," Dan said. "The other Paul has much better advice. We need to do this. I need to, at least... So, what if the Farm is gone?! You heard him, there's tons of stuff around. We'll make our own Farm. Right here. The Farm from Anywhere, located right here on Fairchild Ranch."

"Good idea," Phillip said with a laugh, then noticed something on the far wall. "Hey, the red stag is back..."

Dan looked over, the mounted head of the stag stared back at him. Small and motionless. "Would you look at that, I wonder where he went...?"

"I think he saved my life the night of the attack," Phillip said. "I think I should find a place to hang him up. In the Primafold version of the house. If you're cool with it."

They went to bed early that night. Daniel talked to his mother on the phone for a long time, Phillip could tell he kept the conversation going as long as possible. He understood why.

Phillip laid down on his back. Careful not to hurt his arm, and fell asleep without worries for the first time in what felt like a year.

CHAPTER
41

The Anywhere Club

Things were changing again. The crow could tell these things.

There was no telling *why* things changed. Or *how*. Or what it meant...

He was an old crow. An experienced crow. A careful crow. But even a careful crow had to see what was going on. The nest was changing again. He had never seen the like. The intruder continued to change things, it seemed.

The intruder had made itself quite at home, and was now altering the nest to its liking.

The intruder was inviting all sorts of beasts to its nest.

It was even defending the nest now. The intruder wasn't as dumb as the crow thought.

The crow would expect nothing less. At least this intruder did not see fit to leave a nest when there was trouble, as so many like intruders did...

The crow flew to where he could see the intruder. It was resting now. Perhaps he should be woken. The crow wondered what the intruder would do. The intruder was known to offer food and kinship, would he offer it to the crow?

He watched as the objects moved across the ground. Large ones. Moved like ground animals, hundreds of them. They missed the nest completely and went for the other nest. The larger, abandoned one. They broke in. What odd happenings these were... The crow flew away just as the intruder awoke.

The crow was a loyal crow. He was still indebted to the one here who first fed him, but he was also a curious crow. He would linger here, until he understood what was happening...

— ◦ —

Phillip woke up to the sound of crashing.

He could have sworn he saw something outside his window fly away.

Dan was already awake. "What now?" He said, and went into the closet to grab his rifle.

Phillip grabbed his silver ax. He put a flashlight in the other hand, able to hold it out of the sling. He peeked outside the door. He went into the hallway. Nothing. Then downstairs. Fortinbras was barking out the door. Dan turned on lights as he went.

Phillip pointed the flashlight out the front door. His stomach caught when he saw a shape move across the lawn. *They're back!* He thought, *the creatures are back!* Could he draw another circle?

"Boxes?" Dan said behind him.

"What?" Phillip whispered.

"Boxes, Phil, look..." He was pointing out the other window with the flashlight.

Sure enough, there were boxes.

Wooden chests, moving like buffalo through the yard.

So many they stacked on top of each other.

Phillip opened the front door, and the moment he did so a dozen small chests, three colorful suitcases, and several leather bags fell into the house. They almost ran him over, they gravitated to corners and sat themselves down. There were old armchairs who placed themselves on the deck, throwing aside the rocking chairs to do so.

A grandfather clock, clicking and dinging as it moved, went through the house and into the back room.

Phillip walked outside the house with his flashlight. There were several chests on the grass, but they were moving past the house, heading for the old stone barn.

His feet bare, he followed them, Dan right behind them, neither of them letting go of their weapons. The boxes had stormed through the ivy and thorns, they had broken through the side of the wood door, which now stood agape. A small chest the size of Fortinbras went in with a limp.

"Maybe we should wait 'til morning..." Dan suggested.

"I think they're from the Farm, I saw them running when the Farm unraveled," Phillip said while he walked forward, stepping carefully over the sharp but flattened plants.

He went into the stone barn, it was the first time he was in there. He could barely see a thing. Except on the side stacked against the wall and going all the way up, were a pile of chests and bags and crates. Hundreds and hundreds of them. Some still moving.

"What the heck is this?" Dan said.

Phillip laughed, awestruck at the weirdness of it all. Relieved that the living puppets weren't back. "I have no idea..." He said, as one more leather bag the size of cat went through his legs and climbed to the top of the pile.

"Dryrot!" Dan yelled.

And sure, the massive wooden body of Dryrot was walking into the barn, looking as confused as ever. Making feeble attempts to grab the smaller bags as the wove underneath his feet, before giving up, and looking around confused, not knowing what to do.

He wasn't the only one.

——— o ———

There was no sleeping after that.

They went back and got their shoes and their pink notebooks, Phillip had an intense desire to pull his arm out of the sling, but he resisted the urge. After the boxes and the furniture and the luggage had found a spot, they stopped moving. Dryrot wandered around, not seeming to know where to put himself. He followed Dan and Phillip back to the house, then back to the barn.

"Do you think we should take an inventory?" Dan said.

"It's a place to start..." Phillip said. He managed to open a small leather bag on top of the boxes and crates.

It was filled with doorknobs. Dozens of doorknobs. "Doorknobs," He said. Dan wrote it down.

Only a few bags could be opened, some were locked with silver chains. Every chest was locked with a heavy bolt. The crates might be forced open, if they had a crowbar.

The sun rose, and Dan mentioned that he'd like to try to make it home.

Phillip nodded "Let's go before my Aunt is up," they got dressed as fast as they could. Phillip having a hard time with his arm and the sling. They were out the door in less than twenty minutes, the sun was still rising over the tree line. The crates and bags still moving occasionally. Some of the furniture had left the porch wandered into the woods.

They activated their Many-League Bikes. *Were they allowed to keep these?* Phillip wondered, and then wondered who they would return them too. Haystacks said they belonged to the Pauls...

Phillip had a hard time riding with his arm, Dan slowed down to accommodate him as he led him through his usual path home, Phillip realizing that he had never made his way to Dan's house. There had never been a reason to.

"Yes. Yes! here we are, the path is still here!" Dan said. Phillip noticed that the temperature changed. "I'm sure this is in Knoxville, I can make it home from here!"

"Well let's do it..." Phillip said. Dan's relief was infectious.

"Nah, I'll go home later. I want to go home. But there's some stuff to do at the Dollhouse."

"There sure is," Phillip said, thinking about the boxes, and their books, and what they wanted to try later.

They got back to the Dollhouse before anybody realized they were missing. "I think I left the door unlocked," Phillip said. He was usually much more responsible. But which door did he leave unlocked, the Mundafold one or the Primafold?

Two hours of trying to open every box they could wore them out. Dan was doing most of the heavy lifting as Phillip was useless in that regard. "Let's go do other things right now... I want to try some stuff."

They braked just long enough to get drinks and snacks. Phillip had gotten into the habit of storing sodas and snacks in both the Primafold and Mundafold versions of the home. Right now, the whole house was in the Primafold version. They went upstairs to Phillip's room. Where they were most likely going to get privacy, and relaxed on the floor as they read, Dan wanted to write down some things before he forgot about them. "Remember what the Pauls said about the Bertrand guy? They mentioned another name. I think it was Rox... Did they say Rox?"

"That sounds right," Phillip said as he painstakingly set up a candle in front of himself. He heard a small 'clunk' in the closet.

He already knew what it was.

"You can come out of there, Maddie," Phillip said, snapping his fingers.

The door flew open, Maddie, who was pressed against it, fell to the floor with a thud.

"Whoa!" Dan said. "Did you do that?"

"I... don't know," Phillip said, looking at his hand before looking back at the door, snapping his fingers to no effect.

Maddie jumped back to her feet. "I wasn't spying!" She said.

"Who said you were?" Phillip said, he took a match out and lit the candle in front of him.

Maddie looked like she was about to talk again, but stopped when she noticed the tail of smoke coming out of the candle, which stopped mid-air.

Phillip looked at the tail. He tried to concentrate. Focus. Feel. Grab. He thought, and without any hesitation or too much desperation put his fingers forward and tried to grab the tail of smoke.

The smoke was much easier to grab than the clouds, it came out of the air easily, like a thin length of string, still floating upwards. Phillip laughed and Dan clapped.

Maddie gasped.

"Maddie," Phillip said. "I'm really sorry for gas-checking you..."

"Gaslighting..." she corrected in a small voice, not looking away from the smoke.

"Right. Gaslighting," he let go of the tail of smoke, it floated in the air for a moment before dissipating. "As you probably suspected, that was magic. There's been a lot of magical things happening around here recently. To be completely honest, I'm surprised you didn't notice sooner..."

Maddie was too shocked to take the bait. She stared where the smoke tail had dissipated.

"Thank God you told her, Phil," Dan said. "I was getting really stressed out about it."

"*You* were getting stressed out!?" Maddie said, her trance breaking.

"You probably have a lot of questions..." Phillip said. "Ask away."

Maddie didn't need more motivation than that. She jumped from question to question without waiting for answers. Sometimes she told stories and then asked to clarify what they meant. "Do you know about the birds? And what about the nightmares?" She asked. But before Phillip could answer she took out a doll. The doll that came from the bag Phillip found, he knew he was missing something. "What's with this doll? It moves, look," she placed it on the ground. "Not all the time, but it moves, mostly when I'm not looking... I swear. I swear."

"We believe you," Dan said, and Maddie looked like she was about to cry.

She reached behind her and retrieved a notebook. A *pink* notebook.

"This book is weird, too. It sometimes has different drawings..." Maddie said.

"Where did you find that?" Phillip interrupted, and then checked where his notebook was. It was on the bed. Dan was holding his...

"I found it in my room, under my bed..." Maddie said.

Phillip grabbed the book and put it next to Dan's, it was identical. Every fold and imperfection. Same as Phillip's. He handed the book back to Maddie. "We haven't figured out the books yet..." he told her. Dan was chuckling and writing something in his notebook...

She looked down at the pink notebook before moving on.

"Where have you been going every day? And don't say KHU because I know..." Maddie said.

"We've been going to the Farm. It's like a magical *meeting place*. We were learning magic. We stayed with a gremlin named Haystacks. Nice guy," Phillip said.

Maddie eyes widened.

"Can... I go to the Farm too?" Maddie asked.

"Afraid not," Phillip replied.

"Why?" she asked.

"We blew it up..." Phillip said.

Maddie didn't question what this meant. "Why is the house all different? There's holes in the wall. There's weird stuff everywhere. There's a painting downstairs and a tree that I think is glowing but I only saw it for a second then it went away and the house was back to..."

"Oh, you noticed the house was different too?" Phillip interrupted. "The tree was a gift. There was this traveler by the name of Bert who stayed at the house for a few days..."

"You had a traveler stay here?!" Maddie asked. "You're not making any sense again!"

"You're going to have to get used to things not making sense if you're going to be a part of this..." Phillip said.

"Be a part... of this?" Maddie repeated.

"That's what you want, isn't it?" Phillip said. "To know what's real and what's not? It's your choice though..."

"Can I... can people, *do* magic? For real?" She asked as if she was afraid to sound foolish. "Magic is real? Really *real* real?

"Heck if I know. We can give it a try though. Sit on the floor," Phillip ordered, and took out his skychalk, handing it to Maddie. "Draw a circle on the floor, around the candle. A small one. Draw it in the air..."

"The air?" she asked, and then pressed the button on the side, she put line in the air. She gasped and jumped back like the line would bite her "Wow!" She said, and then pushed the button again, giving it a few more tests before she drew the circle around the lit candle, laughing while she did so. "Magic!" She said, delighted.

Phillip took a lightbulb he was saving for himself and put it on the floor.

"Good, now I want you to think about this bulb. There's no air inside it, it's a vacuum. I want you to draw a circle around it... good, and I want you to draw a line from that circle to the first one." Phillip ordered. "Now, I want you to think about matching the internal state of the light bulb to your first circle. Declare your intent if you have to. Think about the first circle becoming a vacuum. When you're ready. I want you to clap your hands together, and press them into the circle. Say, clap, clap, stamp! When you're ready..."

Maddie didn't hesitate, she clapped her hands together. "Clap, Clap, stamp," and pressed them into the first circle.

The flame went out with a pop.

Dan laughed. "Holy crap!" Maddie said,

Phillip lit another match. Held it into the first circle, it went out almost immediately. It was an almost perfect vacuum...

"That was stupid amazing! Is that what was supposed to happen? Did I do it right?" Maddie said.

"It was... *acceptable*, for your first time," Phillip said, and Dan laughed again.

When he saw that Maddie thought that she was being made fun of, Dan said. "That was perfect, Maddie. We couldn't do any of that for the longest time. Just got the hang of it, like, yesterday. Welcome to the club, Maddie!"

"You have a club?" Maddie asked.

"Of course, we have a club, we're part of several, in fact," Phillip said. "And a Committee, but that's probably gone now."

"Actually, yeah, we have a club," Dan said, giving a look to Phillip. He was serious...

"What's it called?" Maddie asked.

"We don't have a real name yet, but since the Farm is in Anywhere. It's *from* Anywhere. And we want to learn stuff like we were at the Farm. I was thinking we would call it the "*Anywhere club...*'"

"It's perfect," Phillip said, meaning it.

A small bell broke out in the closet.

"What's that?" Maddie asked, Dan was already on his feet.

"It means we have mail," Phillip answered.

Dan came back with a bundle of loose papers.

"It's like... newspaper clippings," Dan said. "A bunch of them. Mostly help wanted ads."

Dan handed them to Phillip. There were seemingly random clippings from a newspaper. One said *'Classifieds'* at the top. Small boxes, some of which were circled, offered jobs like *'Sludge reclamation associates. Paid every day.'* *'Skull merchants with experience wanted.'* Some were personal ads. *'Lonely halfFae seeking companionship.'*

"This is a magical newspaper!" Phillip said. "Look at the top of this scrap, it says 'New Amsterdam Press.' It's yesterday's newspaper! Who sent this? The Pauls? Do they want us to go here?"

"Can I join the club?" Maddie burst out.

Phillip looked at her and dropped the clippings. "Sure," he said, and her eyes lit up. "But first you have to do the ceremony..."

He gave her a can of soda. Grabbed one and opened it himself and handed another to Dan. "We have to drink on it."

"I hate soda..." Maddie said. "It goes up to my nose."

"I don't make the rules, Maddie, I just employ them. If you want to change the rules take it up with Dan, he's the President," Phillip said, and raised his can. Maddie and Dan followed. "Now, to the first official meeting of The Anywhere Club. Dedicated to... *learning*, and stuff, I guess. And discovery! Harrah!"

He took a drink, Maddie and Dan with him.

Maddie immediate spit out the soda. "Sorry, too bubbly... goes up... my nose..."

Dan and Phillip cracked up, Maddie joined in, wiping her eyes. Phillip sensing that her tears were not completely caused by the bubbly drink.

It was just about the best first meeting of the Anywhere Club that Phillip could have expected.

EPILOGUE

Fishing Trip

The warehouse was always a loud place. Machines whirled morning, noon, and night. You could hear it for acres around. And if you couldn't hear the machines, you could often feel them. Buzzing and humming right through the feet.

Fletcher hated the noise.

Hated it to his core. It felt like being around people, and despite the fact that Fletcher disliked leaving the city he also *hated* being around people.

The man—on the other hand—loved it. He was happy to finally hang Fletcher up in the closet, glad to be back to himself, for he could enjoy that wonderful sound. Feel and remember what it meant to him.

What a burden Fletcher was, the man thought.

"That did not go as planned," said a man reading a newspaper on his office sofa.

Bertrand J. Bertrand was enjoying the new suit and hat he wore. The latest style, well cut. A present to himself for traveling so long on the road. *Bertrand always cleaned up when he wanted to*, the man thought, which made his usual state all more contemptible.

"Welcome back," the man said to Bertrand. "And nonsense, nothing goes as planned. We got everything we wanted out of the venture. Maybe more. Enough to work with, at least. You're a cynic, old Bert. Be careful about that, it'll kill you young."

Bertrand grunted and looked over his newspaper.

"A fishing trip not always about catching fish, old Bert," the man said.

"Sounds like the excuse of a bad fisherman to me," Bertrand said. "I miss Fletcher. Less dramatic, no delusional optimism."

"I think Fletcher is going to take a rest for a while," The man said.

Bertrand grunted again. "Quick question..."

"Yes?"

"Why are there sections cut out of your newspaper?"

The End.

Dan and Phillip will return in Book 2,

'THE CITY OF NO REFLECTION'